A Sea of Straw

julia sutton

CHEYNE
WALK

Copyright

Published by **Cheyne Walk**

www.cheynewalk.co

Acknowledgements

I should like to thank my early tutors Sarah Bower and Ian Nettleton for their critiques and their patience. I am grateful to The Arts Council, to Evie Wyld, and to Sam Ruddock of the Norwich Writers'Centre. And to talented writer friends and colleagues for their reading of early drafts and encouragement: Claire Hamburger, Yvonne Johnston, Anton Baer, Sylvia Jobar, Ron Askew, Kristin Gleeson, Caroline Scott, Marlene Brown, Jill Marsh, Katriona Troth, Barbara Emmett, Dave Ingham, Kit Habianic, Amanda Hodgkinson, Georgia Garrett, Gaia Banks, Donald Winchester, and to Roland Denning for his film maker's perspective. To fellow inmates of the Bookshed and Lorraine Mace's Writing Asylum. To Sofia Carlos, Joãna Aranha, Pavlina Zourkova. And lastly to Glenn Haybittle for his editorial input.

You cannot assume

that futures will resemble pasts,

just because past futures

resembled past pasts.

Karl Popper.

One

Lisbon, October 5, 1966

SHE AND ANNA ARE inseparable. Of that much she can be sure. The clothes she makes for her — toddler versions of her own offbeat creations — are the visible, the living proof. Like the matching dolly-print PVC macs she dressed them in this morning, ready for the early downpour. Hand in hand, they stand and wave from the glass lobby of the airport, while they chant their goodbyes to Lisbon. White knee socks damp, the odd drop of rain trickling to the floor.

Having lifted Anna higher so that she can see the palms waving from the forecourt, she feels a tug, as she lets her down again. And they are stuck together by their coats. The rip she hears, when she tears them apart, seems to echo through the vestibule. Its bank-holiday emptiness is as quiet as the grave.

It is Republic Day across the land. And the airport is short-staffed apparently. She waits at an abandoned check-in desk, and opens her passport. Its pages still smell new. But her face is pallid in her photograph; it was taken when she had the pleurisy. *Name: Jody Proctor. Married. One child.*

And soon to be twenty-three, she thinks, as she thumbs her only visa stamp, dated six weeks ago, for Portugal. Well, at least she can be proud of that. That they flew there. British Airways, too. No one else in her family has ever even been abroad.

On entering the main hall she finds it, too, is all but deserted. She squeezes Anna's damp hand and lifts her eyes to scan the arches of the mezzanine. Turning slowly in the glare of the lights, cloistered as well as overlooked by the surrounding colonnade, she longs to catch the merest flicker of a human movement from above. In the War, and probably afterwards too, this place was teeming with spies. Elegantly dressed. Sophisticated. *Casablanca* style. Strange that such an edgy atmosphere as this blithely escaped her notice on the night they flew in.

Zé, for goodness sake, where are you? You can come out now. There's no one here.

She lets her eyes rove the arches until they tire of peering into shadows. And she has spotted not a single corner in which a grown man might hide. Not even one as thin as he is, or as inconspicuous as he would be standing next to one of these pillars. In his long, classic British mac. All the Lisbon men wear them. She rubs her neck and, as the stiffness eases, a conversation from weeks ago begins to echo in her ear.

'Anyone with good ears and eyes can make a living here, and there are plenty who want to do that.'

'Do what?'

'Make a living.'

One last turn before she gives up. She catches herself sniffing hard, as if truffling for a lost odour: of kerosene; of sardines cooking; of the salt air alive with gulls. And then of turpentine, of pencils and rain-soaked gabardine. Centre-stage, the light glancing off their macs, the two of them are unmissable in their shiny, stiff garb. Although apparently not to him. Everything she has been straining on tiptoe to catch a glimpse of: his face grinning round a pillar, peering through a glass display cabinet — is nothing but a mirage. His smile is everywhere she looks, in every reflection, in the slightest hint of a movement. But then it isn't. It isn't him.

The first time she wheeled Anna to the beach alone without Leonora, was the day that she met him. Late in the afternoon it was, when she spotted him from the parapet above the first zigzagging slope. The only remaining sunbather on that small white pennant of a beach. Lying on his belly, flat on the sand, toes grazing the tidemark from where the loose white grains were blowing down across the rinsed grey of the shore. A man, an older man she took him for at first, wearing Buddy Holly glasses. A businessman, a director perhaps, sleeping off a long lunch. Or trying to read an aerogramme that kept on flapping in the breeze.

He was watching her; she could feel it, as she pushed Anna's trolley round the agave plant that listed over the slope. The orange cactus flowers hid her from him until she rounded on a back wheel the starched sea grass lower down. Her wooden *Scholls* clattered on the concrete, while her cheeks flushed and she was conscious of her every movement. At the bottom of the ramp she left their borrowed trolley axle-deep in sand. And barefoot, carried Anna over the burning sand towards the mooring post, which still offered a small and diminishing patch of shade. Once within its range, she spread their towels in the lee of the sea wall.

Later on, glistening wet from a spell of playing on the rocks, they stopped on their way up the beach again, to watch some balls of dried sea alyssum tumble over the shore. While Anna chased one, she shouted to him, but the wind snatched away her voice. So she mouthed while pointing to her wrist:

'What's the time?'

'*Quatre heures,*' he called downwind, raising four fingers as he watched.

'Thank you,' she shouted back.

She was immersed in her new paperback, when she turned a page and, out of habit, glanced up to check. But — no Anna, just a heap of sand where she had been. She had trotted off, the little rascal, and was hurtling down the beach, holding out her pail, straight for the crashing surf. But in a flash, he was on his feet, and then he was lunging down the shore after her. To place himself like a goalie between Anna and the open sea. And to think that she forgot to thank him! She just raced blindly down, flapping open Anna's sunbonnet as she went, deafened by her heart booming in her ears.

His wiry sandy-coloured hair was raked through with silt, when, squinting up, she saw him standing by her feet, holding out Anna's toy pail. A silhouette against the low sun and the mirror that was the Atlantic. But close enough that for a second she could see herself reflected in his lenses.

'You are English? I bring her water.' The English words sounded awkward for him.

But soon his gentle voice and kind sea-coloured eyes had

disarmed her, so. He was different from the local Portuguese she had encountered while with Leonora; he was tall, for one thing, with sandy hair, and he didn't lionise Anna. He was attentive to her, though reserved. But then while Anna stomped around to Manfred Mann, from their transistor balanced on the mooring post, he slyly and very deftly lay down his towel next to hers. She hadn't said he could. She didn't ask.

'I'm leaving soon because I have to catch the last post,' she said, while pointing out the airmail letter that showed through her string bag. 'I promised Leonora that I'd post it. Leonora's the English friend that I'm staying with while I'm here.'

'The wait is long. It will be horrible. You will to stand outside in the heat. I am José. They call me Zé.'

'Zé?'

'Yes. I am painter.'

'You're an artist?'

'Yes.'

Her shoulders relaxed then. A book, or rather a journal lay open on his towel, at an article in French.

'It means *The New Young Painters of Portugal*,' he said, watching her read.

'I know. I can read French. It was my best subject at school, after Latin, that is. There's a Zé Rodrigues here. See? In the caption next to that painting. It's not you, is it? Is it you?'

He merely smiled.

'It's fabulous,' she said, stumbling to her feet, smacking sand from her thighs and shaking more out of her denim shift.

'I can walk with you to the *correia*, if you want.' He was scribbling something on an envelope from the back pocket of his shorts.

His name is really long. *José Manuel Rodrigues Oliveira de Sà.* She still repeats it to herself now and then, so that she won't forget it.

It felt then as if the evening tide had made off with their conversation when, bent over Anna's pushchair, they slogged together up the ramp. Relieved to reach the top, she nearly blurted out something about Michael, but stopped herself in time. She fairly sped along the promenade, darting through the dogs and scattering birds. And hurried past the line of old people playing draughts on small folding tables. It was one thing, a bit of flirting on the beach, but did she really want him there beside her while she walked back through the town? Now of course she would give anything for a glimpse of him, however brief ...

Straight ahead for the barrier. A cold hard metal bar. Dispirited, she resigns herself as she trudges towards the gap, stopping only to set her luggage down and peel off their clammy coats.

It was even hotter in the hushed tree-lined road away from the breeze. And something about this young man was irritating her. But what? While they walked along, he kept glancing over his shoulder, but it wasn't that. He would speak and then, when she answered him, would turn away and look at anything or anyone but at her. It unnerved her, made her feel queasy. But with a thud of boots over cobblestones, a brass band was coming into view. And soon a marching column hid the level-crossing at the end of the road.

'They are the Greenshirts. We have them since the Civil War in Spain.'

'And they're still here?' To be honest, they reminded her of the Blackshirts from old newsreels. And their goose-stepping sent shivers through her in spite of the intense heat. Zé had dropped to Anna's footrest and, squatting with his back to the parade, adjusted the rolled towel serving as a pillow behind her head. 'They've gone now, Zé.'

He stood, but without letting his eyes leave her face.

At the corner of *Avenida da República* she took the pushchair, while Zé went to wash his hands at a broken stone fountain. She had noticed them on the beach, his hands; they were dirty like a child's. Anna had slipped low in her chair and was snoring like a piglet. The *avenida* breathed dust that clung to their skin, making it itch, and the hot air was saturated with the sickly smell of the donkeys. Three were hitched to the iron railing round a gouged chestnut tree, and eyed her as she struggled up a high kerb.

The queue stretched all the way along the wall of the *correia*. Its stones were too hot to touch, let alone to lean against for what would surely be a long wait. Zé, who had vanished, reappeared from the next-door *farmácia*, a glass of water in each hand. And while she drank from one, he cooled Anna's flushed face from the other. Birds flew down to the culvert to drink, scattering dust on a growing line of men in blue overalls and women under black headscarves. Some with gaps in blackened teeth and others with their feet bound in filthy rags. When an old man fell off the kerb, two suited men appeared out of nowhere and bundled him away. When someone nudged her, she stopped looking and fished in her bag for a kerchief, which she tied low across her brow. No one spoke again and no one moved unless they too had lost their footing.

She was glad when at last they stepped into the dingy hall of the *correia*, and Zé began to whisper things in her ear. Things about how the system worked and that, and why the clerks behind the counter were so slow-moving and sullen. And that someone should have bound the old man's feet, so that he would not break the law.

It was there in the post office that he began to speak to her in French. Now he uses French most of the time; he prefers it, he says. But she still answers him in English, while he saves his English for the things he thinks are important. And those haughty-sounding statements that have always made her want to tease him, but often left her dumbstruck instead. Or that shattered her equilibrium, like his statement last Sunday night:

'When you arrive to the airport on Tuesday, I will be there. I will wait and I will watch you leave, but you will not see me. Do you mind?'

Did she mind? Swallowing her disappointment that he would not be there to see them off, she had fought back her welling tears. *'Why, Zé? Why?'*

His mute answer, a pained look, was enough to stifle her bewilderment on that, their last evening together. But not to quell the inner turmoil of yesterday, while she packed. And now that Tuesday has arrived she must leave alone from this deserted airport. Both angry and confused. So, where, now, is the evidence? Show her proof that he is there! Because his absence is becoming palpable and as heavy on the air as kerosene. *Tchk*! He just didn't come. He never meant to come. He lied. And like Leonora and Carlos and everybody else, for that matter, he is celebrating with his family on their national day. But then, why cover up? Why fabricate? Why the need to lie?

Anna won't stop grizzling; she is hot. She whips away her sou'wester, dabs the red streak across her forehead, the elastic mark beneath her chin. But then someone is speaking English above her head, and she looks up.

'Mrs. Proctor? I'm your stewardess.' A toothy blonde woman, smart in navy blue, is holding out a gloved hand. 'So, and this must be Anna?'

The union-jack neckerchief has given Jody a jolt. And she can sense the hand of fate tugging at the reins of her life. Anna promptly swaps her mother's hand for the gloved one her stewardess is offering. And Jody turns aside, her eyes filling with a watery blur. She drops her parcels on the flatbed scale and numbly follows the tip tap of the flight attendant's heels. Anna bobs along in front, gloating from behind a smartly tailored shoulder, a wet finger pulling at her mouth. Jody follows on, head bowed, polished granite flowing past her feet. Watching as, one by one, their hopes and plans begin to crumble, to float away on a tide of debris. Did he know this would happen? Had he seen it coming? This imploding of their dreams. Was it this, or at least the fear of it that made him lie to her the other night? If it was, she may as well forget him and just go.

A persistent little red fleck is worrying the outer corner of her eye, as they make their way along a strip of carpet down the middle of an endless corridor. And soon her total field of vision is awash with a liquid redness. *'There's a heck of lot of that red, isn't there?'* The echo of her own bluntness shocks her as, smiling weakly, she recalls her one and only visit to his studio. A small windowless room in the local elementary school. It was his summer studio and soon, at the beginning of October, when his family would close their summerhouse and return home to Lisbon, his studio would revert to being a storeroom again. At first sight she struggled with the images that leapt out from the back wall. From a ruddied landscape, fantastical, self-populating with distorting forms, inchoate half-human beings. The woman pregnant with — a starfish? Like Miro, a bit.

'Why'd you put the title in French?'

'I told you about the censor, no? I cannot expose it here. Maybe one day, in Paris perhaps … But this work I give to you. I think it is finished now. So it is your painting and it will wait with me in Lisbon for your return.' His biggest painting - it covered nearly the whole of the back wall - and he was giving it to her. He locked the door, they scaled the playground wall again and crunched back along the cliff top, over pebbles whited by the moon. Halfway along she shouted back to him, above the roar of the Atlantic:

'I feel rich, like Peggy Guggenheim.'

His laughter galloped on the wind.

And now their plane waits to fly them home again, and her painting seems to be here in front of her, hovering in the corridor, shimmering before her eyes. Like a great red flag that spans the breadth of the tunnel, placed there to halt her progress. Or to dare her to turn back? She reaches out toward the two figures, a human couple crouching on the earth. But they, too, begin to fracture, and then dissolve in a salty blur. She *must* come back for her painting and for him.

And from the plane, there it is again, the painting, his '*Création Fantastique.*' Its vibrant reds and blues reflected in the rolling cloud banks from above. Anna dozes in the seat beside her, cheeks and ears daubed with chocolate. A cabin steward brings a tray of duty-free allowances and a list. She buys a flask of *Mitsouko* and a block of two hundred *Stuyvesant*. And when she peers out through the window again, the picture has vanished.

Manchester, October 5, 1966

Michael is there to meet her. In the Arrivals hall at Ringway. When she straightens up from lifting Anna onto the escalator, she spots him among the crowd on the floor below. Craning his neck and jostling for a place behind a swagged rope fence. With

Anna clamped between her knees she enters the hum of a busy airport. *Telstar* envelops her as the conveyor belt rolls her down towards a panoramic glass wall that draws her, dizzied, into a forgotten season of smoky autumn golds. The Cheshire countryside. Ivy-covered walls. A red sandstone escarpment: it must be Alderley Edge. Below her is a sea of heads. And the Arrivals hall is more soulless than ever.

To think she used to like to ride out there, pillion on Michael's motorbike, on Sunday afternoons. Back when they were courting and the new airport was still a novelty, a magnet to the curious and the young. She would huddle against the wind on one of those bleak, concrete viewing terraces, her tiny transistor radio clapped to her ear. *Radio Caroline* blasting out and then fading out, with the DJ's apologies and the crash of waves against the ship. Michael would be charging round the terrace, hoarse from shouting through the screams of the jets: *'There's an Argonaut over there,'* or, *'that one's a Viscount.'* And he would crane his neck, like he's doing now, at the front of that crowd. But as they roared home past rows of cobbled streets of blackened back-to-back terraces, their exhilaration would evaporate. Lost among the whiffs of sterilising milk and chip fat on the wind.

What the ...? She spins round to face the metal treads as they trundle down behind her. *Lara's Theme* insinuates itself, swelling to fill the space. As if the airport were now a cinema, and the film she saw with Zé in Lisbon, or the orchestra at least, has followed her there. And that long cortège of Russians dressed in black furs is inching through the snow. *Doctor Zhivago.* Zé had already seen it twice before he took her there last Sunday. He seems fascinated by the Russians. She should have told him about the cossack-style jacket she made. Still 'in the film,' they stumbled out through a side alley in the rain. Until standing stock still, and in a voice that was full of pride, he said solemnly: 'My people are like the Russians. We love like the Russians.' While the rain fell in the alley. She was relaxed with him by then, having just spent the afternoon together in a borrowed Lisbon apartment. But still she couldn't laugh. She could see he was deadly serious.

But now she steels herself ready to swing Anna over the gap. In *Arrivals* there is a lit blue arrow pointing up to *Departures*, and a man in a clotted cream linen suit is walking underneath it, swinging a leather grip. He stops at a drinks machine and, when he has a can, turns around and opens it. She knows those heavy, dark features …

'*Are you sure? Perhaps it was someone who looked like him.*'

'*Yes, Zé, I'm sure.*'

And doubly sure she is now. It is the man who sat beside her and Anna while they waited in *Departures* to board their Lisbon flight. Was it only six weeks ago? It feels like another life. She refused his offer of help with getting Anna onto the plane. Instinctively, as it happens. The head steward didn't like him either. She could tell, when they climbed the air stair. And then weeks later, he turned up again at café Nicola in Lisbon. Two tables back from her. A man she couldn't quite place, who sat with his nose buried in a paper.

'*The PIDE. Secret police. There is one sitting right behind you. But drink your chocolate first. You will see him when you stand.*'

And after all the commotion that had ensued, she and Zé were out of there at last and running like crazy through the arcades of the Rossio. Its Op-Art patterned paving tiles making strobic waves across the square. At the far corner she and Zé erupted into wild hysterical laughter, between their bouts of mimicking the bar manager ordering them to leave. Just for gazing in each other's eyes, for goodness sake. They hadn't even been kissing.

'*They come to Nicola for tormenting us and to listen, listen, listen, listen. They did the same in café Brasileira and, when we moved, they followed us here. Wait until I tell Armando. He will cut them up in the theatre; they will be shot to pieces on the stage.*'

They were halfway to the station, when it struck her who the man was. In Manchester for the World Cup at Old Trafford, he'd told her. Portugal against Bulgaria. Had stayed with relatives in Ancoats. She remembered thinking how well dressed he was for such a poor district. But Zé only stared mutely as she spoke and hustled her across a side street where, he said, the *PIDE* office was.

Michael is making progress now. Though corralled by the rope fence, he rubs his hands and makes straight for her and Anna, sizing up their pile of luggage as he goes. His ears embarrass her still. She can't help it; they just do. She stares down at Anna's face. Will she recognise her father? Can she remember that long ago? Having sensed that Michael has levelled with them, she looks up. His face looks paler than ever. Complexion ashen, chin set firm, lips nearly not there. He's biting them. His eyes are not half so tired-looking as they were before she went away. Are less accusing. As if he might have missed her after all. They are searching her face, expectant, but then are lost behind a flitting shadow.

A tiny tremor has taken hold of the corner of his mouth. He stares motionless except for a slight wobble of his bottom lip. And when whatever-it-is dawns, she finds herself shrinking back a few steps, back against the growling escalator. With *Lara's Theme* still spiralling above its split steel treads. But there is nothing left for her to say.

Hasn't he always insisted that her face is an open book?

Two

The same day

AS MICHAEL GUIDES Anna down the garden path towards his parents' front door, she watches from the car parked at the gate, mechanically brushing Anna's still-warm imprint from her lap. And surprised to find herself there. She knows the journey from the airport to the Proctors' house, of course, but it passed her by unnoticed. And for a moment, just then, she felt herself a teenager again, home from school with her satchel full of books and hanging in the back entry to delay going inside.

Sitting up, in the low bucket seat, she rakes her sun-bleached hair. She can hardly bring herself to move. The stained glass of the porch lights up. The coloured image of a tea clipper is projected onto the lawn. But when the door closes, the little sailing ship sinks into the grass. Missing something, she peers between the pairs of houses, looking for the sun. *Where's it gone? It must be somewhere. It would still be daylight in Portugal.*

She taps out the last *SG filtro* and crushes the empty pack. And back creeps the old loneliness of the nights before she went away. The ones she spent in this car. Tearing round the high moorland roads, her spirits lifting only when she could feel the boards beneath her right foot. There was the night the tyre blew out and sent her to the very edge of a ravine. She didn't dare phone Michael. And she managed to change the wheel. But on arriving home, she stayed parked in the drive, darkly chain-smoking while Michael slept inside.

She will stop the stupid night driving. She has more important things to do: decisions to make; plans to finalise, in secret for the time being. A vague awareness of leaf-lorn trees. A dank gloaming. She shudders. Down the road a stand of dark evergreens is closing ranks across St. Ethelreda's, the church where she was married. Michael too, of course, although you would hardly think it now. And it was *his* parish church. The street lights blink on in succession. Michael has closed the curtains.

It was the first time she had agreed to meet him at the café after dinner. A September evening mist swirled around her as she ran towards the promenade. It had cleared, when she reached the end where the wooden beach café sits. Across the terrace, still warm and smelling of camping and sardines, he sat waiting for her at a table next to the low, cliff wall. He did most of the talking, while he watched her fingers tweeze tobacco from her lip, when she tried to smoke his *Gauloise*. She coughed a lot, but then they talked together till the big red sun stopped its shimmering and plopped into the Atlantic. And then he stood and with a heavy sigh, said: *'I must return to Paris. Come, walk with me for a while.'*

They meandered for a hundred yards or so in the direction of the Grand Hotel. As they were retracing their steps, he stopped, hung back and whispered to her, 'Wait.' To let a dog walker who was coming up behind them brush past. They watched the man's white baseball cap bob down the dark slope that led to the beach, and disappear, before they set off again towards the amber light from a cluster of oil lamps on a table outside the café. Café Amarela. The low shack glowed honey-coloured and welcoming in the darkness. The familiar rush of water through the old sluice crescendoed as they passed. It was the first of many an evening they would spend together on that terrace, talking, drinking *Sagres* while the sun bloodied the waves.

But what is he to her really? A lanky Lisbon art student, but with charming old-fashioned manners and quite ridiculously proud? She smiles to herself. No. He is more, much more, the biggest thing that has ever happened to her. She swings her legs from the car, grabs her bag and stands yawning in the road.

Michael had left the door on the latch. Inside, the lounge is strangely darkened. She threads a path to a fireside chair, in which Anna sits toasting herself on her granddad's lap.

'Oh,'allo.' Her father-in-law starts.

'Don't get up, Fred. I'll take her off you for a while. She needs to cool down.' She plants a kiss on a bald head glowing pink from the *Magicoals*.

Michael stands beside a slide projector in the middle of the room, absorbed. Anna chuckles at the dust particles whirling in a beam of light. Michael steps back and curses, when he trips on the brass fender. And then he focuses on a white vinyl screen stretched across the curtained bay.

'Ullswater.' He says, and clears a frog from his throat.

Anna tries to wriggle free. Must Michael do this now, when she has only just landed? And why show these old slides again? They have all seen them before. But she doesn't have a shot of Portugal to show them, never having owned a camera. The lucent scenes on the screen pinpoint the focus in Michael's eyes, highlight the stubborn set of his chin. And makes those small flicks of his hand cast giant shadows like snapping crocodile jaws.

The scene switches to a fishing trip in the Lake District with Geoff. Ages ago, that one was. Geoff, pumpkin-faced, leather-jacketed, poses nursing a crash helmet. Two motorbikes lean together by a wind-ruffled stretch of water. She can feel the bite of that wind. Anna kicks against her hip bone until, sore, she hands her back to Fred, who gives her an old *National Geographic* magazine to play with. Jody folds her arms on the sofa back and leans in to watch the show.

'This one's fuzzy.' *Click*. 'Ullswater.' *Click*. 'Coniston. A bit dark, that.' *Click*. Next, an image from picture-book villagestreet fills the screen. 'Uh-oh. Here's an old one.' Michael takes a more cautious step back to avoid the fender. Her seventeen-year-old self is framed in the entrance to a Tudor inn. A revenant come to taunt her, no doubt. It was their first weekend away together after they got engaged. They had a low-beamed chintzy room with an unbelievably high bed.

'*I want to save you for after the wedding.*' Her colour mounts at this echo of Michael's words uttered in the darkness and muffled by his turned back. While she lay awake behind him, slowly turning her ring on her finger. Perplexed. Feeling embarrassed — for wanting to, for thinking that they would, once they were engaged. Against her mother's warnings: *'Your virginity is your trump card, dear.'* And he, it seemed, would go along with it, insisting that he was sticking to his beliefs.

Viv used to say that they were Green Shield stamps lying in a drawer, waiting to be traded in. Should she be feeling honoured that he respected her so much? Or what she really felt? There was no way to break the silence between them, no way to protest. He knew the times were changing, must have done. He mucked about with the lads. But for her the future still resembled the old films that flickered through her childhood. Was still in black and white, but made to fit her parents' fourteen-inch TV. And there it all is, in Agfacolour now and mocking her from the screen.

'Tummy, my mummy's tummy!' Anna jiggles on her granddad's knee, gleeful at the next slide.

Oh, not that again. She turns from the screen and glowers at the mantelpiece clock. It is time they made tracks for home.

'Michael, don't you think it's time we —'

'Lytham St. Anne's.' *Click.* 'This one was in the sand dunes.' *Click.* 'St. Anne's again.'

And there is Michael's old MG set against a far-off line of surf. The Atlantic! But of course it is; and she swam in that sea with him. Why did she think it separated them? No, the water connects them. But with the land tilting here, the sea recedes to lie farther out each year. And people drive across the beach in Mini-Mokes and beach buggies to reach it. Michael posed her on his car bonnet like that, motor-show fashion, like the girls who work at Earl's Court.

'It's the old Midget. See the twin spots?' He flaps his hand. 'Ouch! I'll have to let it go. The projector's getting hot.'

That Vichy cotton bikini had looked good on her back then. She still digs it out and wears it sometimes, even though it has faded. Although she wished she hadn't, when Zé said his mother wished to meet her on the beach. No, it's time it went in the duster box. She leaves the sofa and opens the door to a kitchen filled with steam. Her mother-in-law is stirring something on the stove in front of the window, and the Venetian blind is redundant.

'Violet! How are you? I'll prop the back door open, shall I?'

'You got here, then.'

'Yeah, and it doesn't half seem strange.' Holding the door ajar, she rejoins the muggy, gravy-smelling warmth.

'Aren't you brown!' Violet shudders as she moves away from the stove. She rarely has a lot to say for herself, but she can be very kind.

'That'll soon fade. Tell me though, how did Michael manage on his own?'

'Fine, as far as I know. He came here for his breakfast. I put up his packed lunches, and he was here again for his tea.'

'Every day?'

'Except weekends.' Violet lifts a leaf of the Formica table and fumbles for the prop. 'He brought his washing on Mondays and took it home with him once his shirts were ironed.' She sounds a little out of breath.

'Here, let me do that. So, there's no food in at our house, and we're eating here tonight. Is that the idea?'

'Probably. You'll soon find out, when you get home. He built a new model aeroplane and took it down to his club. I don't know if this one flies well or not. They don't always, do they?'

A Lancashire village

The stove is cold, but she stands beside it and tries to frisk herself warm. Michael ushers in more cold air along with her luggage. Leaving him to unwrap his gift in the living-room, she goes to switch on Anna's radiator. And Anna, too sleepy to climb the stairs for her bath, gets a lick and promise of a wash standing up in the kitchen sink.

'There'll be no more fighting over toys with little Paulo in the morning. Will you miss him? We'll see.' She watches Anna suck herself to sleep with the corner of her Linus blanket, her once-white nylon cot quilt now blackened from having trailed across two airport floors.

Michael stands at the window, poring over something in

his palm. An antique brass balance rises from a cloud of tissue on the coffee table. She stares at it, recalling scenes from a wonderful fair. High up in the hills, amid the Disney-style pinnacles of Sintra. She loved Sintra. With Leonora and Carlos she walked on the Moorish castle walls. It was a knee-bending climb. A thousand stone steps twisting, leading them forever upward, to then gaze down between the angle towers over craggy, forested hilltops. The Hills of the Moon. Halfway up they sat and caught their breath on a low, tumbledown wall. And contemplated their goal: a yew tree that appeared to grow from a turret in the sky.

Having reached the turret, breathless again, they looked out across a vast sweep of land lush with wild camellias, gardenias, bougainvillea and giant rusting ferns. And then they walked on stones until the wall itself had fallen away, only to switch back again through wooded slopes of cork oak and walnut. Yes, Sintra was definitely the high point of her stay. And yet an unaccountable sadness had invaded in her in those hills, when she found herself inexplicably missing Zé.

All morning, she had checked herself when about to say his name aloud. Leonora and Carlos had had a fight the evening before. And even though they had been arguing in Portuguese, she knew why they fought. They disagreed about her going out to meet Zé. Carlos objected because for him she was a married woman going out to meet a man without a chaperone. And it reflected on him. In the end he stormed off to his brother's house to fetch the car for today, and returned with the ancient Opel that his brother brought from Brazil. Like the one in *Bonnie and Clyde*. On Sunday morning everyone was calm again, but she avoided mentioning his name.

The crowd of day trippers swallowed them, when they left the car by a fountain in the centre of Sao Pedro. She followed closely Leonora's moody back. Round the tarps laid out on the ground to display the rows of patched shoes and clogs and often stacked with cages of live birds. She was sure the smaller birds were owls. Perhaps they ate them there; they ate barnacles, and there was donkey meat in the butchers.

They stopped before a great land army of terracotta pots

that hid completely the cobbles of the town square. She stood quivering at the sight. To choose was simple: glazed or unglazed. She gathered up the smallest dishes she could find: glazed inside and unglazed out, the outsides scrolled and dotted with a pale cream-coloured slip. Now she hopes that her cherished finds have survived their journey home intact.

Michael admires craftsmanship, especially in metal. It is part of his job. He is holding up a tiny weight against the light that falls from a street lamp. She switches on the ceiling spots.

'You can tell they were made by hand from these file marks on their sides. Every weight is marked in drams. I think it's an old apothecary's scale.'

'You're right, it is. I knew you'd like it.' She shakes out the tea cloth she has been wringing as she watched.

'I'll need a loupe to read that one.' He gives up and puts down the weight.

'Maybe I can see it. Let me try later. I could read them all in Portugal, but the light was clearer there.' She has backed into the kitchen, where she fills and plugs in the kettle, wrapping both hands around it as it warms. Through the hatch she can see her suitcase lying flat on the teak dining table. Unlocking it, she releases a whiff of sand with *Ambre Solaire*. Her fingers dig between the folds of her dresses, feel the linen cover of his Art book and prod her blazer for the small folio that is hidden in a sleeve. *Zé's funny old ink drawings. He gave me these, bless him, so that I would have something to bring home.* Smiling absently, she lifts the *bacalhau* from its brown paper wrapping. 'Good! It's still in one piece.'

'Whatever is that?' Michael has crept up behind her.

'Dried codfish salted; we ate a lot of this in Portugal. You have to soak it first for an hour and a half, no more, no less, and then you layer it with sliced potatoes — let me see if I've got an oval dish large enough for it — then you drop green olives round the rim and sliced hard-boiled eggs on the top. It's really yummy and you can't buy it over here.'

'If you're cooking that, you can count me out. I'll eat at my mother's.'

'You're always eating at your mother's. You've never given

my cooking a chance.'

'My mother always has it ready for me.'

'And I don't, I suppose. I'm just standing here, keeping everything hot for you to tell me that you've eaten.'

The kettle screams from the kitchen. She dashes in and quickly swills inside the teapot with scalding water, while Michael mooches about continuing to talking at her through the hatch.

'It's not for much longer any road, because I shan't be working in the daytime. I've got a night job at *The Express*.'

The wall-cupboard door clouts her on the temple. 'Ouch! I can't find the tea. Didn't you order any? Where are this week's groceries?' She moves around the kitchen, opening drawers and banging them shut.

'I'll earn more working nights.'

Working nights, so he doesn't have to face up to his problems. Well, at least he won't be accusing me of denying him his rights again. His marital rights. Huh!

'There isn't any coffee either, only Camp.'

'No thanks. You can drink that muck. I'll be able to save the money up so I can branch out …' She fails to catch the rest of the sentence, when he wanders over to the stove.

'Branch out doing what? Damn and blast! Now there's no milk.' She slams the fridge door shut. The motor revs. Empty stout bottles roll.

'Start my own business. Doing what? I don't know. Whatever I decide.'

The hot drink burns her gullet. She glares at the kilted Scotsman on the bottle. His money won't affect her. She still won't be told how much he earns. He'll still begrudge her the housekeeping and, on top of that, he'll be at home all day. Sleeping upstairs. While she waits to serve him his dinner at whatever time he comes down. Plus her friends will all stay away; they'll be afraid of waking him up. She walks to the living room and stands her coffee cup on the floor in front of the sofa, as she sits. His feet are on the rug; his eyes are burning through the back of her neck.

'Go on, then. Tell us who he is.' He utters it so flatly, so matter-of-factly that it catches her off guard.

It's too soon. I can't tell him yet. When she sits back, he is raking through his iron grey hair, his low brow deeply furrowed. 'Who? I don't know who you're talking about.'

'Don't give me that; you know damned well.' His toe is digging in the rug, parting the fleece, revealing white skin.

She needs a smoke and walks to the table. Fumbling, she scatters packs of *Stuyvesant* over the dusty teak. She leans against the wall, lights up and, after righting herself, blows a lungful of smoke through the kitchen hatch. Just then, when her head touched the wall, she thought it nestled in his armpit and that her fingers held a flattened *Gauloise* that he'd lit for both of them to share. Until recalling they could be seen, he would lift his arm, they would pull apart and then stay luxuriating side by side in the heat from the low sun. Until it melted into the Atlantic. Whatever made her come back?

'*How can you live with a man who does not love you?*'

'*Well, I can't just stay here, can I?*'

'*Yes, stay. Just stay.*'

With Anna cradled in his arms he stood close behind her, sheltering her back. While she watched the flakes of yellow paint spinning down the gulley of the old sluice. The poor storm-wracked and broken sluice. Then she turned to him with her litany, her voice beginning low and rising in pitch with each successive repeat.

'*For one thing, I need to bring our winter clothes and Anna's toys and my sewing machine. All the things I need to work with, so I can make my living over here.*'

The truth was that she had to come home to do what she is doing now. This. Telling Michael. Being honest. Open. She would have told him in her own time. Because she doesn't know, but it's just possible that she still loves him in a way. She dawdles back to the sofa, while Michael bats away her cigarette smoke before returning to his scales.

'So. What's the geezer's name then?' he says, without turning from his scales. He drops a weight into a pan. The beam clangs down, chains a-jiggle. 'Go on, then. Let's be hearing you. The chap you met over there.'

'Over where?'

'You know where. There, where you've just been — Portugal, wasn't it? He's a beach boy, I suppose.'

'I told you, I don't know what you're talking about.' Light from a ceiling spot is dancing on the tangle of brass chains, expanding and contracting with the rhythm of her breathing. 'All right, so I met an interesting painter — and now we're friends.'

Michael turns to face her, sneering. 'Oh, a painter, is he? What kind of painter? Not another blooming artist!' Doubled over laughing, he makes a show of leaning on her bookcase for support. She feels her cheeks begin to flush, but holds her tongue until the mocking stops and he is watching her from the opposite wall.' An artist. I might have known. I bet he's not got two bloomin' brass ha'pennies to rub together. They see you coming, these people. Like I've told you before many times, Jody— you're just a soft touch.'

'You've got it all wrong. You're talking rubbish.'

'All right, I talk rubbish. Tell me then, what kind of a sob story did he give you? Did you go out with him? You did. You went out with him. I can tell, you know; I'm not daft.'

'Maybe I did — once or twice.'

'And you paid, I suppose.'

'For goodness sake, it wasn't like that. And anyway, what if I did? What's wrong with that? It's poor there, don't you realise? And he — well, never mind...' She drops her voice. 'I can't see why it matters who pays for things as long as somebody does.' She further softens her tone. 'You can't buy people.'

'Oh, can't I? Can't I? Where would you be without this house, without this and all this?'

'Ssh! You'll wake Anna. *Will* you try to keep your voice down, please? Things don't matter.'

'Things don't matter. Money doesn't matter. You'll be telling me next, that we can't own 'owt, that everything just lives with us for a while. Well, I've heard it all before, too many times. You're completely up the spout.' He shakes his head and mutters to himself, then turns back to his scales and removes a weight from its slot. Tossing it in his palm and planting it resoundingly on the coffee table, he says: 'I'm going out.' He clatters up the stairs, which rise above where she sits on the settee. Within minutes he is thudding down them again, reeking of Old Spice. And rubbing his hands together while he paces up and down the room. 'Well, I'm not going to worry myself over the likes of him. He can't afford you. So tell us his name. Go on. Has he got one?'

'Zé,' she says. And more warmly, 'He's called Zé.'

'Zé? That's a name? He sounds a right dick head.' He tugs at his suede tie to centre it, flicks his sleeve and grips the door handle.

'And I love him,' she says, turning to the blank doorway.

The outside door slams; the glass panes in her bookcase rattle. And once she is sure his car really has torn away out of earshot, she tiptoes into the hall and puts her ear to Anna's bedroom door. The childish breathing soft and regular calms the tight band around her chest, and so she lingers in the hall. Should she go upstairs and swap the half-crowns in his trouser pockets for florins? No, it's petty and she doesn't need to any more. Didn't she earn enough from her sewing to take them both abroad?

And she's just said she loves Zé. Which she never did, when she was with him. Nor did he. He only ever said, 'I found you.' Which in *her* book is deeper, much, much deeper. Zé found her; Portugal found her. Portugal came looking for her, while she waited in the pitch dark at the local station for her friends to fetch them. It burst into the waiting room, bringing strange and exotic scents. While she was slowly feeling her way round the picture-tiled walls. That station would have been a Victorian gin palace over here. And she smiles as she recalls the villas painted in bright sugar pink, in pennyroyal blue, the warm yellow of melted butter. Their pergolas dripping lush vines, rows of potted flowers squatting on their steps. Everywhere, even out of factory gates, spilled a love of colour.

She lifts the telephone receiver and hears the operator's, Number please.

'I want to send a telegram to Portugal please. Lisbon, that's right. José Manuel Rodrigues Oliveira de Sá. I'll spell it for you and I'll spell the address.' His parents aren't on the phone, the same as hers. A telegraph boy will soon whizz her message round on a bike.

Contented, she sets to calmly counting out her pottery on the rug. One handle has broken off a sweet little dish. She can mend that herself. And satisfied with her purchases, she clears a space for them in the cupboard. Then with the cardigan that wrapped her Art book now balanced on her shoulders, she carries over to the sofa the pride of all of her possessions: his *'L'Art Moderne.'* It was the only book in his studio, as far as she could see, but he insisted she take it, and that she read it. The pencilled note on the flyleaf brings a little stab of fear. The inscription he wrote so thoughtfully before abruptly handing it to her. She knows it by heart by now, and she mouths it as she reads:

Et surtout n'oublie pas, Jody, il faut cueillir ... She understands now that she is here. He was reminding her of their purpose, of the poor hopes they must realise before time and life fall away. She will need him to keep telling her because, destroy them, life really can. Especially here in England. Did he know what could happen here? Perhaps he did. Perhaps it's why he didn't come to the airport to see her off. Or maybe he was there, but just as he'd said, she couldn't see him. She'll know for certain, when he writes.

His French sounds a little odd now from over here, intellectual and literary in a way she'd come to take for granted. She grabs a pencil and writes, *I Love You*, below his inscription. But then, agitated, rubs it out and claps the lovely raw linen covers shut. Now where can it live? She doesn't know. Leafing through the small folio of drawings, she is still puzzled. He said they puzzled him, too. Comic figures with their noses morphing into candles, hands into alarm clocks, bottle-openers, other crazy things. And signs, lots and lots of signs. And they don't have to mean a thing, he said.

She picks up five weights and tosses them. They serve as jacks in a game of Fivestones with herself. Game over, she slots them into a row of lozenge-shaped holes. The smallest clinks in first.

Zé believes in me. He believes in my abilities.

And another: *I could paint, he said, and he would teach me.*

The next sounds more solid: *I have to justify my existence. We all do, he said.*

Now a heavy clonk. *If I work hard enough, I can take us both out of here for good. The scales are levelled and stilled. But not so hard that I get that rotten pleurisy again.*

As she yawns her way upstairs, she glances back at the trappings of her life. Scandinavian teak, vat-dyed hessian, central heating. When all she needs is the love of a poor man with sea-coloured eyes.

Three

Lancashire. October 10, 1966

BROWN AND PURPLE moorland beyond a spate of grey slate roofs. New bungalows and sprinkled sheep reflect a lemony film of sky. The tarn is flashing Morse code. She has spent the week at home, sewing in her room, running up the lemon yellow straw cloth dress that she wears today. To cock a snook at the weather. Grimy gritstone terraces with doorsteps glowing bath-brick yellow herald the approaching mill town and the traffic jams that will follow. The car accelerates. She grips her headscarf. He took the hood down this morning despite the cooling of the air and her almost backless summer shift. The roadsides are now a flypast of blackened red brick, used-car lots, orphaned mill chimneys. Michael at the wheel beside her stares grimly ahead.

You'll get over him, is all he's said about it since; so that must be that.

The car has slowed to a crawl. Anna bounces on her lap, which lets her screen her face from Michael's glances, when they drive by her workroom above a boarded-up shop. She glimpses her sewing machine through the first-floor window. She did cover it, after all. She imagines Zé's letter landing on the doormat on Monday morning. If he writes to her straightaway.

'Back to work on Monday morning early, Anna. Just Anna and mummy.'

Vacant lots proliferate around them, gaping holes in the decaying teeth of a mill town in decline. The town planners are in earnest here, and the traffic has to take the strain. The engine stalls before some roadworks and, still, Michael stares ahead.

'Do you want to call at the market?' he asks, pulling on the choke.

'Why not? They aren't expecting us until three.'

A shiver pierces through her as she wonders if he plans to shop her to her father. Both are pathetic. But it is Saturday and the mood in the town centre is upbeat. Across the open dirt ground raddled with brick dust that hosts the market, a loud cheer rises from an open-air used-car auction at the back. Aisles of covered stalls and hot-dog vans are belching the steamy odours of tripe and onions, pasties and fish and chips wrapped in newsprint. Hissing urns of tea and canned soup. She buys a cabbage, a cauliflower, turnips, carrots and potatoes, and then she and Anna roam the aisles between the stalls looking for the best fruit.

'Look at all these apples, Anna. Watermelon all gone though.' While her coxes are weighed, she looks around for Michael and spots him with a friend of his who is queueing at the black-pudding stall. She waves and mouths: 'We have to go.'

They turn off the dual carriageway into Ashendale, a short cul-de-sac of grey roughcast maisonettes. The entire Smith family is gathered in the living room, her sisters perched on the piano stool, the men slumped in easy chairs. Everyone's attention follows Anna to the middle of the floor. Jody needn't have worried; she faces only indifference. Her tan is noted in an eye blink, while her dress mutely disapproved of. Perhaps they see the defiance in the way she pitches her still-glowing tan against the cooling of the air.

At the first snips of her scissors into that lovely lemon coloured cloth, its fresh grassy smell was overwhelming. She had come across it while out shopping in Lisbon with Leonora, had seen the roll propped against a shopfront across the street from Grandelo's. With the many craftsmen in the city there is little call for big department stores. Grandelo's is the sole exception. Leonora says people even buy their books a few pages at a time and, when they have the right number, take them to a bookbinder to be bound.

As the banter in the living room swells to loud and competitive, she cannot stop herself from sinking into an edgy unfocussed silence. Balanced on the arm of an easy chair, she feels the satin lining of her shift begin to ride upward from her knees. And glances round the group to locate the circulating bowl of trifle. Once it lands in her lap, she hoards it. But her brother-in-law can no longer resist a snide remark. And this time, even she is shocked at the sharpness of her retort.

'What's it got to do with you? I'll wear whatever I like.'

The scraping of spoons on plates is suddenly intense. Her exasperated father is tripping over kicked-off shoes on his way to the kitchen. Anna sidles up, her eyes saucer-like, and dips her fist into the trifle.

'No, Anna, keep your hands out of it. Popsie is coming back.'

And then her dad is by her side, unfolding and flicking out a starched tea cloth, which he lays flat across her knees. Stepping back to make sure they are completely covered, he says: 'There. That'll solve it.' And with a snort into his handkerchief, he sinks into his chair. Michael wanders in after him. She looks from one to the other. It is obvious from their faces that they were talking about her.

'Watch Anna for me, will you, Michael? I'm going through to dry the dishes.'

She whips away the clean tea towel and bolts with it to the kitchen, which is roomier and is warmed by the sun's rays piercing through the nets. Her mother straightens up from leaning on the stacked kitchen table, her spread hands moving to her back. Hurriedly she pins a stray wisp of hennaed hair into her French pleat, smooths her apron and steps back better to appraise her eldest daughter.

'Oh, you do look nice, dear. Turn around and let me see the back. Mmm, very daring. Did you have a pattern for it or did you —?'

'I made my own pattern; I'll adapt it for you, if you want.'

'Go on with you. I need to cover my poor old knees. And my back. If I was your age, mind ... I was quite the fashion plate myself once, to the extent we could be in wartime with the coupons and the shortages. So tell me, how is that friend of yours getting on in Portugal? Leonora, isn't it? Is she settled there yet?'

'Yeah. She seems to be.'

'I can't understand a girl like her leaving her mother like that to go and live so far away. It's very sad.'

'Sad? It isn't sad. She married Carlos, and Carlos is Portuguese. His job's there; he's a surveyor. He's been working on the new *Sálazar* suspension bridge across the estuary. It's finished now and it's amazing, just like the one in San Francisco. You should see it, Mum. Anyway her sister's a lot farther away than her; she's in Kuala Lumpur.'

'Oh, their poor mother! She must be worried stiff.'

'Of course she isn't; she's different from you. Their mother is a magistrate, and her parents went there for the wedding. They had two, you know, two weddings. The one in Rochdale and, afterwards a Roman Catholic one in Portugal, so it's recognised over there. Leonora's been abroad loads of times. That was how she met Carlos — on a package holiday in Estoril. I wanted to travel, but I wanted to do it properly. Work abroad, off my own bat. But the bank told me at the interview that I couldn't even have an application form for the DCO division. They don't let women join. Surprise surprise. You didn't know about that, did you?'

'I don't know what the world's a-comin' to. We never carried on like that. And you were wrong, young lady, going off abroad like that without your husband. I wouldn't dream of going anywhere without your father, I wouldn't want to.' Her mother gravitates to the sink, empties the bowl and runs some fresh water.

'I wasn't completely over the pleurisy, don't forget. The doctor asked me if there was somewhere I could convalesce. And then as luck would have it Leonora wrote and asked me over there and so I went. I loved it there. It made me better. And I wasn't getting on with Michael, so … I paid for it all myself.'

'Not getting on? You have to get on. You'd better not come running back here with your 'not getting on.' Or we'll send you back where you belong, young lady — at home with your husband.'

'Do you want the baking tins and saucepans dried or not? Only the rack is full.'

'Pull the bath-top down then, girl. How long is it since you lived here?'

She unhooks the hinged tabletop and lowers it slowly to rest on the rim of the bath. Then a black and white gingham curtain on elastic stretches round it like a skirt.

'Mum … you know at our old church, where we went before we moved here. You remember that pretty woman, the one with the black hair?'

'Mrs France, you mean.'

'That's right, Mrs France. She used to sit right at the back by herself, away from the the congregation. Mum, was that because she was divorced?'

'Well, yes, I think her husband left her. A long time ago, mind you.' Her mother's chin is tucked back while she speaks. 'She didn't have the right to sit with us anymore because she was a sinner.'

'Yeah, but you let her sing the solos at the front of the hall, didn't you?'

'We did, yes, because, as well you know, she had such a wonderful voice. It was a gift she had. Contralto it was.'

'I always thought she was an alto.'

'No, contralto. She'd bin somethin' on the stage in her day. Myself, I have to sing soprano, but I'm a messa by rights, a messa-soprano.

'I come to the garden alo—one,'

(*in unison*) 'While the dew is still on the ro—ses.

And the voice I hear,

Falling on my ear,

The Son of God di-isclo-oses.'

'I thought it was the Son of Man.'

'Course it isn't, silly girl.'

'A-and — he-e —— walks with me and he talks with me,

And he tells me I am his o—own ...'

At each crowded stop the bus judders and another line of mufflered figures is urged to, Move along inside. Anna sits on her knee, barricaded in by the seat in front of them and the canvas zip that holds her toys. Their first bus journey back to work begins to feel exasperatingly slow.

The key will turn, but the old shop door still refuses to budge. She puts her shoulder to it and shoves. Anna watches with a worried look, when it bursts open and her mother falls onto a pile of slightly muddied mail. The envelope that she is praying for, as she discards each of the manila ones, will be thin and blue with an aeroplane symbol and a Portuguese stamp.

'Strewth! It's not there.' Dejected, she leaves the pile of bills beneath the boarded-up window and goes to warm the back room before unfastening Anna's coat. Then she watches from the safety gate while the coloured wooden bricks she made for Anna are jettisoned from her truck, bitten and strewn around the room. Her feet are leaden as she mounts the stairs. *Why doesn't he write?* The golf-ball-sized lump in her throat is stifling any joy she may have felt at reclaiming her work bench. From her stool, she looks around walls, devoid of heart, devoid of will.

He did mention that he'd go to Coimbra to visit friends, but Coimbra isn't far. The last time he took the train there, he was back in town by the evening. She had slipped out of the house secretly to meet him on the promenade. She knew of course by then that Carlos took their meetings as a personal affront. So she waited till she heard his snores coming through the living-room door. Then she swapped the book she had been reading at the dressing table for her cardigan and, very slowly turned door handle, holding her breath. She would be back before they went to bed.

Seagulls swooping low. Dark figures crouched at the parapet. The clicking of fans. Along the promenade, a hundred eyes watched him as he breezed along towards her, visibly buoyed up by his own rarefied air.

'I just arrived. I thought I missed you. My friends were all there in Coimbra. Look, I brought you a postcard.'

At her work bench she sits distractedly rubbing her upper arm, recalling how his city jacket with its black wool serge felt rough against her newly sunburned skin. And how he slung it to his other shoulder that night, crooked his elbow for her hand before they stepped out together in unison, back the way she had come. She stopped in a pool of lamplight to read her card. Mellow stonework, gaudy flowerbeds, students top-to-toe in black with shiny gold top hats and canes.

'The University there is ancient. I studied medicine there for a year before I moved to the School of Art —'

' — in Lisbon. It can't be older than Oxford.'

'It is. Much.' He waited beneath the giant agave plant forked black like a trident against the risen and fickle moon. She joined him and they sauntered off again along the low clifftop wall. 'Fine mediaeval buildings,' he said, 'monuments they now demolish so they can impose their new Fascist style.'

'Who?'

'The *Estado Novo*.'

'Sálazar, you mean, don't you? Leonora was ranting on about him during dinner.'

Already seated at table, she had watched her friend stoking up for another of her evening rants. Red-faced, Leonora had swept her damp fringe aside, swilled her wine and downed a glass of water in one. And then she was off:

'He can't even behave like a normal dictator.'

Carlos, who sat next to her, groaned inwardly. She could sense it. So she asked him whether his work on the new suspension bridge was nearly finished.

'It is, Jody. Now I wait every day for it to fall down. I have the bad dreams.'

'He's nothing like Mussolini or Franco or any of them. You know where you are with Franco. But this guy is a shifty bugger. He behaves like a neurotic recluse, so everyone will think he's harmless. As if. Christ, he's only ever been to one meeting of his own blinking cabinet. How does he get away with it? He's never even been abroad. So why does anybody listen to him, is what I want to know. And why does Wilson let him meddle in Rhodesia? It's beyond me.'

'Has Our Trev been fed yet?' Carlos was watching wine rise to the brim of his emptied glass.

'I fed him,' she said, while Carlos stared impassively at Leonora. The cat was by her foot, rubbing up against the carved jacaranda table leg. She leaned her own bare back against the cool surface of her chair.

'Why must I keep telling you? We have the *Estado Novo* for forty years now, for Christ sake. We are stuck with it, so accept!'

'It's backward here, that's what. And *he* does everything he possibly can to keep it that way. I'm bringing back a washing machine the next time I go to Rochdale. And then I'll be able to cor—rupt you all with my evil technology.'

'It will cost you to bring one from there. And why bother, when you have Joãna and the *tanque*?'

'Workers bring them home from France, don't they?'

Carlos leaned in and drained the rest of the bottle into her glass. 'The next cat we have, I want to call Clive. I like it, don't you? Clive. You may think of him as like Dolfuss in Austria, Jody, or like Nasser.'

'Who? The cat?'

'Trevor? *Tchk!* Sálazar, stupid.' Leonora shot her a look. 'And everyone knows he's having it off with his housekeeper. Carlos can you find my new Charles Aznavour EP?'

Carlos was beside the radiogram, shuffling through their records. 'It's here somewhere, but I want to play some *fados* for Jody.'

'Amália ruddy Rodrigues? *Tchk.*'

'If you want,' said Zé, in answer to her question. 'Sálazar. The Public Man.'

The tiny cove below the cliff was gleaming whitely through the darkness, and a spring was playing from a cleft in the basalt. Across the *Marginal*, they found a sandy lane between two garden walls. And the light from Zé's pocket torch lit up lizard tracks on the rocks.

'Leonora is frustrated. There's a job, only a few hours a week, at the British Council library. Only Carlos never gets around to signing the consent forms, so she can take it.'

Farther up the lane, Zé began to sing, his voice low until the cut levelled out and strange syllables resonated off its high walls.

'*O Meu Dese-ejo.*'

'You're a baritone.'

'Yes, *baritono*. The *Lacrima* is too sad for you, no?'

'Well, they're all pretty sad, the *fados*. Carlos played me some earlier.'

'*Heu!* The *fado*.' He shook his head. 'But the *Fados de Coimbra* are something else. Choirs of men with *guitarras* and guitars perform them on the stone balconies high above the crowd.' Then he jumped three garden steps and, turning round, drew an arc in the sky. His forefinger wiggling in the crowd. 'Students crammed like canned sardines all swaying in the quadrangle.' He jumped down to stony ground. 'Everybody cries.' He was boyish that night.

'Everybody? The students as well?'

'*Sim*. It is the *Saudades de Coimbra*. I go to hear them every year. I know what I will sing you. The *Serenata da Queima das Fitas*. Listen. You will cry.'

If only all men would sing. If only other men would cry ...

The lane opened out abruptly onto a hillside, in silhouette an unlit villa. Her friends'.

'Damn it! They've gone to bed. Paulo wakes them with his teething pains, so they need to sleep when they can. Heck! I hope I brought my key.' Her fingers continued to prod the empty place in her purse. 'Why is it always keys?'

She whispered to him that she may have left the top vent open in her bedroom. He unlatched the gate. The hedge rattled. They waded knee-deep in grass that had long dried and run to seed. Below her window was a freshly dug trench, amber-sided in the torchlight. A half-wound reel of plastic tubing lay a few feet to the side.

'It is not deep. Here, you take the torch. You can to stand on my hands.' Zé jumped into the ditch and promptly made a cat's cradle of his fingers. 'Put your foot in there.'

'Ssh!' Her finger touched her lips. An owl hooted. She held tight to his hair, while she slid her other hand through the vent. And reached down inside the glass until her fingertips brushed metal. 'Higher,' she called. The handle jerked from her grasp. The window frame hit her face. An instant later she was sitting on him, a bump rising on her temple. He clamped her in his arms and held her there, while she giggled nervously whispering that they would wake the rest of the household. But he was slow to let her pull free.

Standing on his back to reach the window sill, she worried for his clean shirt. Relief came, when she could feel the solid wood floor through her thin soles. Looking out through the window, she could just see the top of his head. The rest of him was in the ditch, strumming an imaginary guitar while he mouthed a song.

'Don't make me laugh. They'll hear us.'

When he pressed his face to the glass to say goodnight, she wished she had let him kiss her, when he could.

'Four o'clock tomorrow at the café,' he mouthed, four fingers raised. And then his back was blending with the hedge.

Drifting off to sleep, half-listening for the hoot of the Lisbon train, she thought how lucky she had been that Zé was there to help her climb in. She tried to picture him in Lisbon, staying over with Eduardo at the apartment that had once been his. Setting off again at first light for an appointment somewhere in the city.

Four

The back end of October

AN EARLY MORNING with smoke on the wind and dark cloud banks breaking up to be dispersed across an oyster sky. Airborne leaves shudder in shop doorways, as she scutters past them, two fingers crossed. Her own door cracks open to shower her with sycamore wings. They collect in Anna's fur hood. Is that a postcard shining through the dead leaves scattered on the doormat? She seizes it and sleeves away the dust.

Red script across some mellow stonework: *Universidade de Coimbra*. Another card says *Oporto* above some painted barques in a marina, and has a yellow tram like the ones she and Anna rode on in Lisbon. She sifts through the rest and, there it is, the blue airmail envelope with, yes, a Portuguese stamp. Her sharp intake of breath causes her to cough on the cold air.

'One, two, three, all arrived together. Let me have a minute, will you, Anna. I want to open my letter, and then I'll get you out of your coat, I promise.'

Blue ink on tissue paper the colour of a summer sky. A passport-sized photograph tumbles out from a fold. A young man's face. His face? She tilts it to catch the light that enters through a chink in the window boards. He looks different with his hair sleeked back. It accentuates his eyes, which without his glasses are more candid than ever. But the white shirt with that dark tie and his sitting there like a stranger ... Except his mouth looks about to break into a smile.

She skip-reads the two closely-written sheets for a word or two in English. *Here's one — Kay. 'Did you see Kay?'* Yes, she saw Kay. She took the train to Nottingham with Anna, last week. And Kay has promised she will drop Eduardo a line, one of these days. Does he really need to mention Kay in the second paragraph? And the rest is in French. But never mind, her old school *Harraps* has been sitting on the bench in her workroom for weeks.

'Now let me take your coat off.' She dances round with Anna's rabbit-fur cape, while Anna whoops with laughter, tries to imitate and falls down with a bump. In the back room is the rag book she made for her with vivid dyes and wax, flash cards with red letters, and a defunct telephone that currently keeps her amused for hours. She locks the fireguard, lets herself out, and waits hidden on the stairs to listen to the start of Anna's play. And from the workroom, she calls down to her through a gap between two boards:

'*Brring, brring.* Hello, Mummy here. Is that Anna?'

From her stool she can see her cards propped at an angle on the windowsill. And she immediately sets to translating her letter. His writing is the very devil to decipher, just like her doctor's.

Chére Jody,

J'ai pensé à toi chaque jour depuis que tu es partie. Tu me manques douloureusement. Anna aussi.

'Tu me manques douloureusement,' she repeats aloud. She understands that; it means he misses her sorely. Has she not ached for him, too?

Dès que j'ai reçu le télégramme, dont je te remercie, je suis allé chez Nicola, mais…

She looks down the list of prepositions at the back of her dictionary. *Dès que…* As soon as.

As soon as I received the telegram, for which I thank you, I went to café Nicola, but I could not support — I couldn't stand — *to stay alone in Lisboa. I passed several days in Coimbra with friends* — who are returned from the vacation of the summer?— *who are back from the summer holidays.*

I stayed long in Oporto and farther north in the Minho. You would like it in the north. The life is closer to nature, the people work hard and they are good people, sympathetic, artisans. I have friends there, a couple and they have a child also. They work together making pottery and jewellery. But the ridiculous red tape here makes it almost impossible to work together in a collective. You return when? December? Say you will be with me in December and permit me to hope, Jody. Lisboa is now a desert. The Nortada has blown itself out, and autumn winds bring the melancholy. I fear for people I know here and especially my friend Miguel. The news is slow to arrive.

Eduardo, Armando and Isabel send you kisses. All wait for your return. I suspect that young Rui writes for you a letter in his room. He must show it to me first, before to send it to you. He is timid and he says the stupid things. I too, sometimes. I am a ridiculous man ...

Muffled voices are distracting her; they are coming from the floor below. Her pinking shears will serve as paperweight, while she goes to peer down the stairwell. Moll is down below with Caitlin who is rattling Anna's gate.

'Yoo-hoo, up there!' Moll calls up the stairs. 'We've been to the Friday market, and I called in at the convent on the way. My successor in the Art room is leaving to get married.' Moll's enthusiasm fills the building, as Jody waits for her to lift red-haired Caitlin across the gate. And then she clatters up the stairs, the pleats of her yellow suit pinched between her fingers, and with her mop of coppery curls bouncing as she brushes by some loose wallpaper.

'Uh-oh, it's Mrs Sunshine again. Heels on today, too?' Jody backs away so Moll can pass her.

'Yes, they're the new shape. The sisters at the convent called them lavatory heels.'

'It's freezing. Have you not noticed?'

'You need some flesh on your bones, Jody. If you get any thinner, you'll disappear when you turn sideways.'

'Don't worry, I'll shout very loud so you know where I am. And I've always been thin, just like I've always had square shoulders and gnat bites instead of breasts. It's why I couldn't feed —'

'*Tchk*. Stop that right now. Aha! He's written?' Moll starts towards the bench.

'Yes, finally. But what have you got in the parcel? Remnants?'

'No, I found a whole bundle of brushed nylon sheeting. Look at this. Direct from the mill.' Moll undoes the string, and pale yellow mousse tumbles from its paper wrapping. 'There's enough to make a pair of sheets and a lovely warm negligée for me.'

'Warm? Sweaty more like. It makes enough static to start a fire and have you committed for arson. You can half-see through it, too.'

'Can you? Len will like that.'

Moll is broad-faced with the plain open features of a Joan of Arc. And with her fat knees and large bones, she would look gloriously statuesque in nothing but a long see-through nightie. Jody can just see her waving Len off on a winter's morning, with the lights on and the paintings that she did in college on the walls behind her. Sometimes, when walking past Moll's house, she feels proud to be her friend.

'So Len might, but winter's coming soon. Leave that and come here.' She pulls her friend towards the window and his photograph on the sill. 'There he is. It's only small, I'm afraid. And quite old, I should think. So, *now* tell me his eyes aren't like Peter O'Toole's.'

His image leaps about in Moll's gloved hand, reflecting light from the street. The traffic rolling by, the silence in the room, both seem to last for ever. She feels relieved to hold the photo in her hand again and drop it into her smock.

'Well, at least he looks intelligent. So, does this mean that you'll eat now, girl? 'Cos that would be a relief.' Moll is staring at some rolled cartridge sheets among the clutter on her bench. 'I don't want to stop you working,' she says, without turning from the rolls. 'I can take Anna to the birthday party this afternoon, if you like. Caitlin would be happy, and you could concentrate on your work.' She sidles up to the rolled drawings on the bench and opens one out. 'Oh, I say. Well done. Are these something new?' She looks through the loose sketches in graphite. 'Shades of Cathy McGowan?' she says, holding up the only finished one in thick black felt-tip. Moll carries it over to the back wall. And once her teeth are free of drawing pins, comes to stand beside her. Together they evaluate the image that now dominates the room. A stylised boy and girl, wide-eyed, with splayed legs and with some wily stick-birds at gravity-defying angles. 'Hmm, I see. Asparagus legs.'

'Asparagus legs? Shurrup, you. I'm doing boys' leather shorts cut high like the ones the French kids wear. And for the dresses, I shall need to find someone to crochet the deep collars.'

Len's mother does crochet. I could ask her, if you like. They'll be in écru, won't they? You don't want them in white.' Jody winces, and Moll continues, 'Is that the stuff for the dresses? Paisley? I'd love an orange one for Caitlin; it would go with her red hair. And I can use your cuttings for my rag dolls, don't forget.' Moll has edged to top of the stairwell and glances down.

'All right, if you're sure about it, I can make my sample in Caitlin's size. Anna will have the deep rose.'

'All's quiet downstairs. So I'll be off, so as not to hinder you. D'you want to take a look at this, by the way? I can leave it with you.' Moll brings a folded newspaper from her bag.

'Is that today's *Guardian*? I haven't got the time to read it.'

'No, it's an old one. I was laying a fire in the grate and had to stop, when I saw this article. It's on Angola. I brought it with me to finish reading on the bus. It shocked me, I must say. The writer refers to Angola as Portugal's Algeria, but says it's worse.'

'There hasn't been anything —'

'No, there hasn't, not for quite a while, but it's still been happening nonetheless. I can't imagine how they managed to keep this out of the news, or even why, but it seems that they did. And now this *Guardian* man's been over there and ...' Moll opens out the paper and reads aloud, at times simply snatching lines from here and there in a long article.

The MPLA accuse the Portuguese of doubling taxes on Africans to pay for military expenditure ... ... seizing African savings ... ... forcing Africans with motor cars to pay taxes on a daily basis ... ... executing Africans without trial ... ... dropping the corpses of political prisoners into the Atlantic, from aeroplanes, flying high, so that there is no evidence of their murder.'

'What? Drop them in the sea? Who? Does he mean the Africans?'

Moll merely nods without lifting her eyes from the page.

'Angolans and political prisoners, both black and white ...'

Jody's mouth has fallen open and it won't let her close it; neither will her lips form a word. Then her face crumples and she bends forward as if she has been shot.

'That can't be true.'

'But I think it is. Listen to this: *Portuguese authorities are making it impossible for these reports to be investigated. The International Commission of Jurists ... ... was refused permission to be present at a mass political trial ... ... the commission's request was described as an insult to Portuguese justice ... ... MPLA leader was only repeating information ... ...which I received, from a source I regard as thoroughly trustworthy, when I was travelling in territories adjoining Angola.'*

'He's been there, you see, this *Guardian* man. You want it? I can leave it with you, if you like.'

'I can't read that!' She waves the offensive article away, averting her face.

Moll is picking up her shopping bags and her face, too, is averted, as she asks Jody quietly:

'Does he still have to go there, your friend?'

'To Angola? I don't know ... No, I don't think so, not now. He says his father will buy him out.'

'Ah, that. And you believe him, of course. Don't bother coming down with me. I can find Anna's coat.'

She follows Moll to the top stair and watches her walk down.

'And don't forget her beaker. But wait a minute, Moll. Listen. Do you think I'm naive?'

'Hmm. Sometimes.'

The shop door bangs to and sends a cold draught up the stairs. She pounces on his letter, on the bench, as if her life depends upon unravelling the only thread that can connect them. She reads through the first part, the lines that she has already translated, and she absorbs the gist of the rest before she tucks the letter and his photograph safely into her purse. And still feeling shaky, but a lot calmer than she was, she wanders about the room.

He still sounds worried about what has happened to Miguel. She doesn't know Miguel; she hasn't met him, but she knows who he is. When she and Zé met, Miguel had already been missing since June. The secret police always arrest students just before exams, he told her. Miguel wasn't just arrested, though. He disappeared. Straight off the street. *Pfft!* Just like that. And even the little Zé has told her, which isn't very much at all, is more than he should ever have risked.

'There will be things I cannot tell you, Jody. If I did, it could be dangerous, maybe even for both of us.'

They were meandering along the walkway in the direction of the grand hotel. Across the *Marginal*, other café customers began to trail homeward. A bit of light was coming off the sea. And they could hear a dance band and spates of laughter as they drew nearer to the hedge that bordered the hotel car park. Flashes of shocking pink and peacock would bob across a yellow floodlight beam, to vanish into the night. A car engine would purr, and Zé would say it was the sound of foreign money. Minutes before, he'd got up stiffly from the table and said pointedly: 'I must return to Paris.'

Curious, she had probed him with, 'When will you go?' He looked flummoxed. But he'd said he lived there once. She was reading at the time: *On the Road*, the copy Alistair had given her. And Zé had told her that he couldn't read it in Portugal. It was banned. So he must have read it in Paris. 'So, when d'you think?'

'When I go to Paris? Not for a long time unless I walk.' His voice was higher-pitched than usual and, after glancing over his shoulder, he took a deep breath before continuing. 'A friend of mine, Gil, walked through the mountains into Northern Spain, and then through the Pyrénées and on to Paris. It was easy then. He was dressed in robes like a priest, and so they left him alone. But Gil went two summers ago. Now the things are more difficult.' And after a glance behind him, he uttered flatly: 'I lied to you. I did not live in Paris. I tried to go and I still want to go, but I have not a passport. I had one, my father helped me, but three months ago, before the holiday, the *PIDE* took it from me.'

'Before I came.'

On their treeless edge of the cliff the faint breeze was all but imperceptible. But whispers reached her from the far side of the Marginal, from the pepper trees and stone pines that stood behind garden walls.

'They will return my passport to me after the military. Four years it is now — in Africa.'

'In Africa? You mean Angola? It was in the news a lot a while back. I remember because the photos used to fill the whole front page.'

'Angola, Moçambique, Guinea Bissau and, recently Macao. Macao is the worst of all. I know men who come home broken and reject their former life. They walk away.' He stopped walking, seemingly reluctant to go on. 'I met a guy the other day. He was just returned from Macau. Blinded! Blinded and broken. Now he turns from his family and only drinks.'

His hand alighted on her shoulder, where it stayed until they reached the end of the path and stood before a tall hedge, its lower limbs set against a yellow light. He looked preoccupied as they turned. The stars lit their way back.

'Oh, I've got it now. You mean your passport has been confiscated. But why? And who are the *PIDE*?'

'Secret police. The Gestapo trained them, here and in Germany before the war.' His arm dropped from her shoulder and, hands in his pockets, he began kicking stones against the low wall. Then he moved a few feet away and stood staring down below the wall at the undulating sea. '*Bem*. My professors recommended me for study at an Art school abroad. Paris, London, no matter where. I gained a scholarship, too, but then the *Instituto* — the political police that set our academic standards — they refused me a permit to leave.'

'But I thought you were a student here.' She sidled over and joined him in his gazing out to sea.

'I am, or rather I was until ...' He was searching in her face. '*Bem*. You understand about the censor, no? I told you about that, about Joan Baez, the banned books ... So, why try to be a painter here, if I am not allowed to be a good one?'

'I see.'

An eerie blue light was suddenly glazing the waves.

Seconds later, when it melted away, the ocean was as dull as lead. Surf deposits like white treacle streaked the rocks that lay below the parapet. And then a clatter came from the café terrace as a shadow moved between the tables.

'António is keeping watch for me,' he whispered, crossing to the outside of the path before they walked on.' And so I tried again this year to go with another student, Miguel. But this time it was only for a summer school in Paris. Montparnasse. The *Alliance Française*. It was in French Cinema and Political Theory. All year we spent chasing after the permit and we succeeded. We had a sponsor, also. A Paris critic well-known in Portugal, a Portuguese. He invited us at his expense and he guaranteed our return. He wrote for us a testimonial.' He said all this with quiet pride.

'Well that's great. So you could go.'

A crack behind them made him turn around, as a dog walker hawked and spat.

'Wait until they go down to the beach.'

Later, as he walked her home, she sensed that he was glad of her quiet openness. And she distracted him by talking about the music scene in Manchester. 'The club is called *The Twisted Wheel.*'

'*A demain*?' he whispered, when he left her at the gate.

'Perhaps. I don't know.'

The next morning over breakfast, Leonora was curious.

'Did he kiss you?'

'I forget. No, he forgot, I think. But he wanted to. He nearly did.'

All she knows of what happened next to Zé and his friend Miguel, she has had to piece together from fragments. They caught the night train from Lisbon to Paris, but at some point, at the border perhaps, the *PIDE* agents came on board. And they refused to accept their papers, or maybe didn't even look at them and then sent them both back to Lisbon. Apparently their funds were thought insufficient for a month in Paris. Zé said they had plenty and, in any case, they had a sponsor.

'The student restaurants are cheap, and you can do a lot with drawings; you can exchange them for cheese, other things.'

Miguel must have disappeared soon after, which would have been at the start of the long summer holidays. Once, she recalls, she and Zé were on the way to Lisbon and their train stopped for a long while at Caxias. She didn't mind the wait. Through the window, she saw a white marble fortress, odd but beautifully ornate and standing right in the middle of the beach. A dreamscape. But Zé was agitated, seriously so until the train had pulled out. And even then he didn't speak.

Eduardo seems to be the friend that Zé relies on to bring him information. To find out things he wants to know. Once, after they had shaken hands, because Eduardo was about to leave, there was a tiny shred of white paper that was stuck to Zé's palm. He let her peep at it quickly. It said Caxias → Aljube. She didn't ask him what it meant. Perhaps he's lucky after all that his only forfeit was his passport. But it means he's stuck there, so that she must go to him. But first, she needs to earn the money for their boat tickets and a trunk.

The quickest things to make to earn some money with will be the boys' leather shorts. They're a cinch. She can stick the seams back. And they'll sell like whinberry tarts. Bound to. She hugs herself from side to side, which sends a box of pins flying off her bench. And still teasing out pins from cracks between the boards and sucking her finger, she remembers that she has the afternoon to herself entirely free of Anna. And urgent things to do in the city.

She loves her trunk. It is British racing green with sturdy brown leather straps, a lock as big as a porthole and eight shiny gilt corner pieces. The largest one they have in *Futter's*, and they can deliver it C.O.D to her workroom within the week. She will pack it there, a few things at a time. It will be closer for British Rail to collect. And Michael mustn't know yet. But what's that flutter in her chest? She tries to rub away a scuff mark from the lid with her glove.

While nipping through Cosmetics and then a side door to the street, she begins to worry that the *Rockin' Horse* will have sold nothing of hers. And if so, how would she find the agent's deposit by five o'clock? The *Royal Mail Line* doesn't wait for people like her. She fairly zips through the quiet back streets behind Deansgate, wishing hard. And nearly falls into the boutique, where she waits beneath the glassy stare of the wooden piebald in the window. A door curtain parts, and Olga slips in, leafing through her order book. The boutique owner is small enough to wear the kids' clothes herself. Today it is a jersey pinafore with wide multicoloured bands.

'Yes, Jody, I sold all of the PVC macs.'

'All of them? You mean that?'

'Yes, and I'll take repeats please. That's one of each size. What's that you're holding? Leather shorts? Oh, brilliant! It's so hard to find cool things for the boys.' Olga pulls her sample this way and that. The softness of the leather and the cut appear to satisfy her. 'I'll have a go at these. Two of each size, one brown, one black. The dresses are excellent, but I can only take the larger sizes.'

'Olga, I need to tell you I may be moving after Christmas. Abroad.' She watches Olga's pen as it begins a new page. 'But only to Portugal. I can still come over on visits. It's known for leather goods, isn't it? I might learn something there.' She hopes it sounded casual enough.

'In that case, I had better keep a stock.' Olga licks a pencil stub, blacks out the quantities and writes X2 at the side. 'Let me alter yours before I write you the cheque for the last lot.' And she melts again through the draped purple chenille. 'I wish I could take more, but you can see how it is.' She calls through the curtain and then is back and ducking under rails. 'Have you tried the *Futter's* childrenswear buyer yet? I think you could.' She blows on a cheque and flaps it. 'They're more switched-on than they were; they stock some of my labels, I see, and they'll do better than me.'

She's postdated it. Now what? 'I'm surprised. I was just in there and I didn't think to look upstairs. I could ring them.'

She watches from the kerb as Olga locks up. They walk some way along the warehouse fronts.

'The Beatles are in the Algarve. It's a tad wild there, I hear, but it must be warmer in the winter.'

'I should think so. I'll be in Lisbon and even that's warmer than here.'

'Best of luck, then.' Olga blows her a kiss as she veers off.

Back on Deansgate, she puts down her bag. She wants to read through her order, to be sure she hasn't got it wrong.

Oh boy. Get that. I think I must be going ...

She likes the atmosphere in the back streets that she passes through next. Here the textile converters cram their basements with taffeta for linings, poplin shirting, raincoat gabardines and nylon for umbrellas. The haberdashers' dusty windows are choc-a-bloc with metal handbag frames; gilt and silver chaining is sold here by the yard, metal studs and brass eyelets by the pound. Some lend money too. Today she heads for her favourite dealer in leather skins and pelts.

The Twisted Wheel club is boarded up and fly posted with the line-up for a session at the new venue. Tib Lane is fairly booming with the mounting strains of *Believe Me,* which she traces to the *Cona* coffee bar, the place where she and Michael met.

'You don't have to say you love me, just be close at hand.
You don't have to stay forevvah —- I will understa-and...'

She forgets whose idea it was to dive down those steps that night. Whether hers or Viv's. Certainly it was hers to walk up to one of the two decent-looking lads seated at the next table and ask him a favour. *'Would you mind pretending you're my husband? And quickly please.'* Quickly, because the rough-looking types that followed them, were already peering down the steps. And so, she and Viv got some frothy coffee and motorbike rides home. Who would have thought that such a random thing as that could have changed her life? And how prophetic that innocent request has turned out to be. Michael can go to the new *Twisted Wheel* on Friday nights with Geoff now ... But she must hurry.

A more plaintive wavering song is curling up Bernie's warehouse steps, and she skims down to the basement to *My Yiddishe Momma.* She doesn't recognise the words. She only knows the Aznavour recording in French. She has to duck at times the low-ceilings and she breathes a musky animal smell, as she paces methodically the aisles of rolled skins. Dust triggers a cough. The warehousemen gathered round the wireless look up, tip their homburgs and glance pointedly at the clock. She nods; she knows the score. At school on Friday afternoons they'd all watched with envy as the Jewish girls ran out of class before the last lesson.

With an eye to speed, she hauls down the skins from a rack marked, *reduced,* and then hefts her selection over to the counter. Bernie looks them over and drops them onto the flatbed scale. She waits, fountain pen in hand, while he scratches his scalp.

'Boy's knickers, huh?' He frowns at the dial.

'Yes, they're small enough that I can cut them out of the good bits between the holes. How much for the seven?'

'*Tchk.* Take them and run along with you, go on. They're nothing but holes.'

'You mean you don't want anything? Gosh! Thank you, Bernie.' From the exit she can see her benefactor now knee-deep in used brown paper. She waves and slowly mounts the steps, the weighty roll balanced on her shoulder, counting out the lucky breaks she had today. Her macs sold out at Olga's, an order for the shorts and dresses, a cheque, and now these free skins. Her confidence mounts with her. Until out in the flood of sunlight on the pavement, she wavers. A doubt has dogged her. Is she fooling herself? Can she really support them both this way? Sure, she's already taken them to Portugal, on a plane, too, but it wasn't for very long, and she still had Michael then.

Now I have to find the place where they dry-clean Michael's stiff collars.

She sees the flyer in the window, as she is leaving the Chinese laundry with a flat box attached to her wrist. *Mini skirts dry-cleaned – 2d an inch.* She catches her reflection in the gleaming plate glass. They look incongruous now, the box of stiff white collars and her skirt. She and Michael always cross each other on their separate ways. Tomorrow is Saturday, his day off. It would be good for both of them, if he would spend some time with Anna for a change. And she could make a start on her order.

Five

Next day

'NEARLY HOME, little one.'

It has been a long, fraught Saturday at the workshop with Anna, and it is with mixed feelings that she greets the light from her own kitchen door. Anna, still whimpering beneath the blankets round her trolley, could have played inside in the warmth with so little inconvenience to him. Out of breath from having pushed her uphill and upwind, she stops on the crest and watches the bare saplings as they thrash about on the row of front lawns. At least the wind is not so piercing here as at the other end of the estate. There the navvies square up to boulder clay, millstone grit and purple grassland open grazing for sheep.

Light from the kitchen window falls on a concrete fencing post in a newly dug hole. The clods in a heap beside it are shiny from a spade. The doorstep is slippery, the kitchen floor too muddy for Anna to walk over. She calls to Michael who comes to the other door, rubbing his eyes.

'Hullo, little girl.' He stoops to tickle Anna's face, as she unwraps her from the blanket. And while she stows the trolley in the hall, he leads her to his armchair beside the stove.

'Hey! Don't let her walk in that.' She snatches up a newspaper from the floor and tears off a back page to wipe the mud from Anna's shoes.

'Hey, it's the racing page, that!'

'She's tired out and she's starving, and how am I to get her fed and ready for bed in all this dirt? Does the poor child have to wait while I get down and clean it all up?' The floor sucks beneath her slippers as she makes her way to the corner and drags out the high chair. Through the window, a cement mixer, and the kitchen floor invisible beneath a chalky grey film. 'This isn't just mud, Michael. Is it?'

'What have you done with the biscuit barrel? I couldn't find it anywhere.' The question rises from the armchair.

'It's where I showed you, on top of the wall cupboard, out of Anna's reach.'

'What for? She can't get the lid off.' He is sprawled, legs stretched out, with Anna pummelling his chest.

'You've forgotten what I said about her donkey-riding on it. She sits bouncing on the blasted knob. Can't you saw it off, like I asked, before she does herself an injury? Now, will you let me get on? She'll be crying soon, and I can't ...' A flood of tears escapes her control. 'I'm sorry, I'm tired ...'

'That's right, turn on the waterworks. You're setting her off now. Will you take her off me please? I'm going upstairs for a bath. I need my tea early, by the way. I'm out tonight with Geoff.' His galoshes hit the floor and then he creaks up the stairs.

She carries Anna through the mud and buckles her into her chair. A soft-boiled egg with bread and butter soldiers, orange segments left aside for the sugar to melt in, rose hip syrup in her beaker. While the milk warms on the stove, she draws a pail from the cupboard under the sink. The mop will be worse than useless for ground-in cement. She throws in the stiff scrubbing brush and runs hot water from the tap.

'Nothing's changed since my grandmother's day,' she mutters while rummaging for a bar of carbolic soap. 'Never get married, Anna. You're not listening to me, are you, love?'

Anna drops an eggy bread soldier to the floor and leans out to watch it. 'Dada.'

By the time Anna has eaten, the carpet by her door is dry, and she can play awhile in her cot. As she screws up the newspaper from under Anna's chair and bins it, she is wishing she had done the same with the one that Moll left at the workroom. It saddened her and there are still times when it really plays on her mind. Kneeling on an old jumper, she surveys the tiles within her reach. She attacks them with the soapy scrubbing brush, rinsing and wringing the floorcloth over the bucket, and catches herself answering aloud her mother's imagined jibes.

'I've got a mind, you know, Mum. I just can't see what there is to think about in polishing a floor. I feel wasted.' But soon her thoughts are galloping to Monday, when her trunk is due at the workshop.

The men will carry it up. It'll seem even bigger in her room. And what will she pack first? Not her sewing machine; that will go in last. She has to work until the day it leaves, six weeks before her sailing. She can pack the spare rolls of cloth, books, one or two of Anna's toys. If she will let her. As she imagines herself packing, she can sense someone watching over her, not exactly in her workroom, but somewhere off to side. As if Zé were there, standing guard. Not criticising, not judging, watching over her secret preparations to leave. What a shame she didn't sense his presence at Lisbon airport before she left. Because his letter says he was there. And just as she imagined, concealed behind a pillar, his mac collar up to hide his face. The ache has lessened, and now she's on her way to the life she really wants. So, she mustn't let Michael weaken her. Cold sludge half-fills the bucket. She starts up to take it to the sink, but a whiff of *Old Spice* is competing with the vapours from the floor.

'Go on then. Play the martyr. You don't have to do it that way and you know it.'

'I do, you know. This dirt is ground into the surface.'

'Give over. You're spinning it out on purpose. You want to make me late.'

'What?'

'Where's my tea, then?'

Her knees are frozen stiff and pins and needles have obliterated her feet. As she tries to stand, the sight of Michael's best suit triggers something inside her. Something wants to erupt, demands that she let it. Rage is coursing through her veins. The orange bucket blurs and then it reddens. She kicks it. A thud, a whoosh, a slap. The bucket on its side is rocking. A tsunami of sludge and foam is swirling outwards across the floor. Michael's turn-ups are full of muddy water and his tan Chelsea boots are grey. Her toe. It's broken. No it isn't, but she can't put it to the ground.

'Damn you!' His face is thunderclouds.

Go on, do it; just do it!

She grabs the bucket, shoots the rest of the dirty water at his head, drenching him through his shirt to his string vest. She bolts to the sanctuary of her kitchen. Where she shakes as she tries to stop the bottom of the door with her foot. Can she hold it shut and still stretch far enough to lock the door to the hall? She kicks a stool across and manages to ram it fast against the handle. She holds her breath. Listens to the cursing, the stamping upstairs and across the floor above. A sudden shaking of the ceiling makes her wonder if the house will stand it. But then a stream of babble comes to her from Anna's room, and she relaxes. A surprise attack of the giggles follows, which she tries in vain to stifle, but has to mask it by blasting on the radio.

'Knock, knock, it's only me.' A woman's shadow is splayed across the reeded glass of the front door. 'It's me-ee!' The letterbox bangs shut.

She squelches back into the kitchen and silences the evening news. She has missed the latest bulletin from Aberfan because of him, because of listening to his car engine as it tore off up the road, holding her breath until she heard him turn the corner. And she was safe. She lifts her chilled feet from boggy slippers and tiptoes round the puddles to answer the door. Moll stands against the garage light, a haloed Botticelli angel holding out her ancient floor polisher.

'I've brought you this, like I said. I can leave it with you till Monday, if you want. Hey, you've been crying, girl. What's up? Where can I walk? There's muddy water all over your floor.'

'You should have seen it earlier, before I started cleaning up.' She leads Moll across the living room to a dry patch at the end. 'I can't do this any more.'

'Can't do what? Has there been an accident?'

The two women sit close together on the bottom stairs.

'No, it was me; I did it. I tipped a bucketful of dirty water over Michael.'

Moll's hand claps her mouth. 'Has he gone now? Are you

sure? Where is Anna?' Moll unbuttons her roomy old grey coat and drapes it on the banister.

'Still playing in her cot, bless her. I need to get it mopped up before I can put her to bed.'

'You carry on. I'll see to her.' Moll is striding through to Anna's room. 'Squelch squelch. It's like the seaside in here. I do like to be beside the seaside ...'

Jody is on her knees again, back where she left off. But her hands are shaking, which makes it difficult to wring out the cloth. The shakes remind her of the one time she very nearly walked away from Zé.

It was the day of the big storm. In the morning she had done the market and bought the vegetables for Leonora. But an ill-tempered wind had suddenly blown up on her way home. The light was eerie at first, then hyperreal with purple shadows and everything in sharp focus, like a migraine of all the gods.

Back home again, having battled through the wind, her dress flapping like a sail around her legs, heavy thundery rain was now sluicing the garden. Leonora tied on a rain-mate and dashed to her appointment with the doctor. Jody winched the iron storm covers up and spent the next few hours playing with the two children on the floor. Leaving them from time to time to open the door to a Friday beggar and hand them a few escudos.

In the afternoon the children napped for an hour, oblivious to the thunderclaps that rolled over the roof to finally disappear out to sea. And when she wound the shutters down again, sparkling clean light flooded the room. And rainwater was clattering off the roof as she roused the children. A siren blast. A raucous bird chorus. Then Leonora was home again and throwing off her dripping wet clothes.

Jody slicked on some lipstick. 'Do you think it's over now, the storm?'

'Yes, that's it. The air is quite cool.'

'I'll slip out for a walk then, to get a breath of that air.'

Drifts of sand on the storm-wracked sea wall had made her turn back. But walking now alongside the steaming tarmac of the Marginal, it was as if she were the first human in a newly wrung-out world. At the café, she found their table empty, so she sat facing the way she guessed that he would come, her ears attuned for the hooting of the incoming Lisbon train.

'*Limonada por favor.*' Now she could practise her Portuguese on António.

She was going through the events of the night before in her mind, smiling at his mock serenading, his raised four fingers as he left. Four o'clock, four-thirty, and then five and getting stiff from waiting … At last she spotted him on the pavement with a short, dark-haired man who was grinding out a cigarette. And standing back a bit from the men, an English-looking girl with long fair plaits. Later, of course, she knew them as Eduardo and Kay. But Zé neither introduced her nor brought his friend to the table. Had he not seen her? She waved. Eduardo gave a curt nod to her, embraced Zé and then backed away while Zé walked alone towards her. There was something forced about his bearing, and a marked difference from the way he had walked towards her the night before. His eyes shot in this and that direction apparently at random. And judging by the stains and creases it showed, he must have slept in his shirt. Without a word to her, or a look even, he jerked his chin at António. '*Um galao, por favor.*'

António put a tall glass of milky coffee in front of her. And Zé sat without a drink, watching her intently, too intently, not speaking and, to her mind, not seeing her. As she stirred the long-handled spoon round and round her glass, she could feel her cheeks begin to burn. To hide her face, she delved down to fetch her bag from under the table. And saw his hands shaking uncontrollably on his knees.

When she dips the floorcloth in the soap suds again her hands are steady. But she recalls vividly that his continued to tremble for a long time. It made her wonder until she realised with a shock how little she knew him. What a short time it was since they met. The next day on the way home from the beach she asked him about it, but he insisted it was just a chill. She knew it wasn't, but he seemed better, and so she left it at that.

'Did you have a nice time in Lisbon?' she asked, brightly, to hide her fears. 'What are *you* having to drink?'

And leaning back to balance on the hind legs of his chair, hands clasped behind his neck, he said: 'I drink only absinthe.'

Absinthe? The DTs? Surely not. No one drinks that now, although being such a romantic, he —

Thwack! His front chair legs slammed down onto the terrace. And leaning to one side, he very noisily hawked and spat. She nearly walked away then. It was gross. It was an insult. But something was amiss. So she sipped her mellow drink and waited, while he sat before her examining the backs of his hands. For ages. And then she realised …

'Zé, where are your glasses?'

'Broken.'

'You broke your glasses?'

His look said, Don't be stupid. He was angry, she could tell.

'Was there a fight last night in Lisbon?'

A bar brawl perhaps. But Zé? In a fight?

António came back and slammed a glass of water down in front of Zé. And then she understood. He was broke. He'd lost his money with his glasses and was too proud to let her pay. Discreetly she slid her purse across the table. It was shunted straight back.

'I drink only water.'

Now what do I do? But it was touching. When he could only pay for one drink, he'd bought it for her. She pushed her glass to the middle of the table. 'We'll share it.'

'Nao.'

That pride of his. That ardent heart, she thought. And she'd been right about his eyes. They *were* like Peter O'Toole's. Slightly mad though, the way they followed her about, clocked her every movement. Hunched over, fingers laced round his glass, he gazed into her face. His eyes imploring her and not a drop of anger left that she could detect. But something was behind it all and it was making her uneasy. She longed to leave.

She was missing Anna. But she stayed in her seat for fear he was about to crumple. And she watched. Something in him had shifted. And an entity that hadn't been there before, dark, frightening, was of a different order from the other things that he'd always said he couldn't tell her. Or the things she'd never quite got, because he always spoke to her in French. *Don't get out of your depth,* she told herself. Anna must come first.

'I'm going home now. I've left Anna too long. I have to go now, Zé.' She slipped an arm into the sleeve of her blazer and pulled it on.

Leaving the table, she tripped and bruised her shin. She caught sight of his reflection in the glass door as she was hobbling off. He was coming after her, but his image in the glass was watery and blurred. She hastened on. But swung round when she heard him coming up behind.

'I want to walk home alone today, Zé.' He shrank from her words. 'You'll be all right, though, won't you?'

'Of course. I am fine.' He turned and wandered off along the Marginal in the opposite direction.

Tchk! He couldn't even walk straight.

Next day on the strand, surrounded by his family and with Eduardo, the light returned to his eyes. And while his mother, with Anna's 'help', brought out the picnic lunch from the bathing tent, Zé led her through the banks of sunbathers, down to the shore. And there, knee-deep in surf and with his back to the public spies and the swimsuit police ... It was their first kiss. Sea-salty and warm. Her lips can still taste ...

But Moll is back from Anna's room and watching her. 'She fell asleep in her clothes, bless her, so I covered her with a blanket.'

'Dammit, now she'll be awake half the night. Still, I had to press on with it all, so thanks a lot. You're a brick. But Moll, wouldn't you have thought he'd want to be with his daughter on his day off? Just sometimes. Now and then.' She shakes her head. 'But no, he always says he isn't there to babysit for me. I need another load of water and then I'd better see to his clothes.'

'Bugger his clothes.'

'Yes, bugger them, for now, even if I have to do it in the end.' She manages a wry smile for Moll on her way to the kitchen sink. 'You realise I'm leaving, don't you?' she calls through the open hatch. 'I told you, when you arrived, I can't go on like this any more.' When she carries in more hot water, Moll is sitting on the settee.

'Leaving? You can't do that. Don't you realise? This is nothing, Jody! Len's underpants stay on the frozen hawthorn for weeks after I've hurled them out the bedroom window. You mean you've never noticed? Well, I'm blowed if I'll bring them in. We all do it, love. Maureen scrubs the toilet bowl with her husband's toothbrush. It makes her feel better. But you meant you're going — you're going over there to him. You're going to Portugal?'

'You said it, not me. My trunk arrives on Monday, and I can't wait to start packing. You'll never guess what my boat is called. It's a mail boat, the *SS Amazon*. Isn't that just —?' She's saying too much. She quickly hides her face in her apron.

'So Michael knows?'

'No, he doesn't yet. He knows I met someone, but he doesn't seem to care. He seems to think I'll just forget about it. But he's wrong, though. I never will.'

'He *must* care.'

'Well, you'd think so, wouldn't you? But though I hate to say it, the only thing that man cares about is money. And the house. It's all in his name.'

'And Anna, surely.'

She gives a wry nod. 'I know I have to tell him, but whenever do I get the chance? All week I walk about on tiptoe because he's asleep. And in the evenings, he's gone. The weekends are awful now, just one great, long row, when we're not with family or out with his friends. But I will, when I get the chance, don't worry. Coffee? Or there's Sherry? Have a Campari with me, come on.'

Moll shakes her head. She's staring at her as if she were about to vanish. So she pours herself a Campari and brings the soda siphon from the cupboard.

'You should have talked to me before it got to this.' Moll is fiddling with the coat on her lap.

'Yes, but I couldn't.'

'You've got a radio. Have you heard what the psychologists are saying now? That it's healthy to talk about our feelings.'

'Sure, I don't doubt it is, but it's impossible with Michael. He just refuses point-blank to talk about it, or bolts to the pub. Or he'll suddenly be working overtime. It's not like with you and Len, the way you wave him off in the mornings in your floaty nylon negligee. That could never happen here. I did right to go away, though. Before I went, the atmosphere was so tense, it had become unlivable.'

Do I have to spell it out to her? For Zé, it was simple. He could see what was going on.

'Jody, why do you live with a man who doesn't love you?'

'Sure you don't want one?' She waves her glass. And then, Campari in hand, goes to sit beside Moll. 'I've never felt like this before, you know.' She sips her drink and watches her toe doodling in the hearthrug.

'You have got it bad, haven't you?'

She nods. 'But it's true. And it's real. I think I knew even on my wedding day that I couldn't be what Michael wanted. I'd already tried to break it off, but it doesn't work like that in my family. So I braced myself, fixed a smile on my face and acted out the role. Even driving off on honeymoon, I was wishing I could stay behind at the dance with my friends. Coming back, we stopped off at Mum's house. And now she says she could tell right away that something was wrong, just by looking at my face.'

'You should have talked to her.'

'Yes, but, how? When I fell pregnant with Anna, that was the last time we did it. And even then it was because I made him. I think we were both drunk. He's got a problem, but don't ask me to talk about that, please. He used to say it would get better, but it didn't, or I don't think it did. I don't really know now, because it went on for so long, and I was so hurt that, in the end, it was me that was blocked. I felt rejected. I lost my confidence. And I threw myself into work, at least, until I made myself ill. Now I think that marriage is just a role, not a relationship. And I've made up my mind I want a man who treats me as an equal.'

'You'll be lucky. Don't we all ...' Moll is drawing in the condensation on the tiles beside her feet, her face hidden by her scarf.

Her head is swimming after bending down to stand her glass on the floor. She must be overdoing it again. Moll's size nines are shuffling impatiently on the rug. She's looking down at her the way Michael did. She wriggles on her hands.

'I must go. Len wants me at home. I'll call on Monday for the polisher.' Moll has changed her tone. She waits by the door, drawing on her gloves, pushing down one finger at a time. She seems to be killing time. Then she grips the handle hard. 'You see, Jody, this man in Portugal — I don't think he's the answer. What *I* want is for you to find a different kind of love. Get your bible out at the weekend, eh? You never know, it may help. See you Monday. Bye-ee!'

Six

Early December 1966

THE WINTER'S FIRST real snowfall is a foot deep against the picture window, when she pads down the stairs. Still in her shabby housecoat, she stands drinking cocoa in the kitchen, while a robin hops, across the blanked-out back garden, to the hedge. The sky is low and leaden with the promise of another snowfall. It is a day to stay inside and prepare to break the news to Michael when he wakes. The letter that she takes from her pocket has a ringed number seven on the envelope. That was Zé's idea. To number all their correspondence on the outside. She scans the pages for something he wrote in English. Here it is: *I will wait for you on the quay.*

She tries to picture the quay. She has only seen Lisbon docks from the coastal railway, as her train pulled in. But she can conjure up a dockside scene with him waiting on a quay, while she waves to him from a deck rail, elegant in a hat with a wide brim. But to conjure up his face, especially his eyes, or to picture his hands as she knew them and loved them, is becoming harder by the day. She tries to fluff up her limp, straight hair, noting how it has grown and trying to recall the way his wiry mass would spring back from his fingers. She runs a forefinger down over her lips to rest on her chin. Strangers have stopped her in the street to say she is the spit of Rita Tushingham. She taps her nose and tries to gauge the distance from *his* nose to his jaw, which would be lower than hers. There was something primitive about his jaw. And thus, she has a sketchy image of his face to hold to for a while. She plants a kiss on the ringed number seven, drops his letter in the other pocket and, arms crossed, begins to massage some warmth into her shoulders. *His* shoulders slope. They often do on tall men.

The squeak of Anna's cot springs calls her to her room, which is warm enough. But Anna turns on her a furious look and flings her doll to the floor. She wants her teddy, but he is packed in the trunk, ready for the off. She rummages in a drawer for a wool vest and Anna's warmest jumper. She will bath her in the kitchen sink today so she can watch the snow through the window. It is falling fast again, and thick.

The little girl's eyes are wide and shining as she tries to catch whirling flakes. Jody wraps her in a warmed towel to screen her from the icy blast that hits them when she opens the door. And gropes for the milk bottles with her free hand. So, the farmer made it through the drifts to bring their milk. But frozen cream coils from the bottle necks and is pecked by hungry birds. Michael's car is at the bottom of the hill, blanketed by this morning's fresh fall. By leaving it there and walking down to it, he spares himself a lot of shovelling. She hopes it won't be like the winter of sixty-three, when the pipes burst and the water tank froze just as they were moving in. She wouldn't want to be at sea in weather like that. She toes the door shut.

'Now you can have your cereal, Anna, and I can get dressed.' Her blue Shetland sweater dress is itchy, but she doesn't want to wake Michael by looking for something else. He pads downstairs eventually, bleary eyed and blinking at the sunlight streaming through the window, while Anna naps after her lunch. Jody brings the oxtail from the oven and feels a little apprehensive as she serves potatoes onto his plate. She leaves the casserole in front of him and goes to open the fridge. 'A brown ale do you?' She struggles to sound normal.

'Yes please.' Michael always drinks mild at the pub, never bitter, like his mates, so she keeps a stock of bottled brown ale or stout.

She must wait until he is recovered from sleep. Hunched on the bottom stair, she stretches out her feet to warm them in the sun, but turns her face from its sharp rays. Across the room, the stove is belching hot air, much of which escapes up the open stairs to the floor above. She glances down to where Michael sits, his nose buried in the paper. His tough, iron grey hair. An old friend of Michael's often teases him that he was born middle-aged. She doesn't think so. He just turned prematurely grey, so people think he's older than his years. And being Michael, he obliges by fulfilling their expectations.

His paper rustles. 'Is there pudding?'

'There's a baked apple in the oven.'

'No thanks.'

'It's what you need in this weather.' But he is back behind his paper, lifting and setting down his beer. 'You'll be wanting a cup of tea, I take it.'

'Yes, ta.' She collects his empty plate on her way to the kitchen.

'Did you like the oxtail?'

'Yes, ta.'

While the kettle heats up, she takes her *Mrs. Beeton's Cookery* from the shelf. Here's another book she must pack, but not yet. Now that Michael has no choice but to eat at home, he's finding she can cook. And she can; everybody says so. She gives him the tea and carries her coffee back to the stair. 'I want to talk to you, when you're ready.'

No reaction from behind the paper. Normally she loves the peacefulness that follows a fall of snow. She has been thinking while she waits about Michael's apparent passiveness. Perhaps it was an attraction, when she was young. Perhaps it gave her the chance to exercise new powers that she was discovering, that up to then she didn't know she had. In the lower sixth when they met, she was feeling daunted by her school work, disappointed in friends who seemed not to harbour her desires for freedom. Her blithe disregard for obstacles. But she was blind then, to the danger of her freedom as a target for his taunts. Michael will agree to anything to keep the peace, for a quiet life. But behind the act, he can be vicious when he wants. So, what can she expect now?

'*You're bleeding me dry. You're milking me white.*' He can't say that again. She couldn't cost him any less. She already raids her dress allowance for housekeeping money. 'Michael would you come here a minute, please. I've something to tell you.'

And once again he towers over her; she is so close to the ground. She hugs the baluster and looks up at him.

'Go on then, surprise me,' he says. 'How much do you

want?'

'For goodness sake, Michael, nothing. I just wanted to tell you that I've decided to go away. I'm going back to Portugal. I think I'm leaving you, Michael.'

She waits quietly for the explosion, but brings an arm across her bowed head. There are red flecks in the floor tiles, some blood red, like gashes. Nothing happens. Was that him walking away? She drops her arm. He is standing by the window, looking out, jingling change in his pockets.

'Go, then. Go on, leave me.' He juts his chin. 'See if I care.'

She lets the seconds reel by and then she says: 'You mean — you mean you wouldn't mind?'

His back is like a blank wall. A small hole in the welt of his blue pullover needs darning, she notes. Why doesn't he answer? He only needs to say it's true that he doesn't mind, and it will all be over. But he shuffles the weight between his feet while staring mutely out through the window at some paw prints in the snow. Next door's cat? Here comes the neighbour, past the garden wall, a Manchester City scarf wound round to cover much of his face. Michael has stopped jiggling the loose change in his trouser pockets, and he doesn't jut his chin. He gives a shrug. 'I couldn't care less what you do. You're free to leave when you want.' But then he wheels round, and his lip clearly quivers with emotion: 'But you are NOT taking my daughter.'

The air has fled the room. The clonking of the stove has ceased to be replaced by a long hiss. She tries to breathe normally, but something hard and bulky like a hockey ball is stuck beneath her sternum. A pin wouldn't dare drop in there. Is he playing her? No. But if he means it, then NO. Absolutely NO.

'Of course I'm taking Anna with me. She comes everywhere with me. Even to work and on a Saturday, too. You could have had her easily, but you don't want to look after her. And besides, you haven't got a clue.'

'Haven't I? Then I'll bloody well have to learn.' His eyes are steely. Blanked against her. Impenetrable. Illegible. 'It so happens I was putting up a fence in the garden for her, like you asked me to, so she can play safely outside in the spring.'

'Yes, and you were here all day. You can't take her to work with you, like I do. Not at night! And not even in the day, come to that. So what would you do?'

'I can find a way.'

'Your mother, I suppose. You seem to forget your mother has a job. The things you ask her to do, poor woman.'

'She only works for pin money. She can stop it any time she wants. But I may as well tell you now, Jody, if you so much as try to take my daughter out of the country, you'll soon discover that you can't. Not without my written consent, you can't, and I shan't be giving you that. Over my dead body.' A pause, and then more quietly: 'You can't take everything away from me. I'm not being left sitting here with nothing, like a lame duck. What kind of a fool do you take me for, eh?' He stops again to wipe some spittle from his chin. In spite of the tired words he uses she can see the pent up emotion. His mouth has gone a funny blue.

Her mind is whirling. She struggles to make it grasp what is happening. Now, think. Anna's father is her legal guardian. That is normal, she knows. But is it irrefutable for ever? And what is *she* in the law? Without him beside her, nothing, as far as Anna is concerned. Nothing without a man. She has thought about it before, about being on her own with Anna. Has wondered if she would thrive better with one parent who is happy, rather than two who are not.

'They're changing all that, soon. Next year, when the divorce laws are reformed, it'll be different. And I would get custody. The judges always give it to the mother.'

'Not if she's the guilty party, they don't. Ever.'

'But there won't be any guilty party, soon. And I'm not guilty, anyway. I didn't do anything wrong.'

'Who's talking divorce, any road? What would I do with that?' He turns to the window at a thud of snow from the roof.

'I didn't mean —' A squeal from Anna's room, and pounding cot springs are too hard to ignore. She runs to her room. And with the child balanced on her arm, fumbles in a drawer for her special comb. The warm smell of sleep and baby lotion, she inhales as if it is about to disappear from the world. Then Michael's shadow falls across the doorway and, for a moment, he looks disarmed at the sight of the two of them together.

'I want to take her outside before I go to work, to make a big snowman.'

'A little one would be best.' Her fingers tremble on the toggles of Anna's anorak. And as she winds a knitted scarf twice round the hood and knots it at the back, she has to fight back tears of outrage. Blind outrage. Dumb fury. How dare he do this? How dare he try to break them apart? He can't. He never will.

Like the ghost of herself she stands behind the dining-room window, watching father and daughter play together on the snow-covered grass. Father stretches wide his arms as if he is a scarecrow in a field. Daughter runs to him repeatedly and whoops with glee, when he spins her round. Over and over. A sacred ritual is enacted. Michael checks that she is watching before each time he turns his back. This is Michael in his element. Not admitting to anything and yet emitting all the signals. The expression on his face, for instance. She cannot look him in the eye. Anna points to the light reflected in the glass, but not to her mother. Gosh, her face even has the same expression as his.

She wanders back to her stair. There is no denying it, this father-daughter thing. If she is honest, often when they've played together, something as yet undefined has made her turn away. She hugs herself into a ball. Hears them coming back inside. And goes to take off Anna's coat and hang it to dry on the hall stand.

From the living room, a noise that tells her he is dragging out her old playpen. 'Anna doesn't need that; she's too old.' But she refrains from interrupting, when he lifts her in and gives her toys. Placing them around her, as if for a baby. Anna looks alarmed at being fenced in. Still, it is a first for Michael. And in a minute he will leave for work.

She listens to the crunch and slither of his boots fading down the hill. When she can hear no more, she lets Anna out to run around the room. Once she is tucked in for the night, she softly shuts her door and dismantles the old playpen. And standing by the back window, she looks out at the stars. The ones high in the sky, the ones that have fallen into the tarn. The Plough and The Great Bear are holding up above a *Reckitt's* blue moor. Moll's battered old floor polisher is leaning by the back door. She wants to hear the evening news. She turns it on, but keeps the volume low.

Aberfan: the Welsh mining village that has just lost its children. An entire generation smothered, buried by a slag heap on the move. The tribunal is still sitting, trying to decide who is to blame. People always seem to need someone to blame. And out there in the darkness the hulking crags loom behind the tarn. What if they had been slag heaps?

'In that stillness, that silence, you couldn't hear a bird or a child.'

She makes herself turn off the broadcast. Her brain is shutting down. She needs some time alone to think now, to decide what is best for Anna. And then to accept the consequences of whatever that should be.

Seven

Mid-December 1966

THIS MORNING ANNA had a hearing test at the clinic next to the council offices. The district nurse tiptoed about her office, striking a triangle, while Jody pinned Anna's arms behind her back so she could only move her head. Inked crosses fill a grid while she answered yes, no. And finally she was assured that she had a very healthy child.

'And now, what about Mum? Getting our orgasms all right, are we, Mrs Proctor?'

'Erm, I don't know, sorry. Yes. Yes, of course, thank you.'

Perhaps the nurse's clumsy but well-meaning attempt to appear modern was what had fired her up so fast. She was livid, so livid that she ran blindly home. Not stopping till she reached the last stretch of the hill. How dare she? Stupid woman. And on a whim, she left a note for Michael to say his dinner was in the oven. And ran to catch the bus to her workshop for the first time in weeks. Working will bring her confidence back. It has to; nothing else will. How could any mother face this? Decide such a thing? Since the day when Michael shot her life to pieces, she has been afraid to tackle him, but has watched him for clues.

Anna is producing a daily torrent of new words, and each one is a fresh surprise. And a pretty free-flowing monologue is rising through the floorboards today. And something even more exciting than Anna's new words, is being understood by her at last.

'Da-da Teddy no Teddy he sick no Teddy, dere.'

She raps on the partition beside the stairs. 'Knock, knock. I'm the nurse.'

'*Wheeh*! Teddy be-wy sick.'

'Poor Teddy. Kiss him better.' The bear's limbs became squashed while he was packed inside the trunk.

She goes back to fingering the flimsy envelope in the pocket of her brown smock. She needs another peep, to check that she was right about his change of tone.

My Dear, she reads.

He always used to address her, *Cherie*, or *Chère Jody*. And he only ever used English to say things he'd thought about. Important things. Or to make something clear. Admittedly she has paid less attention to his letters lately. Even though he writes the French she learned at school, translating it is still a chore. And what does he write about? His despair at the state of his compatriots, their poverty, the misery of a people being silenced. And yet it doesn't reach her, not really. Not now. And for all she knows, it could all be in his mind. Besides, she desperately wants to hold to her own memories of Portugal: the lovely painted villas glowing in the late afternoon sun. The nourishing soups she and Leonora made in Leonora's kitchen: *caldo verde; açorda*. She loved *caldo verde*. And Anna loved *açorda*. The children always do, surprisingly with all the garlic. And the fruit heaped in piles on the ground at the weekly market. She'd like to paint that. The flower market, the fish market, and the local people with their soulful eyes and their overwhelming love of children. And, of course, going out with him: his loopy gallantry, his concern for her and the quiet closeness they found in the end. Has he really grown that distant?

My Dear,

Your news gives me a shock. You face a terrible decision. I am naturally distrait, but it is necessary that you decide alone. For my part, I will be patient. Take the time, all you have the need of, and know that I wait patiently.

I need you as the air I breathe, as the water I drink.   Your José.

'*I need you as the air I breathe, as the water I drink.*' She wants to hear it again as it was the first time he uttered it, quietly in the half dark as they ambled up the empty beach. How can it sound so trite now, as in the signing off of this letter? And Zé waiting patiently? Hmm. So, what now? Will his letters simply stop? She folds it back in her pocket and listens out for Anna. She will go downstairs and see her in a minute.

As she glances round her workroom the ageing wallpaper

seems to darken. Was it this small and dingy before today? She lost the heart to work and stayed at home. And now her new-found courage threatens to desert her again. She will tidy up, create some space. She blunders about the room, overturns a chair laden with sewing and then trips over the ironing board. She will leave it where it fell, collapsed on the floor. No, she won't; she rights it again. Her mind is elsewhere today. It keeps wandering off to Lisbon. To the city. His city.

Terraces of blank workshops, tall, flaking homes. Overarching gas lamps strung with lines of limp washing. And still there was no breeze. Neighbours watched them from doorways, while cats padded in and out, pawing at buzzing flies. She turned round to look at Zé, the silent plodder at her side, eyes down before his feet and following the flow of cobblestone steps. Was it the blistering heat that was making him so withdrawn? Did he regret his offer to show her Lisbon on such a sweltering day? His fingers pressed her palm, as if he knew her thoughts. She pressed back and searched his profile for signs that he was feeling better.

On their way into the city, when their train was held up at Caxias, he'd fallen silent in the opposite seat. He'd told her before, he thought his friend Miguel was being held in Caxias. As a prison it was notorious, he'd said. For what, she didn't really know. She'd been glad to stop and crane her neck to see that surreal fortress on the beach.

When they emerged from the main station at Cais do Sodré, their faces hit a blast furnace. She crossed the burning hot tramlines, with the muslin lining of her white piqué dress sticking to her thighs. It was embarrassing. She'd had to keep lifting it away. She had lined it with a soft muslin, but the facings still chafed her skin around the armholes and the neck; she must have starched it too well. The fabric, which, before she left England, she had thought too thin, felt as thick as cardboard in that heat.

After climbing all the way up alongside the terraces, they stood together on the crest of a cobbled roadway. Glancing back down, she saw the tram driver leaning from his yellow cab, deep in conversation with a woman at an upper window of a dwelling next to the funicular. If Zé had not suggested walking up the parallel stone stairs, they would still be waiting by the telegraph office way down below. Exploring Lisbon is hard on the legs.

Tiny *tascas*, dark *tavernas*, doors open to the roadway. And all Lisbon peeling from lying long in the sun. Church bells pealing out, calling to the locals as they walked their dogs. And down they went to a teetering square paved with black and white *calçadas*. In a roped-off corner workmen lifted out, tapped and replaced the stones. Limestone and basalt they were, and they were laying them as if a hopscotch tournament were about to start.

'They do it every Sunday morning, when the streets are quiet like now. All over the city. They have a job for life and they know it. They smoke; they take their time. You know Fernando Pessoa?' He was pulling her by the arm over to a life-size bronze tableau: a male figure with a long, doleful face shaded by a fedora, was seated at a bronze café table outside a real café. A poet captured with a raised right hand, from which a wine glass was missing or a cigarette had dropped to the pavement. As she swung by with Zé, she asked if he was drinking absinthe, the poet. But probably he didn't hear. They were entering a dark interior, passing a carved oak bar with chandeliers reflected in its mirrors. 'Pessoa's studies were interrupted by a student strike, also.'

'Is that why he wrote in here?'

'In here and other places; anywhere that had strong black coffee, cigarettes and —'

'Absinthe?'

'I like absinthe.' He was fishing for his cigarettes.

'Have you ever smoked a pipe?' She watched him light up and take his first draw before he answered.

'No. Have you?'

'No, but I smoke *Tom Thumb* cigars sometimes and at school we took snuff.'

'Is that how you got these?'

'They're called freckles, and I hate them.'

He grinned as he pinched his trouser legs and sank into the banquette. The early- morning clouds had passed; they could sit a while and cool down. They ordered *pasteis da natas*, which came dredged with so much icing sugar that she sneezed. And *bicas*, shots of kick-back black coffee with iced water. She said she liked seeing him at home in his own city, where he grew up.

'You could have seen my old school from the train. A small Jesuit community school behind that pink palace.'

'The one with the guards in tight, white breeches, Cuban heeled boots and helmets with yellow ponytails at the back?'

'Yes, the navy.'

'Funny-looking navy.'

And that was the day she fell in love with a city for the first time.

Her elbows have gone dead from leaning on the ironing board, dreaming. She sighs, folds the legs, traps her fingers and gladly props it by the stairwell. *Procrastinating won't do.* Having cleared a space, she sets to picking up pins, sorting cut leather shapes into sets and adding them to the pile next to her sewing machine. She sweeps a pile of off-cuts into an empty tea chest; it booms. She polishes her scissors until they shine. Snap snap snap; her pinking shears are like crocodile jaws. She rips a docket from its staple on the wall and ticks off the first few items. But a door has opened downstairs.

'Hail stranger. I saw your light on.' The thud of gum boots on bare wooden treads, and Moll emerges from the stairwell, apparently out of breath. 'Glad to see you're back at work now, lass. Are you ready for Christmas?'

'Am I heck as like. Nowhere near. I haven't even made up the first half of Olga's order yet. She'll be waiting for it, too.' The phone is ringing downstairs. 'Excuse me a sec.'

From the telephone by Anna's doorway, she can watch her playing with Caitlin who is older and bigger. They are getting on well today. The travel agent is on the line. She keeps referring to a sailing next March.

'I can't think so far ahead. It was just a casual enquiry. For information, that's all. No, I'm not making reservations. Not yet.' The children are taking bricks from the truck and throwing them about the room, while she is listing the advantages of booking early. 'Yes, I know, but the seamen's strike could start again before then. I'd — I'd rather wait and see.' By the time she is walking upstairs again, she has a new timescale in view. March. Next year. 1967 it'll be then. It has such a far-off ring to it, remote, like a lost land.

'Does this mean you've decided?' Moll whispers as she backs away to let her pass into her workroom.

'Decided what? I've decided nothing. The travel agent rang me for a chat. She's a nice woman and I like talking to her.'

'You're lonely. You're on your own too much. It's not surprising that you're thinking about —'

'Him all the time? I'm not now, so you're wrong.' Holding Moll's wet coat at arm's length, she casts about for a hanger. 'I only think about Anna. She's talking well. Have you noticed?'

'You've lost weight again.'

'No, I haven't. I'll make us a pot of tea.' She stands at the sink and watches cold water splash from a brass tap.

March. What about March? It seems to leave enough time to decide without a lot of pressure. And if she cancels, there will always be another boat later on. But there won't be another Zé. But Anna has begun to talk. It must be an important time in her life. She backs away as icy water drenches the front of her smock.

'I brought us some whinberry tarts because you need feeding up.' Moll is opening a cake box and licking her fingers.

Jody lays out mismatched cups and plates on the trunk lid. Moll hasn't noticed it; a trunk standing in a workshop is not such an uncommon sight. At one end of it, heaped on the seat of a rickety chair, some all-but-finished garments are trailing loose threads. They must have sat there for weeks, waiting in vain to be pressed and laid in the trays that fit inside the lid. A March sailing would mean the trunk would have to go very soon. Early in the New Year. Whatever she decides, Moll will know nothing of it and that's for sure. She brings the teapot and stands it on the trunk.

She is remembering the cruise ships and ocean liners she saw in Lisbon. That same Sunday, with Zé beside her, gazing from the castle ramparts and out across lots of red pantiled roofs, to the Alfáma. The estuary lay beyond, and an ocean liner happened to be passing right then, escorted by tugs. Magnificent it was. Heroic. She'd love to live in a seaport. There's Liverpool, but it's dirty. Manchester has got the ship canal, but no ships. Lisbon is a shimmering place, seductive. It really tugs at you inside, forcing you to return. The Alfáma district possessed such a pull, and she promised it she would go again the next day.

'Being built on so many so many hills, this city must have a thousand views of the sea.'

'More, I think, but this one is the best. And Jody, that is not the ocean. It is the estuary of the Tejo.'

'The Tagus.' She could sense his growing impatience with his role as her guide. But it was his idea; he offered to show her. 'I can't see a river bank.'

'It is hidden behind the mist. The river is so broad here that it makes natural harbour. It is the *Mar da Palho*, the great Sea of Straw. Why it is called so? Because its surface is calm like the sheen on a blade of straw. All seven hills are mirrored in it, so the city is a Narcissus constantly admiring itself. But you don't want to look at that.' And he pulled her down behind the battlements. 'No one can see us here.'

A wordless current had been passing back and forth between them since the early morning, when he met her at the local station and they rode in along the coast.

'I want to see the Sea of Straw.'

'One minute.' His arm was round her shoulder, pulling her close.

'All right, but I don't want to miss it. It'll soon be getting dark.'

He stood abruptly, pulled her up after him and re-assumed his role: 'There is my father's ship.'

She tried to brush the red sand from her dress and looked to where he pointed, to some moorings beside a pillar of the high arch underneath the bridge. This time she didn't miss it because of speeding past it on a train. It was white and sparkled in the sunlight, but not as big as she'd expected. 'A tramp steamer,' he said, and pointed to a white building with a flat roof on the other side of the tramlines. 'My father's office. And I was born there in that hospital, so I am native of Alfáma.'

'You've never lived there, though.'

'No.' An indulgent smile. 'It is the Kasbah, and the oldest quarter of Lisboa. It speaks to me inside. The Moors had built it on granite, so it was the only quarter of the city that survived the great earthquake. Poor people, mostly migrants, live there since. When the tsunami came in, the rich moved out, and so they were drowned along with the rest of the population.'

'I forgot about the Lisbon earthquake. Was it Voltaire who wrote about it?'

'You read Voltaire?'

'We read *Candide* in French at school. But Montaigne was the one I liked; I still do.'

'And yet you never answer me in French?'

'Heck, no. Would you want to go around talking in the English of Shakespeare?'

'And with my horrible accent ...'

She skipped off along the battlements, her palm paddling the stones. He caught her up, and then they hurtled down the prickly grass between the bougainvilleas. She can still see that blurry mass of magenta, smell the scorched grass and feel the thorns pricking her legs where she fell.

'I like your accent.' She'd turned to answer him and skidded over a bare patch of hard ground. 'It makes you sound like a Russian,' she said, brushing off more sand. She was breathless by the time they stopped and stood hand in hand before an arch.

'The gate to the Alfáma.' He curled a mock flourish of the hand. Footsteps were echoing along the base of the castle wall. 'Give me your purse before we go through. There are pickpockets. And never ever walk here alone at night.'

As if I would.

From doorways with stone steps down into deep, dark tavernas, came the quivering throaty notes of *fado* singers warming up for the evening. Zé had gone into a trance. One side of the narrow street was a swathe of reflected light, while the other was dark and dank. When he turned into an alleyway too narrow for two to pass, she walked quicker so as not to lose sight of his back. Through a never-ending maze of blind corners, winding steps. Overhead, geraniums fluoresced on broken balconies, while canaries trilled from tiny cages hung on thickly peeling walls. As they climbed, free-roaming cats watched from the sloping pantiles, slinking, snaking down steps. She could still see him ahead.

Doors gaped open everywhere; neighbours talked, exchanged commodities, or mended motorbikes on cramped living-room floors. Old men sat at cards, their backs up against the house wall and their feet dangling in the gutter. They all spat. Whole families cooked sardines outside. Here, dilapidated walls were covered in political slogans she hadn't seen anywhere else, except in the shantytown down the train line to Cascais. And, for once, no one pestered them with offers to clean their shoes or to guide them or to sell them anything at all. Their silent rebellion was to return her rude stares with dignity. In spite of their sour smell the twisting alleys drew her in like a magnet. Beckoned her to explore. But she had caught a whiff of something else running through the litter in their gutters. An undercurrent of unease, of alarm, of latent lasciviousness.

'Are you sure you know the way out, Zé?'

'Of course.'

They were passing through empty passageways that magnified all sounds, now a blast from a football screen, a revving motorbike, a siren. And somewhere still hidden from her, consternation was breaking out. Sharp shouts and a walloping on doors that she couldn't see. When a gang of children running wild crossed their path, Zé clutched at her arm.

'We take another street. We must have come a little too far in.'

Oh God, now he's got us lost. Still, she followed him through a crumbling arch and down yet another smelly alleyway, one with a bearded rabbi chanting in a tiny cave of a synagogue, ablaze with lit candles. Daylight was fading fast, when at last, they stumbled on the *Miradouro*, a look-out point in a rose garden with a view down to the estuary. A passing ferryboat hooted.

They sat on a bench by a church wall facing a small wading pool, to which elderly inhabitants came and bathed their feet. Perspiration trickled down her back. On either side of them stretched a pair of ancient, blue *azulejo* panels. She watched as the small figures in them turned to violet in the growing dusk. Something passed between them then, invisible but palpable. Something luminous with inner light. She looked at him, and he nodded. He must have felt it too.

Deep among the narrow streets again and having lost sight of the sea, they descended into a cave. It was a restaurant with only one table and one candle in a bottle. A few dozen sardines with lemon and a bottle of *Dão* between them.

'In the week, the street is filled with fish and fishwives who stand talking gutting the morning's catch straight from the sea.'

She loved the way his face shone in the candlelight. It was the face of a wholesome man. Outside again, they set off down a slope blanketed in mist. Thin blades of light escaped from under heavily curtained doorways. They stopped on some stairs and listened to a sad, wavering song. Two prostitutes brushed past them on the steps and walked away from them, teetering on white stilettos, towards the docks.

'It is time to go. You must to help me look for the rua da Saudade.'

Eight

A Saturday in mid-January 1967

THE NEW YEAR found her raring to crack on with Olga's latest order. The leather shorts and girls' pinafores, in leather too, were next on her list. But there were parties and club nights to go to with Michael's friends, and both their families to entertain. She will start work again on Monday, she promises herself. She can use a clear adhesive to stick back the seams; it will help to make up for the lost time. She sits twirling her wine glass, while the men talk around the dining table, and takes a few minutes' rest. Alistair's frizzy mop of grizzled hair bobs around beneath the spotlight, as he rasps on about a book he is reading: *Catch-22*. She likes the way he gestures, but his fingernails are chewed to shreds. And he is blaming the advertising world in London for his heavy drinking. 'You see, I'm in a catch twenty-two. I need the job. And Neil, here, wants to follow me, but doesn't know what a jungle it is.'

'Is no-one eating Michael's birthday cake?' she asks. In answer Michael leans back in his chair, rubs his tummy and blows. Alistair rolls on with his account. His brother Neil merely wags a finger. 'I'm still listening,' she calls back from the kitchen, where she leaves the dirty dishes. 'Carry on. I need to wake Anna, then we shall have to make tracks. The 'Wheel' opens at eleven, and I can't rush dropping Anna off. I need to see that she's settled before I can go.'

Alistair propels them all along the Manchester-bound carriageway. She sits in the front of his Mini Cooper, holding Anna on her knee. Looking out at the heavy rain. Anna shakes her box of breakfast cereal in Alistair's face, but she cannot wrest it from her grasp. Michael tries to take it off her from the back seat with the same result.

'Nana Pops! Nana Pops!' Anna says, pointing outside long before they have reached Ashendale Crescent.

It looks as if she will settle.

'I'll come for her in the morning, Mum,' she says, and waits while her mother tries to coax tomorrow's breakfast from Anna's grasp. At last she succeeds and Jody is able to transfer her warm bundle: fleecy sleeping suit, Linus blanket, teddy and all. 'There you go, my great big girl.'

'Go 'way.' Anna pushes her and pouts.

She leaves the room, walking backwards, blowing kisses.

'Go 'way.'

'Why don't you let her stay with us until Monday,' says her mother. 'Then you and Michael can have a proper lie in of a Sunday morning.'

'I'd have to fetch her in the morning before Michael leaves for work, and there's no way I can manage her on my own in the two-seater.'

'Maybe Alistair can bring you,' says Michael from behind her back. 'We can ask him on the way there. Come on. We need to get going.'

They find the rest of their crowd in *Rowntrees*, where a horde of noisy 'Wheelers' have begun to invade the bar. Some are parking mud-spattered scooters outside against the plate glass, or peeling off plastic macs in the vestibule before they walk in, if they've hitched it here from Sheffield, or Nottingham, say. Or else they're surging through the double doors, bragging at the tops of their voices about being searched in the toilets at Piccadilly or Victoria.

Michael holds up her Campari and soda above the crush. She takes it from his hand with care and sips it while attempting to shield it from a likely jolt to her arm. She tries to catch the titles on the covers of some EPs, which are currently changing hands under her nose. A few Tamla Motowns, some well-known local floor-shakers, no doubt foraged from rainy record stalls during the afternoon. From time to time she casts a slightly anxious eye across to the swing doors, in case Kay appears amid some new arrivals, some fellow passengers from Nottingham. All she can see of Michael is the back of his stiff collar, and beyond his shoulder, Geoff raising a glass in his direction.

'The Twisted Wheel opens at eleven,' she shouts to Alistair who stands a foot away.

He feels for his wallet, takes out a press card, giving her a wink. 'I'll go across now and try to wangle a couple of late tickets,' he says. His brother leads the way out.

Alone among Michael's mates, she tries to keep up with their constant banter until, not for the first time with that crowd, she starts to feel like a foreigner. The thought comes to her that Zé's friends, when she met them with him in Nicola, had always tried to draw her in and keep her in the conversation all evening. Never leaving her out, even when they spoke in Portuguese. Armando and Isabel are good people. Eduardo too, probably, but he takes a while to get to know.

Halfway along Whitworth Street they are forced to stop before a mass of badly parked Lambrettas and Vespas, some of which look about to fall. Ranks of them have their handlebars jammed together to keep them upright. At the front of the club, only its illuminated wooden cartwheel is visible above the mass of metal that is half-burying the door. Scooters trail along the kerb and into a side lane, further blocking it so that nothing can pass through.

'Reverse!' Michael stares past her and out through the rear window, while Alistair turns back and forth keeping one arm around the wheel. They park on a cindered waste ground and walk back to the club. 'Can't these pillocks see the cop shop across the road?' Michael rights a fallen scooter and attempts to clear a path for them all through the tottering heap.

They duck through the open doorway and are instantly mugged by a wall of fleshy heat. A battery of lights attached to the low black ceiling is bent on blinding them. Once her eyes have adapted, she follows Michael inside, shooed along by the scores of bodies that are pressing at her back. They fight their way through the soft drinks bar and conga past a line of card tables stacked with cartons full of forty-fives.

'We're stymied,' Michael shouts back over her head.

In front of Michael she can see through an open door into

the cloaks cupboard, which is stuffed to its ceiling with identical blue airline bags. She watches over his shoulder as spare clothes and bottles of *Brut* are zipped into more bags. And another group of dancers, mostly wearing new Sta-Prest slacks, are pulling on their leather biking gloves before heading off to the floor.

Michael leaves her to join Geoff beside a flashing wrought iron gate. They seem to want to stay and peer at a record turntable through the bars. The labels on the discs have small conical covers placed over them. She hears Michael say: 'They must be rare, so they'll be worth a few bob.'

Does he ever stop? She sidles up to him and slips her clutch bag into his armpit. 'Hold it for me, will you, Michael? I want to dance. I'm going in to find Neil.' Michael doesn't answer. 'Don't lose my bag.'

She follows the line of dancers tramping through a dark, twisting passageway, until the cramped tunnel opens out into a sagging, low-beamed cavern. Around her is a labyrinth of low-ceilinged, low-lit rooms, all with wooden cartwheels embedded in the walls. Her breath tastes like her own again instead of borrowed from the crowd. And at last she has found an opportunity to lose herself in something.

Neil is dancing in a group of eight lads, their leather biking gloves almost up to the elbows of their Ben Shermans. They need the gloves for their backdrops and for the one-handers that Neil calls his sticky-concrete-floor spins. She likes the way the lads are more inventive here than in the other clubs in town, where they are banned from dancing without a female partner. And it leaves her free to dance alone.

Tentatively she lets her body move, snaking her hips, circling her waist, shimmying self-consciously at first, while frequently hitching back the shoulder of her slippy grosgrain shift. In the end she lets it fall, fascinated by the way the moiré pattern swirls in the light. Gradually she is easing herself back into her body, after what feels like an interminably long absence. By reining in her wayward limbs she gains control and starts to invent steps. Meanwhile her skin can breathe again. It tingles from the vibrations that are pulsing up through the floor, an electric massage to soothe her jangled nerves and set free her mind. She opens her eyes, and Neil is there, trying out some jerky string-puppet moves, his face glowing soda pink. While Alistair, against the wall, watches through his blue John Lennon shades.

Upstairs again, she gulps the overheated air and stands watching rivulets trickle down the back of the stage. She is still humming the Otis Redding song: *A Change is Gonna Come*. By the time the *Ferris-Wheel Band* has finished playing the warm-up a muddy puddle surrounds the stage. Behind her back a familiar voice is still debating record prices. By one-thirty the room is buzzing. Not a soul can bear to stay seated. She decides to get her feet wet, and goes to join the crush before the footlights.

A raised saxophone, a drawn-out note, *The Allstars* springing onto the stage, and Junior on the horn in a rendition of *How Sweet It Is. Cleo's Mood, I'm a Road Runner,* and later, *Cleo's Mood* again. An assault of pore-boring rhythms; an ear-splitting high note. Then a grunt escapes from her throat and, from deep within, a rampage of long-imprisoned feelings breaks free. Impulses that unsettle, sentiments that call fury, are stinging their way through. And from elsewhere, long-banished yearnings are sheepishly returning home. In the hush that follows, when the music stops and the rush of sensations slows, she feels cleansed. Energised. She is on the untravelled road, the one she has always known she must take, even though she cannot see where it leads.

Lads who left in twos and threes a while ago are running back inside, producing boxes of Benzedrine inhalers from their jackets. In dishevelled corners, penknives wink and lumps dissolve into Pepsi, while bottle swillers argue heatedly over where to go to next. To *Stax* for the Sunday morning session and on to the *Shakerama* from two o'clock until late? Or straight to Blackpool *Mecca?* Jody wanders off to queue for her coat, and then to search around for Alistair. It is time for him to drive them home.

Nine

Monday Morning

'I COULDN'T FINISH *On the Road*, by the way. I took it with me to Portugal. It's too chauvinistic for me.'

'Portugal? By yourself?' Alistair, her prolific furnisher of paperbacks, has cocked an ear. She turns sideways, so that she can watch him as he drives. She just can't quite picture him in that isolated village where he and Michael grew up. Or at school together till Alistair moved up to the Grammar School when Michael started at the Tech.

'Not completely by myself. Anna came with me.' She hopes Anna is all right. She felt a twinge of guilt as they flashed past the turning for her parents' cul de sac. But Alistair insists on buying her another book before he leaves. And so, here they are on their way to visit a bookshop in the city.

'Sorry, but I just couldn't see Michael there. But why not? The boring old fart.' He throws her a hurried glance before he brakes to join the rush-hour crawl. But her eyes are welling up. He's turned to her again. 'Jody love, what have I said? Here, have a good blow.' A brown spotted silk handkerchief unfurls from his breast pocket, and she takes it quickly from his chubby hand.

'I've just told him I'm leaving him.'

A low whistle escapes Alistair's lips. 'And there was I, whingeing again. But why am I not surprised? No kidding, I thought you would have upped sticks a long time ago.'

'Well, I probably should have, but there was Anna to think about. Not that I regret … I'm sorry, I shouldn't talk about it while you're driving.'

'You call this driving?' His elbow rests on the side window as he scratches his stubble, checking from time to time that the lights have not just changed to green. 'It was a good night on Saturday, kid.'

'Alistair, he wants Anna!'

Another whistle. She tries to gauge his reaction, but they are off again and, soon, it is time to try and find a place to park.

Their table in the *Kardomah* overlooks the now tranquil city square. She can see the Corn Exchange steps now that office workers have abandoned the open space to a flock of pigeons. The fragrance of coffee beans calls her attention back to the interior and its animated clientele.

'What language is that?' she whispers to Alistair across their table, her elbow resting on her new novel in its *Sherratt and Hughes* bag.

'Dunno. Arabic? Greek? Yiddish?'

'No, I can tell Yiddish. I think it's Arabic. I like this branch the best because you could be anywhere in the world, in here. So, did Michael not tell you, then?'

'Tell me what? That you're leaving?'

'It's not definite! It's not decided yet, and *he* can't know anyway, till ... I just thought he might have —'

'— said something? No, he wouldn't, not to me.'

'Come on now, you two were friends once.'

'Yeah, I've known him for ever, haven't I. You never really know Michael though, or I don't.'

'My mother says that.'

'We were at school together for a while, but after school he was always down the shed, talking to that old owl of his. I reckon that's who knew him the best.'

'Of course, his pet owl. I hardly see him myself now he's working nights.'

'Well, he can be a stubborn customer. But he's only spiting you for leaving him by saying he wants Anna. His pride's taken a knock. After all, he married you to make the rest of us jealous. You're the boodiful wife to go with his sports car and his house. And that's the pathetic truth. I doubt he'll ever leave that house. I know. We'll fetch Anna, then you can come down to Earl's Court. Crash at my place for a while. Give yourself time to think. And I fall in love every day, you know.' He winks.

'What? Sleep on the floor in a freezing bedsit? I'd planned

on moving to Portugal with Anna, until he said he would refuse his consent.'

'A guy?'

'Wait.' She brings out the small photo from her purse and lays it on the table.

Alistair squints at it without picking it up or touching it. 'What's he do?'

'Artist. And I think he's a revolutionary,' she whispers.

Alistair chuckles. 'Trust you.'

Then she is grinning. It is a new dawning. Here is someone who understands.

'I can never be what Michael wants, Alistair.' She shrugs.

'What he thinks he wants, you mean. Listen to me, kid. Just this once and then I'll shut it. Michael will want the house. And why shouldn't he? It's his. Like his sports car and his … Sorry.' He swallows, looks away. 'What I'm saying is, if you want to keep Anna with you —'

'*Tchk*! There aren't any ifs about it. Anna stays with me.'

A waitress walks up, dressed in black with a white cap and frilled apron. Thick blue cups appear in front of them. A steel coffee pot and hot water jug are laid down on a tray. The waitress moves off, a pencil stub swinging from a string across her skirt. She could pass for a housemaid in Lisbon, she thinks. The waiters there are all men. Alistair yawns. She hopes he's fit to drive to London later, after they've collected Anna. He is dressed ready for his office, in a grey checked suit and button-down grey shirt that came from *Mr. Fish*. A yellow fine wool tie trails from his mac pocket to the floor.

'It doesn't matter where you go, love. Whatever you decide, you'll have to leave her behind for a while. Temporarily, that's all. Until you get a home together for you both. Because *you* need a home, too. It's rough, but that's the way it is now, love. Otherwise, if you took her with you — Christ, it'd be *Cathy Come Home* all over again. Shoved around from pillar to post and ending up in hostel. Anna taken away from you. You think you could survive that? You've only lived with your parents, and then Michael. A private landlord wouldn't look at you; they want tenants they can evict easily. Families are out.

And on your own with a child without a man behind you —
jeez ...'

'You mean that documentary? We haven't got a television.'
She shifts her bottom on the backs of her hands. 'I've got a
headache. I can't think. Can we drop it now, please?'

She didn't expect to hear such things from Alistair of all
people. The lines in his face are deepening, she sees. His skin is
dry; he needs some cold cream. She could give him some to
thank him for her book. She glances round in an attempt to
dispel the daze that is creeping over her. The Arabs are still
arguing. A bearded chap in purple cords is engrossed in *Oz*
magazine. The door stays closed behind her while canted light
from the leaded windows warms the empty tables. A ray of
sunshine lights up the Demerara sugar in their bowl. She
watches her spoon heap the golden grains into sand dunes,
while her swirling coffee releases the aroma of Blue Mountain.
Across the square a man leaves the bookshop, stuffs a parcel in
his briefcase. She slides the bag from her paperback: *The Ginger
Man,* it is called. She turns it in her hands and listens with half
an ear to Alistair's description.

'... it's a gas. There's this guy Sebastian Dangerfield and
he's me, I tell you. I'm him.   When you've read it, I'll get you
one that's even more of a gas: *Meet My Maker the Mad Molecule.*
In fact, I might get it now.' He lifts his shirt cuff from a green
fluorescent strap and squints across the square.

'No, there isn't time now. Leave it.'

Alistair is kind, as always, but she is restless and itching to
stretch her legs. Besides, she is missing Anna, and it is time they
went to collect her. A pigeon struts across the pavement
outside, a twig clamped in its beak. Then along comes a smaller
female and the twig is dropped and ignored.

'Can we go soon?'

'You want rid of me?'

'I thought you had to go to work.'

'You're dead right I do. I ought to be in London at the
agency by now. We'll fetch Anna from your mother's, and then
I'll drop you off at home. I'll be whizzing off again smartish,
mind, back down to the smoke. Try to come down to see me

before you run away. You know you like London. And I didn't mean all the bullshit, kid. I'm just an old bullshitter. You're not obliged to listen.'

'Now you talk as if I'm going.'

'Aren't you? You told Michael you are. But honestly, you'd do well to ask yourself where you can best survive. Get real first. Step back a bit and look at your situation. The guy was right to say it's your decision. It's nothing to do with him. Or me.'

'I haven't involved Zé. Though he does care about us both. But over there without Anna? I can't see me finding the heart to work, if she isn't with me.'

'Not if it were only temporary? It could motivate you, you know.'

She holds his gaze for a moment before she says as softly as a whisper:

'They say it only happens once. And when you find the one, you should take the chance.'

Alistair has turned pensive. He taps his little red *Rizla* packet on his tin of *Old Holborn*. Screws some papers into balls, flicks them into the ashtray. And then he rolls himself a thin one and reaches for her matches. 'You could never rent in London. It costs. Whew!' He rubs his thumb across his fingers. 'Rachman may be dead now, but he's not short of successors, and they aren't all in Notting Hill.'

'Well, I can't stay here, either. I'd be ostracised, if I did. In fact, it's already started.' She pinches her bottom lip. She meant Moll and her husband Len. And Carlos came to mind as she spoke. But Leonora will answer her letter soon. Her letters. 'Can we go now, please?'

'You slay me, you do. But send me your address. My agency does work for the big airlines now and then. So I might come out on a visit; see you're all right; get to meet the guy.' He winks as he knots the belt of his mac, and helps her into her coat.

Pacing up and down the living-room, hands deep in her skirt pockets, she stops. How could she forget? The hurried call at the workshop just to whip the letter from the doormat. Driving off again with Anna on her knee, and Alistair's constant wisecracking … In two strides she's by the hall stand, and pulls the letter from her coat. Anna is sleeping soundly in her room. Alistair will be halfway down the A6 by now. And she is running out of patience. Something has to give soon. This letter is thin and has the number nineteen on the back. A single page. And with only one line? She trembles as she reads:

'*Now Jody, I cannot wait for you forever. I need to know.*'

Once the shock has dispersed, she rereads it several times over. In fact, this is more like him. More like the man she knew. Impatient and proud. But then, what has happened to his promise? The one he made that night on the beach.

'*Even after ten years, I will come there and I will find you again. I promise.*'

It was a Sunday evening. They were back from Lisbon, where she'd been for the first time. He was still staying at his family's summerhouse across town, so they took the early morning train together into the city. And walked around until they were light-headed from the heat. They must have climbed a thousand steps, the mound up to the castle and the alleyways of the Alfáma. The magic of the Alfáma stayed with them into the evening. She would say now that it protected them, when they walked into café Nicola.

An atmosphere of faded grandeur filled the arcades of the Rossio. Lottery touts swarmed over it, waving fistfuls of tickets. Women carrying infants lagged behind with old men on crutches, and legless people scooted along on fish boxes with wheels.

'Run,' said Zé, and pulled her with him.

She hardly had the time to throw a handful of coins on the ground. At a vacant shoeshine stand she stopped and shook a stone from her plimsoll, while she questioned him about the *saudade*. Could it not have come from a collective memory of the earthquake? 'I mean the sense of loss would be tremendous; it would reverberate for centuries.'

'Well, that is an original idea,' he said, amused. 'No one

knows its age. I believe it is as old as the soul.'

'Can I get it?'

'What? Catch it?' He laughed, and ushered her past a line of tables on a terrace. 'You told me once about feeling homesick while living in your own house, remember? The *saudade* is like that. But look, this is real contagion.' He nodded to an open doorway. 'Paranoia is contagious. Look at how they block the entrance. They are a virus. A disease. And if they wait for my friends to come here tonight, they have no luck.'

'Is this a café? It looks beautiful, really elegant,' she said, suddenly conscious of her dusty, blackened feet.

Zé clutched his jacket collar to his throat and snaked his way through the group of dark-suited men gathered round the entrance. One had the grace to step aside for her, but others closed in, forcing her to press against their bellies. The interior was quite shabby, but opulent nonetheless. Some darkened canvasses, huge ones, were hung unframed above a long bar. Painted images of hooded monks and soldiers of The Inquisition were set against a vast square, alarmingly like the one they had just crossed. The one she could see through the front window. The sinister figures added to an edgy atmosphere around the bar. They passed along the brass rail to a square pillar with, built into it, a railway-station clock. The clock pillar separated the bar from the dining space behind, where tables were filled with men engaged in either writing or reading, while they blindly stabbed at little dishes of seafood, or drank. And from the back of the hall, another dead-eyed poet stared from his plinth into an atmosphere of genteel, well nicotined decay.

She followed a sign, down some steps to a powder room in the basement. There, she lifted each foot in turn to a basin filled with cold water. Next, she splashed her face and armpits, taking care not to spoil her dress. And recalling how September evenings can rapidly cool, she unfolded a mercerised cotton cardigan from her bag. It was fine like Anna's layette, and the sleeves clung to her arms. In the mirror, they had a blueish tinge like a veil across her tanned skin. She felt confident enough. Leonora's mother-in-law was with Anna and Paulo, while Leonora and Carlos caught a film in Cascais. They all knew she was in Lisbon, nothing more. Upstairs again, she found Zé seated near the clock pillar, in front of him two glasses of hot chocolate.

'It is full tonight. We cannot talk,' he said, and slid her purse across the table. She would have liked some iced water, but Zé appeared agitated, so she thought it better not to bother him. Soon, though, he calmed down, and the Alfáma magic was back, draped around them like a cloak. They fell to licking their long handled spoons while gazing in each other's eyes. Happy to be isolated in a world of their own dreaming.

'Just to look and to dream. To dream is all we have.'

His hand edged across the tablecloth till his fingertips touched hers. A minute later, a tall, suited man was hovering behind his back. The restaurant manager. He must have walked over from the bar. At a sharp tap on his shoulder, Zé's hand shot away from hers, and he sat to his full height. The manager stooped and spoke in his ear, then walked round to the other side of the pillar, where he stayed. Hands clasped behind his back, and bouncing on the balls of his feet.

'He said we must to stop what we do or leave the restaurant now.'

'Stop what? We weren't kissing.' She felt her ears burning, then her cheeks.

'I know and so does he. He knows me well. But if he doesn't do as those thugs at the door say, they close his place down. They watch him every night only for the opportunity to do that.'

'But what have we done?'

'I looked in your eyes.' His tone was clipped. It hid his anger, she thought. But then he raised an eyebrow and drew in the corner of his mouth.

'That's not a crime, surely.' She looked around the room, trying not to laugh at the solemn faces. Diners eyed each other knowingly or studied their plates. A pipe-smoking newspaper reader began to stare her out. Should she stare back? There was something about him ... And there he was again, her well-dressed fellow air passenger from Manchester. Zé said she should forget him, because even the *PIDE* like to follow football and take holidays.

They rode home on the folding wooden seats beside the driver in his cab. Zé chatted with the man in Portuguese, while she yawned. '*Dormirá bem esta noite,*' the driver called, as they jumped down to the track. And alarmingly she saw that Zé was veering towards the promenade.

'Come to the beach and trust me,' he said.

Running blindly down the slope to the beach, everything was shades of black. They blinked hard until their eyes could use the light coming off the ocean. 'See the phosphorescence? Out there.' He pointed out to sea.

'Where?'

'Wait. Now. There. The green flashes. Too late. They have gone.'

The sun had gone down and left the heaving surface lightly burnished with gold. Undulating, lapping near the shore at rocks of the deepest jet. A lone angler waited at the waterline, a dark silhouette cut from a wrinkled cloth of gold. His frugal movements made the only sounds to compete with the lapping water.

They stood watching him in silence and then backtracked up the beach. Huddled together, laughing secretly until they came to the concrete overhang from the promenade. Zé, his back against the wall, pulled her towards him. And, bra-less in the heat, she could sense his words forming in his chest, feel the vibrations through her cotton dress. He spoke quietly in English:

'I found you.' His chin nudged her cheek. And again, 'I found you. Years and years, I found you.' He spoke slowly, deliberately and not without some effort. Her chin was raised on his knuckle. And with his face so close to hers that only fine perspiration slid between their cheeks, he said: 'If you go away to your country and you do not return here to me, even if it takes ten years, I will come there and I will find you again. I promise.' His breath was hot in her ear. But then she slipped lower when some sand fell from under her feet. 'Live with me. Be my woman.'

She waited.

'Okay, but for how long?'

'Forever, if you want.'

'And Anna?'

'I will love her like my own daughter. '

'I know you will, but there's still the problem of the military.'

She moves away. She wants to see his eyes. A shadow clouds them for an instant. But then he startles her by adopting that reverent pose. She has seen him do it once before, when he was describing his father. 'My father can buy me out. I will speak with him at his office in Lisbon as soon as he returns home from Brazil.'

'And if he won't? He may not. And four years is a long time.'

'Even after ten years, I will come there and I will find you again. I promise.'

Again she finds herself staring at the stark message of his letter:

Now Jody, I cannot wait for you forever. I need to know.

He's got a cheek. But she nearly lost him.

Ten

England, 11 March 1967

FIVE MINUTES TO nine by the mantelpiece clock. It is ticking slightly out of time with the one above the kitchen door. Their syncopations distract her from the tension that is in the air. While Michael studies her, wraithlike, from the dining area wall. She stares past him to the darkened window, to the glistening drops that tremble on the outside of the glass. In the silence left by an earlier fall of rain. Tomorrow's date has been circled in red on the kitchen calendar since the middle of January. And somehow she and Michael have got through until tonight, the eve of her sailing.

By February her trunk was ready for forwarding to the docks: the packing, and then the re-packing of it minus Anna's toys. The writing of the inventory; the frantic search for receipts; she had completed it all in the privacy of her workroom. The worst part had been having to begin by tossing out Anna's things. She shivers at the memory. But she soon found that, without Anna's toys, the trunk had room to spare. And as an afterthought she had folded in an old army blanket of her dad's. The one her mother had dyed maroon and used for their curtains after the war. In case she has to sleep rough; you never know. Where will she go, for instance, if Zé is not there to meet her? To Leonora who never answers her letters? No.

So the men from British Rail collected her trunk and carried it away. And now it will be in Southampton, maybe already stowed in the hold of her ship. *The SS Amazon.* She pictures one of those tall cranes as it lifts her trunk in the air, swinging it aboard and dropping it on deck with a resounding thud. There can be no backing out now. Nearly nine o'clock. Maybe Michael will want to listen to the news? He shakes his head.

When she tries to walk to her suitcase, on the table in

front of Michael, her knees turn to jelly. And when she trips over the edge of the grass mat, he makes a move to help. She scoops up her vanity case; she needs her brush and comb and makeup.

'You won't need the bathroom in the next half-hour, will you, Michael?'

'Don't you worry yourself over me. I never need anything.' His voice is thick.

But now is not the time to start pitying him. She holds her skirt to climb the open stairs, while he watches from below. It is warmer inside the bathroom. And she can afford to take her time. The taxi is not due for another hour.

At a click followed by squeak from downstairs, she turns off the tap and listens. A thud, followed by footsteps, tells her Michael is going out. *That's funny. Where's he going?* She hears the choke cough, then the engine revving, the car backing out and tearing off round the corner into the night.

Anna will be sleeping soundly now at her grandparents' house, and he won't want to disturb her. So, he must be heading for the pub. To avoid seeing her leave? Feeling lightened at the thought, she ventures out to fetch her leather satchel from the bedroom. Perching with it on the side of the bath, she marshals her thoughts. She stands it in the washbasin while she checks the documents inside. Her passport, visa, boat ticket and receipt for the fare. The bill of lading for the trunk, which she will need at the other end, when she collects it from customs. Plus a single ticket for the train journey to Southampton. She slides out her leather glove case; it was a present from her godmother and is stencilled with a crinolined lady watering some flowers. One of its silk pouches holds a thickish wad of tattered notes, which she counts out on her knees and, satisfied, puts them back. The other pocket holds papers she could be asked for at some point. The crisp new fiver in her purse will cover her for taxi fares and refreshments, and her jam sandwich is safe inside its *Tupperware* box.

She stands at the sink. Having things to look forward to is exciting in itself, although the vaguenesses of her imaginings have left her feeling anxious at times. She who always laughed at others for their fears of the unknown, especially at her parents, who seem to make a fetish of security. Security is death. Who said that? She doesn't remember, but she needs to make herself believe it. In fact, her future is a blank, except for her image of him waiting for her on the quayside. It won't be long now. Only five days at sea and then she will be there. Part of her is there already. He'll come to meet her on the seventeenth, no doubt at the last minute.

She leaves her satchel in the washbasin and walks downstairs in her stockings, intoxicated by the airy sense of detachment she has now. Her shoes are ranged against a table leg, and are polished to a high shine. Amazingly Michael must have cleaned them for her before he went out. She walks through to the hall and stands at the mirror, tail comb in hand. Its teeth graze her ear. Her fingers are all thumbs. A car is pulling up outside, stopping in the roadway out the front. She checks her watch; nine-thirty. Her taxi isn't due yet.

Footsteps, a man's, are coming down the garden path. Why would the taxi driver come to the back door? It's strange. He's much too early; she will have to send him away. Perhaps it's Michael after all, but she is sure it wasn't his car. And crikey, those footsteps are coming in to the house. They are right behind the kitchen door.

The cheeky sod has gone and let himself in ...

A sudden movement is reflected in the hall mirror. A man's silhouette, a dark spectre staring mutely from behind her shoulder. The eyes piercing straight through her. Dissecting her reactions, as she grapples with the shock. The hefty weight she can sense behind her back, while she doubles over, winded. Straightening, she does a second double-take before she can turn to face him and quell the quaking from deep inside her, enough that she can stare back. He is waiting for her to crumple. But instead she tries to stand taller. Her stiletto heels are in the other room, beside the table leg where Michael left them. And this is all Michael's doing. He is responsible for this. She must show this man who she is now; a grown woman, not a child. And not his eldest daughter any more, not after this.

She bites her lip so hard her eyes water, but she isn't

shedding any tears. Her father steps back, the better to scrutinise her face. He wants to make her feel guilty. He thumbs open his tobacco tin, while his free hand brings a pipe from his jacket. The smell of damp tweed, Virginia Flake and sulphur from several matches. And then the pipe stem hovers at the side of his mouth, where it will stay until he's said his piece:

'You must be feeling guilty, if you break down when I so much as look at you.' He leans in so close that he is speaking into her face.

He rehearsed that on the way here.

'I haven't broken down.' She hasn't. But he wants to play the great psychologist, when all he is is just a clever dick. And Michael should never have called him in. He doesn't want her to stay; he's said so. So why ask her dad to come here to stop her from leaving him? Her dad can't stop her. It's ridiculous. And what gives him the right to let himself into her house? Because it *is* hers. She hasn't left it yet. 'And neither do I feel guilty.' She doesn't.

Her father's shoes are always polished, and they creak, as he leads the way out of the hall and across the dining room. She makes a beeline for her shoes and slips them on, which brings her up to his level. And while he stands rocking on his heels, repeatedly kissing clouds from his pipe, she follows the direction of his gaze over to her luggage. The lid is closed but the case is still unlocked. And his eyes are on her shoulder bag, which is hanging open on the chair back. Her passport is in there. But he wouldn't … She is aware now of having followed him in here too obediently. And she resolves not to let herself revert to reacting like a child. She's not in *their* house now.

Smartly shouldering her satchel, she locks her suitcase and drops the keys in the pocket of her coat. They are safer there than in her bag, she thinks, as her hand returns to guard the clasp. The windowpanes are cleared of raindrops now; the night could turn out fine. She lifts the fox fur collar of her best coat to feel it touch her ears, and places herself squarely between her locked luggage and him. But he keeps moving about and doing that thing he does with his eyes.

He must have begun to practise that look a long time ago.

All through her childhood, that look had been omnipresent. It had set the parameters of what she could get away with. And on the Sunday evenings when he took his turn at the lectern, it was there, as he searched the faces of the congregation for the moment to bang down his bible and thunder over their heads. While she blushed for him, wriggled on the hard seat of her chair, and grew impatient for the chance to sing.

Afraid of him and yet confusing him with the God he'd told her she must love.

Perhaps it was the old drill sergeant's voice that made the congregation cower. A voice unsuited to peacetime and yet, finding renewal in the images that haunted their lives: fire raining from the sky, whole populations on the road, a man struck to the ground, blinded by a blast of light from the sky. A Jew changing his name.

Watching for further signs of rain on the darkened window, she waits and steels herself for the sermon that surely is to come. The one he concocted just for her. The hedgerow is gathering a bluish mist around its thorns. It could soon thicken into fog. Even smog, when she reaches Manchester. She wishes that she had allowed for such delays, when she booked the taxi.

'You see, I believe the relationship between mother and child is sacred.' Now a spiritual twinkle is holding fort in his eyes.

'I dare say, but it doesn't mean you can assume that I think the same.'

So there.

The twinkle vanishes. The clouds roll in. Blood is rushing to her cheeks now. And she is four years old again, bent across his knee and waiting for him to slipper her a second time, for turning round and answering him back. '*It didn't hurt, see.*' And of course, the second hammering was guaranteed to bring the tears. Everyone says now that he was too strict.

Your beliefs are nothing to me now. I go by my own experience.

'And even if it is sacred, which I'm not saying I accept, it doesn't mean that the rest of the family can't help. Because that's all it is; it's not as if I'm abandoning her forever. She's got

Michael. She's got you and Mum; she's got Violet and Fred. Between you, you can manage till I've got a place and can come back for her. And anyway, I could always come back to Michael.'

'Don't be daft; he wouldn't have you. And *they'll* take her. She'll go to their side, and we won't get a look in.'

'I'm leaving Michael in charge of her, because he's her father, and she needs him. She needs me as well and I'm coming for her just as soon as I can.'

Her father is getting nervous now, pacing back and forth, hands in his pockets, tossing back his hair in frustration, when he stops.

'Well, don't imagine you can come to our house. If you walk away now, I shall go straight home and burn every photograph we've ever had of you. Everything. Every sign of you gone. Your name will never be mentioned again. You leave the family, you haven't got a family. So don't even try to cross the doorstep; you're a stranger.'

This is hard. Raw. Wild horses trample on her gut.

'I'm still going,' she says, as calmly as she can manage.

And she pictures herself gliding down from her ship into her new life. Zé walks towards her, smiling at her, tall and upright as he is ...

'He's a pimp.'

'A what? Now you're being ridiculous. Zé could never be a pimp.'

And now he is the all-knowing cynic. The one who always sees the worst in everyone, especially her, or any young man interested in her. The one who left the room whenever a new date came to collect her, when she had already told him, many times, that she was no longer engaged.

'I don't need you to tell me his name, because I know him.'

'You know him?'

'Well enough to know it won't be long before he has you on the streets. I don't need to travel; I can read the papers. I know exactly what goes on in a country like that. Is he solvent?'

'That's none of your business. Nor mine. I intend to look after myself.' And her responses then become a litany: 'I'm still going. I'm going. I don't care. I'm still going.'

The sound of a car pulling up outside, an engine left to tick over, brings relief from the current toll on her nerves. Her dad goes to the window, flicks the curtain back. She sees nothing but yellow mist swirling round the street lamp outside.

'It's your taxi. It's getting foggy out,' he says, as if he's talking to his shoes.

Five past the hour. Already five minutes late. As she drags her luggage from the table, her father takes a step back, both hands raised in mock surrender. Yes, all right, he will let her go, but he needs to ask her one last favour.

'It would make such a difference to your mother, if you'd call, just to say goodbye to her on your way to the station. When I left, the doctor was with her. She collapsed, when Michael brought the news, and she begged me to come here. But don't think I'm blaming you. I expect she'll pull through. I'll drive you there, so she can see you, not for long, just five minutes. And then I'll drop you off at Piccadilly.'

What's wrong with Mum? Has she had a heart attack, or what?

'All right. Send the taxi man away. But keep your foot down all the way there. And I can only stay five minutes, if that.'

What began as a swirling mist in the old Hillman's headlights, is a nose-to-windscreen pea-souper by the time they gain the dual carriageway that will take them into Manchester. Soon a double line of brake lights has slowed them to a crawl. A Shell sign glows orange through the fog, and Dad flicks on his indicators. Fog seeps in, when he hand-signals and pulls up at a pump.

'You can't, Dad! There's no time for this. I'll miss my train.' Glancing back, a trail of fog lights fades. 'They'll never let us back in.'

He ignores her and ambles over to a haloed vending machine. Then a pump attendant is rattling a nozzle into the tank. She fidgets in the front seat, her mind racing to the worst scenario: they find her mother lying dead. While another part of her is opening the boot and running off as fast as her legs will go, hugging her suitcase.

The fog lifts, as he said it would, when they turn into her parents' cul-de-sac. There is no doctor's car that she can identify in the road. She tilts her wrist to the light escaping from her mother's open weave curtains. Gone half-past and going on for twenty-five to eleven.

'Five minutes at the most. My train leaves at eleven and, if I miss it, I can say goodbye to my connection for Southampton.'

In truth, the sight of the curtains is filling her with anxiety. That heart attacks can be fatal, is all she really knows. She runs ahead of her father down the path and waits at the door. In the overheated living room she finds her mother seated, fixed, transfixed, in her usual position: swollen knuckles showing white as she grips the arms of her chair; slippers dangling from feet propped on the old leatherette pouffe. Her cheeks are flushed, but only from the heat of the electric fire. Her hair is not in disarray; no new prescriptions lie along the mantelpiece, on the hearth, or in her lap.

'Don't stay because of me,' Mum says, without turning round. Her eyes are glued to Hughie Green. 'It's a gas mask, you ninny!' she scolds, presumably to a contestant. 'Fancy not knowing that.' And then she turns to her for confirmation. 'What say you, Jody? There's a good job for you, don't you think? What's the matter with you? You look as if you've seen a ghost.'

'Aren't you ill, then? Dad told me you'd collapsed.'

'Ill? Me? 'Course I'm not ill. When do I ever have the time to get ill?'

'He said the doctor was with you, when he left you to come to mine.' Her mother swivels round, directs a withering look towards her husband. She can only guess at the meaning of that look. Dad is over by the china cabinet, his eyes resolutely lowered. She stares at him in the awfulness of second sight. He tricked her. Her own father has betrayed her and, not only that, he planned it. Meticulously. All the details. All done to stop her going.

Double your money and try to get rich. Double your money without any hitch.

Mum staggers up from her chair as the blaring theme abruptly stops. 'That's over then. There's nothing on that telly.'

The scene before her is taking on the unreality of a film, while she tries to overcome the shock. The shock of knowing that he lied. Because he did. Blatantly. And not only that, he hid behind her mother. Hid, while he used her mother's health to manipulate her feelings. Her legs are buckling; she stumbles, but she fails to stop them giving way. She grabs the nearest support, a floor lamp. Light bounces round the wallpaper, casting horrific shadows. Normal vision is deserting her, however hard she tries to hold onto it. As if an unseen hand from behind her is tearing away a veil. From a tableau of, well, evil; there is no other word for it. There is whispering going on around her, but it comes and goes in waves, and disappears into a sea of voices …

She has forced herself back to consciousness. The hands of the clock are still. Five minutes to eleven. Her train leaves in six minutes. Her boat sails at five a.m. So, if she misses it, her dad will just have to drive her south to the docks.

'Is that clock right?'

Her father flicks his wrist. 'More or less. You'll just catch that boat, if you run.'

If I run?

The stocky man stands, his feet apart and planted firmly in the Axminster. He's not going anywhere. She rapidly decides she'll run to the main road and flag down a cab. There's still a chance that the train will be late. They nearly always are.

'My case is locked in the boot.'

'Is it?'

Down the path, keeling over on her heels, at each step she takes her legs feel ungainlier and weaker. Her case is waiting, all alone in the middle of the pavement. She reaches it and, even with the strength of both hands applied to the handle, it refuses to lift off the ground. On stopping suddenly she falls across it. The trees are whirling, the houses waltzering. All dissolves into darkness.

Eleven

Lisbon, March 17, 1967

HE LIKES IT HERE in his own dishevelled corner of Lisboa.
And so will she. Up since first light, and dressed against the
cold, he watches the pale sunlight patrol the walled terrain
below. By shedding light into dark corners it fools his eye into
seeing them as if for the first time. Yes, he thinks, she will like it
well enough. Although a little threadbare, and parched, she will
like the ivy-clad enclosures laced with spindly, eclectic trees.
And the empty house across the way with the glazed verandas
at the back that he has long coveted as studios. It seems
significant today that there are two of them side by side. Shrubs
have blundered through cracks in its walls, so deregulated that
they bear seed pods in mid-March. And the tenants who,
though possessed of gardens, hang their washing from
windows, will amuse her. Jody — her name has a new ring —
will be here in a few hours. His mother can get used to it. She
got used to him, didn't she?

As he fastens back the other shutter, a jet thunders
through the sound barrier, reminding him that he lives beneath
the flight path of travellers. Passengers with passports, free to
leave, to come and go. Neither barred from the airport, nor
forced to watch from the shadows while a loved one disappears.
Immobilised within his anger, as the gap widened and she
walked away with little Anna, out of his life. And now that she
is coming back to him, he is still grounded, the docks as far off
limits as *Portelo* airport was then. There is time to walk to the
dock along the quays. It will do him good. A glance at the little
brass clock behind the bowl of nodding blue anemones, tells
him to be on his way.

The tiny lift cage rattles him down to the ground floor, he

unlocks the door to the *avenida* and sets off. He'll take the bus he caught as a boy, when he went to meet his father from his ship. He used to alight at the little model shop in Rua Alcántara to buy some parts that he needed for his sailing ships and galleons. The patience he possessed then. As he lopes along, he imagines her wandering in the side streets, where the chestnut trees stretch their limbs to touch the house walls on either side, thereby creating shade. Shelter for the *tascas*, the upholsterers, the cobblers. Enough cobblers to shoe an army. The neighbourhood is not a bad one, with the book market and a swimming pool. And he needs her so badly. She will laugh him right out of himself and into her world, mocking his self-pity and goading him to do better. And this is just too easy, to be walking to the docks, when she has spent five lonely days at sea. Without Anna. That, he doesn't like at all; it worries him. They must get organised, and soon.

At the intersection, a sign-writer is brushing something in above the door to the wine merchants' shop. From the bus stop he can just read it: *Estabelecido 1967*, in gilt on a green ground. He doesn't like, *Established*. His co-operative will evolve out of affinities between friends. *Created* would be better, with *International* in it somewhere. He has the people, now he only needs to find the right location, where they can live and work above a gallery.

The bus speeds half empty underneath the Free Waters Aqueduct, its arches making giant strides across a cerulean sky. The sky has not been as high as this since he met her last summer. It was diamond bright then.

It was early September. The tourists had almost gone leaving him the beach to himself. That afternoon the sun was low, but still burning hot against his back. Cool air rushed in on the surf and fanned the soles of his feet. But the loose, white sand was blinding him as it blew down across the shore. And the breeze made it impossible to read his aerogramme from Gil; it flapped and beat against his hands. So he slipped it into the journal Gil had sent, to mark the place of the article that he would read later at the studio.

The sea wall rose up in front of him, a stone's throw away.

And she was standing at the parapet, wearing something billowing and blue. It was the turn of her head. Her closely-cropped hair. The stillness in the air surrounding her, while the blood tingled in his veins. He swiftly used the crumpled shirt beside him to rub the grains from his lenses. And then he watched her glide along the wall and pause before she took the slope that zigzagged down to his end of the beach.

When she disappeared behind the orange-flowering cactus, his chest thumped. When she reappeared round the clump of sea grass, he saw she wheeled a child's trolley. So, who was she? With that asymmetrical, geometrical haircut, she was far from local. And the spring in her step confirmed it. At first he thought she was a Frenchwoman sent to trap him. Having stopped him on the train to Paris, knowing that he tried for years to get a permit, it was exactly the sort of thing they would do. Except, what else could they want from him? But for them, he could be in Paris and, like Gil, working like a madman at Studio 17. Or on the summer course in Montparnasse. Talking with other foreign students without the fear of persecution. Well, no one could have tried harder to go there than he and Miguel.

As he watched her carrying the child across the burning sand, he thought of the survivors from *The Raft of the Medusa*. She made straight for the vacant mooring post, before the row of beached fishing skiffs, where the beach narrows to its end. She must have been there before. Later, standing with her back to the wall, she became a carved figurehead. And when she led the child by the hand, down the sandy bank, he strained to catch a word on the wind. One word would have been enough for him to know where she was from. But all he could hear was music from the transistor radio she carried. She looked so free. And not because of the shocking pink stripe around her navy blue bikini. There was command in her firm stride; it steadied the little girl each time she faltered at her side. Her love for the child radiated from her, plain to see.

He should have guessed she came from the land of The Beatles and pirate radio. Normally he could spot a British girl breezing down the promenade the way they do, oblivious to the stares. Who else would go around barefoot in a short denim shift like a man's shirt buttoned up to her throat? But it was striking and it suited her with her square shoulders and her flat chest and splayed legs that had seen the sun. She had style, his kind of style, and she made him walk tall.

She was mouthing something and pointing at her wrist.

'*Quatro. Quatre heures*,' he shouted above the tinny sounding song.

Her eyes widened, so she understood French, but she answered him in English, as, alas, she still does. But at least it made him more relaxed.

'*Monday, Monday* ...' He crooned along with the song as they passed. The little girl stared back, dragging her feet, tugging at her sunbonnet, while her mother, with the radio strap slung across her bare shoulder, padded on, down to the shore. To where the ocean had exposed the ridge of black, green-fringed rock. Heads of white *lobularia* rolled around on the packed sand, as they do there in September. He watched as they chased them, laughing when the wind snatched them from their palms. Stumbling back up the beach, glistening wet, they stopped to wave to a schooner that had its sails lowered for cruising along the coast. While out at sea, the two grey carrier ships waited still. More requisitioned liners ready to head down the coast to Africa, or farther, to Macao. Timor even. Or it was just another military exercise in disguise. Even the sea has become a prison.

'Avenida da Ceuta!' He jumps up from his seat at the announcement from the driver. And there it is still, the dusty model shop. So small and neglected. Crossing high over Avenida da India by the footbridge, the sudden panorama of the docks gladdens his eyes. And his heart beats faster at the thought of soon seeing her arrive. Then begins the old hop and scramble over metres of massed railway tracks. Cranes everywhere and small craft bobbing, buffeting in the basin. Blasts puncture the air. And two tugs head downriver.

At the Sálazar suspension bridge, smoke belches from an arch. Coal tar stings his eyes. From now on he must be vigilant. This bridge is manned by spies and they keep his details on file. Now that buses cross the bridge they open up a new route to the Alentejo, the region that spells Communism for them. He hangs back as a crowd gathers to watch while an ocean liner clears the underside of the bridge. Ears are stopped against the horn. To better spot an informer among the crowd, he stands apart.

When that *bufo,* the one with the frayed panama and grubby sneakers, had leaned down from the parapet, a darker than dark shadow fell across her, below. Where she sat reading on a narrow band of shade. He was the last informer to be still lurking at the café at the season's end. And when he leered at her from behind a stupid magazine, the clear blue sky he stood against abruptly darkened to Prussian. The *filho da puta.* It was her innocence that drove him off. Head thrown back, arms waving, shouting out against the wind. Her full-blown anger against that wheedling male voice. *She* hadn't been planted.

But where was Anna, then? He caught the sound of a child's voice coming close to his ear. Anna, red-faced and tripping on her bright striped dungarees, thrust a toy pail in his face. She wanted water, and him to fetch it. But her glee was already focused on the water's edge below, a sudden dip in the sand propelling her out of control towards it. In just a few strides he blocked her off from her careering course and the sea. The crash of breakers was deafening. She sat down with a bump and looked at him through eyes screwed against the light.

'Where is your sunhat?'

Where is her mother? Her mother stood below the parapet, a hand clasped to her mouth. She had rid herself of the rat, so, clearly, she wasn't working for them. In any case, what mother could involve a child like that with their darkness? She arrived beside him breathless, having sprinted down the beach. 'Anna! You naughty girl!'

But now Anna isn't coming with her. Not yet. On the board fixed to a wooden hut beside the yacht basin is chalked: *High tide: 17 March 09-30.* A peal of bells from Santos-O-Velho joins the chanting of the pennants. And their combined music carries him down the length of the blind wharf fronts. He loves this part of town. She will grow to love it too. The great ships steaming in and out. The long quays infused with the lovely blues of jacaranda blossom in May. He is coming up to the Rocha da Obidos, the port of entry. He stops and lights a nervous *Gauloise*.

A small lock separates him from the *Terminal de Cruzeiros*. Officially the building is off limits for him, like the bridge. He lifts the collar of his raincoat to clasp it tight around his ears. Across the lock, beside the entrance to the terminal is a sign: *Embarque*. And the *PIDE*? Where will they be this morning? Do they watch this place as closely as they do the airport? Probably even more closely, because of all the containers. All about him is a forest of them, each one a place to hide. But this time he cannot hide. He promised her he will be there to meet her from the boat, and he will. Eduardo begged him not to come, of course. But let wild horses stop him now.

Faced with a deserted forecourt and half an hour to wait, he decides to try and calm his nerves in the riverside café. If the pigs are lurking at the door, or anywhere near it, he will spot them. Once inside the bar, he breathes more easily and walks along it to install himself on the glazed veranda at the back. Visibility is good today; he can see across the estuary. And downriver to the bridge. From here will see the SS *Amazon* approaching well before her siren is booming underneath the arch. The Royal Mail Line steamships, the *Amazon* and the *Aragon*, have been familiar to him for years, as they are to everyone here. She chose well. That ship suits her. In tonnage she is little bigger than his father's old tramper, but is built to carry more passengers and refrigerated cargo. *Papäe* is carrying sheep to Cabo Verde today, and it is fine sailing weather. Too excited for his morning *bica*, he sits and smokes before ordering himself a soothing hot chocolate.

The bar is hung with framed photographs of the great military embarkation for Angola in sixty-one. That enormous quayside parade. He watched it with his family, and half the population of Lisboa, and waved to his cousin Helder while he boarded the *Vera Cruz*. Impossible to find his cousin's face among the ranks of soldiers in the photographs. And Helder was not the only mother's son not to come back. The crowd thought then that they were watching the only ocean liner that would carry young recruits to Africa. But a long trail of requisitioned cruisers has followed her there since. At first, only to Angola, but then to Mozambique, to Guinea Bissau and now they go to Macau.

A dapper waiter lifts a steaming glass from a tray and places it in front of him. Impossible to find his cousin's face among the soldiers in those photographs. If he goes across to look, he will be searching all day. The aunts and his parents, they all know he was there, though they would never come to look themselves. And he would like to tell his aunt he spotted him. Cousin Helder. It was when the *Estado Novo* would not repatriate Helder's body that the aunts stopped haranguing him with their, The army will make a man of you. And instead swivelled their sad, blanked eyes, or turned aside on hearing him or seeing him approach. And Helder's ghost began to haunt him as a chameleon of many guises. More lately disguised as friends of his embarking on the same journey. And as the wars sink to deeper depths of depravity each year, it is now the image of his own unseeable future that comes to haunt him.

The hot drink burns his gullet. He shakes out a *Disque Bleu*, and blows with the cellophane strip pressed against his lips. The bark of a ship's hooter is quickly followed by a shrieking whistle. A flock of schoolboys runs down the riverbank in the distance and is lost in the crowd at the bridge. He stands to have a better sighting of the ship. And there she comes, *SS Amazon*, breaking through a light mist. The front tug has just pulled her great white bows safely through the undertow. The foc's'l follows, and the mast with its insignia comes slowly through until the bulk of her has emerged. Her yellow funnel glows greenish through the haze. And now some black specks have just begun to appear at the deck rails. Whether passengers or crew, he cannot tell.

Once the stern is through and its cranes have cleared the underside of the bridge, a mournful bass note drones all along the surface of the river, a low moan beneath the screech of sea birds that circle in the vessel's wake. What a spine chiller of a horn. His neck a-tingle, he sees and hears the cafe windows vibrate, the glasses singing on their trays. Rising nimbly to his feet, he dashes out and round the back of the building. He will lose himself among the raucous crowd that is overspilling the quay.

Excitement mounts all around him, as he gazes out across the flow. Everyone waits to see the ship steam past the *Christo Rei* monument, their 'traffic cop' across the river, veiled from the west and currently blotted out by the advancing ship. A radio blares from somewhere. A whistle blasts from on high. A second tug is nudging and buffeting with its fenders, putt-putting as it turns in ever-widening circles. Two beeps before both tugs draw a wide arc in the water surface, then wait. While the shuddering great hulk finally comes to rest at the quayside. Sea birds soar above the pilot as he scales down the side of the ship and drops to his waiting tug. Zé cups his hands and cheers his heart out along with the crowd. His love for that pilot is overwhelming. Amid the mounting noise and much directionless milling about, he shades his eyes to scan the rows of portholes, catching every slightest movement, lingering at each opening to search the darkness for a face. One face, which is taking rather a long time to appear.

Restless now, he watches as the gangplank is lowered, and the harbourmaster hovers with some other braided officials all appearing keen to put a foot aboard. The crowd has turned and, in one body, is heading for the terminal. He tacks himself onto the back of it and, when he reaches the revolving door, averts his face, as if he has spotted someone outside. A few passengers are dribbling into the hall, all of them comically unsteady on their legs, until borne away by exuberant friends and relatives. He paces up and down the vast expanse of floor, painfully alert to the menace of the *PIDE*. Up and down it, forward and back. Until the porters waiting at the exit have begun to throw him wordless glances.

Meu Deus, how she can take her time. What has she done this time? Lost her cabin keys? Locked herself in?

But, of course, she will be on the forecourt, having left by another door. He revolves back through the doors again, but into brightness this time, now that the sun has burned off the mist. But even in the clearest daylight, he stands immured in an empty hush.

Twelve

England

THE SLOPING ceiling looks familiar. The sun is streaming in, bleaching patterns on the deep rose distemper. Are these her own bedroom walls? On the empty side of the bed the clock says it is coming up to eleven. So, where is Michael? She shakes the drowse from her head.

Ah, yes, he's gone back to working days.

The telegram: she needs to send one from the phone in the hall. When she attempts to prop herself up, she ends by sinking farther into the pillows. She was on her way down the stairs to dictate the telegram, when she fell, she recalls. Forward probably, because she remembers groping for the rail. On the floor at the bottom, full of hot aches, and no one else around to hear or see her, she simply wailed. Can it be five days yet since her boat sailed away without her? She thinks not. There should still be time to warn Zé. But now her legs refuse to respond, when she attempts to swing them out of bed. Perhaps if she lifts one leg at a time … she tries, but the effort it takes exhausts her. Eventually having wriggled to the edge of the mattress, she can touch the carpet with her toe.

'Mrs. Proctor!'

'Who's that?'

Two taps on her door, and Dr. McBride is peering round the edge. Pale and puffy-eyed, he brings the odour of a vestry into her room. He drops his bag on the ottoman and then perches next to it, cross-legged, his foot tapping to the puffs on his pipe. He makes her jittery, this junior partner from the surgery. She mistrusts his nervy diligence, his over-earnest probing. She has at times thought that he is just the type that would have her put away.

'Any more fainting fits? We can't have you falling down the stairs again, so no getting out of bed just yet. Can someone help you to the bathroom?' His stethoscope is now hooked behind his beard.

'No,' she says, while he moves the end around and taps her chest and her back.

'Headaches? Dizziness? Still sad, Mrs Proctor?'

She nods. And while a cloth is tightening round her arm, and he is absorbed in gauging her blood pressure, she wonders if she ought to mention her legs. She still remembers his response when, quite late in her pregnancy, she told him that she wanted to go for natural childbirth. 'A wacky idea,' he scoffed, and gave her a note to take to the hospital. She had steamed open the envelope, but resealed it when she read … *query personality disorder* … He was just a student doctor then, and a somewhat awkward presence at the surgery. Fortunately next morning, before Michael had the time to talk to him, he rushed round in a panic and asked her for the letter back.

'My legs are heavy and …'

But he is yards away, on the ottoman again, trying to kiss his pipe back to life and scribbling on a pad on his knee. He drops a slip of paper on her night table.

'Stay in bed until I come again.'

And while frowning over his scrawl, she hears his Morris Minor choke into life, leaving her entirely and thankfully alone. *Nervous debility,* she reads. And then some long, exhausting names. *So that's the end of the telegram.* Her fingers feel inside her bedside drawer. The writing paper she finds there is too thick to go by air. The extra weight will mean more delay. It takes five days for an airmail letter, five days for the boat to arrive, and who knows how long it takes for a letter by surface mail. Whatever day it is today, it is too late to forewarn him. He'll go to meet her from the boat. He'll be angry. He'll want to drop her. And who could blame him?

Dearest Zé,

I am writing this in bed because I am ill. The doctor calls it nervous debility. I tried to send you a telegram, so you wouldn't go to the boat, but I fainted on the stairs and fell before I could get to the phone. I'm truly sorry, but please believe that I would not have hurt you for the world. You must be angry now and want to drop me, but it wasn't my fault.

The chewed end of her pen leaves a bitter taste on her tongue. She doesn't want him to think that there is bad blood in her family. Because there isn't, or there wasn't, until Michael interfered. And now they make her want to puke, both of them, Michael and her father. But at least she knows now that it isn't just Michael she must leave; she must leave her father, too. But how can she tell Zé that? *His* family are so kind. She can't expect him to understand.

I don't want to speak ill of my father and, I hate to say it, but he tricked me into missing my boat. Yes, my own father, and deliberately. I was so shocked, I broke down.

It sounds feeble put like that. But she can't seem to remember. Except that Michael was in bed asleep, when her father dropped her off at the door. And that she bolted upstairs, straight for the bathroom, and threw up.

I was ready and waiting for the taxi to arrive. But unbeknown to me my husband had asked my father to stop me going. I still don't know why he did it, because he'd said he didn't mind my leaving. And when I ask him now, he only says he did it because he thought that he ought to. It's what he's like, I suppose.

I shall try again, when I'm better, but the next time I shall make sure that I don't tell a soul. I have to wait now for a friend to post this, so don't know when it will arrive.

I'm really sorry.

Love, Jody.

Exhausted by the mental effort, she dozes softly in the sunshine. When she wakes she thinks she smells burning. But it is only her cotton pillowcase. That sun is strong for March. For a moment, she imagined she was lying on a beach, the sun scorching on her old gingham bikini.

'*I stay with my family on the other beach across the rocks. My mother invites you to join us.*'

'*I can't go to meet your mother dressed like this.*'

It being Saturday, Leonora and Carlos had other plans. And so, she and Anna set out earlier than usual for the beach. By late morning, turmoil was piling in from the city. Families arrived arguing. Children and dogs ran amok scattering sand. She looked up and saw him standing by the wall, the ghost of his deplorable state of the day before. His black shorts hid his hands, which were pressed against the flaking wall; and his feet were on the ribbon of shade that underlined the wall.

'Zé!' Her arms went to her midriff. And she turned aside to watch Anna, who was digging in the sand. Yesterday she had decided that she must run from this new entanglement. So why the butterflies in her gut?

'You're not going to the studio?' she said, picking up Anna's bucket.

'You did not come to the café last night,' he murmured, in English.

What? Is he mad? How could he have expected her to go, when only that afternoon she'd walked away angry and in tears? Did he lose his memory along with his glasses and his money?

'No. I didn't go.' It felt like speaking through molasses.

A fisherman was labouring up the sandy slope to his skiff, a Portuguese water dog at his heels. She greeted the man, and turned to pull down the sleeves of Anna's dress. The sun was high and getting hotter. And Zé was still there. 'My mother invites you to join us. She wants to see Anna.'

'Heh? She knows about her?'

'Yes.'

It was then she noticed his lisp. She glanced back toward the green-fringed rocky causeway he'd just crossed. Beyond the rocks were ranks of red parasols that stretched along the strand to the private beach below the hotel.

'It's even more crowded over there.' She shaded her eyes to look at him.

His back had found a hollow place in the wall, as if he needed a shell. And with his denim shirt flapping loose, he looked a little thinner round his ribs. Not haggard though, like yesterday, but still not quite himself.

'I can't go to meet your mother, dressed like this.' She tugged at her bikini, wishing she could rid it of the silly frill.

'It is Anna she wants to meet.'

'Anna hasn't any water left for her sand pies and her castle.'

'Come Jody. We go. I fetch her water on the other beach.' And he was off, swinging their packed string bag, striding past the ramp where Anna's trolley stood axle-deep in sand.

The stood and pulled on her beach robe; the rough towelling scratched her shoulders. It was too hot to walk. The midday sun was blitzing the rocks, penetrating through the crevices, to light up the former ocean floor through a wash of swirling foam. He called back to her that they were walking on an old underwater volcano. Ash black and pitted, it griddled the soles of her feet. Especially when she stopped to lift Anna over a wide crack. And her arm was wrenched down. She tripped on something. Anna fell and banged her knees.

Damn! The rock will burn her skin!

Anna wailed, and sobbed tears down her neck to be absorbed into her robe. And then she pawed at it, and bit it.

'Here, take this. I will carry her.'

She felt the handles of the bag suddenly hooked over her finger. Her sobs abating, Anna hiccupped, and reached out for Zé. Safe in his arms, she watched Jody ease the grit from her palms and knees. And having wet her cheeks with snot, held out a hand for Mum to kiss it better. Zé strode ahead with Anna looking back from over his shoulder. While she dragged her toes through a fringe of fluorescent algae, exposing barnacles on the seaward side of the rock. As she crouched to buckle on her sandals, she heard him shouting, 'Whoa!' in the distance.

'Ever the follower,' she muttered to herself. But she had to admit that she was curious about his mother. Perhaps she could shed some light on Zé's strange state of the day before. She still felt raw, she noted, as she checked the hem of her beach robe and tightened the belt.

'Come. We are nearly there.' He was pretending to bite Anna's fingers, when eventually she caught them up. 'My mother speaks English, and my brother speaks French,' he said gently. 'Don't worry.'

Anna chuckled and snatched away her fingers from his face.

'You mean I've got to speak French?'

'Grrh!' He mock-frowned at Anna. 'Come, Jody. Come.'

'So what do I call your mother, then?' They were progressing along the coastline.

'She has the same name as me.'

'She can't have. You're teasing me.'

The putt putt of an outboard engine partly drowned out his answer. ' — José. Maria-José.' He stood on the last boulder, silhouetted against a dazzling, a riotous stretch of beach.

Leaving him on the rock, she slid down to cool, caked white sand. And stood amid a strangely distant-sounding babble of foreign voices. Ahead of her a fête of windbreaks, of oiled bodies and women shaking out their thick, dark, glossy manes. A girl, tall like a mannequin, was eyeing Zé as if she knew him. But as she took Anna from Zé, she saw the long pony tail bob away.

'When the Portuguese are tall, they're really tall.'

He laughed and clasped her on the shoulders as he jumped down to the sand. But his warmth against her back quickly became an edgy, uncertain space. She ducked to let fall a hand. And they walked together without speaking, over soft, sinky sand. And on, between the ranks of canopies, towards a bathing tent of sorts with wide vertical ice cream-coloured stripes. A wisp of smoke curled from the door flap. A woman's hand appeared and batted it away. The hand of a small, slim woman with a nut brown chest and wearing a regulation black wool swimsuit. Shielding her eyes yachting fashion, she squatted on a low stool.

'My mother.'

'*Encantada*. I am Senhora Maria-José.'

'*Encantada*. I'm Jody.' She was grateful for the beach babble and the sough of the distant waves. His mother's hand had left hers with a reptilian sensation. But her face was youthful in expression despite some deeply etched lines, her brown hair loosely braided and lightly salted with grey. Anna strained to catch the light refracted from the crucifix round her neck.

'Ot.'

'Yes, hot.' The Senhora leaned down to Anna's level,

holding out the jade pendant.

'Ot.'

She laughed brightly, his mother, but the next instant, looked grave. Her face was hidden while she slid a flat, wooden box from underneath her stool. Its lid inlaid with a monogram in mother of pearl. A teeny button flipped it open. 'Cigarette?'

Jody turned to Zé, puzzled.

'Take one of my mother's; they are not so strong as mine,' he said, and fished a crumpled pack from his shirt. He spoke to his mother from the side of his mouth while sheltering a flame. 'Jody could not believe that you and I have the same name.'

'José? Well, we were all called Maria then; it was the law here. So most of us used our second name, which in my case was my father's, because my mother was dead.'

Again the disappearing smile. Maria-José's attention was back with Anna, but whenever Jody spoke to Zé, a glance came her way. A boy and girl ran up and showered them all with sea water and laughter. Rui, thin and gauche, peered at her through splashed, steel-rimmed glasses. He could end up taller than his older brother before long, she thought. Then a girl of around twelve, with braced front teeth, rushed to pounce on Anna. 'Aa-ah!' Stooping, she tried to lift her, but her plaits touching Anna's face caused her to splutter. When Zé spoke in Portuguese to her, she desisted.

Senhora Maria-Jose shaded her eyes and said to Jody: 'What a lovely little girl you have. Do you think she'll come to me? Zé tells me you design the clothes for you both and make them all yourself. So unusual. So pretty.'

Anna tugged at the hem of her robe, but Jody urged her forward.

'She's playing shy.'

'Today is my son's birthday. We make a picnic instead of taking lunch at the house. Sixteen today, aren't you, Rui?' Rui was preoccupied with dragging off a stray dog. 'Bring Anna into the shade. Zé, take the little girl inside and give her a drink. Here, I'll do it. I have some grenadine. I keep it by for my grandson.' As she spoke, she fastened back the flap.

Her oiled back was the mahogany of a summer spent at

the resort, and nothing about her figure hinted at the four children she had produced. A flock of nuns passed behind the tent, each sister carrying a pair of stout black shoes. Seagull cries soared to fill the blue. Football crowds roared from a good hundred transistor radios. With Anna safely inside, Zé passed the string bag to his mother. And then his arm reached across her shoulder.

'Zé, don't.' She brushed his hand away and freed herself, while his mother watched them from the tent.

He presumes too much. He hasn't even apologised yet.

'Did you make this, too?' He tweaked her sleeve. 'It looks nautical with the navy blue band round the edge. Anna is happy in there. Come for a swim with me.'

Never apologise, never explain. What's the third? Never complain?

She let him lead her to a sand bank; it was teeming with sunbathers. He threaded a descending pathway through the jutting orange legs of families, as they passed plates around, dripped juice from half moons of bright pink watermelon, or fanned themselves with comics. Dark men stabbed knives in the sand, lolled on their elbows while they tossed each other cigarette packs. And dogs shook sand onto her legs. Slowly they meandered down to where great waves crashed onto the shore, and then stole away with their voices, to toss them back again as echoes from deep inside a vast conch shell. Glancing back, she saw his mother's bright, striped tent crowning the ridge.

'You take after your mother. You've got her eyes and you've got these.' But she quickly pulled back her finger from the crevice beside his mouth. 'You move like her, too.'

'Like my mother? She was a dancer once, a long time ago in Brazil.'

'What kind of dancer?'

'Nightclub dancer, in my father's club, the one he owned in Rio before the war.'

'I thought Portugal wasn't in the war. Can your mother do the Bossa Nova? It's all the rage now. I want to learn it.'

'Probably. You can ask her. I know she once did an extremely athletic type of samba. She was young when my father married her. The convent where she lived was punitive, and so, one day she jumped the wall.'

'Jumped? You mean she ran away?'

'Yes, when she met my father. I never knew my mother's mother; she was English, but she died.'

'And her husband put your mother in a convent?'

'He could not care for her alone.'

'And he was called José.'

'Yes, and *my* father, too.'

'I see. Jody started as a boy's name, you know. And my parents married young. So did I, but what was right for them wasn't right for me. They were the no-fun generation, straight from school into the war. I was engaged, when I was still at school. It was silly. I hid the ring behind my school tie.'

Zé looked unfazed. 'My father went to Italy with the Brazilian navy, and returned to Portugal after the war.'

She dropped her robe onto hard, corrugated silt and skipped to the water's edge. He picked it up, dropped his glasses in a pocket, left it lying on the shingle. Sea foam licked their ankles, and they charged into the surf.

'Zé, you've still got your shirt on, you ninny.'

'It is fine.'

'Are you cold? This Atlantic water's always cold. It's blue today. Why's that?'

'Look at the sky.'

'The sky's yellow.'

'It is all sun. The blue is just its complementary colour.'

Hitched on his back, clutching at his hair, she realised it was the first time they'd had the chance to play like this. And that it was a measure of his patience with regard to Anna. She watched a few more doubts fizzle out and drain away in the surf.

'I must put you down. My back is sore.'

'I thought you didn't get sunburned.'

Her feet found the rippled seabed and she kept her balance in the waves. There was a dark patch across the back of Zé's dripping shirt. As the sun gradually dried it, the damp cotton lifted from his skin. The patches had fused into a dark horizontal band.

'Hey, whatever have you done to your back?'

He swung her round to face him, while his back was to the shore. And there, knee-deep in surf, and hidden from the public spies and the swimsuit police, he kissed her for the first time. And with salt tears of relief, she kissed him back, beneath a blurry sky. Their secret murmurings inaudible amid the whisperings of the surf. Sea spray wet their lips and all became a shower of white light. Then, heads down, they swam out together to the warm swell beyond the breakers. When she circled back, he overtook her as she slowed alongside the coastline. And they rode into shore to stumble out, knee-deep in laughter and breathless. Water dripped on the shingle as he wrapped her robe around her shoulders and reined her in to dry her hair.

'Zé, that's not nothing, is it, that stripe on your back?'

'Trust me. It is nothing. The salt water has done it good.' As he was massaging her scalp, she broke free and said into his chest hair:

'Zé, are you a revolutionary?'

He laughed and flicked away the towel.

'I am an artist and that is all. But that means I belong to the whole world, which in itself can be dangerous. Art must break down the boundaries, and there are some who object to that.'

'Your mother was nice to me, wasn't she?'

'Yes, because she assumes it is just a holiday romance.'

'Hmm.'

By the time they were back at base, they were dry and nothing showed through his shirt. The family was ranged on the sand in front of the tent. They were passing round tin plates. Anna coolly ignored her from where she sat between his mother's knees. Jody knelt and read aloud the blue letters round the rim of her plate: *M.V. Castelo São Jorge*.

'They are the plates from my father's ship. His steel castle.'

'She was built in England, you know. On the Clyde. My husband could tell you all the other names she had, but he is currently away on business, in Brazil.'

'I used to go with him sometimes, to Brazil, before they

took my —'

'Zé!' And deftly his mother switched the conversation back to Portuguese.

When lunch was over, Eduardo arrived on a visit from the city. She saw him waving from the parapet.

'I'll join you later,' she called, as Zé climbed the steps to meet Eduardo at the café. 'I'm going back to fetch Anna's trolley from the bottom of the other ramp.'

Zé's mother rose from her low stool and held out her hand.

'You do well, my dear. So pretty, so talented, and kind. What a pity, Zé is just a poor boy. A pity.' And whatever his mother meant by that remark, she still cannot fathom.

She dozes through the afternoon, in and out of thoughts about Zé's family. She only met his father once, at their apartment in Lisbon. The tallest man she's ever seen.

At last, Moll arrives, flustered. 'It has to be a flying visit,' she says, refusing to sit. 'I'm not supposed to come at all. Len would hit the roof, if he knew.' She crosses to the window and looks out.

'Why? What's wrong?'

'He called you something unrepeatable. I didn't like it when he said that.'

'What did he —'

'I can't tell you. I can't bring myself to say it. Gosh, it seems so stupid now, but he forbade me to see you.' The agitation lasts until she comes to stand beside Jody's bed.

'Tell me. Go on.'

'No. Okay, he called you a prostitute among other things.' Moll's eyes are showing flecks of yellow. She looks tired. 'But you can make it work here, with Michael, you know, Jody, if you try.'

'I'd have to want to, though,' is all she can reply. For her the matter is sealed.

'*Tchk*! You may not think it now, but you'll get over it. You'll see. I want you to find a different kind of love.'

'You've already said that: you're repeating yourself. Are

- 119 -

you going to the village?'

'Yes, but quickly in and out. You need something?' Moll settles on the ottoman, her ankles crossed, lips pursed, and fingers laced in her lap.

'I need you to post a letter for me, but you mustn't put it in the pillar box. You have to hand it over the counter, ask to send it airmail and say it's urgent.' She watches her letter slip from Moll's gloved hand into her handbag.

'You can count on me.'

The bathroom door swings shut behind her and, by holding onto things, she makes it to the window and looks out. She is bored with waiting for Michael to come home from work, and she is hungry. She stares out at the row of porch lights already lit. At the cars with their lights extinguished, parked on steep drives. She lets the sill support her weight. The lights are blazing at the Calvi's house, Mrs. Calvi's house now. Ever since her husband's accident, Mrs. Calvi keeps all the lights on. They blaze the whole night long. It seems she still cannot bear to sleep alone in the dark. That awful night, when the police had been and gone, and Jody went across to stay with her, she will never forget. The older woman's body racked and torn apart with animal cries of grief. Lying there beside her, not knowing what to do except to just stay. Until her son arrived the next morning.

'Blast you Michael!' He's really late now. She's tired of listening for his car. And yet, her ears won't stop doing it. She cannot stop herself either, from leaning outside so that she can see past the end of the street. It may never come. He could have had an accident. It can happen easily, so why not to him? A tyre could blow. No, that's not enough. A wheel could spin right off, making him skid around and then spiral completely out of control. Maybe somersault and then land upside down. Bang. Bang. Bang. And then silence. The police will come, and she won't be able to get down the stairs to let them in. Her brow is pressed against her forearms. Her face is hidden; she is wishing. Wishing and feeling sad. The sadder she feels, the harder she hopes. The harder the hopes, the louder she sobs.

She throws herself face down on the bed. And cries herself to sleep.

Thirteen

Lisbon. March 17. 1967

HIS CHEST IS pumping out panic rhythms. He casts about him for a seat. The official-looking plaque beside the revolving door is emitting danger signals. He leans with his back against it and glares at the dusty tarmac. Looking up, he sees in front of him a long, low concrete building. The Colonial Navigation Company shed.

In sixty-one, while still a schoolboy, he knew the fear he feels now. The military police filled the flat roof of that shed, and from there they controlled the embarkation on the ground with their guns. They filled the iron steps that mount the tower from which they controlled the crowd. Today he sees a bare concrete shed, nothing more. Round the edge of the roof, they stood, feet placed apart, pistols raised, glaring down at the march-past of the soldiers and the new recruits. Those saluting, goose-stepping boys. While eyes, from the tower steps, were trained on the noisy, agitated crowd. At his mother's side he stood and watched it all and wondered how he would protect her. Today containers dwarf the building, stacked on its roof. Yet more imported goods.

Back inside the embarkation hall, a smiling African attendant sits in the middle, on a high stool. Zé sidles up to speak to him.

'*Senhor*, I need to check a passenger list. My friend did not come off her ship.'

'Certainly, *Senhor*. See the staircase? Go up, and left along the corridor to the office marked *Escritório.*'

He runs up two steps at a time, and taps on a wired window.

'*Sim, Senhor?*' A male clerk appears.

'I wish to check the passenger list for the *SS Amazon*. She docked this morning, but my friend did not —'

'Name?' The long-faced clerk eyes him coolly, his pen tapping on a clipboard.

'Jody Proctor.' Strange to hear himself say her married name aloud.

'Nationality?'

'English.'

'British, then.'

'Yes, British.'

He stares in blank disbelief at the only box that doesn't have a tick beside it. Her name is entered on the log as *passageiro 19*. In place of a tick a ringed handwritten note: *failed to embark*.

'Failed to —?'

'*Sim, Senhor. The Senhora* failed to embark in Southampton. Will that be all, *Senhor?*'

'*Sim, Senhor. Obrigado.*'

Possible scenarios interspersed with highly unlikely ones begin to reel through his head, as he stumbles down the stairs. A train crash on her way to the boat. A sudden illness, the pleurisy perhaps. But no, he knows what it was. The scenes before his eyes are slowing him, as he drags himself towards the café. *The Pide. They have arrested her. They have kidnapped her. Interrogated her. Interrogated HER?* He trips over his feet at the thought, the blood freezing in his veins. *That agent she saw in Nicola. What did he want? They were watching her even then. Meu Deus!*

On reaching the café door, and seeing that the space around it is empty, he realises that his thoughts are moving into spy-thriller territory. What if they simply refused her a visa? They could have done so easily. He spits an order for a Pernod across the bar, and moves along it without a glance or a nod to the waiter. On the outside veranda again, his seat is still free. He sits hunkered down inside his raincoat, hands buried in his pockets, and glowers through the plate glass at the unforgiving bulk of her ship. All the to-ing and fro-ing aboard her has now ceased. Nothing stirs on deck. *This is it. Reality.* She won't appear at a porthole now, however fervently he wills it. A lone sailor at a deck rail has started feeding out a coil of rope. He watches it as it writhes against the hull and, in the end, is left dangling. A dull ache begins to gnaw his bones. A muzzy feeling fills his head. And he succumbs to full-body wipe-out like the onset of influenza. He can hardly move. He has no wish to move. Why should he move? He can suspend himself in time.

Towards lunchtime he stirs. He is hungry. Ravenous. But he doesn't want to eat. He staggers stiffly to his feet. He crosses tramlines, unseeing, and is strap-hanging in a carriage before he notices that he is riding home on the metro. Walking down the *avenida*, with its stark, modernist apartment buildings, the pavement clings to his soles. He is home again and, at last, he can close his door on the world. He rests his head against his jacket hanging on the peg, and exhales. The hunger has passed.

He brings out an old attaché case from under his bed. Lying open on the counterpane, it spills letters in blue envelopes, each with a royal stamp. There was a time in January, when their letters crossed in the mail. He sifts through a pile until he finds one dated the twenty-fourth, and holds the envelope to the light. This arrived here the morning after he had posted one to her. And yes, there it is, her decision, with the date of her sailing from Southampton: the twelfth of March. And she signs off with a promise to write again on the Tuesday. That would have been January twenty-eighth. He rummages. And here it is.

'... *Anna is watching me write this letter in my workroom. By the look of it, she is trying to chew the ear off her Teddy. When the two men from the railways arrived and carried out my trunk an hour ago, she looked ready to burst into tears. The first time I packed the trunk, I left her Teddy out until the last. And when I did put him in, she sobbed so hard I had to leave him out altogether. Later of course I had to unpack everything of hers. And then I was the one sobbing. That was the hardest thing I've had to do.*

I spent the last few days squeezing in some kids' clothes that I can sell in Portugal. I even fitted in some bolts of cloth and some sample lengths I'd been given. So now, without my machine, how shall I spend the next six weeks? With Anna, I expect. I can't believe it. I don't know what to do with my hands.

Well, that confirms that her trunk was forwarded, and she intended to come. If she changed her mind about Anna — But her later letters never hinted at it. Or did they? He will go through them all again. As he throws aside the earlier ones an aerogramme slips out. He picks it up, thumbs the French stamp and the little indigo plane symbol. His last letter from Gil in Paris, but what is it doing here?

I was reading this on the beach, or trying to, the first time I saw her.

He unfolds the aerogramme and reads:

Atelier 17, Boulevard Montparnasse, Paris.

Zé!

Your group exhibition was well received by the punters and the press. I enclose a copy of the article, 'The Young Painters of Portugal,' in the French edition of the Journal. As you will know, The Portuguese Jornal de Letras will never print it there.

I go well here in Montparnasse. I live on fish and Coca-Cola and I work like a madman. At Studio 17 I learn the new viscosity printing from the Englishman who invented it. It means that I can now print in full colour from a single plate. No more registration. It is all attractions and repulsions now. Did I tell you Vieira da Silva came in with her husband, and we talked?

So, Gil is happy in Paris, the lucky devil. He meant to answer that letter, but he was miserable last summer. His painting in a Paris show that he was not allowed to visit. The summer school they were blocked from attending even though they had a permit and a guarantee for their return. And then Miguel disappeared, arrested on the street just before the summer vac. Their names added to police registers, relayed across borders. Passports, papers, currency all confiscated. He was sick of it.

And now Jody hasn't come.

He sits and stares at the old beaten up case lying on his bed, and sees again the callused hands of a Portuguese labourer. *What happened to that man?* June it was, when they took the night train to Paris, he and Miguel. The labourer's persistent drumming on the lid of a cardboard valise had been disturbing his sleep. And then the guard jolted him awake again with his stupid lecture to the passengers. It was just before the Spanish border.

'*Documentos!*' The *PIDE* agent was one of three that had

ambushed their carriage.

The two sulphurous faces that loomed over Miguel, plus another on the running board, still swinging from the handrail. Miguel beside him clutched their papers. The carriage bristled with the sound of papers held ready in trembling hands.

They kicked the labourer, the pigs. Kicked him all along the gangway and out into the night. A poor man he was, a stunted workman with callused hands and his threadbare green suit worn to a shine, and yet so lovingly darned and pressed. They had threatened him with a wrench, his own wrench, confiscated from the case that lay open on the empty seat. Clean blue overalls unwrapped from round a few tools. Just enough tools for a keen man to find plumbing work in Paris.

Nothing but a sneer from the agent scrutinising their permit. He held it out like a stinking fish. Miguel handed him their testimonial and waited with a smile on his face, hands clasped between his knees.

'*Uma falsificaçao.*'

A forgery? Their letter was no forgery. But apparently it was their turn to be 'helped' off the train. The sight of the last coaches disappearing into the darkness, leaving nothing behind them but a trail of throat-stinging smoke. Being kicked over the tracks and onto a coal-dark siding. Then manhandled up an iron ladder to the headquarters of the *PIDE* inside a disused wagon-lit. A rat scurried underneath it. A shortwave transmitter rose up against a star-washed sky. He remembers glancing at the mast, oblivious to how it was to ensnare them.

'Sign these two statements, then I return the passports.'

The liar. What else could they do but sign underneath the pigs' blatant lies? Stand by and watch while the agent locked their passports in a safe? He locked them up anyway, once they'd signed and emptied out their francs.

'Insufficient funds for a holiday in Paris.' He seemed not to want their permit, because he threw it back at Miguel. Miguel must still have it. Wherever he is now.

He stuffs the aerogramme into his back pocket, kicks the case back beneath the bed, leaving Jody's letters spread on the counterpane. And then he reaches down the Journal from the shelf. It flops open at his article, now paint-stained and grubby.

Zé Rodrigues - peintre Portugais. He was right to introduce himself to her as painter, not art student. His studies had been cancelled, so it seems he told the truth by default. He all but smiles as he catches himself mouthing the words again.

'*I am Zé Rodrigues. I am painter.*' Or was it **a** painter? He still doesn't know! '*I am painter,*' he decided, although he doubts now that she could hear him through the jangling of that radio. He caught the gist even so:

'*This is Roger Day on swinging Radio England bringing you the Space News from the north-west-east-south...*'

The pirate radio ship that broadcast it had been blown into Lisbon harbour in a storm. The *Laissez-Faire*, the ship was called, she said. She seemed to think that he would know it. He pretended quite a lot on that first afternoon.

It had touched him to see the two of them, so small and unprotected, the way they hunkered down against the wall, while the world passed above their heads. He wondered where the child's father was and whether he should even ask. She sat in full sun, a book, *On the Road*, propped against her knees, while she absently stroked sand onto a small, damp mound and patted it. She shaded her eyes to look at him, and they were startling, of the darkest dark, forever shifting and curious. And when she said she couldn't stay long, he thought she was expecting someone, a husband perhaps.

'Is your husband with you?' It must have come across as blunt, because she turned her face away and watched the slope. And he could trace the lines of her profile, the shape the bones made of her nose.

'My husband's at home in England.' He can still see her brushing sand from her knees as she said that.

And then she abruptly rescued a hat from under Anna's feet, shook it, and scolded the child firmly as she tied it on. *Her hands are large for a woman, like sculptors' hands,* he thought then. 'May I join you one minute?' That was pretty blunt too, but he was returning the child's bucket after saving her from the waves. She looked flustered and said she had to go the post office with a letter. And there was his opportunity. 'The wait is long at the *correia*. I can walk with you, if you want. I am José. They call me Zé.'

'Zé?'

'I am painter.'

'Artist?'

'Yes.'

The relief he felt, when her shoulders relaxed.

'Say thank-you to the nice man, Anna. See, he's brought you some water. She can say it when she wants.'

His cigarettes were too strong for her and, while she rummaged for her own, he very quickly and deftly laid his towel down next to hers. And sat on it, bolt upright like a man inside a statue, while she fished out a box of cooks' matches and he caught her glancing at his hands. Then... *music, more music, moremusicmoremusic with Boom Boom Brannigan and Everybody Must Get Stoned*. They had to shout above that radio.

'Wait. Anna loves this one. She'll be dancing in a minute. Watch.' The little girl danced and scattered sand on them while they laughed and covered their heads.

'How old has she?'

'Twenty-one months.'

'I have twenty-one years. But you do not say me your name.' It was hard to make her say it. He said her book looked American from the bright colours on the cover.

'These beatniks go on a road trip across the States to the West Coast. Why does everyone want to go west? They all do now, don't they?'

Not him. He'd been trying to go east. She said she thought he must have read it.

'I cannot read it here,' he muttered. And there lay his first mistake.

'Why not? Is it banned? It's not like *Lady Chatterley*.'

He sat watching an oblique shadow unfurling over the sea, while the sun hid behind a cloud. He was saved from answering, when Anna broke free, tipped her water on the mound and bashed it. And Jody crawled to her on her knees. And shifting back again, pulled on a robe, bright white against her tanned skin, and tied the sash round her narrow waist. 'I'm not keen on that book,' she said. 'The friend who gave it to me told me that Allen Ginsberg was in it, but I can't find him anywhere. Is it really banned?'

And then he made an even stupider mistake. 'I read it when I was in Paris. It is not obligatory here, and all that is not obligatory is forbidden. Especially if it is foreign and speaks of freedom.' He didn't mean to, but he uttered it like a litany, while he slid a glance up the wall. 'You know Joan Baez?'

She had that effect, of making him say things he shouldn't. But Anna's skin was reddening, and the child struggled as she gently creamed her skin. No, her hands are not her best feature, but her eyes ... her eyes are mesmerising. Huge and yet deeply set. Brown shadows melting into black. They made him think of Montparnasse. It was Modigliani, of course, the way he did his eyes like black thumbprints in clay.

Le Journal des Lettres, des Arts et des Idées. He caresses it, where he stands.

She liked it too, the plain buff cover, the red typeface. She said they had these editions in her French class at school. Her lips moved while she read his article, just like a little child. And all the while, kneeling next to her, he was smelling her clean hair.

'Are you in it? Look here. It says *Zé Rodrigues*.'

He longed to tell her what it meant to him, but he couldn't. The Jody he knows now would have understood. He returns the Journal to its shelf, leaves it hidden behind a vase. And the Jody he knows now would never let him down as cruelly as this. Something made her miss the boat. But what? *Christo! The woman lives in a free country* ... His brain aches and he is trembling slightly. He is tired, and it is turning cold. A short sleep is what he needs, and afterwards to talk with Eduardo.

Fourteen

EDUARDO'S BELOVED linotype machine is already silenced. Switched off, he sees, when he slips discreetly into the typesetters' room. His friend is standing at the sink, busy sluicing kerosene from his hands, his overalls discarded and hanging on a peg. Eduardo sees him coming, grabs a pumice stone and, after greeting him, uses it to attack the yellow crusts on his thumb and two fingers.

'They're the ones I use for lifting out hot slugs after a run-down,' he says, towel-drying his hands. Then Eduardo leads him to the crucible and, together they stare down into the chamber of molten metal. 'Touch wood, it hasn't given me a splash for a long time. The nurses at the clinic know me now by the metal stuck to my jeans. Lead, antimony and tin. Though I still have to remind them every time I need treatment for a burn.'

The cacophony in the room eases off, as operators drift out, leaving their machines ready for the night shift. He sees how tenderly Eduardo lays the cover over his. According to him, no night worker has the patience for her. He is right. Not a single character can be read on its worn keys. Apparently they had all but vanished, when, long before Zé knew him, they had sat him down at the keyboard as an apprentice and left him to work it out for himself. And he deliberately played dumb, to hide his former training, as a lithographer, by the party.

He looks back from the bottom of the metro steps, at how Eduardo skims down them on his short legs. At work, seated on his stool, Eduardo is the same height as the others, but when he stands he is at once the twin of every stunted waiter in Lisboa. And the majority of them are Alentejans, too. *He was lucky to be born into a family of communists. He doesn't seem to have the conflicts that others have with their parents.*

They surface in the student neighbourhood where Eduardo has a small apartment. Eduardo, who was always denied a formal education because his father's papers were confiscated, can now afford to pay the rent. While *he* can't, and is obliged to continue living with his family. But Eduardo is unlucky with women. Maybe he is inheriting the trait himself. Will he never ask about Jody? He knows she was to arrive today. Leaning against the door jamb while Eduardo fumbles with the keys, he notices that he is calmer now that the decision is made.

He must have stared at that empty grate for a full fifteen minutes. Lost in memory. Of how she was with him the last time he sat here. He lit a fire to dry their hair and their clothes. Chuted coal from that scuttle. She was sitting on that stack of old magazines next to the hearth, while the rain came down in torrents. Which is why Eduardo lent him the key. It was so peaceful in here with her. When the flames began to lick, his trousers steamed, and she rubbed her hair with a towel. But when he crouched to unlace his shoes, her question sent ripples through the calm. *'What's that on your turn-up, Zé?'* She'd seen the bloodstain, on the bus, and she didn't want to let it go.

'I told you on the bus. I did a year of medicine at Coimbra, and so I know enough to be useful sometimes. While I was crossing town to fetch the key today, I saw a demonstration from the tram.' In fact, it had been a trap. And having spotted the provocateur he'd jumped off the tram to go and warn the students. But she was happy with his explanation. He can see it now, his wet socks hanging from the mantelpiece clock, the firelight playing on her face. He can hear the hissing of the coals and almost feel the stirrings he felt then, when she turned around and caught him watching her. And he was filled with an overriding need to know everything about her. In what order she paints her nails. What her eyes are like without the kohl.

'I will make us some tea.'

'Can you manage? You're used to having a maid, aren't you?'

'You think I cannot make tea? What a low opinion you have of me.'

And he went into the kitchenette. Where Eduardo is now, bringing a pan of water to the boil. Tipping in a glug of olive oil. He must be making *Caldo Verde* for his supper. Jody loved it. So did Anna. *Eduardo still doesn't mention her, but then he knows me better than to probe.*

'Do you realise it won't be long now before we're all photo-compositors? Not that it affects me. As soon my machine becomes obsolete, I shall buy her from the firm. And, so long as I can transport her under cover back to where I came from, then I can start to become free. I shall keep my own press running by typesetting for *Avante!* Everything under wraps. In the long term, it should give me enough to live on in Alentejo. Just.'

Isabel has started calling Eduardo the 'malchemist.' Because he works at the official newspaper *Diário Noticias.* She says he turns base metal into fools' gold, meaning state propaganda.

'I set twenty columns of tabloid today and half or maybe even two thirds of them got the blue crayon. Cross cross cross! Stamp stamp! *Censurado.* They've run out of blanket articles now and keep having to repeat them. But that job has provided good cover for me over the years. You want some music? I borrowed the new Stones album, *Paint it Black.'* Standing in the kitchen doorway like that, polishing a glass, who wouldn't take him for a waiter. 'Well, maybe not today. I know what we can listen to. Climb onto that stool, Zé, so you can reach up to the classical stuff. Right. Now find me the Bartok. Got it? He'll do you good.' Then Bartok rhythms shred the air in the room. 'Aperitif?'

'Yes please.' He knocks back his dose of port. 'Do you think it was the *PIDE?'* he asks at last.

'What d'you say? Hold on a sec.' And Eduardo appears to float through the bars of sunlight falling through the shutters. He stands behind the door, his shoulder to it, holding it ajar. 'I thought I heard someone on the landing. Turn the volume up, would you.'

By now Zé is sitting hunched even closer to the grate. He rouses himself and goes to turn up the gramophone. 'You remember the agent I saw in Nicola that evening, when Jody was there with me. The one she said had approached her when she left the airport in Manchester.'

'Coincidence. He fancied her and, like Armando said, he saw an opportunity to belittle you in front of her.' Eduardo turns the sound even higher. 'Why bring it up now? It was last year, at the end of summer.'

'I went to meet her from the boat today.'

'You — I told you not to go.'

'She wasn't there; she didn't come, Eduardo. And all it says on the passenger list is, *Failed to embark*. It was them, of course. They intercepted her before she could go aboard.'

'*Não, não*. Look here, don't you think it's possible she changed her mind? I mean, come on now, it's a huge thing for a woman to have to do. Enormous.'

He stops fingering some scorch marks on the floor in front of the grate, pulls the letter from his jacket pocket and, having verified the postmark again, puts it back.

'If she changed her mind … I can't lose her.'

'Perhaps she didn't want to tell you. Women are like —'

'Jody isn't. She would write or she would send a telegram.'

'Well, yes, she probably would. Even I could see that she is honest. And kind. She went to Nottingham to talk to Kay for me, as you know. But Englishwomen are different. They oil their own wheels over there.'

'Jody is nothing like Kay, so don't even compare them. And how about you being honest and telling me what they'll do to her. Interrogate her to find out about me? When they see how innocent she is, they'll think they've got one of the great naïves.'

'Heh? They haven't got her. And they already know more than they need to about you.'

'Do they? I told them nothing during that interrogation last year.'

'Forget that, right now. It didn't happen, okay? Anyway, it wasn't even an arrest. They've got Miguel, and now they only want you for the military.'

'Only the military? You see, that is why I decided not to join the PCP. They are militarist now. Not so long ago they supported defection; they helped deserters. But now they seem to be encouraging everyone to join up.'

'Okay, but before you say it, it isn't hypocrisy. It's the new policy, to infiltrate. To spread the message from within the barracks. And we've recently built a whole new strategy for the colonies. But this is neither the time nor the place. Come over to the window. That door is giving me the creeps'

'They tried to get information out of me about student groups. They had a list.'

'But you're not a student anymore.' Eduardo is closing shutters.

They lean, backs to the wall, one at each side of the tall window. A chink of light is falling on the table press, which is pushed up against the bed. He recalls how she had stood playing with the letters in the firelight. Having made the tea, he brought it in on a tray. And found her leaning on the press with one arm buttressing her head. Her eyes lowered while she moved the type around the flat metal surface. Tiny buttons, on a white cardigan she liked to wear back to front, had slipped from the curve of her spine. Her summer skirt, hanging limp from the rain, stuck in patches to her thighs; her brown skin showed through as red. And black gondoliers punted round the hem of her skirt.

'*I know a bit about presses. This is a Stephenson Blake relief press. It's English.*'

He left the tray on the safest chair. And then he took her in his arms and breathed in the warm smell of her skin.

'*Never mind about presses. I want to talk about those men running round your skirt.*'

'*I think it's meant to be Venice. It's an old skirt, but I like it.*'

It felt silky.

'I will take you there.'

'To Venice? You'll need a passport.'

'*You know what is a skirt-runner?*'

'*Mm, no, but I can guess.*'

And he talked into her still-damp hair, saying anything and nothing.

'*Bem.* Here's the score, then. The same as for Miguel,' Eduardo says, across the window. 'Legally they can detain you without charge for up to ninety days, and then a hundred and eighty more. Renewable indefinitely. They can incarcerate you anywhere, or deport you to the Azores, Cabo Verde, São Tomé. Where d'you want to go, man? But if you're English, there's bugger all they can do. And certainly not in England. They can't touch her. So, now will you shut up?'

'Sure, it's a free country over there. But *they* don't give a monkey's for international law. Look at all the duplicity in the way they carry on with Nato, the games they play with them. And that agent was in Manchester to watch the emigré community there. If he wants information ...' He screws his eyes shut and shakes his head. 'I go mad now, Eduardo. Sorry. I'm not myself.'

He walks back to his chair and fishes in his jacket for his cigarettes. Eduardo has directed a reading lamp onto his press. The galleys and some scattered metal type gleam underneath the light. 'Come over here. This is English, look.' Eduardo stands by the filing cabinet at the foot of the bed.

'I know. She told me.'

'Jody knows about presses?'

'Yes, everything.'

A dozen or so printed sheets are curling up their corners on the counterpane. Infernal thing. That slippery green satin kept sliding down from the bed, but at least it made them laugh. Lots. And the rain worked in his favour for the rest of the afternoon.

'Have you seen these poems yet, Zé? They're Isabel's. She is streaks ahead of the rest of us in her thinking. Read this.' Eduardo passes him a poem, and he unfurls it to read. 'I'll distribute them in Alentejo, but only to my known subscribers. I'll slip them inside my Journal. Don't fret, Zé. You'll probably get a letter from her tomorrow.'

Will he? He rubs some ink from his fingertips. There were small dents from that metal type imprinted in hers, when he pulled her to him, with the heat of the fire on her body and her face. *'Do you want to be my Modigliani woman today?'* She was cross with him for saying that. And so she should have been. She wanted to be herself.

'*I hate you.*'

'*I hate you, too.*'

Hugs and laughter and the tea going cold. That bed is like an early operating table, high, narrow and uncomfortable. But they managed, and it didn't go too badly.

But if she doesn't write, and my body won't forget, what do I do?

He clamped that damned slippery stuff beneath his jaw to stop it sliding off them and leaving them to freeze. At first he thought she was refusing him, when she turned her face to the side. But no, she was only telling him to kiss her neck. He found the smooth hollow there, bit her earlobes, kissed her face and her mouth. The sounds she made. Yes, she answered him. Her black eyes, his black eyes. His bones, her breath. Her flesh and his blood. Her turning head. His lilting heart. Their peace.

'*Now I feel like an animal. A good animal.*' He must have said that later, in the cinema queue.

On a bench that overlooks the boating lake in the Jardim do Campo Grande, the two men sit close together in the encroaching dusk. A few other park benches are similarly occupied. Their muffled conversation falters at each footfall, on the lawn behind them, of a student or a group of students from the *Faculdade de Ciências*. Even though the white mist lying on the lake deadens all sound.

Zé holds out the envelope. 'This letter here was delayed. By the censor, I suppose.' He shrugs. 'It ought to have arrived two days before I went to meet her boat. It confirms that up until the last week at least, she still intended to come. She hasn't changed her mind, Eduardo. I have decided what I shall do, and I want to tell you my plan.'

Eduardo's head just sank deeper into his coat collar. He can sense him bracing himself.

'I walk.'

'You walk. You walk where?' Eduardo sounds more resigned than surprised.

'To England. I walk to England. I go North across the Spanish border, then through the Pyrénées and into *França*. I have a friend Gil, who learns the new printmaking methods at an atelier in Montparnasse. He's made some good contacts there in the last two years. And he will know someone in Paris who can make me a passport, so I can cross the channel to England.'

'You wouldn't be much use to Jody without one, believe me.'

He pops a match on the bench and cups a cigarette in his hands to light it. 'You remember when Gil left. He took the pilgrim route through Santiago de Compostela. Cigarette?'

'No thanks. Disguised himself as a priest, I suppose. That's an old one. And good, too, while it lasted. But it's too risky now that they exert so much pressure on the priests. Every one of them is an informer. But rest assured that I don't blame you for wanting to go. You can achieve more politically by working from abroad.'

'*Tchk*! It's not because of that. I don't want to work politically abroad. I may not know what has happened to her, but I am sure of one thing. She won't stay with her husband for much longer. And I can't ask her to go through all that again.'

Eduardo sits staring out across the water, at the white mist that is disembodying the trees on the far bank. '*Não*,' he says at last. 'We'll cut across the Alentejo to the Serra de São Mamede, where the border with Spain is at its highest. You go over on a cloudy night. Winter would have been best, when it was too cold for the border patrol to venture up to the top.'

'You just said, We.'

'Did I? Well, I have some holiday owing to me and, also I could do with visiting my sister.'

'I can't let you do that. If you take your holidays, your job won't be there when you get back.'

'I know, but don't you think I ought to stand up for my rights? Think about that young Alentejana, a few months ago, murdered by the authorities because she asked for a pay rise. And that's only one story of many. Workers like her, they died for nothing, if none of us will ever start to insist on our rights. On the other hand, you may be right. But I can find another solution. I can revert to what I've done before.' Eduardo looks along the path to where the mist is rolling in from the lake.

'And here's the superintendent coming up the path. Be sure to call in at Nicola tonight, otherwise the pigs will miss you there and they'll send out an alert. Plus it won't be safe to write to Jody again, once you leave Lisboa.'

'How the devil can I find out what happened to her?'

Fifteen

HE STOPS WALKING when he finds himself in a pedestrianised street, and opens the bag containing the maps. A road map of Alentejo and some precious military photostats of the Serra da São Mamede. It was worth going the extra kilometre for those, and amazing that the army's geographical institute let him buy them. But on inspection he sees that even they stop short before the border. He crosses to a narrow side street and, turning this way and that, watches the needle on his new compass. He took the best one they had, but it is crucial that he test it thoroughly before he sets off tomorrow. He knows for instance that the bullring lies north-northeast of here and is on his way home, so he will see how true it is by —

'*Merda*!' His shin. He jumps back from the path of a large wheelchair, while the old lady in it turns round to stare. 'Zézinho! Isabel, stop. Stop. It's your friend Zé.'

Isabel has passed by him without turning from a shop window or acknowledging her mother's cries. But now she sees him, she reddens. Splutters. Laughs. 'Zé! What's that you're holding? Have you lost your A to Z?'

He bends down to rub his shin. 'This is so lucky! It was too risky to tell you anything in Nicola last night. Has Armando told you my news? No? I just need to test this before tomorrow.'

Isabel's eyes are half-closed. She is digging deep. She is such an old friend he can't recall a time before he knew her. Perhaps there never was one, because their mothers have been friends for ever. Isabel, always with a look of goodness about her, the expression of a sage. She can see straight through him and is doing so now.

'Perhaps I didn't want to hear it,' she says. 'Perhaps it's why I didn't stay. But don't tell me now.' She cocks her head towards her mother. 'Meet me later on today. I need to give you something important.'

'Isabel, I have to hurry now. I have just remembered an appointment. I have seen your new poems and I shall give Eduardo the key. You can trust him completely.'

'Sure, we'll talk later. Don't be late for your appointment.'

They walk together just a little way, and then he needs to strike out alone. Now he must forget the bullring and find another way to reach the *distrito*. His signature in the police register will buy him a month of freedom, before the pigs decide to smoke him out. A reflex kicks in once he is out of the city centre, and his mind turns to listing his activities of that month. A mechanism that will stay for as long as he is obliged to report. It was implanted in him last September, when Jody was here, although she knows nothing of it.

He had gone to visit friends in Coimbra, to hear the annual *Saudades*. Returning the same evening to meet Jody on the promenade. It was the night she locked herself out, and afterwards, he caught the last train to Lisbon and slept on Eduardo's floor. His appointment was so early in the day that he was still half asleep as he walked across the dewy Campo Grande. If he'd been more alert he would have clocked the black Mercedes that was parked right across the entrance. He even squeezed round it, to pass through the district station door. He was signing in, when the agents burst from the office behind the counter. And accused him of spending the night in Coimbra without a permit. And he went there to agitate. What rot.

A day-long interrogation. And when he woke in that filthy alley at the back of their headquarters, he was clutching a list of associations he was now banned from. A proclamation of his doom had been written into each line.

But here comes his sweet revenge. Just let them find a reason to interrogate him today. He's been nowhere. Except the docks... No, he wasn't at the docks he answers, with a quickened heartbeat, to the duty officer's prompts.

'Still at the same address?' Et cetera, et cetera.

Having signed the ledger, he bolts. And he runs until he

can no longer see the lamp above the station door. When he must stop to catch his breath, he knows for sure that he will need to be much fitter. Soon he must put a mountain between himself and the police. But only the passes of the Pyrenées can sever him from the *PIDE*. Walking slowly, he gets a sense of the future clutching at his sleeve. Demanding that he follow a certain path, cross a certain line. That he apply himself and learn a mode of life unknown to him as yet, but known to many before him as the life of the fugitive. From today there won't be any need for permits for overnight stays; he will be sleeping out in the open. Two men beneath the stars. And then just one man and a very, very long walk.

The *avenida* has come to life since early this morning. He thinks he can see Eduardo waving to him from the entrance to his building. As he approaches, his friend waves back. But when he is close enough to see the bandage on Eduardo's right hand, he scowls. He doesn't want to hear him say: 'I've come straight from the hospital. I got a splash first thing this morning. It will give me at most a week away from work. You got the map, I see. Good. And guard those photostats with your life, *amigo*.'

They walk together in silence and take the turning for the Campo Grande. He doesn't need to ask him to know that his friend's burn was deliberate. He should not have let him be involved. And in fact, he already knows there will be more to thank him for than this.

The sunlight glancing off the lake already has power enough to warm them, as they gaze across it to the stand of poplars ranged along the far bank. Through the odd gap between their trunks he can see his city start to steal away from him. His gaze follows a container lorry as he wonders where it is headed. At last, he turns to Eduardo.

'Can you tell me why a military map would stop short before the border? And why is it so impossible here to buy a map of Spain?' But Eduardo is preoccupied with adjusting his bandage. He tries again. 'Guess who I ran into on my way back this morning. Literally. Isabel. I fell across her mother's wheelchair. She was pushing her round the Baixa. How often does something like that happen in Lisboa?'

'All the time with Isabel. She's always there and she doesn't look where she's going. She likes the smooth, flat pedestrianised streets in the Baixa, so she brings her mother in from Chelas on the tram.'

'Did you know that she is teaching illiterate adults to read? In her mother's attic in the Chelas. It will be highly dangerous for her, once her students have made some progress. They are unlikely to want to go on pretending they are still illiterate. And the change will be hard to conceal. We'll meet again this afternoon because there wasn't time to tell her of my plans. And I must give her Gil's address in Paris, too, in case she ever hears from Jody. She gave Jody her address. And now she wants to give me something. Some useful contacts in Spain, perhaps? What d'you think?'

'I always forget she's Spanish.'

He lights two cigarettes and slips one into his friend's good hand. It is such a simple gesture, but one his lips and fingers recall. He wants to shout out across the lake to her, 'I am coming. There is hope!' But she, too, is disembodied now, like Lisboa, like the trunkless poplars reflected in the lake. And those he knows and loves in this city. Except Eduardo, who is blowing smoke into the front of his floppy hair.

'So what stopped her, d' you think? Her husband? Her family? The *PIDE*? I shall walk away now, if you tell me again that she changed her mind.' He brings a key from his coat pocket, keeps it pressed against his warm palm.

'I thought that husband of hers was in favour of her leaving. Or am I being naive?'

'He was, but he seems a funny type. She says he seems passive and compliant, but can be vindictive underneath.' He slips the key into Eduardo's pocket on the side of his wounded hand.

'He could do well in business, then. What was that?'

'A key. And as soon as you take your coat off at home, hide it in a safe place. I've looked after it for years for Isabel; it's the key to where she hides her poems. She will give you the address. Memorise it and never ever let her go there alone. Not even if she asks. And something else has come to light since I saw you yesterday. My mother wrote to Jody's father, begging him to intercept our letters.'

A lone canoeist, a dark silhouette, is lapping up the water, a string of ducks bobbing on behind.

'Your mother?'

'Can you believe that? I caught her kneeling on the landing outside my bedroom this morning, intent on telling her rosary.'

'But Jody doesn't live with her father.'

'He won't reply. My mother is mad. She wanders through the rooms, praying all the time. She is reverting more and more to her former life in the convent, while my father is away more and more often with his mistress. I can't imagine how she found their address. Smith is such a common name over there.'

A skiff is passing. He stops to listen to the dipping of the oars.

'What's the fastest route out of town?'

'That'll be the ferry.'

'Informers travel back and forth on those boats. And Alentejo spells Communism in red letters for the *PIDE*.'

'So, we leave at first light and don't go aboard until the last minute.'

The lone sculler is now behind the islet, out of sight. Three students just left the library, weighed down with books. The lawns are bristling with expectancy at the start of the Easter vac.

'Terreiro do Paço terminal then, tomorrow morning at six.' Eduardo leans across to offer his good hand.

Fear of the unknown, the conjuror of ghosts from the known past. From where he sat, in the blacked-out back seat, he could feel the engine turning, could sense when the lights changed to red. He could hear the sighing of the trams, the clip clop of hooves, the rumbling of the traffic. And in the silence, when it all stopped, he concluded that they must have parked in a backwater somewhere.

Soundlessly the car door let in eye-watering sunlight, and he was manhandled outside. They marched him across a pavement then pinned him fast against a wall. The wall fronted a tall building indistinguishable from the others that lined the narrow street. He looked around for a nameplate, but the entrance was unmarked.

A few metres back, an old woman dropped her oranges. And let them roll into the gutter, while she hobbled on her way rather than stay a moment to retrieve them. A trudging labourer averted his eyes, and crossed over the street. Passers-by turned back before they had reached the end of the block, and chose the pavement opposite, instead. He knew then whose building it was, whose wall his back was against. On the street he never, ever took because it housed the '*Olho de Judas.*' The notorious interrogation centre at the headquarters of the *PIDE*.

Inside the building corridors stretched away, empty and echoing. Keys jangled, and a cell door opened to an unholy stench.

'You wait in there.'

A darkly-stained wooden pallet covered over half of the floor. Flies buzzed around a bucket in a corner. Condensation was chasing down the green painted walls. But the sight of all that was preferable to standing in the pitch dark alone, once the cell door had clanged shut. A spy hole allowed a single ray of light to pierce through it. And in its moulded glass he could see himself tiny like an earwig. But then the light shrank to a crescent and melted into total blackness. He leaned, palms against the wall, fingernails making dents in his forehead, and breathed in a little cool air from the wet surface of the wall. Until a blood-freezing scream ripped along the corridor beyond his door, and he gave thanks that he was inside. Then came the thud of boots followed by a grinding noise in his lock.

A wide staircase with rough gashes in its walls. As he was bundled up its steps, his stomach was telling him it was lunchtime. And that he should have been eating with Martins at his local bar. Martins went in for long lunches, and he would find him later fairly easily, but he needed more time to get the collector over to his studio. And Jody would be expecting him at the café at four.

Closed shutters in a bare, first-floor office blotted out the street. A dig in his ribs, as he trembled before a large, grey metal desk, made him stand to attention. Behind the desk, against a closed shutter, sat the flabby agent with the pale face, a bulky file propped against his belly. White skin between his shirt buttons. The escort had moved off. And when he risked a glance across his shoulder, another agent stared back at him from either side of the door.

'A-gi-ta-tor. Communist.' The pale one behind the desk hawked and shot phlegm into a metal bin. 'Who sent you to the University of Coimbra yesterday?'

'No one.'

'You lie. You are an agent provocateur, and I want the name of your outfit.'

'I went to Coimbra for the day to visit friends and, also, to make music before the new academic year. It was the *Saudades de Coimbra* yesterday.'

'I know it was. I also know that your no-good friends are here in Lisboa, and not in Coimbra. You went there with the sole intention of spreading poison in the crowd.'

'Many students leave Lisboa in the summer. There is no one here. I have friends from when I studied medicine in Coimbra.'

The box file on the desk had an enormous spring clip. 'And you left something behind, Doctor? A thermometer perhaps? Coimbra has enough hotheads and they don't need help from you.' His fat fingers opened the clip, and he licked them before removing the top docket. 'And what does the doctor prescribe for poor, misguided hotheads, *heu*? Run amok? Set fire to cars? Rail against the State? The State, *heu*?'

'I am not an agitator. You can ask my friends.'

'We did. And believe me when I tell you they are not friends.'

Canted light cut the printed camel on a cigarette pack in half. The lid of the box file banged shut. The camel and the pack were shunted into the shade. The agent began to read from a flimsy paper held to the light.

'Injunction dated June the twelfth and issued at Vilar Formoso border post. Two of you were caught attempting to run from the draft. But my men brought you home.'

'We weren't running from anything; we both had return tickets and we would have come back.' Another paper on the desk was proving hard to read upside-down. Two names had been inserted and one of them was his.

'A week later we were called out again. We quelled your fiery little insurgence on a thoroughfare of Lisboa. A main thoroughfare at that. But then my Coimbra colleagues had the honour of a visit from your tribe. Denouncing our Overseas Wars with anti-Portuguese sentiments. Is that what you call making music, Doctor? I call it treason. *Treason.* Think on that and what it means for you. And your comrade; what's his name? Ah, but we've got him, I see.' He stopped speaking and took a manila folder, crossed in blue crayon, from a pimply youth beside the desk.

Is that Miguel's file? Can I at last find out where he is? There must be thousands of lives lived in the folders in these vaults. He watched holding his breath as puffy hands untied the narrow pink ribbon.

'Miguel. That was his name. Arrested on the 28th of June in Lisboa. He told us all we need to know. We have it in here. We don't need your information, Doctor, so just sign this statement.'

'What have you done with Miguel?' He took a sheaf of stapled papers from the lackey and flipped through them. Meanwhile the agent had drawn a toy car, a Mustang convertible, from his desk drawer. Lead showing through its red enamel caught a ray of light from the shutter. As he read the papers, he asked through his clenched teeth: 'Where is Miguel now? Where are you keeping him? When will you tell his family?'

The heavy silence in the room was shattered by the creak of shoes behind him. While he read:

José Manuel Rodrigues Oliveira de Sá. June 23rd 1966. ORDER for annulment of student status, due to participation in activities contrary to the security of The State.

Signed: agent Da Costa. Coimbra division.

'You should have signed it at the time.' The agent brought a tiny key from the drawer and nudged it shut with his belly.

'It was issued to me on the street. I dropped it in the commotion.'

'So now you see how the power falls to the street. Just sign the statement, will you.'

He sensed the other two agents were closing in behind his back. He asked about Miguel again and, in the absence of a response, flipped the page and read on:

Subject banned from affiliation with:

*1 Sindicatos. (*Trade unions.)

They're all illegal anyway, except for the travesties that are run by the State.

*2 Grémios. (*The craft guilds.)

Also run by the State, and membership obligatory, if you want to practise a trade.

3 Ordens. (Associations for professionals.)

The same thing. Managed by the State. Posts offered to obligatory members only.

In other words they had removed his right to work, to add to the existing annulment of his student status. Their student union was long gone, crushed by force of law. But artists and writers had need of no union, nor guild nor organisation whatsoever. And that was what they couldn't stand. It infuriated the *PIDE*. Incensed them. To them, he was the monster of dissent. The only possible and, as yet, unextinguished voice of dissent. And so, yes, he would sign their statement, but he wanted something from them first.

'This is not my statement and you know it.' He pushed the papers over the desktop. 'I want the truth about Miguel.'

'Your Miguel is safe with us. But you want to play it this way, so, undo your belt.' He felt the air leave his lungs, sensed a rising kernel of fear. The toy car's wheels were pressed into a fat palm to stop their whining. How childish these people were.

'What for?' He knew what for. He hooked his thumbs into his belt loops and dug in his heels.

'You want me to undo mine?' The voice behind the desk crescendoed; its owner nodded to the other agents.

He gripped his belt until his fingers ached. His belt would hold him up, would keep him erect. His belt would contain his tremblings, would prevent them from breaking out. Stars he saw, as a foot stunned him in the small of his back. The metal edge of the desk sliced into his gut just above the pelvis. Nausea. His head swimming. His belt was whipped away, ripping off its cloth loops before he could stop it. His trousers dropped, but he caught them in time when he felt the draught. The little mustang overshot the end of the desk and crashed to the floor. And he stood, elbows out, clutching bunched cloth, a whine rising from the boards.

'Now the shirt.' The agent gave the henchmen another of his silent nods, while he unscrewed the lid from a silver toothpick that lay on the desk. Then lifted his top lip, clamping it open with his free hand.

Manhandled round, he now faced a blank wall with two doors. One door was closed; the other swung open onto a small room. A wooden rack stood in the middle of the room, the floor badly stained beneath it. Warm breath brushed his ear. And hands opened his shirt, slowly, like a lover, while a man's face leered into his. He tried to conserve his breath. The shuffling of papers on the desk behind his back. The sound of a mechanism winding up.

'I want the name of the outfit. Just the name.'

Sixteen

Lisbon, March 21, 1967

HE WRAPS THE bar of soap in half a towel with his toothbrush and his shaving gear, and puts his knee down on his rucksack before pulling hard on the cord. What can he take out? His razor? His shaving brush? He needs to stay clear of barbers' shops, so he'd better grow a beard. With a backward glance at the note lying on his pillow, he leaves his door ajar and tiptoes across the landing. Snores are coming from his parents' room, but his mother's eyes are wide open. He looks away and treads as lightly as he can going down the stairs.

The *avenida* is deserted, and the first metro train of the day has yet to rumble beneath the pavement. As he walks he can feel a jagged ridge cut across the ball of his foot, reminding him of his responsibility, to himself and to others, to keep the thing safe. At their meeting yesterday, while Isabel was slipping him the half-innersole, she slowly spelled the address of a safe house directly in his ear. He repeats it now several times and vows that he will not let himself forget it. And that nothing, not even torture, will wrench it from him. He prays also that the pattern of the cut edge will survive intact throughout his long walk across Spain. And will serve him well, when he knocks on that door in Pamplona.

'You must present your half-innersole at the door to the safe house. The guides there will have the other half, and will want to see that the two interlock before they will let you in.'

That sole is his only passport and will stay where his foot can feel it inside his boot, even while he sleeps.

Footsteps. And the panting of someone running up behind.

'Zé, it's me.'

He stops, fastens the belt strap of his rucksack and turns around. Rui, his face anxious, is shivering on the pavement, clutching an envelope to his pyjamas. '*Mamäe* said to give you this. She said ... She said ...'

'Get your breath first. And tie your shoelaces or you'll trip.'

'She said for you to please forgive her. She was worried for the little English girl.'

'Yes, yes, Rui. Is this the only letter? Are you sure there isn't one from England?'

'No, there's nothing else, only that. It's a thick one. There may be money inside. Open it and see. Where are you going dressed like that? Where did you get those commando boots? I know, you're going camping, aren't you. Can't I come, too?'

He tries to read the seal on the envelope, but the light is still dim. It looks official.

'Never mind where I go. I will write to you soon. You will take care of Inês for me, and all will be fine. You can tell *Mamäe* that I was worried about the little girl, too. She's called Anna. Remember?'

Rui nods and pulls his pyjama jacket tight around his chest. 'I'm coming with you to the bus stop.'

'Rui, there are no buses at this hour of the morning. You know that. You're not a child.'

'You're mad. I'm going to follow you.'

'Go back inside. Now.' He turns his brother round by the shoulders and pushes him away. And he slides the envelope beneath the top flap of his rucksack. He thinks he knows what it is. All the more reason to hurry.

From over the dark waters, the sound of coughing hacks through the mist. And then the *Madre de Deus* ferryboat is pulling in beside the jetty. It is the first ferry of the day, bringing in the earliest of the commuters. The two men stay out of sight behind a wall, from where they can glimpse the workers as they hurry through to the terminal. And they wait to see who else will pitch up before they venture down the quay.

From the jetty they can see the necklaces of lights that loop the length of the suspension bridge. Fog lights creep along the road bridge, blueing swathes of the tarmac. On the far bank their 'traffic cop', the *Christo Rei*, emits a yellow aura. While closer at hand, the river itself is far from silent for the hour. The putt putt and smell of boat engines, the clank of chains against concrete. Rasping voices, vibrations, all deadened by the fog. As birds on the wing slice through refrigerated vapours, the boat below them fills with labourers. And now the gangplank waits for them.

Some workmen drop their tool bags on the deck and stride aboard after them. Huddled on the outer benches, they smoke or drum on their lunch boxes, impatient to cast off. Lastly an old man drops in a half-full sack and sits upon it, wrapping it carefully underneath his long, ragged coat. Zé relaxes, screened by the workers gathered in the stern.

'Did you remember to bring the torch?' Eduardo whispers in French.

'Yes, but it's so cold, I wish I had put on the rest of my clothes. You have the matches?'

'They're wrapped in plastic in my pocket. I see you won't be parted from your umbrella.'

'No. It doubles as a walking stick.'

The skipper climbs aboard, the engine splutters, and they cast off into a greeny dark expanse. The estuary is calm. The *Trans-Tejo* ferry will dock at Alcochéte within the hour. About five kilometres out, the morning mist begins to thin around them to reveal patches of colour that hover just above the water. And some luminescent painted fishing *barques* are gliding silently along to port. As the fleet diverges it displays to him the entire range of the shipwright's art in carved figureheads so gaudy they would outdo any gypsy caravan. Painted irises, gladioli, red and white striped carnations all softly veiled by the mist. And when the boats have dispersed completely, they see the oil terminal and stark apartment blocks ranged along the far bank.

A rotting green stink has seeped aboard the boat. A crack and slap from the bulrushes on either side of its hull. The deck lurching, and a booming noise as their fenders buffet the landing stage. Zé walks unsteadily ashore, his boots thudding on the boardwalk as he heads towards a public toilet. His teeth are chattering incessantly while he whips on some more clothes. Outside again, feeling warmer and relieved by a lighter pack, he looks about him at a strangely flattened world just beginning to stir.

'We needn't have worried,' says Eduardo, as he comes to stand at his side. 'At this hour the local *bufos* are heading in the opposite direction. They'll be setting out now to meet with agents in the cafés in Lisboa. And they'll be coming back this way, snooping on the workers on the boats tonight.'

They stand now on an unfamiliar peninsula. Salt pans lie shimmering about them, laid out in grid patterns that extend as far as he can see. 'Is this what they do here, spend all day tending the pans?'

Eduardo answers that reputedly they make guitars and guitarras. It is getting light as, buoyed up and swaggering a little, they march through the still sleeping small town of Alcochéte. Low sunbeams ricochet off painted ceramic house fronts, flinging a blaze of colour into the evaporating mist. He is glad to leave the sour odours of the brackish waters behind, and to exchange them for a sharpening taste of salt. He wets his lips as he walks. A colony of house martins, clinging to the wall of a church, reminds him it is the first day of spring. He skips a step. He is on his way to find freedom.

However winter seems to return, once they leave the town. Multitudes of water birds are gathered on the mud flats. Ahead of them is a salt marsh and, as they walk towards the low sun, Eduardo spots a flock of spoonbills in the distance.

'I do know the names of *some* of the birds.' Zé begins to feel the city dweller that he is.

They take a quiet track that runs well below the level of the road, along a dyke fringed with purple sea lavender. Its surface is a flashing mirror coated green by trillions of tiny leaflets, and is joined at intervals by tributaries full of white cotton wool clouds. The crunch of their boots on gravel is their only companion, apart from birds that liven the air and that he isn't quite alert enough to spot. But Eduardo still recalls his roots. 'Look at those flamingos; they're like flying pink umbrellas.'

Thudding over a small wooden bridge, Eduardo turns a dead snake belly-up and kicks it into the dyke.

Meanwhile Zé is cutting himself a fistful of reeds: 'To make pens.'

'Folk normally cut them in September,' says Eduardo, coming up.

'*Tchk*!'

'Well, you need them to be dry, don't you?'

'I hope you're not going to do this all the way.'

They crunch along below road level to the east of Alcochéte, through an area of salinas, which have been converted into fish ponds. From some of them, the deeper ones, comes the joyous noise of fishing terns. At a junction they take the main road, which will lead them on through the wetlands. He can feel himself becoming part of an ever changing panorama filled with water birds, water weed, waters merging into sky. He tries to adapt his steps to fit with the staccato bristling of the reeds.

When they stop to rest on the edge of a water meadow, both are tired. They sprawl on a grassy bank to eat bread and cheese with olives and sardines. Down below them yellow irises are opening in the late morning sun. And black velvet oxen graze on the greenest of green shoots beside a whole field of yellow lupins.

'It'll be as green as that all over *Inglaterra*, when you get there, but I shouldn't think they have oxen like these to do their ploughing. This herd is getting nutrients into them before the season starts.'

Moving on again, their boots are at last treading red sandy soil. They have reached the land of the cork oaks, which is another country all together. On either side of them the thick bark has been cut away from tree trunks, thus baring reddish coloured wood, which darkens downward to the roots. At intervals a lone tree, and sometimes a group, will have a number daubed in white halfway up the stripped flesh of its trunk.

'The smaller ones look young, don't you think?'

'*Não*, they've been harvested already, so they're twenty-five at least.'

'It takes such an age for the bark to grow back that I don't see how anyone can make a living out of cork. Whether landowners or labourers.'

'Not when just four families own the whole of Alentejo? They'll be doing all right.'

They are crossing over a track and stop to watch the way it winds up through the cork oaks, then holm oaks, to a *casa da quinta* ringed by stone pines. The farmhouse and its approach lined with yellow shredded palms, could almost be a transplanted bit of Africa.

'The folks on the hill can visit to inspect the harvest, and then take off again, back to where they came from. Africa or wherever. And between-times our farmworkers must survive in hovels with the animals, if they're lucky. And if not, sleep on the roads as they do, forever looking for work.'

'It was like this in Russia before the Revolution. But with cork, there seems to be no choice other than to manage these plantations over ever-increasing areas.'

'It could work in collectives, if the workers were organised,' says Eduardo.

'Perhaps, but not by the State. And they would need specialist training. The logistics alone are daunting.'

'It depends what kind of state. I love the cork woods. Our Whistlers. There's not another country has them.'

White and black storks have quit spiralling above them and now perch, one to a telegraph pole, alongside their track. 'They're claiming poles to build their nests on. Look there, Zé, the strawberry trees planted in between the oaks. That's good land use. The black pigs can still eat the acorns. Though apart from chickens, what else can anyone raise in this sand?'

As if answer, they stumble on a sandy hollow filled with rows of beehives, all made of cork. They slither down its bank, and watch their track switch from cinnamon to creamy white. But it is not until they have progressed further into horse and bull breeding territory that he relaxes and decides to let Eduardo's commentary soothe his nerves. Their surroundings have been blitzing his senses all day, and now his words provide a welcome distraction. From his nagging worries over what could have happened to Jody. And from the doubts.

His mind is still lurching between fragments of conversation from his last days in Lisboa. And last night at café Nicola, Armando's rallying words belied the fear he recognised in his eyes. When will he get to see the great Armando again? And projects that were germinating there, for paintings or for new ways of living, now erupt brutally and half-formed into his conscious mind. Hastily made projectiles to an uncertain future. If he is granted any future. Will they really let him walk away?

In the lateness of the afternoon the cork woods are generally deserted. But a clearing come upon suddenly can suggest a village or a town. And every village in the land has somebody who is working for the *PIDE*. For the locals, the informers are easy to spot: a man with no apparent means of support, a priest who always quizzes servants about their employer's views, enquires after visitors to the house. But without the local knowledge, he and Eduardo are as blind innocents. Glancing back, he sees Eduardo's pace has flagged and put him out of earshot. He starts to climb more slowly onto a ridge.

He smokes standing on the crest, while the sun burns through his jersey. He peels it off, and then his shirt, and lets a strong breeze fan his itching skin. Spread out across the paddy field below him, women stoop to plant rice. Women wearing mannish black brimmed hats pulled down over headscarves. One has spotted him. She lifts a muddy skirt and kicks out a booted leg ringed by welts. In a lightning flash, a hurled rock has knocked the woman down to the muddy ground. A male supervisor fires obscenities at her from an adjacent bank. Furious, Zé is glowering, as the man advances, animal-like, his eye kept on the women. At a whistle, Zé looks round. Eduardo is at the bottom of the ridge, beckoning him down.

'You idiot! Are you mad? Do you deliberately set out to attract attention to yourself? We'll be followed now. We need to leave this track and look for another route.'

'That's a bit extreme. The girl was only having fun.'

'Yes, and that supervisor will be making phone calls tonight.'

'Well, I was thinking it must be time we looked for somewhere to spend the night. But I can't find where we are on the map and I'm afraid we are lost. This map hasn't seen a reprint since nineteen thirty-six. But if that bridle path is the one I think it is, it goes to Branca.'

'And if it isn't, what do you suggest? The track on the other side of the road is out of sight from the paddy field, but it changes direction. *Christo*, we could be lost hereabouts for days.' Eduardo walks across the unmade road and disappears down a bank. 'There's a lake,' he calls back. 'Can't you find a patch of blue on that map? Here comes a friendly looking goat girl. I'd better ask her.'

Zé folds the map and runs down the other bank to join Eduardo. The young goat girl is parting some low scrub with a stick. From the underbrush a small fountain appears, entirely made of cork bark. Ingenious. And the girl stands beside them keeping watch as they drink the fresh cool water.

'She said you're right; the path leads to Branca. Not much has changed around here, since that map was printed. A bit of road widening for tractors ...'

The bridle path has brought them up short before an ancient stone settlement. Outside its falling walls they stumble on a long, low, broken shed. Sheets are drying on a paling to one side of it, and they wander inside, blinking at the gloom, a hound sniffing at their heels. Light falling from a hole in the roof catches bales of straw and a broken cartwheel on the floor. It is perfect. They drop their bags on the packed earth floor and wander off towards the settlement.

The low sun is projecting shadows like giants on stilts in front of them, as they walk towards an empty farmhouse, past workers' hovels and some rougher looking labourers' shacks. More dogs come to join the hound. A young woman with an old face comes up and shoos away the hound, before leading them to a small whitewashed well. They scoop its water in a cork bowl, which they leave on the low wall after they have drunk and refilled their bottles. Barefoot children come running through an ancient arched gate.

'Where are you going? Where?'

'Mora,' he says.

'Say it again.'

'Mora.' He feels well with the children, especially when they laugh. But Eduardo says they ought to stick to their plan and speak only French.

More women lead them through the gate to a square with a deeper well and a place where they can buy kerosene. They try to lift more water, but the well shaft is too deep, until the women jokingly pass on to them the knack for jiggling the rope. A skeletal, toothless girl runs off, stockings flapping round her ankles, to rush back with an oversized cabbage under each arm. She will take no money, and he thanks her in Portuguese.

'These are good people.'

'Sure, but you should still be careful. She's a worker from that paddy field.'

Eduardo is too much. But continuing to speak French with him is bringing back his time with Jody. Perhaps it makes Eduardo think of her too. Why else would he fall silent, as they make their way to the barn? They eat a wholesome supper of sardines with lemon and cabbage. He sees the sun go down and, with it, his last ties with Lisboa. From tonight, after such a peaceful day and safe passage, he will be free to think of other places. Of Paris. Of England. Of Jody waiting for him there. Except she won't be waiting, as she doesn't know yet that he is coming. Just as he didn't know that she had 'failed to embark.'

Those images still stalk the periphery of his thoughts, as they have done all day, and now they emerge fully blown. Like that huge phantom of a steamship, deserted and silent. Like the pounding in his chest while he waited for her to appear, and the faces he searched as they came towards him through the arch. Her face looming like a film still across the vast floor of the terminal, while the porters whispered at the exit. His heart heavy with dread. His fears ——

Eduardo has just suggested something. That they set off early in the morning, before breakfast.

'Why?'

'To see how far we can go before we feel hungry.'

'As you like.' *Has Eduardo done this before?*

Lying down inside his sleeping bag, with his boots on, he stares out through the hole in the roof, at a single bright star. An inner dialogue is throwing up a few things he wants to say to Jody. And now that he is on his way to her, he could write to her in instalments, which, one day he will be able to post. But to wait until he reaches *França* is too long. She'll have forgotten him by then. He could try to post it from an outlying village in *Espanha*. One without a civil guard, if such a place exists. The other side of the Pyrénées would be the only truly safe bet. And probably the only place that Eduardo would approve. Meanwhile she can leave home without his knowing. They are one day's walk closer today and, some day, he will find her, even if it takes ... The star is gone. He is staring at a black hole. Is the star out there still? Or has it moved on?

Seventeen

Alentejo, March 22, 1967

HE LEANS ON the paling, watching as Eduardo spreads their map on a flat boulder. Children crowd round, elbowing to get a glimpse of the map. While others, the ones with pinched faces, hang back. 'Are you spies?' they ask in chorus.

'No, we're Frenchmen,' says Eduardo.

He goes to join the ragged circle. 'Boys, do you want to see where you are on the map?'

'Where's my house? Where's Luis's house? Where am I?' Where?'

Pointing to where the bridle path ends, he shows them where they are. 'Can you read? Do you go to school?'

'*Não não não*. It's Saturday.' And the children surge towards the settlement.

He chases them. 'Saturday is tomorrow.'

And as the children vanish through the gate, he feels the stern mask fall from his face. He used to do that once to imitate the expression of a Russian. He did it on that first evening at the café with her.

He ambles back to the paling beside the rickle where he and Eduardo spent the night. In the enclosure three women work the hard ground with their mattocks, bent, lifting out large, rounded stones. The morning sun has begun to dry the dew from the wild asparagus. He inhales its sharp scent, holding it in his lungs as if in an effort to conserve a memory.

He couldn't bear to sit on the terrace, straining for a glimpse of her on the horizon, so he chose a table at the back and sat facing the other way. Listening to the rush and fall of water through the sluice. Noticing how the sounds are weightier, more vocal in the evenings and, as dusk approached, how the big clifftop hotel receded from his view. Soon he began to fear she wouldn't come. They'd had a hot day with clear skies again, but she hadn't come to the beach.

Just inside the café door António was tending his vat. Goose barnacles were steaming in a broth of wine and herbs. The terrace lit up, startling him, and a shadow fell across him. It was António collecting glasses from the next table. A damp cloth swirled in front of him.

'You lost everything on the Loto, or what?'

'What? No, I was practising looking stern. Does this look like a Russian?' He quickly retrieved his last facial expression and held onto it.

'You're crazy.' António shook his head, flicked his wet cloth across an empty chair. Then he shoved the chair beneath the table, catching him on the shin. '*Desculpe.*' Since the long summers of his childhood, when he first got to know the café owner, António's eyes and mouth had spent a decade sinking downward. It gave that odd twist to his smile. Ironic for those who knew him. 'Either they come or they don't. Is it the English girl? She comes in the afternoons.' And hissing in his ear, as he brushed past. 'They were here again today, scaring off the girls, making me lose business. Don't they know it's the tail end of the season and it's hard?' The swimsuit police had always been the thorn in António's side. And for a café owner, he took too many risks for his own safety.

He asked for a *Sagres*, and then stumbled over to the men's room. A local man with a girl and her chaperone occupied a table, which was blocking the narrow door. He watched the man parse a lobster in the glow from their oil lamp, and prepared to squeeze through a gap. But when he looked up, she was there, smiling at him from the kerb.

She was an island of calm. A navy blazer, very British-looking with a badge rested on her shoulders. Beneath it she wore the sundress she'd bought from the gypsy on the beach. Its deep blues and purples made her seem quiet and mysterious. And she was different without the pushchair and that beach bag full of encumbrances. She clutched a bulging household purse; a silver charm bracelet jingled as she walked. He caught the scent of clean hair, when he stood back to let her pass. And she made him stand taller.

As he led her to a table by the parapet he felt his masks fall away, and he forgot about looking stern. But the Russians *are* more gallant than the general run of Portuguese. And the last thing he needed then, and now, was a Portuguese coquette. That afternoon at the studio he'd been looking at the new paintings from the Anti-coquette Group. *The New Lady Godiva.* Their latest works, brutally frank.

She sat facing him. He couldn't think any more. She drew him into a perfumed space, and life became close range. He sat following the sheen along the slope of her nose, waiting for a single dimple to appear beside her lop-sided smile. Snips of her brown hair lifted in the breeze, and then settled like the wing of a small bird. That was not desire. It was hypnotism.

In his imaginings he is always in control, and on guard. But that night he kept falling victim to a sudden urge to tell her everything, but then would catch himself in time, becoming tongue-tied as a result. He told her that that part of the coast was famed for its resplendent sunsets. She knew that. So he rambled on about his grandfather on his father's side who wore a monocle and who penned a good line in railway-station fiction. And how sunsets always featured in his novel endings. She said *her* grandfather worked on the bookstall at their local station. 'Isn't that funny? They could have done business together.' And they laughed, not that it was funny, but because they were talking that way. 'Your eyes are really blue, aren't they? Not like a Portuguese,' she said, looking at him straight.

It felt to him as if a door was opening and beckoning him to enter. And he was gripped by a strong desire to shower her with everything he owned: the paintings in his studio — and the ones in Lisboa — his paints, brushes, canvas, all bought with money *papäe* had given him for prostitutes ever since his fourteenth birthday. She could take it all.

Suddenly he felt exposed, and hot from the rush of sentiments. And the lobster eaters were still blocking the way to the men's room. But he squeezed through and, once inside, found a piece of aluminium for a mirror and rehearsed what he would say next.

'I must return to Paris,' he said, casually, on returning to his seat. Night was pulling in, and she was doodling in the condensation on the tiled tabletop. So he checked to see if she had heard. He doesn't know why he said it. It was an affectation and it could have got him into serious trouble.

He joins the queue at the bakery just inside the settlement gate. On the bare ground beside a hovel door an old woman sits twisting used paper bags into flowers. He stoops to take one. It has one petal torn from a sugar bag, another from *Grandelos* wrapping paper. *She went to that store to look for material to make a dress.* With his warm bread beneath his arm he leaves by ducking under the arch. A stunted old-timer is coming up on his bent legs, bowling over to Eduardo to join him in poring over their upside-down map. Eduardo points to a road: '*Foros da Salgueirinha Senhor?*'

'*Sim, sim.*' The old fellow's directions come with energised graphic gestures, which send them on their way with their enthusiasm renewed.

'*Obrigado Senhor. Bom dia.*'
'*Boa viagem.*'

They are still in rice-growing country, although the paddy fields are beginning to look increasingly dried up. They trudge alongside the railway line until, at Quinto Grande, they stop. Eduardo sits on his rucksack at the roadside and smokes. Higher up the steep embankment, Zé begins to rummage in his bag for a new pack of *Disque Bleu.* And there, slipped beneath a shirt, is the forgotten manila envelope.

With his back turned to Eduardo below, he shuffles through some typed papers. He was right; they are from the *distrito.* And yes, they are his marching orders. A shiver runs down his back. And as he skip-reads through the sheets one by one, his breathing contracts. The date of his appointment at the barracks has him staring in disbelief. *The twenty-first of March.* That was yesterday.

It can only mean that his mother pocketed the letter days ago, weeks ago perhaps. But why? She and *papäe* are liberals and against suppression in the colonies, BUT ... Was this the trigger for her recent fervent praying outside his door? Was it for him she wore out her rosary? Except the seal on the back flap had been intact until he broke it. Had she simply guessed what it contained? He checks the date again and rereads:

... is required to: *present himself on the training course for new recruits. At Escola Prática de Cavaria, Santarém, at 17:00h on the twenty-first of March 1967.*

Everybody knows the Cavalry School in Santarém, the stage of so many crucial moments in the country's history. He unfolds a printed slip, a travel warrant for the train journey from Lisboa to Santarém. And no longer valid. He scrambles up to the crest of the ridge and stands looking down the Lisbon line gleaming in the morning sun. If *mamäe* had been asleep when he left the house, what would have happened? She couldn't post the papers on to him without an address, which means he never would have received them.

Staring back down the line towards where they came from — Was it yesterday? — the city seems another world, and so very, very far away. He stuffs the letter in his back pocket and slithers down the dusty bank. He squats beside Eduardo at the roadside, his new pack of *Disque Bleu* lying unopened by his foot. Eduardo greets him through narrowed eyes while pulling on his cigarette.

'I want to move on quickly now,' says Zé.

Eduardo looks askance. 'We haven't eaten our breakfast yet. Aren't you hungry?' And receiving no answer, he slowly shoulders his pack.

Zé lopes ahead, past a shantytown of corrugated tin shelters, past field after field of crops like potatoes with sprinklers. At last he slows his pace, lets down his pack and, leaning with his back against a stone ruin, lights up. While he smokes, he broods above an anthill. His blood is starting to itch with some early inklings of his criminality. He has dodged the law before, several times, but this time he knows a line is being irrevocably crossed. And it disturbs him. He takes the papers from his pocket, reads through again, breaking off at intervals to stamp on fallen ash. '... *will be considered as a breach of military law* ...'

What does that mean? Court martial? Being shot at dawn as a deserter? But can they call him a deserter, when he is not yet a soldier? Or is he one already in the law? He moves around to try and free up the tension in his shoulders. Then he blows the dust from his lenses and polishes them on his sleeve. Thud thud thud. Eduardo's old commando boots are coming closer. Should he tell his friend or should he not?

Eduardo comes to his side, breathless, and leans with him against the ruin, his face flushed and moist. His bandage is unravelling and streaked rust red from the sand. As he winds it round his wrist and ties it for him, he thinks about the sacrifice that his friend has already made. Really, he should not have let him risk losing his job. And telling him about this would only implicate him deeper. If Eduardo knows nothing, he cannot be charged as an accessory. He forces a smile.

They eat a late breakfast, hidden in among some densely piled heaps of cork. From their hiding place he can gaze northwards over vast, open plains, which are crossed only by animal tracks as far as the river *Tejo*. And Eduardo has just enlightened him. The landowner thereabouts has prohibited the laying of roads.

'So, when the revolution comes, the workers here will know absolutely nothing of it.'

Eduardo's concerns are once again becoming distanced from his own, his running commentaries harder to follow. His thoughts are fleeing to the banks of the river *Tejo* in the distance. Does it know that it will soon be carrying his footsteps across *Espanha*?

'If the men are all away in Africa, you may as well forget the revolution. That settlement back there housed only women, children and the old. Where are the younger men who are capable of making something happen?' He tears the bread and passes half of it to Eduardo. They both devour it greedily, while he sets the stove on the ground and shakes their water bottle to his ear. 'About enough to make us some coffee.'

'Between you and me,' Eduardo says, while the stove hisses and they wait for the first water bubbles to rise, 'with the Party's new strategy for the colonies in force, the revolution is more likely to start there, out there in Africa.'

'*Heu*! Is that how they recruit these days? Come to Africa and help start the revolution at home.'

'They've discovered they can learn a lot from the African freedom fighters, from strong leaders like Amilcar Cabral in Guinea and Cabo Verde. He's more interesting than Che Guevara. His troops live off the land while they work side by side with the farmworkers, teaching them the new farming methods at the same time as they fight. And what's eating you this morning?'

'Nothing. Cabral is great. I've read *The Weapon of Theory*. It's like I said, the workers need training. It's just that here the men who make the new party rules are all like you, Eduardo, ex-servicemen who did their soldiering in Angola early on, when we still had authority. And that is light years away from the degradation that is rife now, when we are only just hanging on. The men return now, if they return at all, too broken for anything, let alone to make revolution.'

'All the new anti-fascist writing is coming out of Africa.'

'And Brazil. And the anarchists are all in Paris.'

'In Paris, they have the CGT.'

'And that is still the best way.' He watches Eduardo limp away and empty coffee dregs on the grass. 'Have you a blister, *amigo*? You need to walk another day in order to harden your feet.' As he speaks he presses the envelope deeper into his pocket. He wants desperately to be rid of it, to burn it in the ring of flames. But Eduardo is watching. He would have to explain.

'You go on ahead. I'll catch you up, once the fire is safely out.'

He stands awhile watching print dissolve. And when nothing remains but charred flakes, he whistles his relief, and extinguishes the stove.

***

The maize bristles as they trudge through it on a narrow track of red sand. He is listening for the tiny animals that scurry among its stalks, when church bells peal the Angelus, and they wonder how it can be noon. Soon the never-ending cork woods and olive groves will give them the cover that they will need, because Couço cannot be far. They aim to reach it by nightfall, which will leave them with just eleven kilometres to walk in the morning. They come to a mound, and climb to the top from where they can survey the red and white village. It makes him nervous.

'There'll be the Civil Police. And they'll be hard to spot because their grey uniforms will blend in with the olive trees and eucalyptus,' says Zé.

'Yes, and *bufos*. It would be best to cut through the woods and stay wide of the perimeter.'

'All the olive trees hereabouts are flattened on top,' he says.

'They were sat on, when they were little.'

They find a path along a churchyard wall under cover of some pines. And having followed it to the end, they duck to keep their heads below the hedge line, as they skirt round a parched field scattered with thin, dust-coloured cows. Smoke spirals from the village. Soon after they have rejoined the road, a cattle wagon overtakes them, bringing labourers from the fields. Women and old men are dangling their dusty feet from the tailgate to the rhythm of some raucous singing.

Somehow they thread their way round the outer edges of the village. But seemingly out of nowhere a ruined hamlet comes to encircle them. And a group of children dressed in green shirts and forage caps turn and stare. All have the silver 'S' buckles glinting from their belts. Behind the staring group, some older looking youths are playing a game against the wall of a derelict house. One stands apart, his finger pressed against the wall, while the others move around taunting him and laughing.

'You know what they're playing at? They call it, Doing the statue.'

'Children playing at torture in the name of Sálazar,' he

seethes.

'They've just come from their Youth Movement. We had to go too, remember. *Viva Sálazar!* Marching up and down, three afternoons a week plus Saturdays.'

He claps his ears. He wants to tell them all to stop. And starts to walk over to the wall. But Eduardo pulls him back. Except it isn't Eduardo's hand that is tugging at his sleeve, or Eduardo's voice that is calling softly, 'Bread. Cigarettes.' He frees himself and turns around. The arm has shot back, behind a barred window on the rounded corner of a much dilapidated building. Behind the bars is a man. He is sitting on a broad window sill, repeatedly touching two fingers to his lips. Along the street at the side of the building, men are scurrying away. The building is of course a prison. He shakes two cigarettes from his pack, lays them on the sill and is about to say they have bread, when he feels a hand across his mouth and hears Eduardo's voice hissing at him: 'You idiot. Come, we're out of here, now.'

They catch up with the field workers, who are easing themselves down from the wagon, clutching at their backsides. He watches from behind a tree, as Eduardo sidles up to a woman who stands apart from the group. They talk together, then the woman points across the fields towards a eucalyptus wood.

'The smell of eucalyptus will deter the insects while we sleep,' Eduardo says. They find it difficult to keep their feet within a furrow as they walk. And sharp-smelling wild rosemary helps too, they discover, while they are draping a plastic sheet over a bough and fetching up stones. Both too tired to cook, they finish off the last of the bread with a few cheese rinds and olives. The squeaking of bats, the sudden rush of air from a swooping owl, are to be the only notable disturbances of the night.

With a full morning's walk behind them, they approach the small town of Mora. Eduardo says that it will now be safe to board the three-o'clock bus from Lisbon. Mora is giving his perceptions a jolt. He finds he is in the main street of a

Mediterranean Lilliput, amid rows of scaled-down houses and squat, shaving-brush trees. Windows bordered in ochre and umber, besides the ubiquitous devil's blue. A sudden urge makes him want to walk and not to stop again before the Serra. But Eduardo tells him they are sure to blend in with the other passengers.

'Look, the bus stop is right outside a really busy café.' It is Sunday lunchtime. Men fill the bar.

'There is bound to be a *bufo* lurking somewhere here,' he says.

'Yes, you're right. But it's a problem only for the locals. For you it's when the police pitch up and ask to see your papers. But for now you're fairly safe. The café owners won't ask you for anything; they never do.' Eduardo mounts the step into the dark interior of the bar.

Eduardo must have been here before. At a trestle table on the pavement, two old men are passing a tot of clear liquid back and forth between them. *'Modronho.* From the strawberry trees,' they chime, their gestures taking in the swathes of orange groves that are the fringes of the town. Eduardo reappears clutching two tickets for the bus. A waiter follows on behind, holding up a tray with four tots. The old men are lavish with their gratitude and make room for them on their bench. Between the Judas trees across the road, not yet in leaf but bleeding red flowers from their trunks, Zé spots a male figure, in pale grey, crossing open ground.

'From now there's nowhere to hide,' Eduardo says, knocking back his shot.

Zé's first taste electrifies his veins. The old man beside him hitches a thumb towards the back of the building. *An illicit still in the courtyard? A place to hide, perhaps?* He promptly excuses himself and walks round to the back yard. There is nothing promising except perhaps a creeper-covered door. When Eduardo sticks his head round the corner, he nods to him. But Eduardo shakes his head and beckons him to join him at the kerb.

'The bus is in,' he says. 'The passengers are off and piling into the bar.' Then suddenly Eduardo pushes him against the side of the building. And keeping his back pressed against its stones, he peers round the corner, but immediately springs back.

'I'll be off now, *amigo*,' says Zé. He doesn't want to wait to see the man inside the grey military jacket, with the unbuttoned vest, the holster, and his pockets bulging with oranges.

'He's on his own,' Eduardo says, firmly through clenched teeth.

'I want to walk there. I'd rather walk all the way and meet you in Castelo da Vide.' He lifts his back pack, shoulders it and hooks his thumbs beneath the straps.

'No, wait. The passengers are all aboard now. Hold on. Just let the doors close and then ...'

A sigh from the closing doors reaches him. The rumble of the bus approaching. He knows for sure that that policeman will be watching it from the rear. But then Eduardo sprints along the courtyard kerb, waving wildly and calling out to him:

'You go first. Go on! Run!' The bus has rounded the bend by now and is out of sight of the café. 'I said, You go first, Zé. Run, I said!'

The brakes squeal, as the bus slows and its doors open halfway. The driver's eyes flit between the rear view mirror and those on the sides. He squeezes himself through the gap and onto the platform, yanks his rucksack from the jammed doors and drags it inside. Eduardo squeezes through after him, edging round his pack. 'Duck,' he says, as the bus lurches. 'He's coming round the bend.'

He ducks, moves along and swings himself into the seat in front of Eduardo. 'That policeman will radio through to Portalêgre from there.'

'Maybe, maybe not. It's Sunday.'

He no longer needs convincing that Eduardo is an old hand at this. The orange groves are well behind them, and the bus is straining uphill alongside an off-the-scale dam. Low mutterings in French are telling him that water is being wasted because they don't teach the peasants how to ... His eyelids droop. He's thinking how a full bottle of *modronho* would be good for the ride. He drowses and, when he wakes, he finds the earth and sky are switching their colours. The sky slips on a stunning evening red; he locks it into his colour memory for his future use. Hills with black goats, chopped branches and slopes of vines roll by. And when a road sign for *Espanha* leaps out at them from the darkness, he sits up straight and draws the cord a little tighter round his pack. At Portalêgre market, they have to wait outside on the pavement, but no police arrive to disturb the calm of the unlit street. And when the bus pulls away, it feels as if they are entering another region. Flowers carpet the orchards here; outcrops of white granite crouch at the feet of the Serra. He stares ahead to the mountain range, where his destiny is hiding behind its darkening crags. The mists swirling round the peaks. And he wonders if it would be possible to see a man up there, on the slopes. On a cloudy moonless night.

Eighteen

Castelo de Vide, Alentejo. March 23

'THEY'RE HERE!' Eduardo's mother's voice floats down from the Almeida family's apartment above their newsagents shop. In the pool of light at the door to the ancient town house, a mere stone's throw from the back of the town hall, Zé lets down his pack. And taking it in one hand, he follows Eduardo up the narrow staircase to the dining room. On seeing them, Eduardo's father folds his newspaper and levers his loose frame out of his chair. Eduardo drops a small parcel at his feet, and they embrace.

'A few copies of *Avanté!* They're in production again, *Papäe*, so keep them under the counter.'

'I could have brought more,' says Zé.

'And if you were stopped with those on you, it would be the end of all your plans,' says Eduardo's father.

'Oh, Zézinho! How are you? The last time we saw you, you said your young friend was coming from England. But now you're leaving us, I hear.' Senhora Almeida lays a tureen on the table.

The men choose their chairs and sit. 'It's probably for the best in the end. Zé needs to get away. They have made his life here impossible, as they do with all our best talents.' Now seated between them, Abel Almeida cuts himself some bread and passes round a dish of olives. '*Vinho verde* with the olives, Zé? You can relax here, at our shop. We are not restricted, like we were. How we managed, when the children were growing up, I don't know.'

'I wanted to start a gallery with Jody and some friends. A co-operative; it could have worked.'

'Yes, it might have worked until they shipped you off to the jungle somewhere. Although I do wonder sometimes, if they really want you in the army. They're not keen on intellectuals spreading poison through the ranks. Especially officers. And they do seem to be dallying.' But Abel finds that he is hungry too, when he lifts the lid from the casserole.

'Did you have a good trip?' Eduardo's mother looks from one to the other.

'Yes, but we missed lunch,' Eduardo says, spooning stew onto his plate.

'We lunched on *modronho*.'

A cackle from Eduardo's father.

'We made good time, didn't we Zé? Thirty-three kilometres in one day is quite respectable.'

'I'll say it is. Take some bread Zé.' Eduardo's mother sits at last.

'When you walk across the Alentejo instead of driving, you move at the normal pace of the life there and you come to understand things you miss from a car or a train. The bread basket of the country it is, but not just in the material sense. The Alentejans harbour a resilience, which the rest of us sorely need. I see the workers there as the fermenting yeast for the future.'

'Oh, Zézinho, we shall miss all these ideas of yours. Fermenting yeast for the future; I'll must try to remember that.'

'*Mamãe*, I need to change my bandage.'

'I expect I can find a clean one, but first thing in the morning it's the nurse's office for you. What is it? Another splash? You should be careful with lead. So. What are your plans?'

'Zé needs to do some hill climbing first; he needs to be fit.'

'I am fit.'

'You'll take a rest though, surely.'

'There's no time for that. We start tomorrow,' says Zé.

Fired up for his journey, his vagabondage as he calls it now, he taps the barometer on the wall of the shop. *Change*. Eduardo insists they wait for a dark night with good cloud cover. And annoyingly, he is right. There will only be the one chance. One night to climb the nineteen kilometres to the top, find his way down the other side, and be clear of the border by daybreak.

In a day or two he will be fit enough. At first light today, they set off to climb the road of martyrdom to the tiny chapel on the ridge, *Nossa Senhora da Peña*. Looking out from that shrine towards the three highest peaks of the Serra, he could even make out the path he would soon take. It was exhilarating, but made him feel so small. He lit a candle for his mother and set the jar among the others in the chapel porch, out of the wind. But his prayer was also for himself.

A customer has come in. A small weasel of a man with a trilby pushed back from his face. Without removing the hat he stands at the counter, hands in his pockets.

'No, we don't sell *Avante*! *Adeus*.' Eduardo flashes Zé a warning look before the man is out of the door. '*Filho da Mãe*. How does that one make a living? Not from hanging on the steps outside the fire station all day. Have you seen him there? Fucking fireman fancier — Ah! *Bom dia, Senhora Maria -Joãna*.' Eduardo dips behind the counter and comes up with a folded tabloid. 'One *Correia da Manha* with a supplement inside for you, *Senhora*, because I trust you not to open it until you are home alone. Where's Abel, did you say? He'll be back at lunchtime with my mother. *Obrigada, Senhora. Adeus.*'

Zé, halfway up a stepladder, is losing track of how many sheepskin shepherds' vests he's counted, and stands on a rung, scratching the new stubble on his chin. He takes the stock ledger from Eduardo. Recipes, herbal remedies, horoscopes, farmer's almanacks. *Toto Loto, Toto Bola,* envelopes for posting film. He counts them all and records the numbers, while customers come and go. The suspicion he harbours about Eduardo is growing. But if his friend really makes a secret practice of aiding defectors, he will neither mention it nor probe. But clues appear, as they did the time when they met to talk about Miguel.

Earlier that evening he'd taken Jody to his summer studio. And they were crunching back along the track. The moon had not yet risen, but her loose white shirt was blueing with the cooling of the light. He watched from behind, wincing as she dragged a stone along the wire fence. The grating noise only aggravated his nerves. The time was racing by. He wanted to make sure she would come back.

'I wish I'd worn socks, with all these nettles growing near the fence,' she called back.

'Here, let me go first.'

After changing places, he could no longer watch her hips swaying in her jeans. And he launched into his idea for the co-operative. 'More tourists will come now that the regime is changing its attitude and starting to invest.'

'Huh! It's just because The Beatles are living in the Algarve. But do you honestly think your government would lend us money for an artist's co-op?'

They both laughed.

'Of course not. And we must guard our independence too.'

She sounded keener, when he promised he would teach her to paint. She said she'd tried to go to Art School to learn painting and sculpture, but the principal had been condescending and enrolled her in Fashion. So she started turning up at school in enormous hats just to make a point. 'I didn't stay for very long. I seemed to know as much they did; I'd learned it all off my mum.'

'You come back when? December?'

'Possibly.'

At least possibly was better than perhaps. He'd hated perhaps. When they reached the schoolyard wall she wanted to climb over by herself, and so he vaulted, and watched her try. The playground swings were all padlocked and looped together with chains. A slide was mummified with sacking, and the building was kept locked. So he put his arm through a window vent, climbed inside and pulled her through after him. The corridor reeked of disinfectant and the floor had just been polished. Reminding him of the coming changes, for which he was not ready. At the weekend, he would return to Lisbon, when his mother closed up the summer house.

She seemed to feel more at ease in his studio than he did.

He was worried that the painting wouldn't be enough to bring her back. But she was overwhelmed, when he gave it to her. Well, it was his biggest and was only just finished in time. He was so moved, he hugged her hard and very nearly crushed her to death. She said his rough tweed jacket made her sunburned skin sore. The moon bobbed along behind them, as they walked back along the track. It made the wire netting shimmer. He tasted salt in the *Nortada* wind that was blowing in across the cliffs. And the Atlantic roaring down below reminded him Eduardo would arrive soon.

A light sea fog. The distant murmur of the surf at low tide. A tinkling sound like glass breaking, as he felt his way along the cliff face and moved closer to the spring. Bare rock then seeded rock, and he stopped just before the cleft where its water splashed from the basalt. The noise it made as it fell was just the kind of cover they would need. Leaning into a fissure in the rock, he lit a cupped cigarette. Eduardo could be a while yet, if his train had left Lisboa late.

  While he waited he checked at intervals that the cliff top was still invisible, to reassure himself they would be safe. The worst time, that of not knowing Miguel's whereabouts, had passed. The next big question was, Could they try to get him out of Caxias? Standing flat against the cliff, he made himself imagine what it must be like to live within the four walls of a cell. A confined space in which nothing ever happens but the passing of time, and where each ambient sound becomes a significant event.

  The crunch of boots on sand was followed by a shape advancing through the mist. Bizarrely he mistook the figure for a waiter he knew from Nicola, and had to suppress a laugh when he realised who it was. 'Eduardo, you made it.' He came up breathing fog into his face, and stood beside him leaning flat against the dark wall of the cove. While he listened through the steady fall of water from the spring, he saw Eduardo patting pockets, so he brought out a cigarette.

  'Here, take one of these. So, what's the news?'

  'I did my best to talk the others round, but in the end they all said they can't afford to get involved in Miguel's case. Student activists are high risk and not essential party workers.'

He kept his cool by blowing smoke at a trailing succulent. 'I didn't know Miguel was in the party. He never said.'

'*Não*. He kept his oath.'

'They know more about him than I do. I should have guessed though. He's from the Minho, so like you —'

'He was raised with it.'

They stopped talking while they listened.

'So they moved him from Aljube to Caxias for what? For —?'

'He's in the torture block now.'

His chest had suddenly tightened and his breathing was becoming shallow. 'I can't bear it.' He was agitated. 'I'd really rather it were me. I can stand bit of pain, but Miguel ...' Long green tendrils brushed the rock above him, watery and blurred. 'Miguel is diabetic.'

Eduardo's boot was scraping back and forth, making sparks fly from his stub.

'Afterwards they can release him, or else send him back to Aljube. They could also keep him in Caxias, I imagine.'

'What? Without a trial?' said Zé.

'They can. Has he done three months yet? What's the charge? Don't you know?'

'Couldn't you find out? He was arrested while we were out collecting signatures for the petition to the Conference for World Peace. I was there, but I spotted them first and I hid.'

'The one that asked for the release of all those poets from Aljube?'

'Ironically, yes. And now who will petition to free Miguel, an unknown painter? They've got to give him a trial.'

'Come on now; you know the score. Just look at Tojo. With all those British writers, Canadians and South Africans too, petitioning for his release, and he's still in there. Indefinitely.'

'They're all in there indefinitely and they all have tuberculosis. A writer, thinking he may never be released, marries in his cell. I can't stay still for much longer. Can we walk?'

'To the sea, or back up?'

'Better go back. The tide is turning and will soon be filling this cove.' He hopped around and then edged some way back along the cliff face. And stopped dead, when a boulder crashed down, just missing Eduardo who was right behind him. He waited. He strained to hear. 'Ssh. Blend with the wall.'

He felt his way along, from time to time checking back on Eduardo. Some way ahead, a rail was gleaming like a charmed snake in the darkness. Just a few steps more, and he was leaning on it, ready to climb the steps. He waited for his friend to reappear. Eduardo was born a communist. He was born into and, therefore accepted as certainties the very notions that he questioned, and would likely question for ever. Because certainties are death to the imagination. But on the other hand efficient organisations got things done; and something had to be done. He mounted a high step, to leave the one below him free for Eduardo.

'Listen. On Friday I return to Lisbon. Jody flies away on Tuesday. My studies were already cancelled and now I am barred from working as well. And from tomorrow, I'm without a studio. So, I thought ...' He hesitated. The tide was coming in. 'I have the time now and I am strong enough, so why don't I work for Resistência?' He tapped his temple to indicate that by strong enough he meant mentally.

Eduardo let out a whistle. 'For a start, you'd have to join the party.'

'I know. But now that I have the status of a peasant by default ...'

'My guess is that they won't have you.'

He climbed a number of steps, all the while cursing to himself. Was it his family? Their history? Did they sense his Galician roots? Looking back, he could see Eduardo's white bald spot and, set against it, the dark water's edge creeping up the beach. 'They consider me too bourgeois?'

'It's not that. It's like you said yourself, you haven't got cover. And without it you are risky, and not enough use to them. They need members who are workers, who can give them access to a network. I can give them one because I work at *Diário*. The job gives me the cover to run my own clandestine press. But I can also access services. In other words, it brings resources that they can make use of.' Eduardo carried on talking into his chest. 'And you know as well as I do that Resistência is for life. Or the other. Look, you're better off working from within the student organisations.'

'Yes, I could try and get myself arrested again.' They were avoiding each other's eyes. 'The universities, the school of Art, all are out of bounds to me now. They arrest me just for seeing friends in Coimbra, so how can I attend their meetings? *Bem*. I need a beer before António closes the bar.' They were breathless when they reached the cliff top. 'You see; the sea is up,' he called, and led the way along the cliff wall towards the café.

'I've heard they think you're too conspicuous and you attract too much attention.'

'Because I'm tall? Because I look Russian?'

'*Tchk!* Because artists stand out. Because there's something about you. You look different; you look cultured. And Jody turns heads everywhere she goes, by the way she dresses. The little girl too, the three of you ...'

'They go to England on Tuesday.'

Eduardo fell silent, and then went to sit on the wall. It was a while before he said quietly: 'And you can't go to the airport to see her off because it's out of bounds. Is that what's been eating you?'

'*Heu!* Never mind. I go anyway. I hide.'

'Are you mad? What will you tell her? She'll be looking out for you, drawing attention to where you are. And suppose she tells that couple she is staying with? Because she will. The guy works for a company that obtains a lot of State contracts.'

'No, she won't tell them. Look, the lights are on and there's António.'

Just before they reached the café terrace, Eduardo's tone became kinder:

'You know, *amigo*, you can still draw your political cartoons. You don't need a studio for them. Will you do some for me? To print in my journal? And don't forget that your name is next to Miguel's on that register. You must be extra vigilant now.'

At one o'clock the shop doorbell rings. The Almeidas are back. He follows Eduardo upstairs, behind his parents, to the dining room, where they eat a lunch of fish soup. The maid carries it to table wearing woollen mittens and a red anorak.

'You must be careful now, *Papäe*. A *bufo* was in the shop this morning, asking for a copy of *Avanté!*'

'Don't worry, your mother and I are always on our guard.'

'After lunch we go to Portalêgre. I want to talk to Rosa about the press. There are some things I need to rush through in case *Avanté!* disappears again soon. I like to cover their production gaps, but it's harder now to find advertisers that haven't been scared off. This month we get the seed potato merchants, and the hay train in April. But after that I don't know. I don't like anonymous subscriptions.'

'Do you like the venison soup?' says Abel.

'The best I ever tasted.'

'You only ever taste it here.'

Crumbs litter the tablecloth. The maid carries in a fresh loaf.

'We change the name; we memorise the lists. That way we're never raided, but it means we can't expand. And now look who's here.'

'Taxi?' Eduardo's uncle Luis appears in the doorway.

As they walk to the taxi rank, Zé says to Eduardo: 'I left Lisboa a fugitive, and now your parents make me feel wanted again.'

'You're not a fugitive here. The locals are used to seeing you about the place with me. And with my parents, well, there's never any tension between them. Surprisingly, when you remember they are Catholic and Jew. I guess the politics helps. And we must keep an eye on the weather. Saturday will be the best night for what you want to do.'

Nineteen

ROSA AND DIEGO Almeida da Sousa live in an ancient stone farmhouse in Portalêgre. The entrance is diagonally across a cobbled yard from the gate. On a disused stable block with low, lime-washed windows, three cinder-blocked doorways are still visible through the creeper at this time of the year. In a month, thinks Zé, the only clue to their existence will be the vines that straggle up next to places where the cobblestones are worn flat, and even dip a bit.

Rosa comes to the door and ushers them through to the kitchen. A back slap for Eduardo betrays a feistiness in her, which is missing from her brother. But like Eduardo she is short. And her thick shoulder-length hair adds to the impression of stunted growth by completely hiding her neck.

'*Mamäe* sent these.' Eduardo tosses her a parcel.

'Oh no, she hasn't been crocheting already.' Rosa holds up some tiny white garments, edged in the same yellow ochre as the windows in these parts.

'Who's expecting? You?' Eduardo beams. 'Will I be an uncle?'

'Just go through, will you. Tiago is in the print shop. Watch your head, Zé.'

He stoops to enter a succession of small, low-beamed rooms, through which he can see the cast iron press at the far end. Tiago, who is laying proofs along the sill of a blind window, flicks his hair back, which adds another black smear to his forehead. Zé gently rubs the corner of a print to gauge the weight of the paper.

'I've at last found a stronger rice paper, Zé. I hope it stands up better to our primitive distribution methods.'

'Eduardo! At last.' Tiago comes to greet Eduardo and hands him a proof. 'The writer's permission came through eventually, so I've gone ahead with the extract.'

Eduardo passes it to Zé. 'See who wrote this? It so happens that he is living not far from here. These are reprints from his article in *Diário*, but I'm hoping to persuade him to write something especially for us. He's in the *Unidade*, or was until we lost Delgado last year.'

Zé flinches at Eduardo's mention of their opposition leader's murder. Just as he is about to see for himself where it took place. Yes, Delgado took the same well-worn track, the path of clandestines or, coming back the other way, of secretly returning exiles. Their late leader and his secretary, found dead beside the path, had been trying to re-enter Portugal in time for the last elections. And on Saturday night, with luck, he will escape along the same track. Eduardo is still talking.

'I don't want to keep republishing stuff from those hyenas. I need an appointment with him while we are here.'

When Rosa comes in, Zé spreads out his drawings on a flat surface. 'I've some cartoons for you, Rosa. I'm doing more of this type of work now that I'm travelling.'

Rosa slides the cartoons around like playing cards on a table and, finally selects three.

'How long can I keep these? We need to make a line block from each.'

'Not long at all, I'm afraid. I'm setting off for Paris at the weekend.'

What a ring it has for him to say, I'm setting off for Paris. It sounds so easy all of a sudden. He will draw a few cartoons along the way, and hawk them round the cafés when he reaches Montparnasse. The freedom in that is giddying. Until Tiago brings his thoughts to earth.

'I only need to lay your drawing on the board of the copy camera to make a glass negative. I can transfer it to a plate tomorrow morning before you go. Or you could etch a plate by hand tonight, if you want.'

'I'd like to make one especially for you, while you work on two of those. I'll need a needle. Mine is in my rucksack in Castelo de Vide.'

***

They are back from a simple supper at the *pastelaria* across the road. The goat pasties were good and so was the beer. He follows Tiago into the print shop. The odours in the last room nourish him: kerosene, burnt stand oil, fresh Indian ink. They produce a plate of Sálazar setting sail from Lisboa. He is off to fight in the colonies, when there are no soldiers left. And they set the caption in type: '*I have the right to self-determination too.*'

He adores the peace in the stable block, once the others are in bed, and he can go on with his work alone. He lays a hard ground, blackens it with a flame and blows out the candle. A doodle starts off the process. This time Sálazar is fleeing Portugal along a mountain track. He finds a title, *The Path to Victory*. And he listens to the old house frame shifting as he works. Satisfied, he cleans up the place with kerosene on a rag, and sluices cold water on his hands before opening a window and lighting up.

Darkness dissolves boundaries. With all the lights out, he feels closer to Jody. Cloistered like this, he could be anywhere in the world. He still associates her, though, with his old life in Lisboa, which is retreating and will soon be lost to him, perhaps even for ever. He pushes out the window, to feel closer to the stars, those twinkling brass buttons in the black cloak of the night. And as he smokes leaning on the sill, he tries to imagine her asleep, a sight he is yet to see. And *will* see. It will happen. One day they will wake up together in the morning sun.

But then a real image from the past appears to replace the one he imagined. She is striding down the promenade towards him, the sun blazing white-hot beside her, until she blots it out, when she stands in front of him with face flushed and her eyes burning black as liquid coals. She throws a glance at the waves. Their rhythms that day had mesmerised him, while he sat at the table, waiting for her, scraping paint from his nails. Cadmium red, Naples yellow. He could eat Naples yellow.

He caught that angle of her head again, like the first day they met. While the hush that had surrounded her now enveloped them both. And he saw in front of him the opening up of a long, long road. The same road that had brought her to him, from way back down the ages, like someone he used to love once, a long time ago.

'I missed you,' she said, leaning on the trolley, breathless and laughing at him as she watched him spring to his feet. She had been to Sintra for the day with her friends. 'I missed you, but it's bonkers, you know. I only saw you yesterday.'

When she was seated, he sat again and prepared to light two *Gauloise*s. His fingers missed that small ritual for quite a while after she left. She held hers cocked to her ear and blew away the smoke without inhaling it.

'Now you're a Modigliani. No, you're not; you're a Max Beckman. With that pink scarf you've got tied like that, right above your eyes.'

'I like Modigliani. Those women with the black holes where their eyes were meant to be. Did he do them like that because he used to be a sculptor?' Her eyes were turned from the blinding glare that was bouncing off the waves.

'Yes, it was exactly that. But Jeanne, his model, really did have black eyes just like you. It must be why you kept reminding me of Montparnasse, when we first met.'

'It's the kohl, or the mascara, or both. Or maybe it's you. Yes, it's you. You burned my eyes out with all your staring.'

'It is the only thing I do well, now. We can only look and dream. You know it is against the law for me to kiss you in a public place, don't you? And even the sea is public.'

'Is that the regime?'

'No, it has always been so.'

'Would they fine us?'

'No, not you, but I could go to prison.'

'Don't worry; I'll come with you. How long is it for?'

She could be funny sometimes, but right then her blithe remark touched a nerve. *Miguel — Aljube — Caxias*. Names on a shred of paper and that was all. But he shivered as she mentioned prison. Miguel had been banged up in Aljube about three months, then. And Caxias was not far from there, just a few stops along the train line.

But then the sun sent a jagged line down her nose in imitation of Picasso, with his piercing eyes and his staring Demoiselles. And that Andalusion saying he was so fond of repeating: that if you stare a woman in the eyes for long enough, you can have her. Or something to that effect. Well, whatever it was, Picasso was very good at it.

Anna was lifting her arms to him, expectant. So he gathered her up from her trolley. She infused him with such warmth; and she accepted him unconditionally. He sat her on his knee, while Jody told him of her climb on the Moorish walls in Sintra, her purchases in terracotta. She had a passion for pottery, as did several of his friends. It had already set him thinking.

He paid António and followed her down the steps, carrying Anna. He stood behind her at the broken sluice, listening while he looking out across the rocks and down to the waterline. A lone surfer pulled his board from the sea and walked dripping up the beach. Jody didn't want to venture down the slope. The recent storm had smashed its surface, and water gushed from a hole. Anna pointed to some flakes of yellow paint spinning down the gulley. He pulled Jody round to face him and he couldn't stop himself from asking her: 'Jody, why do you return to England?'

She looked flustered, shocked. It was broad daylight; they were surrounded by a crowd. Perhaps it was too abrupt.

'Because I have to. You've always known that. I've never suggested otherwise.'

She was right. She never had. But he whispered forcefully in her ear: 'You cannot live with a man who does not love you.'

Her eyes stretched wide at hearing it. 'Please don't, not now, Zé. I can't just stay here, can I?'

'Yes, stay. Just stay.'

But she launched into a list of things she said she needed for her work: her sewing machine, patterns, pinking shears whatever they are, while her voice rose in pitch. He watched her cheeks flush, saw the pulse beating in a vein in her neck. He eased her body round until he could fit her underneath his armpit, and no longer see her face. And glaring at the black rocks beside the sluice, he tried to force his brain to think, while his free hand raked her hair. When he stepped aside again, her expression was altered.

'Well, maybe he does love me in his own way.' Her voice had changed and she set her face away. She sounded unconvinced, he thought, and so, too, was he. They turned together and wandered to the end of the promenade.

'There are many kinds of love between a man and a woman.' He watched the cracks between the paving stones as he walked.

'I believe that,' she said quietly, as she joined his study of the pavement. 'I'm older than you, aren't I?'

'Are you? A year, a year and a half at most. What matters? At times I feel really old, like an old, old man, or somebody who knew you in another life.'

'I know.' She drew closer, but almost instantly pulled away. She had remembered what he said earlier about being in a public place. He wished he still had the studio apartment in the city. But if he'd spent the summer in the city …

Writing to her and reading her letters are what he misses. Even now, smoking at the window, his fingers itch for something else to do. And what if she leaves home before he arrives? What then? He is as powerless as when he watched them walk through the barrier at the airport. The pigs divided them then and they will try to do so again. His dreams for their future together, they would brand as treachery. And there is nothing more subversive, it seems, than to dream. He pulls the window to and fastens it shut for the night.

In the kitchen, Rosa makes breakfast, while he draws into his hard ground with a darning needle from her sewing basket rammed into a cork. When the image is complete, he coats the back with wax, and leaves the plate on the bench ready for Tiago to do the rest. Tiago will know exactly how long to let the acid bite. He needs to do some more training with Eduardo before his climb.

The sun is blitzing the cork oaks. The ancient mule track is barraged with arrows of white light. Ever since the Middle Ages the mule trains have slowed here. Where the stones are laid in a wheel pattern at a sharp bend in the lane.

'Have you thought about how you'll get through the Pyrenees, yet? I'll write to Gil for you, if you want.'

'How can Gil help without a passport?'

'*Tchk*. Does anyone have a passport? Well, for one thing, he could raise the alarm, if you don't arrive.'

'Absolutely not, *meu amigo*. No alarms, no explanations. Not to anyone. I am a clandestine and I accept the risks and the consequences of that.'

'I know, but I just thought —'

'Don't.' When a sunburst lights the lines in Eduardo's face, he feels his gratitude and is sorry. 'Don't be worried, I have the password to a safe house in Pamplona.'

'From Isabel?'

'Yes, from Isabel. She said that guides who know the terrain well will help me through the Pyrenées from there. You'd best look after her for me. Talk to her about the danger of the reading lessons in her mother's attic.'

From their vantage point at the bend in the lane, he spots a thin white light. It looks to be snaking upward, but then it vanishes behind the mountain.

'And you'd best remember that, in spite of the current stand-off with Franco, the *PIDE* in Portugal and the Civil Guard in Spain are still hand in glove. Don't forget it for a minute.'

He nods. Three peaks thrust skyward into an electric blue sky. The highest of them is the one.

Twenty

Saturday

SHALE GREY MIST is rolling down the mountainside when he wakes. From his window it looks as if the sun fled the earth while he slept. Today he could legitimately doze until noon. But Eduardo's face has just popped round the bedroom door. 'Catch!' he says. 'Courtesy of the shoemaker's guild.' A package lands near his feet. He opens it.

'Innersoles? But of course!' He hits his temple. 'Ordinary standard innersoles. Genius.' *The left one will hide the cut edge of the half sole underneath it and thus save its pattern from wear. But how does Eduardo know about this?*

'Have you thought about what you'll do, if by any chance they don't let you in?'

'Then I find my own way. The mountain passes will be marked on a map. I have a French identity card and, with the beard, they won't tell the difference.'

Dusk is falling when they leave the lay-by and, one behind the other, march down the narrow road to Spain.

'We've done five kilometres already,' Eduardo calls from the rear.

He is coming up to a signpost. It says *Espanha,* pointing straight ahead. He stops and waits for Eduardo who tells him this is where they turn right. For Galegos, a small village close to the Serra.

'I doubt that you'll be running into any of the border patrols, once you've left the river bank and the woods. It's too high for them and too cold up there and, anyway, it's a Saturday night. They're probably all drunk. But if you do meet a guard, stick your hands up before he unslings his rifle. Smugglers are another matter though; you just can't predict what they'll do.'

They are come to the edge of a village. The word *Café* is painted, tall and black, on a whitewashed gable end.

'What do you think?' he says.

'It looks abandoned.'

'If it isn't, I could do with a drink.'

Down a step and through a plastic curtain of red and green plastic strips. They are knee-deep in bed linen and tea towels with gaudy toreadors under cellophane wraps. A high mahogany counter could be taken for an altar with all the candles flickering on it, their flames reflected in some gilt-coated plaster animals of the neighbourhood: deer, salamander, foxes, a hare. And a semi-circle of lanky, Disney-faced, glazed porcelain Virgins is deferring to an open box that spills cartons of long-life milk. While Eduardo buys milk, he praises the statues to a group huddled at the end of the counter.

'Smugglers,' Eduardo mutters, when they are out on the street.

Leaning against the side of a bridge, and deafened by the raging torrent, they drain their cartons of milk. The world is darker now, the moon a hazy white spot in a starless sky. They cross the bridge towards a public lavatory, and Zé leads the way inside. He drops his rucksack, opens it and takes out a few essentials, which he quickly stuffs into his belt. Swiss army knife, torch, a whistle and a few squares of chocolate. He pats his pockets for the compass, and checks the photo-stated military maps are dry and easy to reach. Lastly he clips his water bottle to a belt loop before walking out alone, lightened, into the damp evening air.

Eduardo will be carrying his pack through the legal checkpoint. And they will meet again across the border in the morning, in *Espanha*, all being well. And if by any chance they lose each other, well, too bad, it would be mad to hang around. Eduardo must keep the rucksack. And he has just emerged with it, evidently struggling beneath its weight.

'You'll soon be used to it,' he says, as he raises his rolled umbrella. 'Until the crossroads, then.' Eduardo nods, and walks away.

He feels so light, and the noises coming from the river below have lessened. But it rushes by him as he walks along the bank, repeating to himself: *'We meet again at the crossroads, between El Pino and La Casinas. Between El Pino and La Casinas. Between …'* His thoughts are still with Eduardo. He imagines he should be veering upwards from the river bank by now, and onto the cobbled lane that runs between some falling drystone walls. There are boulders as big as houses. A stream down in the ravine. The main thing for Eduardo is not to lose his way in the dark. Pitch dark. He shouldn't do; they have walked it together many times before now.

Fontanera should be lit up, when he gets there, but only from the houses, which are well spread out, with haciendas hung with lanterns in the Spanish style. And that lugubrious café. He is welcome to wait in there. If he can climb the massive stone step, that is, and part a really heavy door curtain. It would be shelter for a few hours. The locals would be playing cards and wouldn't even look up from their hands.

No, Eduardo will be fine. *He* will be the one exposed. Completely exposed, too, once he gains the highway that goes to Spain. And then the lower slopes of the Serra, where the guards patrol in threes on horseback. He shudders. But here, so long as he stays on the north bank, the cover should be thick.

He is heading steadily upstream along a rough, pinkish track. The river that flows along beside him has now narrowed quite a lot. And its banks amplify the rushing noise that the water makes between its stones. He welcomes that noise; it drowns out the crunching of his boots on gravel. The moon has just bobbed out again from behind a passing cloud. It lights up the mica in the granite chippings that they've used to fill the potholes. And, high up on his left, it floodlights a moss-covered stone frontage. Tall cacti stick their hands up like prisoners and hold them flat against a desolate, black sky. He can profit now from the swirling stream of sounds and, also, from the shadow thrown down by a tall, thorny hedge.

But suddenly out of nowhere, a pack of dogs is barking in the distance. And then a voice joins in, an old woman's voice, and curses come hurtling like missiles through the void. He stops and listens to the dogs as they become increasingly excited. Although they still sound far away. He just prays it isn't Eduardo that has strayed across the old contraband route. That kind of thing could well precipitate him into the ravine. And if he can hear the racket this far away, so can the patrols.

He decides to walk along the riverbed itself and jumps down from the bank. Then steadying himself, he sets off again along its large, flat stones. The moon is hiding again as he picks his way along the waterway, lunging from stone to stone, hopefully unseen and unheard. And without getting his feet wet. Pleased with his own cunning, he is even gladder when some goat bells chime in with the water's jabbering. Shadows flit past, eyes gleam low. A deeper clonking comes from higher up a field, where cow shapes are darkening the ground underneath the oaks. *It may well rain, but please, please, do not let there be a storm.*

The stream has turned into a moat alongside the driveway to a house. An upper window is lit. He clambers out, and removes his boots under cover of a tall hedge. Fumbling in the dark, he peels back his wet innersole and lets his fingertips find the cut edge underneath. *Still bone dry.* His trouser bottoms and the hem of his raincoat are splashed with mud. But no dogs bark at the house. He tiptoes along a sandy track, in his socks, and on until he finds himself bathed in strong yellow light. The glare is coming from a sodium lamp beside the highway into Spain. He waits for a single car to flash past and scuttles over the shining tarmac, hugging his boots.

Crouched, and lacing up his boots, he listens with his ear close to the ground. A low hum is coming from the highway, an eerie buzz from the lights. He hopes Eduardo is safe and that he still has the rucksack. Straightening up again, he glances back at the rock face of Pitaranha. That way would be impossible without climbing ropes and hooks. He must stick by his decision.

Alone on a bare slope with nothing but the most sporadic of tree stumps, he is alarmingly confused. Are these the lower slopes? Is this the Serra? He pulls out his map, to see, but can't, and has to walk back towards the highway again, to make use of its light. He is wishing that, instead of fitness training, they had spent a few days studying the movements of the patrols. But then, it might have looked suspicious. And from now on, it seems, he is going to be off the edge of the map. But at least, he knows the way back now, so he could always start again.

Diabo! He forgot to tell Eduardo what's inside his pack. Will he think to look before they question him? If he gropes around and feels wood, surely he will guess it is a small canvas. And if he touches cold metal bolts in the wood, he'll know it has to be a sketching easel. And Eduardo is not dumb. He'll say that he was hiking in the Serra and he needs to catch the train home from Valencia de Alcántara. Although in Spain, it is the nearest station. He tries to picture the situation. A customs officer, a hut, a rubber stamp, a torch shone in Eduardo's face. The beam swings back and forth, between Eduardo's features and his passport, and lights up an area of cinders and shallow flooding. A red neon sign: *alfândega.* But that customs shed is really long and he'll be watched as he walks the length of it. Unless they are asleep. They could be dozing under their gold-braided caps, their feet resting on the table. It must be boring for them at night.

Eduardo said he'd wait the night out inside the all-night café, the one that stands across the car park from the money changer's hut. If the guards are drinking in the bar, there will be horses tethered to the doorpost. And if Eduardo sees them, and they're tall enough to be police horses, he will know. He reassures himself by picturing their pistol belts hanging loose, their rifles upended and leant against a card table. Eduardo at the bar, willing them to keep drinking throughout the night.

Wrapped in white mist, he is bent double over scrubby ground, searching in the underbrush for his track. His lost thread. Nineteen more kilometres of this will definitely kill him, assuming that he isn't shot first. *Is that the track?* He must find it. He dare not stray a centimetre from the well-worn path. Others before him have found the way, and lost it, too, probably. He is not the first fugitive to take the 'green route' out of Portugal. As he searches, he tries to keep his spirits up by thinking what lies ahead. The road to Paris, the boat to England, seeing Jody again. He should focus on that. *Is that the path?* Over to his right, the forked, bone-white trunks of lightning-struck trees. A ghostly defeated army. Were they all struck at once? he wonders. Or did they die slowly from exposure? As *he* will, unless he walks faster. *It does appear to be a path.*

Goat bells come ringing, echoing on the thin mountain air, as he passes below a compound. A barking Estrela, chest puffed out, patrols behind a wire fence. He darts towards some dead oaks, but they are too thinly spaced to hide him. And when no human presence manifests, he rejoins his path. The dead oaks are gone. The stumps have gone. The vegetation has thinned to nothing but the odd white, knee-high stick. And, before long, even they are lost in the burgeoning bank of mist.

He is on a rough-pelted hillside, when a drop-dead hush begins to usher in the low moan of the wind. Animal tracks or human pathways? He crouches down to find out, but he dare not light his torch. The moon has shown him that the hill he is on is not the highest after all. Beside his narrow path, the land falls away to disappear into a fog-filled hollow, out of which it then rises to become a distant peak. Ahead of him, a steep ravine. And a second peak emerging from the mist. Should he run down and start to climb the great stony giant over to his right? How far away is it? And will it give him better cover? The moon is now laying out a network of silvery white threads. Tracks, all of them, but where do they go? And how far away are they? He is edging closer to panic. One wrong move and he could blunder round in circles for days. But one track is beginning to stand out from the mesh of trails. Was it human feet that wore it wider and whiter than the rest? But then the moon deserts him, taking with it his choices.

Too cold to stand still, he follows on, obedient to where his feet lead him. They take him onto a plateau, where he comes across a shadowy enclosure. Built from tree stumps, it consists of two interlocking L-shaped stacks. He runs between the stacks. Instantly it is warmer out of the wind. With shaking hands, he pulls out his torch and, shading it with his coat, he flicks it on and shines it on the gap. But then, thinking better of it, he strikes match after match, until his supply has nearly all gone. Then one stays alight for long enough that he can read the compass. He was right. He's heading South East. And he should stay on the same hill.

He is desperate for a smoke, but his teeth are chattering, clattering loudly out of control. He could pee for Portugal, but his fingers are by now frozen enemies that won't unbutton his flies. Smoking up against the stack helps to mask a smell of musty decay. The worst thing about it all is the complete absence of life. But to wish to meet another human being would seriously tempt fate. *One step at a time from now, and in a south-easterly direction. Here goes.* An act of sheer will wrests him from seclusion, and safety, and he sets out again, vulnerable and exposed. He chooses paths by instinct now, reminding himself frequently that what goes up must come down. Until his legs are numb and he can no longer tell if he is moving up or down. And a freezing, oily blackness has swallowed him whole, and is killing off all sound.

Ahead of him looms an ill-defined shape, a low hillock, a rickle maybe. The one-boot-wide gulley he is in is turning him into a robot. Moisture trickles off the ends of his hair and freezes into his collar. The wet tweed burns his neck. His feet merely tread water. Wet cloth is chafing his calves. He swallows gulps of fog whole. The chocolate is now nothing but a ball of tinfoil in his pocket. None of this was in their training.

Fatigue dissipates, leaving him a well of loneliness instead. His thoughts are gnawing at a question, just one. How long would his body lie on the ground here, undiscovered, if he simply lay down and died? Would the day come when a search party found nothing but a heap of bones? His grimace is so wide it reaches to his earlobes, and they pain him. But the sharpness of the sudden pain draws him to the present.

Afraid now of hallucinating, he tries to concentrate his mind on catching the threads of an old song. It is an Alentejan folk lyric, and he must sing it coherently. He will force himself to remember every word and keep to the strict quatrain pattern, repeating the lines backwards, then forwards again. The sheer difficulty prevents his imagination from overwhelming him, throughout the longest night of his life.

He is still singing, when a faint ribbon of light streaks the horizon. Within the hour, he can begin to make out the gentle downward slope in front of him, the hoar frost that coats the ground. He tugs the rime that clogs his beard. Can it be that his tormenters are now in another country? Are they behind him? Is he free? His entire body convulses in a great trembling of relief. And he breaks into a run, the fall of the land dictating his pace. He is light enough to fly to England now, never mind to walk. She must know now that he is coming. She will feel it. She will know ...

From the mist down in the valley ahead, a dark shape is emerging. A silhouette forms before his eyes. He stops. He waits. He hardly dare breathe. A cloaked man on horseback, standing still, perfectly at ease. Watches him, as he creeps slowly forward, willing the dawn light to clear. Something moves. There is a beating sound like the flapping of a cloak. It flaps awhile and then it settles, to be again a part of the whole.

'If you meet a border guard, stick your hands up before he unslings his rifle.'

He lifts his arms, still with his umbrella in hand, and edges slowly forward, incapable of tearing his eyes from the dark form. The horse looks so solid. Like the stack did from this distance, the stack of wood. And wood left out to dry on a windy hillside will turn black, even on a south-facing slope. Or a south-east facing slope. He stands still. It is a stack. Just a stack after all. Cuboid, raised on pillars, four of them, to let the air currents through. A pyramid of logs with, laid over it, a flapping tarpaulin.

At the bottom of the hill, a tarmac road. A man-made road; he relishes the road. It winds away among some fir trees and then is lost in a forest. But its newness brings with it dangers. With the daylight will come the Spanish police hunting down smugglers. Around here they stop and search anything that moves, with a pack or without one.

There isn't even birdsong to celebrate the dawn. The first creature he encounters is a stork. Perched on the first telegraph pole in the newly-made world. It flies down from its nest, begins to encircle his head. Six more storks arrive to join the first, surrounding him, blessing him. He is São Francisco. He understands the language of the birds. He speaks in the tongues of all winged creatures. Raising his rolled umbrella, he draws a perfect circle in the air, in answer to the clattering of their bills. All the birds will know soon that he is walking to England.

Long before his throat has thawed, before he can speak again, he recognises the magical figure. Seated on a fallen tree trunk, encased in the morning light. Through the gaps between the pines he catches flashes of a single-track road.

The road that runs from El Pino to La Casinas. Can it be? It exists?

The sun is low behind the pine forest. Soon it will be up and strong enough to dry the dew from the wild rosemary. And it will warm his back while he sits beside his friend Eduardo on that fallen tree trunk. And devours greedily the chocolate from the all-night café.

'I swear, I will never ever do that again.'

'You won't ever get the chance again, so I wouldn't worry your head. I'd like to move on as soon as you can manage it. The border patrol were in the café last night, playing cards and drinking. But it's rapidly getting light, and they'll be coming out on their rounds. Without a map, we'll just have to chance it that Las Huertas de Causa leads away from the frontier.' Eduardo holds out a fistful of Spanish pesetas. 'These are marked down to my passport. I don't know how you'll get francs. Can we go now, Zé? There's a super-efficient smuggler hunt in progress around here. We absolutely need to stay wide of the road.'

There is also a nonchalance towards the land in these parts, which could not exist at home in Portugal, he says, where every square metre is cultivated.

'You see the same old cork oaks, but they're nothing like our Whistlers.'

'And the storks. And the same river *Tejo*. I'll follow the river to Toledo, or round it rather and, after that I can skirt around Madrid by walking on its banks.'

Eduardo is apparently pulling out the lining of a pocket. 'Here, does this belong to you? I found it underneath my bed when I spring-cleaned.'

He feels a cold spot in his palm. A button. A pearl? A pearl button. From a white cardigan worn back to front with too many buttons. He touches it to a tooth and then, as he walks he rolls it through his fingers.

Twenty-one

England. April 1967

THEIR TRAIN HAS been threading in and out of the forest for a while. It should be Nottingham next. She stands with Anna by the window from where they can see the other carriages veering round a curve. 'We'll see the cranes soon,' she says to Anna. 'The sky will be full of great big yellow cranes.' She recalls how the cranes were like a second forest, last time she was here.

'Cows.' Anna, gripped by a state of wonder, points through the glass.

'No, cranes I said, not cows.'

'Cows.'

'All right, cows too. But now your hands are black.' She takes out a damp sponge, dabs it over Anna's face and hands. Such a conscientious housewife she is these days that she hardly knows herself. Michael can't remember when he ate so many homemade cakes. But when the phone rang at home, late last night, and Kay was urging her to come, it felt like a blessing, an opportunity to breathe. An escape route from the well, and the not so well meaning advice.

The neighbours had meant well:

'*We'd been listening for the taxi and were so relieved, when we heard you sending it away. Your father was there, wasn't he? Thank goodness he came. We both think you should be studying. At Art school, and full time.*' An easy thing to say, but quite ridiculous. Who would mind Anna?

But Mum's reaction, floorcloth in hand, was far from well meaning: '*I'd like to see you tied down with four or five children, my girl.*' And, if looks could kill ... '*You don't know what love is.*'

Her mother-in-law had surprised her with a hitherto unknown stubbornness. Like mother like son.

'My son is NOT weak.'

'He is.'

'You're wrong about that.'

When Mum comes to visit now, she goes around fingering for specks of dust. And she can't stay long at their house before it's: *'Go home and start cleaning that nice house, you ungrateful girl.'*

Thankfully, her dad stays away. He came once, when she was ill, and showed her a letter from Zé's mother begging him to intercept their letters. And he promised he wouldn't, as if he were doing her a favour. Anyway, what letters? Zé doesn't write now. Their compartment door slides open, letting in the rattle from outside. The man who enters doffs his trilby, then drops a bulging briefcase on the opposite seat.

'You look whacked, luv. Will you let me bring you a pick-me-up from the bar?'

'Do I?' Her fingers brush imaginary shadows from under her eyes. 'No thank you.'

'Would you mind watching the bag, a sec? Oh, sorry. Didn't notice it's first class.'

'Is it? Nor did I.'

'Well, if they say owt, you tell them it's dirty enough for second.' And then he shuts out the din and disappears towards the front of the train.

Anna, bored with the view through the window, sits chewing on her rag book. Peace. Except her mind keeps returning to the polishing she's been doing for days. Rhythmically, mechanically, trying literally to see her face in the floor. What is happening to her? She stopped going to her workroom because she can't face the empty doormat. She looked in briefly on her way to the station this morning. But she won't hear from him now. He's too angry, too hurt. And it's her fault. She's to blame. She should have just stayed there, like he said.

The door rattles and the man holds it back with his elbow; in his hand are two cans of shandy, and he drops two paper cups. She bends to pick them up and swaps Anna's chewed book for a bunch of keys. She sips the unwanted shandy and tries to listen with one ear. He sells knitwear; he's been banned from driving; his wife drove him to the station. But her thoughts are drifting off to Lisbon. They are following a young man on a sad journey home from the docks. She tries to name all the tram stops that he would pass on his way home, but is obliged to leave a lot of blanks. *What's the one near the aqueduct?* Anna throws away the keys, thankfully not through the open window. The train slows, and the necks of brontosaurus cranes are coming closer. She sways along the corridor, holding onto Anna's hood. The salesman steps down before them and takes the axle of the chair. She leans hard on the handle and they lower Anna to the platform. 'Thank you. I can manage now, thanks.'

Kay is waiting at the ticket gate. They both wave. She nearly takes her for a schoolgirl today: the long, fair plait hanging down her back, the white knee socks, the plimsolls, the crammed duffel bag spilling books.

'Hi, Jody. Hi, Anna. Gosh, don't they grow fast!' She is brushing down a green wind-cheater faded around the welt. 'Well, anything makes a change from that starchy uniform I wear at work.'

She is surprised at how glad she is to see Kay. She isn't someone who would shower her with sanctimonious advice. 'There's room for some of those books in the pushchair, if you want. But hey, I thought your exams were over.'

'No, only Midwifery. I got my badge, by the way. It won't take long to drop these at the library; it's by the Council House.'

The rain has stopped, the sun is out again, and she needs to stretch her legs. They set out against a blustery wind, through the racket from the bulldozers, across a vast, open ground.

'I see what you meant about it being just a great big demolition site.' They pass along what had been a street of red brick terraced houses, and then a three-storey row along a walkway with most of its railings missing. 'Look at all that washing left to trail in the cinders. There, by the empty coal merchants. They're never slums though, are they?'

'No way, but they still call it slum clearance. See there?' Kay is pointing to a cloud of brick dust. 'It's where they filmed *Sons and Lovers*. And so many old caves have come to light, they don't report them any more. Time is brass, so they fill them in with rubble and say nothing. I've been out with the protest group. What went on beneath this city would amaze you. Barber shops they had and everything. It was a second city underground. I love history.'

'Do you? I can never remember what followed what. And I'm sorry, but I'm not going in caves. I once went potholing and completely freaked out. It would be nice to find somewhere quiet.'

The Kardomah coffee house is empty, as is the booth from her last visit.

'Jink,' says Anna, from the seat beside her.

'So what's new? Have you been to Manchester? The Twisted Wheel maybe?'

'No, I've been too busy. But listen, I've had a letter from Eduardo.' Kay's eyes are ablaze and she is fidgeting in her seat.

It must be about Zé. 'What? For goodness sake, tell me quickly.' She pushes the cutlery, the cruet and the ketchup out of Anna's reach.

'Jink.'

'I'm looking for your drink.' She slaps down her purse and cigarettes and searches furiously in her bag. 'Here it is and there's a rusk for you. Now will you be quiet? So, what did Eduardo say? Are you two still in touch?' The waitress comes up to Kay. 'Order Blue Mountain again.'

'No, hardly ever. He only wrote to ask me to get a message to you.'

'But why couldn't Zé write to me? He doesn't write!'

'I assume it's about Zé. He didn't give a name, though. All he wrote was: *'Tell Jody her friend is on the way.'*

'Her friend? He *must* mean Zé. But on the way to where?'

'To here, to England, I suppose.'

'Can't be. Zé hasn't got a passport. The police are keeping it until they …'

'I think that's the whole point. It's why Eduardo doesn't say his name. I think it means he's done a bunk, you know, left illegally. Escaped, in other words. You do know about the censor?'

Jody lets her arm fall around Anna, drawing her close. The waitress is moving some cakes around on a tea trolley. She watches her replace the glass dome. *'A friend of mine walked through the mountains … he was dressed as a priest …'* The coffee machine gurgles in the background, hissing steam. The waitress puts down her tongs and then walks back behind a screen. *'Not unless I walk … I promise, even if it takes ten years …' He can't be walking here!*

'Yes, but what else did he say?'

'Only that he's been hiking in the Serra with this friend of yours and that he left him in Valencia da Alcántara. And that's in Spain, see, near the border. I know because my brother told me. He's been there.'

'Don't tell your brother anything. Don't tell anybody anything. Not a thing. Promise me you won't.'

'Okay, but what's the matter? Something bad has happened, hasn't it?'

Her eyes are brimming with tears. 'But why didn't Zé write to *me?*'

Kay shrugs. 'I don't know. He was forced to leave in a hurry? He doesn't want to leave a trail?'

Their waitress lays down a coffee pot, a jug of hot water and some thick blue cups and saucers. Anna grabs for the spoons. Jody holds her fast, and moves the creamer, till Kay has poured the scalding coffee.

'But why would he need to leave in such a hurry?'

'Listen, Jody, I've been thinking. I'm not at all sure about what you told me last time, on the phone. What your husband said about you needing his consent to take Anna abroad. My brother says it's not true. And he should know; he's a law student.'

She freezes. 'I don't understand, then. Are you saying Michael made it up? Surely he …' She looks at Kay who is tentatively nodding. 'Well, perhaps it's changed then, the law. But crikey! If Zé is on his way, maybe later we can all go to live in Portugal. The three of us.'

'Can you heck as like. You don't get it, do you? If he's left the place illegally, it means he can't ever go back.' Kay is shaking her head, wagging a finger. 'Not in the normal way.'

Then she cannot stop herself from smiling, as her coffee swirls around her cup in the wake of her stirring spoon. *Even after ten years, I will come there, and I will find you.*' She is imagining being found. It'll be just like in the film. He'll be riding on a tram like the one that just slid past their window. He'll be looking out, and he'll spot her among the crowd on the pavement. But then she'll turn into a side street, with her skirt swinging as she walks. Her summer skirt with the gondolas. And Zé will jump off the tram while it's moving, running and calling out her name. And when she turns ... Except they don't have any trams where she lives, so he can't. So that means that he'll pitch up at her workroom one day. Just like that, out of the blue. When he writes — because he will soon — she'll draw a map of where she hides the door key. Otherwise she'll have to hope he thinks to throw some gravel up to the window. He will. Imagining the noise it makes against the glass makes her spine tingle.

Twenty-two

Spain

THE SWISH OF wheels over tarmac, many wheels, lots of raised voices. Male voices, shouts muffled by the damp morning air. To his ear, they sound French. French cyclists? What luck! They are bound to have a good road map. He rolls onto his side, so that he can see through the pine trees, to the road. There they are, at the bridge. Men in shorts and bright wind-jammers propping racing bikes against the arch. While he rubs the sleep from his eyes, they leave their bikes and stomp around on the verge. And brandishing water bottles, they slither down to the stream.

On standing up, he winces a bit. His knees are as stiff as iron. Last night he was loping like a man possessed, his sole aim to be a long way away from the border before dawn. He thinks he can hear Eduardo, and turns, but finds it is only the plop of rainwater from the pines. Then he remembers how, after waving him off at the station, he felt suddenly unprotected without his presence. So he just kept on going, thinking that Eduardo would have slowed him down by forcing him to take breaks. Eduardo will be back in Lisbon by now and setting up the evening edition. Of course, getting a splash on his hand was deliberate. And of course, he regrets not having been kinder to his friend.

He wakes up his circulation by pummelling his thighs and calves, massaging his painful knees. And then, on peg legs, he wades into the sunlight beyond the trees. The cyclists are setting off again, the leaders already swallowed up by a dip in the road. But as the last one cocks a leg over his saddle, he glances back.

'*Bonjour*! Do you have a map? A map!'

The cyclist returns his wave while steering blindly with his straight arm, and then, head down, begins to pedal furiously in pursuit of the others. When the last one of them has shrunk to a speck, he runs into the road to watch the speck dissolve into the horizon. He kicks a stone across the roadway and lets it roll down the bank to stop short of falling into the stream. As he watches the stone roll he sees again Eduardo who is pulling down the window of his carriage. And he shudders as he remembers that the train stops at Santarém, home to the Cavalry School, on its way to Lisbon. A soldier with his bed roll had boarded the train before Eduardo. And if Eduardo suspected anything of his conscription, he didn't show it. He leaned down from the window to drum into him the last instructions: *'Don't forget now, there is only one way across the river, if you want to stay south of the Tejo. And that's through Cacéres and then on as far as the bridge.'*

With that last scrap of information he can perhaps get by without a map. But there is something else he could have asked the cyclists, had he been more alert. To post his letter to Jody, from França. Or from Belgium. They could very well have been Belgians. He splashes icy cold water on his face and works the soap into his beard. It grows fast; it no longer irritates and with the shades it changes him completely.

While he brews his coffee and breakfasts on the last of Eduardo's biscuits, the wood begins to grow increasingly sun-spotted and warm. And packing up his equipment, he resolves to himself that he will keep to the cover of the pines. For one thing, these valley slopes are prone to very frequent showers. He checks his compass, and sets off.

The pine needles are soft underfoot. And when at last the old Roman town of Cáceres is spread before him, it is an architectural feast for his eyes. A walled multi-layered city guarded by a regiment of storks, platoons of them standing to attention on its walls. Some he recognises as the storks he spoke with after he crossed the Serra. He appointed them his guides and protectors, and they know it. They honour it by coming here to show him the way. He stands still while he mentally describes the sight to Jody, and imagines little Anna's excitement. 'Storks,' he says, softly. She can speak now, Jody said, and he imagines her lisping, Storks. But then another voice is taunting his thoughts.

'*You don't think it's just possible she changed her mind? It's such a huge thing for a woman to do.*' And if Eduardo was right? It no longer matters. He is gazing across fields, as far as the ancient town walls. To the baroque churches within them and back again to the hectares of abandoned orchards without. If this were Portugal these almond groves would be tended, used for grazing, and would be planted between the trees. It feels alien, this neglect. And yes, Eduardo *was* right, it *was* an enormous thing for her to do. Although he still believes she didn't waver. She will be there for sure, and he will find her. As he walks on he is steeling himself to brave what lies inside the walls. He mustn't forget to watch out for the Civil Guard.

To reach the orchards that surround the citadel he must cross the lunar white rocks. Boulders as big as circus tents are all around him, some with smooth mushroom tops. The territory is known to shelter many caves. He will search for a good one, so he can sleep soundly tonight.

Neglected growth has its uses. As he darts from tree to tree, he welcomes the cover it gives. The Moorish terraces rain down white petals on him from the almond trees. And he has never felt so exposed as when he makes his way up its many levels, towards a tower. It must be thirty metres high, the tower. Built to ward off foreigners by the Amohade, no doubt. At the gate he stops to brush the last of a white shower from his shoulders and to tease out stray petals from his hair and his beard.

Once he is within the walls, more towers overlook the cobbled street, with only alleyways between them. With what hostility did the inhabitants build fortresses against their neighbours? The old Jewish quarter is the closest to the wall. And in its passageways he thinks of Abel, Eduardo's father, and of the ancient synagogue at Castelo da Vide. Of the centuries of skull caps hidden underneath black hats. And how Abel was persecuted all through Eduardo's childhood. Not because of his race, nor of his supposed religion, but for nothing other than to maintain the power of the strong above the weak. He will stay close to the perimeter. All he needs from this town is to buy a map and a few provisions.

French voices? Again? Around the next corner, a tourist couple sit beside a brazier, beneath an arch cut into the wall. The man is fanning off smoke from an enormous black iron fryer. Farther along the wall, beside another arch, a scruffy recruit stands with a rifle against his shoulder. He pulls back behind a horse trough and watches, while the soldier ambles in the opposite direction. The French couple sit on a bench within the arch, eating something fragrant. He sidles up to them and asks in French if they can tell him where to buy a map. They are sorry; they are strangers here; they are only passing through. He buys a plate of chorizo with fried breadcrumbs from the trader, and eats it seated by the woman. Licking off his fingers, he takes in their bright anoraks with grouped badges sewn on the sleeves. Sitting there next to them, he hopes to be taken for a tourist. He should try to look more relaxed. The man opens out a map and, while he is offering some suggestions, Zé's finger sketches in a route. The better-known caves situated to the east of the city are marked on the map. But he will look for an unmarked one, a dry one, a secret one. And tomorrow at first light he will find the bridge, and then head eastward.

Since the night when he learned how rough it was to be an Early Christian in a cave, he has walked for twelve days solid. And now with each heavy step he plants on the stone bridge above the gorge, he draws nearer to the dream. The dream that led him on and fed his mind along his walk of a thousand detours. Throughout his many fruitless meanderings. To be able to see for himself the spires of Toledo. And now he is within a bridge crossing of the dream city itself, he can look down and see its lush terraces reflected in the dark river. He can lift his eyes to scale the pinnacles of rock that rise up from the gorge. Or he can stumble on to where the *Alcázar* fortress dominates the city.

Having gained the bridge, he is immediately pressed flat against its walls by a surging mass of sheep. Their fleeces and the coats of the hounds that slink along behind them are raddled with red dust. Their shepherd looks just as weary of goading them on as *he* is of his fruitless search for farm work. And he lets his vain hopes of finding any evaporate into the clear, ringing, intoxicating air. He shrugs off the all-enveloping cloak of wheat fields that was La Mancha. The mountain passes of Castile. The gruelling detours he took in search of anything, any work at all, just enough to earn a few pesetas.

In La Mancha he watched as men drove herds of black bulls to grazing in fields of blood red dust. And he knocked at the doors of ranches, where packs of chained dogs strained at him. And in the end, decided he would chance his luck as a street artist instead. In Toledo he will gain experience in the discreet streets of the Arab quarter. He must: he is out of money. One day along the road back there, he walked into a hamlet to discover that the inhabitants had no food they could sell him. So, from then on he ate the wild figs that he found by the roadsides, along with green ears of ripening wheat from the fields. In retrospect it wasn't bad. The figs especially gave him energy. And the natives told him how they stave off hunger by chewing sunflower seeds and carob beans. It will stand him in good stead while he is mastering his new trade.

Gazing up at the lightning-prone sky above Toledo, he wonders whether El Greco was in fact the first painter to notice it. And one day, while wandering in the outskirts along the riverbank, he stumbles across the gate and shaggy garden of the artist's modest house. He walks up the path, finds the door locked and wanders round to a side entrance. It opens onto a storeroom about the size of the one that served as his summer studio at the school. And, glory be, there are some small canvasses stacked against its walls. They are studies, small sketches of a hand or a foot. For El Greco's works? Really? He picks one up and feels the powdery rough edges of rotting jute. All about him is a musty odour of dampness. He replaces a small study, and stands mesmerised before the iron oxide stains it left on his hands. Red from the rusty tacks. After vowing not to wash the marks off, he slips out through the side door into a badly overgrown garden.

Next day, having spent the night sleeping under the bridge, he climbs the narrow twisting lanes up to the oldest part of the town. Where houses blinded to the streets have windows that overlook secret courtyards. And when he finds the church of San Vicente, he slips inside. And stays to reverence the *Virgin of the Immaculate Conception* in its neutral morning light. He is stupefied by the small miracle of a painted hand. And still entranced by it, he searches the streets outside for a good pitch where he can begin his first day's work. He will study that hand, to know how El Greco re-formed it. He wants to make his sitters' hands just as expressive.

He sets up his folding easel in an oddly-shaped plaza, which, but for its graffiti overkill, could be any one of the teetering squares of the Alfáma. He then takes up position on the low wall of a fountain and tries to look like someone who draws portraits. A few pesetas and little parcels of local marzipan start to tumble from the hands of dark women on an old wooden balcony. But before he can stand to thank the women, the balcony is locked and all he can see is vanishing hands. But what hands!

That the people thereabouts live entirely by exchanges, he has realised by the close of the first day. He saw cigarettes swapped for olives, fresh eggs for bottles of hair oil or books, and flasks of Malaga wine for the more intimate of favours. And as the dusk gathers dapper barmen begin to serve each other drinks, and stallholders stop busying themselves and eat their neighbours' produce.

By day, whenever he can, he exchanges pencil studies of faces and hands for lumps of hard cheese, which he lets collect in his pockets, while he chews on sunflower seeds. Between commissions he tortures himself with his unsuccessful attempts to reproduce Jody's hands and face. The commissioned faces crowd his mind, so his results become more elusive and frustrating by the day. In the end, he resorts to drawing her a dress. It will make her laugh.

Every evening now he calls in at the sacristy of the cathedral to make chalk studies of the drapery in *The Disrobing of Christ,* staring into the robe's deep crimson folds until they start to flicker. They flicker over apostles with chiselled faces, with sinewy arched necks and those greenish honed limbs. The capital would be better for earning money, he begins to realise. But should he go there? Ought he to brave the lions? Instead of skirting round the outskirts of the city as planned, must he now walk openly through the centre of Madrid?

There is money to be earned here in this city. He leaves his room above a cowshed, takes the ladder down and hands over a key the size of a spade. His skin is itching as he sets off through the building sites of its hinterlands for the highest capital in Europe. As he is trudging through its wide parade streets, its political squares, his old fears begin to re-surface. He looks around for cover. Concealed behind all the pomp, he finds a maze of narrow, stinking alleys, filled with beggars and ever-clamouring hollow-eyed children. He keeps watch beside a doorway while an old, old man dies. And later that same day, helps a young woman who is giving birth in a yard behind a disused olive oil plant.

Madrid: city of a thousand taverns, where the men spend half their day hiding away from the sun. Forever sipping pale sherry, or downing cactus juice next to towering platters of seafood. And just as before in Cáceres, or Toledo, he is instinctively drawn to the oldest quarter of the city. The scaffolded cliffs that rise above the Manzanares river where there is hardly any traffic, and the inhabitants are too poor to be going anywhere at all. Old men, content to amble up and down its slanted courtyards, chew carob beans and offer sunflower seeds to their neighbours. And he is popular. He is the only one that has cheese.

His first night there is sweltering. Nobody sleeps. Women sit outside and crochet and talk together on chairs clustered beneath the lamplit arches. Brushing away the fireflies, while they wait for a breath of air to come from the *sierras*. He sits among them, on his rucksack, and waits for the dawn. And thinks constantly of how they always had fresh air in Lisboa.

'*There must be a thousand views of the sea from this city.*' She said that, at the castle, while they stood together on the ramparts.

And it was later that evening that they were thrown out of café Nicola. *'Come live with. Be my woman. For ever, if you like.'* It had seemed so simple that night, as he stood with her on the beach, both of them huddled in the lee of the sea wall. Simple and natural. Uncomplicated. The logical solution. *'And the military?'* That was her. And now his answer to her question doesn't have the ring of truth it once had. *'My father will buy me out. I will ask him.'* He should have known, even back then, that those days had gone. At least for liberals like his father.

He can feel the pull of this city sucking him into itself. Paris does that, too, he is told. And no one is ever strong enough to withstand its centrifugal force. Madrid is hypnotising him. It is making him forget that he is there to earn money, while revealing to him a darker and more fascinating wealth. Goya's models, still living, still breathing, are all around him. And just like Goya, long before him, he starts to draw the beggars where they sit propped against the city's moss-covered walls. Or to rapidly sketch the children who crowd around him daily, rouged and powdered, and tottering in their mothers' or their sisters' high-heeled shoes. He draws the men who lead their asses to the fountain to drink. And in-between-times he learns how to hide away from the sun.

Before long, unused to sleep, he starts to forget it. And one morning, while out walking in a cemetery in the early hours, he stumbles across a stone panel chiselled with a long list of names. Forty-two Spaniards executed by the French lie there before him, all buried in a common grave. Suddenly he breaks off from reading through the list of names. He is startled by the sight of a large painting, on a canvas, which is hung like an altarpiece in its own make-shift chapel. Unbelieving, he checks the title: *The Third of May, by Francisco Goya.*

It shows an execution scene at dawn, in the very light in which he now stands. He is transfixed. Every line of the composition draws his eye to a central figure. The young man who is kneeling on the ground before a military firing squad. The soldiers are all depicted in shadow. The young man's face is sunburned; his hands are worked and weathered. He is a rebel, anyone can see. A rebel in a white peasant's shirt, who has fought hand to hand across the countryside, and now he is in Madrid. Napoleon's soldiers compose a dark, uniform block. And littering the ground between the young man and the firing squad, his companions lie dead.

But Goya himself was a liberal, a keen supporter of the French Revolution, at least at first. The commission for that work must have been awkward in the extreme. He turns his back on the painted scene. And he sets out to retrace his steps along the cemetery path. *At least Goya had a government that commissioned his works. And what a work. He left his own blood on the ground.*

While drawing in a quiet square in the cool of the early morning, a sloe-eyed girl arrives carrying his breakfast on a tray. He thanks her warmly. He is lionised on every day that he spends in this city. By the girls who come out to him from the bar and the brothel, by the shopkeepers and stallholders who keep him fed throughout the day and, in the evenings, by the barmen who cross the pavement to carry him drinks on high-held trays. And by now, he sometimes forgets, too, to look out for the evil sun.

One day, while walking in the streets surrounding the square, he starts to break out in a cold sweat. The sudden head pains are excruciating, then unbearable. He cannot see. He is convinced he is going blind, as he blunders off the pavement like a drunk. And he sinks, just like a fruit peeling, to the cobblestones.

Stretched out beside the cool wall of a fountain, he feels the beads of sweat erupt and trickle from his forehead. Someone must have borne him to the wall and lain him out in the shade, where the water from the fountain would splash him. There are some women standing in a group. And as they talk together, hands on hips, he strains his neck to listen. He catches nothing. A woman at the edge of the group turns around and glances at him before she moves away. And he drowses, at times shivering, while the world chatters and brays.

He lifts his head when, across the cobblestones, a young woman draws his eye. He watches her as she turns off the square and into a side street, with her skirt swinging behind her. The spring in her step. And then the turn of her head. A current runs through his veins, sending him electrifying images. Out of nowhere, he sees a summer skirt hanging limp from the rain, clinging to brown thighs. Gondoliers are running races round its hem. He struggles onto an elbow and stays propped on it for a while. But she has gone. And he remembers where he is.

Twenty-three

Madrid

ALL AROUND HIM is darkness, eerily silenced darkness. Somebody must have come in the night and turned off the fountain. Without its splashing cold water to cool him, it is hot. Too hot. Another somebody has been and covered him over with a clean sack. But he feels angry. His sleep is disturbed, always interrupted by the same dream. Hordes of people burst through the doors into his studio. And in the course of fending them off his physical strength deserts him and he panics. Then he wakes angry at his weakness.

The water trucks have begun to rumble faintly in the distance; it must be daybreak. He tries in vain to lift his head. Whenever he finds that he is drifting off again he fights it, and keeps on fighting it, to stay outside of the dream. If he succeeds or is just lucky, it becomes supplanted by a new dream. He is lying on a red carpet, but when he touches it, it turns to liquid. Jody joins him and lies beside him with her head resting on his shoulder. A counterpane of snow covers them both. He feels her breath, like a warm southerly wind blowing through his chest hair. On reaching out, he touches the cool marble surface of a pillar. All around them are pillars and, through them, walls hung with paintings. It is an exhibition in a sort of palace, with a green-uniformed attendant guarding it from a high, black horse. He recognises some forgotten early paintings of his. Other images that startle with their newness, although somehow he knows they are his own work, perhaps works yet to come. High above them is a vast, glass dome, a balcony round its rim. Ten-metre-long icicles hang down from the glass. The punters, all wearing ski jackets, are running laps round the balcony, their breath steaming like horses' breath, their feet stamping like horses' hooves whenever they stop to rest. Until they all stop and point downward through the atrium to the doors. And Jody whispers in his ear:

'A police inspector that I met on the roof promised he would find my painting. I'm going to the station to ask.'

'No, don't go. They will ask you for your papers. Papers. Papers ...'

The glass dome is reverberating. Sharp sunlight glances off the snow. Spears of light attack them from all directions, aiming for their eyes. He tries to shield them with both hands.

'Papeles. Papeles.'

A noise jolts him awake, the jarring noise of horseshoes on cobblestones. Alarmingly close to his head. All over the square the cobblestones are steaming in the sun. The smell of horse muck stings his nostrils. His eyes stream; clouds of meaty white breath burst over his face. A black creature rears up over him. Jackboots kick, stirrups jangle, studs are flashing in his eyes. *Why did the authorities let the cavalry into the palace?* Why, when they are the last people he wants at his exhibition? They must help him shoo them all away. Jody is calling back to him, as she turns into a side street: 'The policeman promised me he'll organise a search for my lost painting.'

The jackboots are kicking rhythmically now, marking time with an insistent demand that comes from on high. *'Papeles. Papeles.'*

A wave of strength arrives from nowhere, and he starts up just as Jody is disappearing round the corner. 'I told you they would ask for papers. Don't go Jody. Wait; I'm coming!'

'Papeles.'

The dreaded syllables echo across the still-empty square. How vast it is without the crowds. A monster gargles underground and, suddenly liquid retches from the fountain. Falling water settles in its rhythm. But his head is heavy as his mind claws for the last shreds of his dream. Cold water smacks his face. A club is staving in the side of his head. A shower of red sparks before his eyes. Sitting up now, he finds himself before a reeling green uniform, a giddy tri-corn hat, and one eye that won't stay still. The mounted Civil Guard is unslinging his rifle.

'*Make sure you stick your hands up before he unslings …*' His chest booming in his ears drowns out the echo of Eduardo's warning. He stumbles to his feet holding one hand in the air. The horse is brought to short rein. Iron horse shoes come crashing down, while the guard tugs off his gloves.

He gropes behind him for his rucksack. He'll make a run for it. But with this weight? Must he leave it there? Must he? He trips over a bootlace. He cannot stop to tie it, nor can he abandon his drawings. And those incriminating cartoons! As he shoulders the straps, sharp sounds come screaming from the guard's whistle.

The Civil Guards of the plains used to stare at him, confused, when he answered them in French. In the city it is the same breed of men, only wearing smarter uniforms. By now his fingers know exactly where to find his French identity card. And once it is out the letter from a French 'sister' slides out after it. '*Ma carte d'identité Monsieur. En plus, une lettre de ma soeur.*' They never read the address on the outside. He bends down to lace his boot and waits for the customary nod. When he looks up again, the guard is peering myopically at the card. *A fellow sufferer. What luck.* The guard keeps the card and opens the envelope, ignoring the address. And parting his thick, black moustache with the edge of the card, he focusses in an effort to decipher the letter.

At last he folds the letter into its envelope, shaking his head. '*Español empapela sólo*,' he says, and grunts while he waits.

This is the capital, the guard informs him, and its laws say that the papers must be in Castilian. Different rules. And better guards. Pretending not to understand, he puts out a hand to take back his card. But has to stop his ears at another searing note from the whistle, a note so long that the guard's complexion is beginning to turn puce.

A second guard appears from round the corner where he saw Jody disappear. The back-up. The back-up comes with a clinking harness and some sharp shouts as he reins in the other horse to a halt. As the guards confer, fat pigeons come to form a circle round the basin. The sky drops to an ominous low. Indigo, and as lightning prone as El Greco's sky above Toledo.

His watch says five o'clock.

Two *Grises* arrive. Grey shirtsleeves, gloved hands over holsters. One peers too closely at him and twists his arm behind his back, while the other picks up his rucksack. Although his legs are still a bit unsteady, his head is clear, and he knows the fever has passed. As he brushes himself, briskly smacks the streets from his trousers, he is congratulating himself for having burned those conscription papers. And Eduardo too, for having found such a good way to conceal the innersole. He decides that he will keep his mind on his destination, Pamplona, and lets the *Grises* carry his belongings and prod him across the square.

The holding pen is in a building close to the old quarter where he passed his time when he first arrived in the city. Through the bars of his cage he answers to their questioning in French. And left alone, he silently wills his jailers to extradite him to França. Thus sparing him an even longer trek and the climb through the Pyrenées.

The heat inside the station suffocates any worries he may have had of talking in his sleep. He sits down on a pallet and prepares himself for a long, wakeful watch. The two *Grises* arrive, unlock his gate and let it clang shut behind them. One opens out a card table and sets it up in a corner with an attaché case on top, out of which he takes an ink pad. The younger man having locked the metal gate, comes to him and drags him by his wrist to the table. Pins his arm to the green baize. It is a routine familiar to every Portuguese that has had a passport. Which means the *PIDE* posts along the Spanish border have received copies of his fingerprints.

The night is humid and lung-sucking. The Brigade Chief is intent on wearing out the hours by talking on his radio at a table by the corner office. Blowing down into his shirt front as he listens and takes notes. His free arm batting moths, at intervals banging down on the table. And so another day has gone by without his having added any new anecdotes to Jody's letter. This heat seems to stifle thought. And if they catch him writing with his torch lit ... The fever has exhausted him and, too weak to fend off the drowse, he succumbs willingly to sleep.

Glare. The glare from two torch beams is blinding him as he wakes. He flings an arm across his eyes and, with the other, feels for his glasses.

'You are a student?'

He shakes his head.

'You are a student. Get up.' The order pierces through the glare 'You think we like being dragged out from the faculty in the night?'

He half sits, half stands, all the time battling against the torches, while the men behind them are in shadow. Two men, both with polo shirts tucked into leather-belted slacks. Flashes from lenses, from gold teeth, from a gold watch. He is still pulling on his shirt, when they prod and push him through the gate and into another small room. Once they have him sitting down before a desk, they blind him again, this time with an Anglepoise-type lamp from close to the floor. A cracked face looks back at him from behind thick pebble glasses.

Franco's Brigado Politico Social? A faction based at the faculty? They can't be anything else.

'You are José Manuel Rodrigues Oliveira de Sá?'

Why bother to deny it? Why bother to answer this wily Spaniard in French?

For once his cleverly worked out defences seem absurd. Childish even. He clears his throat, while the room shrinks and a curtain slides across his future.

'Is it such a great intellectual feat to know one's name? One's nationality? Has the agitator lost his tongue?'

That again. Agitator, and now active internationally.

The voice across the desk is thin, but oily. 'You came here to make contact with the Spanish student groups, huh?'

'No, I didn't.' He waits as the man's blue-veined hand taps the desk with his fountain pen; and the taps echo from the walls.

'Communists' *tap.* 'Marxists' *tap.* 'Leninists' *tap tap.* 'Terrorists.' His interrogator sighs wearily and, having hawked and spat, mutters to himself as he unscrews his pen.

He shields his eyes from the floor lamp and hopes to hide

the fact that he is trying to read a paper on the desk. Upside down and creased from having been recently opened, words in teletype are pasted on it in short lengths of tape. What has he done to merit a telegram? Now a hand is smoothing it flat, and all he can see is the printed heading, the initials: P... I... D... E ...

'Before we decide when to escort you to the extradition post, we want the names of your contacts in Madrid.'

'I know no one in Madrid.'

Bored with looking through the names and photographs of men he has never met, or heard of, his thoughts turn to Eduardo. It must be at least a month since he last saw his friend. It is so easy these days to lose track of time. Eduardo will be fine; he always is. To think he risks his life every day. Rosa and Tiego also. And yet, none of them is ever caught.

Twenty-four

Santarem, Alentejo

IT COULD BE worse, he tells himself, standing to confront the cracks in the washbasin. Inside a small tin locker he finds a bible with many pages torn out and shreds of dusty tobacco. Whitewash is loosely brushed over some obscene daubings on the ceiling, just a hand's breadth above his head. But he recalls having paid six pesetas a night for such a room as this, at an inn above a cowshed in the hinterlands of Madrid. He will never ever rue his detour to Madrid. Despite the arrest and his extradition. He came home there, in Madrid. It is Madrid alone that can sweeten the bitter irony of having been escorted here yesterday, to Santarém of all places, with its famous Cavalry School.

Looking back on it all, he had a lucky run across the Spanish plains. Once his initial spurt had lessened, he began to feel vulnerable and terribly alone. Until he found his stride. The long, loping stride that he worked up to a day at a time, and that propelled him along the open roads of the plains faster than the mule trains. And he reckons they travel at about four to five kilometres an hour. The muleteers would salute him as he loped by them on the road. He was unaware at first that their fraternity would turn out to be his closest ally. If the Civil Guard was about, the drivers would stop him in the hills and carry him to some high, sheltered spot, where he could be hidden for a while. The same muleteers would gleefully mock his French act, when they swapped their cucumbers for his cigarettes. And they never failed to ask after the *pequeña Inglesa*. Almost making him believe that he might have news of her along the way. As if he could.

The mule carts carried charcoal, oil and olives, rusty old

iron, newspapers and gossip. The drivers were prolific gossips. He liked to pass the time of day with them before venturing into a village whose streets would be black with priests, while its taverns seethed with atheists. That way, while he caught up on the news and the weather reports, he also got to know the whereabouts and direction of the Civil Guard. In many village streets the children would be chasing piglets in and out of houses that reeked of wine and woodsmoke, and he could pass through unheeded.

But far from the towns and villages, Spain's economic miracle would roar through its outlying parts on shiny new motorcycles. Their fumes would catch in his throat. Car drivers would flash by too, leaning hard on their klaxon horns, desperate to arrive at an already-choking city. But the sloe-eyed muleteers remained outsiders to all that. They carried him through rocky passes in carts painted with vine trellises, striped carnations, gladioli. Every bit as gaudy as the *barques* that had glided past their ferryboat on the way to Alcochéte.

The sudden grinding of a key in his lock jolts him back to the present. A hand waves a sheaf of papers round the door. He takes one and skims through the xeroxed rules for writing letters: the prohibitions, the kinds of statements he *'can be punished for severely.'*

... *criticising his country to a foreigner...*

... *mentioning the circumstances pertaining to his arrest ...*

At least, now he can write to her, because he has an address.

... *leave the envelope unsealed ...*

What envelope? There isn't one. And if he doesn't write in simple English that the censor can understand, his letter will never see the mail box. So, what can he say that really matters? Is there anything at all that can bring her one centimetre closer? He searches every centimetre of the cell for a pen or pencil. There isn't one. Dejected, he flings himself on his bunk. What can he hold to in here? Is there a straw yet to be gleaned from his time in Goya's city? Better to ask what is Goya's legacy to him, and to every modern painter? Blackness. Solitude. Metamorphosis. Is what they say. Blackness and solitude he has aplenty. Metamorphosis? Would that be possible in here? Well, there is time enough to find out if he can make all three things his own.

The light from a bare bulb is scorching the back of his head. He turns away to face the wall. What does he amount to, banged up in Santarém jail and without a pencil to his name? Seeing them remove his work, his drawings especially, had made him feel like a traitor. That in itself is pretty black. But according to Lorca, all the colours are dissolved into and reborn from black. For Lorca, *duende* is the only true struggle.

He sits, head in hands, elbows on his knees, on the edge of his bunk, trying to conjure up that woman smell of her. Trying to get the feeling of her thin body in his arms. But then, in his memory they are walking in the Alfáma, which harbours its own odours that impinge on everyone that walks there. Something wonderful and strange had passed between them that day. Something he cannot name. A body memory of it will be bound to manifest in their lives. He will remind her of it when he writes. And he must ask her not to forget him. He doesn't want to be lost like that button from his pocket. It was definitely there before he came down with the fever.

They won't keep him locked in here for long, he thinks; they will want him for the military. Which is why he must write to her, to warn her. He wishes he could stay and shelter with her while they listen to the rain. Her black eyes; his black eyes. Her bones and her warm breath. His flesh and his racing blood. His long, melancholy road. They will never have the power to stop him dreaming of her.

He is agitated, and has been so all morning. The guards forgot to unlock him for his exercise in the yard. But at last he can hear the grating sound of a key turning in the lock.

'You are the only 'political', so you exercise alone.'

Ah, there will be solitude ... 'All right, but could you please bring me my pen and an envelope? I need to write an urgent letter first.'

The guard produces a pen, not his own, but one that has some ink in it. And he nods to the single sheet of paper as if to say, Get on with it. It pains him to have to write to her so hurriedly and with the guard watching him. Hopefully she will understand the situation and forgive him. When his letter is in the guard's vest pocket, he begins to feel anxious. What if he goes to Africa before she can write back? He could be gone within two weeks, a guard said, in answer to his constant questioning. From now he will be counting days until they bring him her reply.

After the close confinement of his cell, the large open space of the visiting hall is giddying. All around are other inmates, their faces larger than life. The guards escort him to a table near the front of the hall. The rows of eyes behind him are a collective gaze fastened on the vaulted arch directly in front. But who is this mystery visitor soon to appear? Who does he know that has enough clout to bypass the regulations and visit a 'political'? Perhaps the guards made a mistake.

The thud of boots from down the corridor is coming nearer. Through the arch a soldier walks and, at the first pillar, stops and removes his beret. And then he walks towards him, arms held wide as if he's carrying fire buckets. A lieutenant, from his grey leather bomber jacket. Creaking of new leather. A fresh face bathed in the sunlight that is falling from a high window.

'No handshakes,' says the guard, as the soldier steps forward from the pillar.

'Zé? Fernando Maia.' The lieutenant takes the other chair. 'You look different with the beard, and the hair bleached by the sun. We met once, with Eduardo, in Castelo de Vide, quite a while ago now. Perhaps you have forgotten? At the time I was at the Military Academy in Lisboa, but was about to move here, and visiting the folks for the weekend. I guess you were visiting too.' He sniffs the air as he glances round the hall. 'At least you don't smell the horse shit in here. What? From the agricultural fair in Santarém every May. But Zé, I promised Eduardo that I would try to visit you in here.'

'Eduardo? Eduardo doesn't know ...' He sits facing Fernando across the cigarette-scorched tabletop. He vaguely recalls a café terrace with a soldier's face against a row of houses with a mountain range beyond. His visitor's face is open, with a square jaw and a cool, level gaze. *But the uniform.* 'Eduardo has not the faintest idea that I am in here.'

'He found out, Zé, quite by accident. He came here by bus from Lisboa to collect a visitors' permit, so that his parents could see Rosa. Apparently he was kept waiting in the prison yard for several hours, and when a van came in through the gate he thought that it was you he saw getting out of it. He knew he could have been mistaken, but still, he asked for a meeting with me in the public gardens. He was blaming himself constantly, but I hope I put paid to that. We had a private talk, and drank some beers together on my way back to the barracks. I'm at the Cavalry School now, Zé.'

His blood freezes. Fernando knows of his conscription and his missed appointment. Is that the real reason for his visit?

'It's all right, Zé. I —'

'Hang on a minute. What was Rosa doing here?'

'Rosa and her husband —'

'Tiago as well? Surely they weren't — '

'Raided?' Fernando nods. 'From the little Eduardo told me, I think they must have been.' Fernando's eyes swivel, quickly taking in the rows of men behind him. 'Whatever it was, it must have happened not long after you left. But when Eduardo came, they were no longer here. They had been transferred.'

The guard has stirred and is watching them.

Did someone see him leaving Rosa's place? It seems a bit far-fetched. But harbouring an illegal can be a pretext for a raid, if they already suspect …

'You mean they've been released?'

Fernando visibly holds something back. Hesitates before whispering:

'They've gone to Caxias.'

'Caxias? Caxias …' He is struggling to take it in. 'Caxias … like Miguel …'

But Rosa and Tiago are so competent. They are discreet to the last detail in how they run the press for Eduardo. Careful not to arouse even the least suspicion in the neighbours. And

Eduardo's distribution methods are genius. Except he does work for *Avanté! 'I like to cover their production gaps ...' By production gaps he meant raids.* 'Caxias,' he repeats. Sheer abhorrence clings to the name.

'I know.' Fernando's eyes say the rest.

As the guard moves a step closer, Fernando clears his throat. Zé continues to question him with his eyes and his lips. Does he really know so little? If he only knows what Eduardo told him, of course it will be next to nothing.

'I was at school with Rosa in Castelo da Vide; she was in my class.'

He nods. 'I remember now.'

So were they stopped in the street with the *Jornal* on them? No, they can't have been. Eduardo does the distribution. Rosa is the editor, and Tiago handles the production. Did the pigs arrive in the night, break into the stable block, smash the press? He smacks his fist against his palm, grimaces questioningly at Fernando. Fernando bites his lip, nods despairingly. He can picture the amputated limbs of the press lying on the floor. But imagining its shiny black metal parts littering the stable block yard, suggest to him the aftermath of a massacre in Africa. Blankets torn from the rollers leave behind shreds of lambswool fleece. He hears the typewriter, sees it kicked against a wall. Imagines plaster falling, papers shuddering, cowering in corners. But no, they will have seized every scrap of paper, every article, every plate. Including the plates for his cartoons. The *PIDE* will keep them all, they'll catalogue them, list every damned thing. They'll know it all. His cheeks are hot; he is remembering feeling happy working in the print room in the quiet of the night. How it made him feel close to Jody. How it made him feel secure. The cartoon he drew there, the plate he made, the drawings he left with Rosa. Yes, they will have them all. And much worse than that, they've got his friends.

'Tiago's elderly grandmother sleeps in the room above the kitchen. Is she all right? She's very frail. She must have been terrified, bless her.'

'I don't know. Eduardo didn't mention her. He only asked if I could help you. And he'll see someone about your case.'

'I'm classed as a 'political', so I'm not allowed to see a lawyer.'

'Eduardo has a legal friend in Lisboa.'

'Yes, I know. He brought him to my studio, once, to see some paintings.'

'Anyone who tries to leave illegally is classed as a political,' Fernando says, beneath his breath. 'Eduardo has explained to me how you feel about the wars. I feel the same, Zé, but my way is to end it all as soon as possible and bring the men back home. Anyway, what else could I have done? Join the railways as an engine driver like my old man? I left the Academy because I didn't want to be an officer, but then they gave me a commission over here. My dad was a sergeant, a good one, I believe. And now my fiancé is mad at me because, as an officer, I'm obliged to marry someone with a degree. And by the way, you just forfeited your right to be an officer. You'll be a foot soldier.' Fernando's eyes are darting sideways again. 'I'm not far away, Zé. The Cavalry School is a few streets from here.'

'Do you know the recruiting officer?' He tries to picture the man's anger at his no-show. 'I think you'll find you have me over there for training before long. A guard said I'll be shipped out to Africa in two weeks. Will they put me in the medical corps? It's based at Coimbra, no?'

'Zé, don't you know they have penal battalions? And they're not just to threaten students with, to try and keep them on side. They do exist. You know what a rear gunner does? But don't worry just yet. You can't come into the military prison, if you're not yet a soldier. And the armed forces won't recruit you, while you're under investigation.'

'So they can't ship me out, yet?'

Fernando shrugs, and his bomber jacket squeaks. 'This place is out of my domain. But if you're being held without charge, it means that your status vis-a-vis the military can change at any time.'

That sounds typical. The guard has moved to the table behind. He leans forward while he can. 'Listen. I need to find out what has happened to my rucksack. I had it with me in Madrid, until I was arrested, when the *Grises* took it. Everything is in it: canvasses, drawings. *Heu*, and some cartoons.' He cocks his head to indicate the guard. 'Do you think he'd let me have my drawing pen and some paper? When I ask, he won't say where my pack has gone.'

The guard's bulk is now blocking off the end of their table. Fernando stands.

'I'll do my best to investigate it. Our time is up. Go well now, Zé. I'll come and see you again. And I'll tell Eduardo it was you. *Saúde.*'

'*Saúde.*' As Fernando's back disappears through the stone arch, he feels his spirits plummet.

There goes an intelligent guy, but what is he really? A private agenda concealed behind the uniform? A career soldier, but without any social ambition? Or just a young man thirsting for adventure. He doesn't want to leave the men behind and, yet — he will surely go farther than any of us have dreamed.

He stares at the vacant spot beneath the arch, and half-rises to see if he left his footprints on the floor. He is still staring, when a hand grips his elbow.

Twenty-five

England. June 1967

SNATCHED FROM the doormat as she sailed out into the morning sunshine, the letter pokes from the pocket of last summer's plain denim dress. They walk down the hill at Anna's pace and cross the road, again at Anna's pace, even though it means she will be late for her appointment in the city.

'Mummy go shop.'

'No, not today. Mummy goes to Manchester. And where does Anna go?'

'Mmm. Cait'n.'

Garden insects swarm in the rush of an early June heatwave. The Home Service mid-morning news drifts in waves across front lawns. In the city she will buy a newspaper to read about the war. These are worrying times.

Moll appears round the side of the house and takes Anna by the hand. Jody waves as she walks down the hill. Caitlin bends over Anna, shows her how to aim the clothes pegs at butterflies. Moll picks them up to use for her yellow Bri-nylon sheets. As Jody breaks into a run, she is thinking to herself that Anna will have forgotten Zé by now; it has been so long since she saw him.

She enters a carriage, hot, stuffy, and reeking of stale sweat. She watches how the light inside the carriage darkens when heaps of coke glide past, and listens to the other passengers.

'I thought it was about the water carrier, the pipeline, like last time.'

An old man pinches his trouser legs and leans towards the woman opposite him, his feet in black shoes with no socks. 'Nah, not this time; it's Russia what's behind this. Our

Kenneth's worried, and you know how he's never one to mither.'

The woman shifts to make room for the old man's tapping foot. 'Makes you wonder whether to start laying in stores. Myra is.'

'Myra's what?'

'Stocking up on tinned stuff.'

'A few tins of beans maybe, evaporated milk. But this could go nuclear, easily. You'll see.'

The woman pokes the man's knee and whispers hoarsely: 'World War Three.'

Jody pulls out the letter from her pocket. *Wow! A Portuguese stamp*. She rips the envelope, and feels the deckled edge of a card. Well, well. Leonora has got in touch with her at last. First she reads the English copperplate underneath the Portuguese.

Carlos and Leonora have pleasure in announcing the birth of their daughter Constância.

She repeats the name as a succession of green lawns floats past the window. She is trying to recall the day Leonora went out to see the doctor. She wore a rain mate, so it must have been the day of the big storm. The weight of memory forces from her a sigh. That evening, she and Leonora had their last real heart to heart.

'What's up? Can't you sleep?'

Exasperated by her inability to sleep, she'd gone into the dining room. Her small folio of Zé's drawings was in the pocket of her housecoat. She had spread them over the tabletop in the light from a small lamp, and was studying them absently when Leonora came up, making her jump. She can still see the little perforated sheets against the black polished wood, as much black ink as there was paper. She'd been identifying the common motifs: faces, figures, dogs, the moon.

'Where did you get these?' Leonora was about to pick up one of the sheets.

'Hey. Are your hands clean before you touch them? Zé did them for *me*.' She stressed the *me* because she wasn't sure yet that she wanted anyone to see them.

Leonora held a selection to the light underneath the lamp.

And then put them down. 'Hmm. There's no unity. Art has to have unity.'

'Of course there's unity. It just isn't obvious. It's something you have to feel. Anyway, they're only studies.'

'Yes, but even if his work *is* good, he's still a Latin, don't forget. And believe me, they're diabolical with women.'

'You married one.'

'It's different. Carlos isn't like that. And when I met Carlos, I wasn't already married.'

'I haven't got a real marriage with Michael, and you know it. I doubt that it can go on for very much longer.' She gathered up her precious drawings, returned them to their marbled folio and tied the ribbon in a bow. And sat watching Leonora, the little book pressed to her heart.

'I remember being at your wedding, thinking to myself, This can't last. You were in a dream, m'lady. You had broken it off with Michael once, and you should never have gone back with him.'

'Yes, but Dad refused to speak to anyone else who came to take me out. He used to hide in the other room until we'd gone. And when they brought me home, he'd be waiting and he'd say, "Engaged girls don't go out with other men." You're right. I should have stood up to him and not gone back with Michael. He doesn't even like Michael anyway.'

'Yeah. Try explaining that to Carlos, though. Carlos isn't just a Catholic; he's Portuguese. And you don't know what that means, yet. There's always somebody watching you here. They watch you leave the house, find out who you meet. And neither does it stop there. You'll learn.'

'Zé is Portuguese, too.'

'And that's exactly why you must be careful. You've still a lot to get through, a lot of things to sort out in England. It'll be hard once you're back there. I don't envy you. You'll see.'

Probably Leonora still doesn't know how right she was. And a few unanswered letters don't amount to the end of the world. No, the one she should have watched out for was Moll. Because of Len. He still turns the other way, when she goes by. He's even shut the door in her face. Ages it was before Moll would repeat to her his snide remarks. And now she doesn't want to hear the rest. It's all irrelevant now that Zé is on his way. He'll come here and he'll find her and it could be any day soon. It was bound to take a long time.

While the train is pulling in, she stands at the door and plots her shortcut to Futters. Her nerves quicken at the thought of her appointment with the childrenswear buyer. It would be bad to keep the woman waiting. While weaving a way past the station bookstall, she sees a headline: *JUNE 7th. DAY THREE OF WAR. WAILING-WALL RIOTS — Pics*.

She grabs a copy of *The Guardian* and forks up her loose change. And scans through the news without stopping on her way through the blackened arch. In the city centre an unfamiliar lull has fallen on the streets. Inside the store she takes the lift, waits on the third floor, for the buyer, next to a tiny gilt and velvet chair.

'Hello there. What have *you* brought me?'

Held up for inspection in those hands with long, false fingernails, her efforts start to look paltry. Pulled and twisted this way and that. Then scrutinised through red-winged glasses on a pan-sticked nose. She wants to melt into the carpet.

'You can do me one of each size of the plastic macs and the catsuits. To test the market. I like the frocks with the crochet collars. One of each size again.'

'But not the shorts?' She feels emboldened now.

'I can get those from Austria.'

'If you mean the *lederhosen*, these are not at all the same concept. These are Mod. The cut is unique.'

'Hmm. Who else stocks them?'

'Rockin' Horse at the moment, and soon, Liberty.'

'Hmm.'

'I mean the one in Regent Street, in London …'

She zips her new order into the pocket of her holdall as the escalator wings her down to Perfumery. White overalls and false eyelashes bow her through to the exit, where a porter with a, Thank-you Madam, sees her out onto the street. No one is selling hot salt beef sandwiches today, so she goes to Joe Lyons for a Welsh rarebit and a cup of tea. She turns the pages of the newspaper. They are crammed with pictures of soldiers. *Thank goodness Zé isn't out there.* Now she has a new order in her bag, her luck seems to be turning. He won't be long now; she is sure.

The atmosphere in Bernie's leather warehouse today is electric. She tiptoes across to the huddle of men gathered at the counter with their attention glued to the wireless. Some have their brown store coats on, while others dressed for the sabbath in dark suits stand feet apart, rotating their Homburgs against their waistcoats. The crackling broadcast in Yiddish comes across at fever pitch, but then fades in time for the pips that announce the one o'clock news.

'A report just received indicates that at twelve-fifteen today, Israel broke through the blockade of the Straits of Tiran. Israeli forces have taken control of Sharm-el Sheikh from Egypt. Israel now plans to open the Straits to all ships.'

Hovering behind the men, she wonders what she ought to do. Bernie, mutely and with moist eyes, has merely marked her presence with a nod. And realising that no business will be done in here today, she waves a silent accord and slowly climbs the steps up to the street. Her leather skins will have to wait. Besides, an unpleasant task awaits her attention in her workroom. A Pandora's box is about to spill her secrets and her sins.

Her trunk as it turns out had never left the shores of Blighty, and was found abandoned in a railway siding somewhere near the Welsh border. Months after it supposedly had been forwarded to Southampton. She has looked at it briefly. It was badly scuffed and looked damp. But she only lifted out her sewing machine and checked its moving parts for rust. Now she must unpack the rest. Her precious art book will be inside it, a shoebox full of letters too. She hopes the ink isn't smudged, or worse, hasn't been obliterated by the damp.

In the station she finds an empty bench, on which to wait for her train home. She is trying to remember who it was that took her last letter to the post. Someone must have, because she was confined to bed. *It can't have reached him, can it? He would have answered; he would have told me of his plans to leave.* Instead, she had to hear the news from Kay. She is trying to recall the part that Moll had played. Had she come to visit …?

Her train is in, and is waiting. The carriage, though empty, is even hotter than on the train that brought her into the city. She takes a window seat beneath a ventilator, but very soon dozes off. On waking, she feels heavy from having slept in the sun. Her legs are a dead weight. But so is her memory. She stands, brushes down her skirt, and braces herself against the rocking train. She leaves the paper on her seat. There is nothing in it but war.

Letting herself into the empty shop, she treads on a letter. And no, the envelope is thick and white, so it won't be from him, in spite of the suspension bridge on the stamp. She sleeves away her footprint from the seal on the envelope, and waits until she is upstairs and walking to her bench before she opens it.

Pénitencia Distrital de Santarém. The address shocks her; it sounds like a prison.

Santarém? Is that an island? So, it is from Zé after all, even though the handwriting is unusually large and clear for him. But never mind why. It makes it easier to read through her tears.

My dear Jody,

You see from the address that I am prisoner here. I went to the boat and returned home deeply depressed. A delayed letter arrived, and in it, you wrote that you would come.

I --- (erased) ---(erased) to England. I walked through the mountains and in Spain, but in Madrid, ---(erased) ---(erased) ---(erased). I was in Spanish prison two weeks. I am now in Santarém prison. Please, Jody, write back quickly, please. In two weeks, I go to Africa to fight.

My love, José.

She has to read it through a few times before she can grasp what has happened. Then her intuition is telling her that the letter trembling in her hands is going to mark her for ever. She takes it over to the window and tries to make out the date. She can be sure of one thing only: that it was more than a week ago. And with the five days it will take for her reply to reach him in Portugal —— she must hurry. She must write back this minute.

There is no time to lose.

She cranes her neck to see the time on the station clock across the street. Still an hour until the last post. One hour including the walk. Where's her pen? A pencil will do. She only has a pad of tracing paper. Hot tears are blinding her. What can she say? She still doesn't know whether he received her last letter. She suspects not.

Dearest Zé,

I am really, really sorry at your dreadful news. If you received my last letter, which I now doubt, it will have reached you after you went to meet me from the boat. Believe me, it couldn't be helped. I had to wait for someone to post it. And I thought you were too angry to bother with me any more.

Her pencil point snaps. She is thinking while she goes in search of the Stanley knife.

I was waiting for the taxi to come ...

NO. She stops writing. She has filled an A3 sheet, but with nothing that he needs to know, nor with anything she wants to say. The sky outside has filled with scudding clouds that are advancing like marching armies. She tears off the sheet, throws it in the bin. Now to try again.

My dearest Zé,

Thank you for your letter. I am replying by return. I am devastated to hear you are stuck in that prison. I was so happy, when Kay told me you were coming. Were you coming here to see me? Did you still want to be with me? I could hardly believe it. I've looked out for you every day. And now, whatever happens now, I want you to know I haven't stopped loving you. I never shall. If you want to, we can still be together one day. Please keep writing.

I plan to leave my husband and go to London, where I have friends. But I need to make sure I'm not prevented, like before, so I'm telling no one. Only you. Maybe I can come to Africa. I'd like that. I'll ask at your embassy in London, if it is allowed. I need to look at some maps. I was never good at geography. Please send me your address in Africa and try to write before you leave. I am so, so sorry that I had to let you down.

Stay safe for us both. I love you always.

Jody xxx

She races up the road and over the zebra crossing to the

main Post Office. The clerk dips behind the counter, finds her a big manila envelope, which he crosses in blue crayon.

'When's the last collection, please?'

'Six o'clock.'

Phew! Now for her address on the back. She adds a kiss for good luck and waits until the clerk has dropped it in the sack. From a kiosk, she phones Moll.

'I'm delayed. I'll be late back. Can Anna please stay with you for another hour? Sure? Thanks a lot.'

She has less than an hour to unpack the trunk. On lifting the lid, the odour of mildew is overpowering. The bolts of cloth feel damp; the coldness of them makes her spirits sink. She is imagining Zé in prison. He'll be nervous; he'll be chain smoking till they come to take him to the jungle. Zé in camouflage fatigues like the ones the soldiers wear, in the paper. It's unreal.

Unwinding a forgotten length of 1930s green satin, she is reminded of how she packed it thinking it would make a dress for her, for a special occasion. Yard on yard she spools out around the room, loops it over chairs, along her bench, using any prop that she can quickly lay a hand on to weigh it down. She is quick to empty the rest, but even so, the memories keep surfacing. And something keeps making her cough. She checks for mould spots on the silk, on the Madras, and closely on the paisley. Finding none, she begins to lift out books with buckled pages. His drawings were safe, as were her templates, because she wrapped them in the plastic sewing machine cover. Pocketing her keys, she perches on her stool and smokes a menthol cigarette.

When she arrives home with Anna they find Michael waiting in the living room. She had forgotten that his shift changed today.

'My dinner? It was very nice.'

Well, at least, he's trying. While he is putting on his jacket and tie, ready to go out, he talks to Anna. And then, with his hand on the door handle, turns to her.

'Your mother says you shouldn't hang that nude print over the fireplace, when there's a little girl in the house.'

'Well, this is not my mother's house.'

'No, but I agree.'

'It's not a nude. It's a caryatid. They're sculptures; they're made of stone.'

The slamming of the door resounds in her ears. Anna chews on a rusk, while she butters bread and cuts it into soldiers. And while Anna dips them in her egg, she takes down the Modigliani print.

'What do you think, Anna?'

'Mummy.' Anna points an eggy finger at the glass.

A new print slides easily from its tube and into the frame. Picasso's *Paulo Dressed as Harlequin*. They can't object to that. 'Look at this little boy in a cocked hat. He's called Paulo. Do you remember Paulo?'

'Pau-o gone.'

She likes to pass the long summer evenings with the curtains open wide, the sound of Anna's breathing seeping through the wall. Tonight the lambent light has reached its most beautiful by the time that Big Ben strikes nine o'clock. And then the newscaster's voice adopts a sepulchral tone.

Jordan has accepted the United Nations ceasefire agreement. Israeli troops advanced across Sinai to the Suez Canal and captured the Egyptian fortress of Sharm el Sheikh. Throughout the day Syria has continued its shelling of Israel's northern communities.'

Casualties in the thousands on both sides. Whatever can it be like to be a soldier in a war on foreign soil? She knows the countries of Middle East from the diagrams in the newspapers. Everybody does now. But where exactly is Santarém?

Twenty-six

A BALMY DAY in early June. A bleached, melancholy lane. He stands before its only building, a detached single-storey house built with its back against the prison wall. Beyond the high wall, a great metal dome glitters in the sunlight. An unhinged gate, a shaggy lawn, and rust streaking from the padlocked shutters, all suggest that this 'gingerbread house' has long remained unoccupied.

Blocked between his two minders, he watches as a third agent wrestles with the rusty lock. *Take as long as you like,* he thinks. And while he still can, he throws a glance to the top of the lane, where it meets the *avenida*. One or two neighbours stare down from the second floor of an apartment block. He wonders what they say among themselves about the little house, all alone and neglected in the narrow dead-end street. Have they guessed? They must have. Do they refer to it as the *Olho de Judas?* As the interrogation centre for the Santarém branch of the *PIDE?*

A chill pervades the bare room dimly lit by a naked bulb. His back to the shutter traps the only ray of sunlight that leaks through. A desk light clicks on and, as its beam swivels, it momentarily settles on a heap of canvas. The joy, and then the stab of fear. His rucksack is leaning opened against the end of the desk.

All the work he brought with him is in it, or was. The canvasses, a few folios, some small notebooks half-filled. The cartoons! He quickly tries to spot some perforated edges peeping out from between the printed papers on the agent's desktop. Are these people capable of reading captions written in French? Of course they are, but they'll have to read them backwards, so they'll need a mirror. He didn't stay at Rosa's long enough to pull the proofs himself from his plate. And even if the local *PIDE* seized the plates, none bore his mark. Neither do they know his style. But the drawings in that rucksack on the floor — he can't deny that they are his.

'Stand!'

He is standing already, but in answer to the bark, pulls his shoulders back. Immediately one of the minders starts to rummage through his pockets, while the other tips out the contents of his rucksack behind the desk. And the obese one begins to drone from a printed sheet.

'*Primeiro: French identity card in the name of Pierre Marcel de Laon of Toulouse, França. The card, being the property of a person other than the detainee, is appropriated together with a letter addressed to one, Francine de Laon, sister of the above and also resident of Toulouse.*'

His mind is making mental photofits of the unknown French siblings, while preparing him to think on his feet. But what is this now? He burned those conscription papers ...

'*Segundo: Pages one and two of an order signed by the military governor of Lisboa, for the detainee to present himself at the Escola Prática de Cavalaria in Santarém at five o'clock on the twenty-first of March nineteen sixty-seven. The detainee is urged to enrol on the course for recruits and to undertake the training.*'

Merda! He stares at the familiar-looking copies in the flabby hands.

'*Supplementary to the order: notice to the conscript that failure to comply with the terms of the above order will lead to his being tried for having broken military law.*'

So I will at least get a trial.

The monotonous voice is drowned out by the thunder of a jet. And he prays it is the one that is winging her reply from England ...

'*Terceiro: travel warrant for a single journey from Lisboa to Santarém.* Sign here.'

Without so much as a curse, he picks up the pen that is placed in front of him. And as he signs under the names of the three agents, his hand shakes. Is there anything else? Anything he forgot?

'And here. Sign.'

'I haven't read it yet.'

'Read it now, while you sign.'

This typed statement on yellow-squared paper reads oddly. There are mistakes in the Portuguese. He stares at his supposed admission:

... that *he crossed the border illegally with the sole aim of avoiding military service in Portugal.*

And the reason they say he gave:

... '*that he could not leave by the legal route because he no longer has a passport.*'

'Sign.'

A blow to the back of his neck throws him up against the edge of the desk, winding him, searing him in half. His scalp is on fire; his hair is trapped in a clamp. A rustle and much cursing rise from the floor somewhere near his feet.

'Sign!'

He manages to do so in a very spidery script. Now it is agent Da Costa's turn to read.

A lot of mumbling and shuffling behind the desk is followed by a ritual of stamping, signing and passing papers between them. '*Arguido.*' '*Arguido.*' Someone's fingernails are digging into his biceps as he listens.

'The attitude of the *arguido* to his obligations of military service clearly indicates his allegiance to an illegal, secret and subversive organisation, which calls itself the '*partido communista português*', as well as to other illegal and secret organisations engaged in subversive activities, which attack the security of the State.' At least Da Costa, the obese one, is making eye contact now.

He tries to stare back through the glare.

'How long have you been a member of the group that calls itself '*partido communista português*'?'

'I am not and have never been a member of the communist party, nor of any other secret or subversive organisation.'

'You lie. As a known member you are guilty of involvement in crimes of attack against the security of the State.

Your eccentricity and misguidedness have been noted and must be isolated to prevent their influence from spreading. The *arguido* will stand.'

On either side of him the minders lean in.

'The charges against the *arguido are:* 1. exercise of activities against the security of the State. 2. clandestine emigration.'

The room shrinks and darkens. And straining to look back at his long-lost possessions, he is hustled out, down the path and into a waiting black Mercedes.

It is darkest dark in his cell, but his door has just cracked open. He is hungry, having missed his meals today, and somebody down the corridor is creating a mighty din. In the sudden glare, he finds his three tormenters filling up the tiny space and sucking all the air out of his cell. Pulled to his feet, he waits to hear the date of his trial. But then gradually he comes to understand that this *is* the trial. This, here in his cell. And they are already passing 'sentence.'

'The *arguido* is to be held for an indefinite period of incarceration under the regimen of 'continuous isolation'.'

He stares at the slim docket they have just pressed into his hand. His feels his heartbeat begin to race as anxiety mounts.

Incarceration order. Fortress of Péniche. The rest of the docket reads like a courier's delivery note.

'Péniche? I can't go there yet. I am expecting an important letter from England. And what about my belongings? My rucksack. You left it there at the house.'

'This is your copy. Don't lose it and mind you sign it on arrival.'

'Will someone in here forward my mail?'

Péniche.

Once an island, which the passing years have long silted up, the fishing port of Péniche is now the navel of a rocky peninsular, which is joined to the mainland by a barren spit of land. A sudden clarifying of the light that pours through the back window of the van tells him they are now crossing that low-lying, silty strip. And that soon he may glimpse the ocean. He stands, feet apart, and peers through the disembodied square of light. Across a great arc of white, sandy beaches. And as the beaches recede, he retracts his gaze and lets it rove around the rocks, down to where Atlantic breakers come crashing, and then fall.

In no time at all the van is rumbling through some double fortifications. The last time he saw their like was when, with Eduardo, he climbed up to Marvão. The little fortified town perched like an eagle's nest in the Serra, was a good training for his escape. He doesn't regret the escape. Better this incarceration than killing freedom fighters in Africa. Better even the tortures that will inevitably come than being forced by the military to torture other men to death. They are now passing through a no-man's-land of piled sandstone boulders.

He strains for glimpses of the harbour beyond a tumbling spate of small restaurants, amid a whiff of roasting sardines. Being sealed off, as he is, from the cab, he won't see the ancient fortress rising up from its promontory. He's seen it before, several times, from his father's ship. Strange to think that for centuries the old fort did what it was built for: to keep the enemy out by driving off landings of troops and pirates. But now that the country's enemy, —- its intellectuals and free thinkers —- is within, the old fort is asked to keep them in. And, in fact, it has been that way since before he was born.

Perhaps those fantastical, sculpted cliffs are visible today. He saw them once, through the telescope on the deck of his father's tramper. Giant faces, grotesque, superbly menacing in a fog. Fantasies in sandstone whipped up by the frequent storms. And often veiled by sea fog, which can cause the whole town to disappear in the middle of a summer's day.

Now the van has stopped, the butterflies are on the move again in his gut. He stands at the small window staring at a vast military square. A flagpole, a few statues, dilapidated public buildings bearing lines of limp washing. In a tiny yard, an old man is busily sorting through scrap metal, a small dog yapping by his stool. Then they're off again and edging through alternate darkness and light, until they emerge from the last arch. And the van stalls on a bridge. It must have been a drawbridge, once.

He cranes his neck to see, down right of it, a flight of mossy stone steps that lead to a dirty little pebble beach. And through a very low arch creeps the darkened edge of the sea, to deposit shreds of white foam around a young woman kneeling on a rock.

Can that be the arch that Cunhal used in his great escape? Portugal's most wanted man, kept in here since '49, escaped along with nine others on a dark January night. After abseiling down the walls and into the sea, they finally emerged from underneath a low stone arch. It has to be the one. The getaway cars could have waited on this very bridge. But even if it's true the guard helped them, the fellow will have long gone. Still, the arch may be worth looking into, given the chance. According to the press, a Russian submarine waited off the coast and rescued the PCP leader. And good for them. Rumour has it too that Cunhal made a lot of drawings while in here. Perhaps he'll even get to see them ...

A jolt throws him onto his backside, where he stays until they have lurched over the rest of the bridge. On his feet again, he sees a massive stone arch and guards running to its gates. Other guards are hefting iron bars, one bar between two. The engine dies. He is alone in the dark. The notorious escape from Caxias in sixty-one was another coup. Straight out through the prison gates in an armour-plated Mercedes that had once belonged to Hitler. The chutzpah! But anywhere, even here, is preferable to killing for them. Village massacres, Portuguese soldiers playing football with scalps. All in the name of civilising the savages. He shudders.

Bolts shoot back. The van is flooded with light so bright that he emerges wiping his glasses and blinking at his new home. A flat-roofed, entirely white building, bullet-pointed with small windows and dominated by a watchtower that could pass for a lighthouse. They bundle him past some Hortensias beside an ornamental bridge. The little bridge is painted yellow like the old sluice at Café Amarela.

All this must be for the visitors.

A guard leads him through a vestibule. A great din emerges from the open doorway to a medieval hall. Foreign uniforms.

Laughter. Dutch-sounding vowels. He catches one word only — *Afrika* —- before the guard leads him out onto a sloping courtyard with yellowed palms. He makes a mental note to come there again, if he can. Just for the tiniest glimpse of the sea. The guard stops him at an open door labelled *Salo do Governador.*

'Stay where you are.' A nobly proportioned chamber with an open fireplace partly hidden by the governor's desk. The guard hisses a simultaneous interpretation in his ear: 'The Baluarte Rodondo is occupied for now. You stay in the main penitentiary until it is free.'

'What's that? Baluarte —?'

'Place for 'continuous isolationers.' The guard speaks without moving his lips. 'One man only. Over there. You'll see in a few days.' He points along the promontory, to an outbuilding on its tip, enclosed by a high, inward-leaning wall.

On their way up an ever-winding staircase, he strains at every window they pass. But each one faces inward, onto the governor's yard. By time they step onto the third landing, he thinks he has grasped the layout. But this landing, apparently for *Delinquentos politicos,* seems to have no windows, only grilles. Grilles mounted on grilles and covered with double reinforced glass. Was that his last glimpse of the outside world?

'For today only, you are allowed to use the refectory.'

He slips on the white canvas shoes that he finds in his cell; they remind him of Jody's plimsolls. And he manages a wry smile as he stows his razor in a tin cupboard. A bucket fills the lower half of it, so his boots will go beneath the bunk. Absent-mindedly he feels inside his boots for the jagged edge of an innersole. And stops. Its absence is still a shock.

The refectory has the same white-tiled walls as his cell, but a great deal more light. He carries his bean soup and black bread over to a long table, where a lot of coughing is going on. The atmosphere seems friendly. They are all on the same side in here. At the far end of the table, a white-haired old man is fanning his throat with a postcard. 'The soup is scalding hot,' he says.

An old sepia photograph of the *Fortaleza* is passed along the bench until it reaches a man who can read. '*I am in this place I have no wish to return to.* João, have you nothing better to say to your woman than that?'

'You can add, Love to the children.'

'Why don't you tell her she can visit you now? We waited long enough for them to finish the *parlatorio.*'

João, the baker, keeps his eye fixed on the guard and says quietly: 'They've wired up the amplifiers so that only the guards can hear us and the visitors have to shout.'

'I've heard that,' says the scribe. 'Sur-veill-ance,' he mouths to Zé.

'It would be safer just to send a card. I spoke too loudly in a café once and now I'm paying for it in here.'

Zé suppresses his hunger for a while longer to admire the card. 'Can your woman read such small handwriting, João?'

'My boy will read it to her, or perhaps the stand-in baker will. You can tell I was a baker from this.' He taps a purple-veined cheek. 'Rosacea. And it's not from drinking; it's from blasting my face in the ovens every day.' He winks at Zé and then laughs when he sees him clap his hands to his ears.

'*Diabo!*' A searing whistle screams along the corridor. Their drinking glasses vibrate. He looks along the rows of men who are all covering their ears. 'Some fire drill,' he says inaudibly.

Pedro the reader raises four fingers, ten times, and then two fingers more. 'Forty-two times a day. Minimum,' he shouts in Zé's ear while dragging him with him to the counter. Zé feels him edging closer while they scrape and stack their plates. 'A dose of mass torture. Never know when it's coming,' he whispers.

The afternoon is passed in racking his brains for anything at all that he can use to make ear plugs. He must occupy himself and not drown in nostalgia for his old life. A certain afternoon is haunting him though, one when he was as well-surrounded as any man could wish to be. With Jody, with Eduardo, with his mother, brother and sister. It was the day after that surprise interrogation at the *PIDE* headquarters, and the painful scene with Jody afterwards.

He'd spent the morning with his family on the beach and, just before lunch, he and Jody had their first kiss in the sea. There was Rui's birthday picnic, and then Eduardo turned up. He'd caught the train out from Lisbon just to see if he was all right. It was the hottest day of last summer and the promenade swarmed with day-trippers, workers from the city. Jody had to walk Anna back down the promenade to fetch her trolley. While Eduardo waited at the café.

He went up to the terrace and picked his way through the beach bags to where Eduardo sat beneath a parasol, a wisp of smoke curling from his mouth, his elbow resting on a pile of folded newspapers. Bathers were shouting orders while cracking barnacles with their teeth. Eduardo pushed back a handful of that floppy black hair of his and smartly removed a magazine from the next seat. He looked pale, but then he always does; he tends to hide away from the sun.

'How are you, *amigo*? How's the back?'

'Never mind that. Anyone about?' He couldn't spot a single *bufo*.

'Only swimsuit police. They should be feeling good; they just reduced a Swedish chick to tears. What a job for a grown man, eh. But what about your back?'

'It's behind me, where it should be. Forget it. What are we drinking?' He felt the stripes snagging on his shirt. 'Jody and Anna will be along any minute.' He ordered cool beers and, like a starving man, pounced on the newspapers. 'Where's the Trib? What have you done with it?'

What he would give now, in this place, to read any scrap of international news from any old paper. He lies on his bunk and mouths to himself, savouring the repetition, 'Where's the Trib? Where's the Trib?'

'Here,' said Eduardo. 'There's only one small paper missing, but the last thing you need now is to be stopped and searched with that one on you.'

He waved aside Eduardo's words and began leafing through the *Herald Tribune*, his back firmly to the parapet.

'What's this? Are the Americans taking lessons from us?'

'They always have done. Don't you know that? Especially

the CIA. They make efficient use of the skills they acquire here, over in Brazil.'

'*Washington will cancel draft exemption for all students who protest against the Vietnam War,*' he read aloud. 'They'll never do it over there.' Eduardo looked about to contradict him, but let him continue. 'Too many students are engaged now for measures like that. The revolt is spreading through Europe. I heard from Gil; he wrote to me from Paris. It's getting interesting there. The students link up with the workers at the *Renault* plant in the city.'

'We've got *Renault* here.'

'And now *British Leyland* —'

'What was that about *British Leyland*?'

At the sound of Jody's voice, his chair legs banged down on the terrace. And when he stood, he saw that he was not the only man looking at her. At the white shirt knotted just below her ribs, the pink checked cap tipped at an angle, almost covering one eye. She lit him up from inside, that day.

'Eduardo. Jody, Anna.' Once the two of them were settled, he and Eduardo sat, too. And he passed her the centre pages. 'I was saying I could just use one of their vans to carry my paintings.'

'What? A Mini Moke?'

'Can't we keep talking English?' *Trust Eduardo to ask that, knowing that his English is fluent.*

Jody was shaking Anna's beaker, looking round for a waiter, but then Eduardo went to the bar. He explained to her that Eduardo now had his old apartment in Lisboa, that he was well liked, that people often said he was the salt of the earth. He didn't say he was unlucky with women, poor Eduardo.

'There's nothing in the centre pages, Jody.' Eduardo was back and handing her a grenadine for Anna.

'Yes, there is; there's California, look. Hippies burning their flower-power clothes and other psychedelic stuff in public. Why bother to publicly burn them? It's only fashion.'

Then they all laughed at the noise Anna made while guzzling her drink.

'No,' he said to her calmly, 'they make a statement about

the movement. The war has moved on, the times are changing, so some things become decadent. It is time for a different kind of protest. But at the same time, at the end of it all, life is still Man and Woman. Still Man, Woman and Creation.' And he swatted his words into the table with his rolled newspaper.

They seemed to get on well together, Eduardo and Jody. She told him how she'd made *açorda*, which led Eduardo to recite a silly proverb in his Alentejan dialect. He translated it and she corrected his English. *Heu*! He wishes now he could remember all the banter that followed, but it was a memorable afternoon. The world seemed more hopeful then. There was innocence. There was faith. There were still things to believe in, for them to fight for, it seemed. And to think that it was only last year. Eduardo asked her eventually, if she would visit Kay for him, in Nottingham. She said, Yes, she would, that she could take the train there with Anna. He looked happy then, poor Eduardo.

And when the sun was low and had started stippling the wavelets with amber, they saw the crawl back to the city was under way. And they agreed they would walk together with Eduardo to the station.

He remembers moving close to her, while Eduard went to buy his ticket. His need for her was so strong that day. The time was passing, and his senses seemed to know already the void he would need to fill. When she went home.

For tonight only he can spend an hour in the company of others, so he sets off down the corridor for the *Sala de Convivo*. He is gaining ground on a mop-headed young man who is walking backwards and, apparently, conducting a band that only he can see and hear. As he gains more ground, the eyes that look back from oversized glasses are assuming an intense brown. And then the bundle of nervous energy in front stops in an open doorway, and bows him into the common room.

'*Obrigado.*'

'*Senhor.* Just trying out a new medium. And heavens, why not? It makes a change from strumming all day. I'm Carlos. Guitarist. I used to compose on my instrument, but in here, I just move my fingers in the air and hear the notes in my head. The inner ear.' He taps his temple. 'The others think I am mad.'

'Zé. I'm a painter. And cartoonist. Or was.'

'Cartoonist, eh? I bet you're popular. Outside, they used to call me the man with a thousand fingers. And I need them all in here, I must say.'

'So you must be ... Didn't you make a film once?'

'What's that? Have you met Christo yet? You must meet.'

'Sixty-two, wasn't it?'

'What?'

'The film.'

'Hmm. Well ... You'll like Christo; he's a writer. He copies out all the books for our library project. He handwrites them very small, so you need a magnifying glass to read them. He sews the pages in as he goes, one or two at a time. His current passion is a course book for us all to learn English. He aims to make two copies of it, so the script is teenier than ever. You could do the covers.' Carlos shrugs, smiling haplessly. But then they have to cover their ears.

'He is a very good poet, Christo. He's been everywhere, well, everywhere they could send him: Tarrafal, Aljube, Caxias, and here. A truly well-travelled man.' Staring at the parquet floor between his feet, he lowers his voice. 'He was the last man in Tarrafal before the UN closed it down. The poor devil. Alone in that camp, entirely at their mercy for six months. But don't mention it ever. He talks when he is able. You understand? Now, what about you? Will you be staying with us long?'

Later that night, locked in his cell, he sits counting on his fingers. He is determined not to lose track of the days. Her reply to his letter should arrive in Santarém any day. So, the question is, how can he get hold of it from there? He picks up yet another censor's list and runs through it lazily. This one is more restrictive.

'*No mail to or from abroad.*'

And she is definitely abroad. But if he could just write once ... He will ask, if he gets the chance before the start of his isolation. Meanwhile, it seems there are some good people in here. *Diabo*! *That infernal whistle. It drives a man insane.* A key is turning in his lock. The door swings back. A guard appears. He opens his mouth to ask ...   But three men wearing shiny summer suits are pushing past the guard.

Twenty-seven

THE BALUARTE Redondo, round bulwark with tall, inward-leaning sandstone walls, has stood for four centuries on its own rocky promontory, relentlessly pounded by wild Atlantic waves. The wall encircles two sentry towers overarched by a single headstock whose bell has fallen and, silenced, lies beside a locked iron gate.

How long has he been locked in this cooling tower of a cell? Two days? Three? Three days of inhaling spores from the black mould on the walls. His wheezing is now a constant. He gives in to an attack of coughing, which reverberates round the walls, thereby creating a bond between him and the other sufferers back there in the main block. So that is three days without sight or sound of his one invisible neighbour who, supposedly, occupies the adjoining tower. Would they invent a neighbour? What reason could they have to do so? His meals arrive punctually, his bucket is emptied daily and a basin of clean water carried down the path to his door. The door to his sentry box, as he calls it; it is no bigger than one. Each time the door opens it lets in blinding sunlight along with oven heat and the noise of the waves crashing onto rock. The cries of seagulls from the watchtower. And dark guards with pursed lips.

'*Pena incommuniabilidade*'— the only words the guards will deign to mutter to him under their garlic breath. And when the door has squealed shut, once more leaving him alone, he reminds himself that the isolation will not affect him so badly as it does the other men. Has he not forever jealously guarded his precious solitude? The long hours, the whole days spent alone in his studio, often just staring at his work.

But why has no one come this evening? The hour for supper is long past; and his stomach growls like a predator. He hugs himself to try to smother it, while focusing on the ants struggling to lift a crumb from the floor. Standing up, he forgets to grip his waistband, and so his trousers fall in a heap on the stone flags. He steps out of them, scrambles up and stands on his bunk. By hanging onto the window bars, just about within his reach, he can haul himself up the wall. As he expected, the sun is setting, which in June means it must be late. It could even be the longest day. Through the window bars, a gilded sea is taking on a rosy copper. He stares at it until his eyes begin to water, and then to pain him. One set of toes finds and grips the jagged edge of a stone, while the other probes the mouldy surfaces for any kind of a hold. He clings on. He can make out a ship, a dark shape against a sea of light. A tramp steamer, is it? Count the funnels. Two? Three? What colour are they? He cannot tell and his fingers are numb. He lets go and falls onto the mattress.

He sits erect on the foot of his bed and faces the blank wall. Composes himself ready for a routine of his own invention. His imagined camera obscura is set high up between the window bars. It will soon transpose its view of the ocean into light, which it will project onto the drystone wall in front of him. There will be purple pillars, floating orange bits, and then the after image giving way to the world outside the bars. Wait for it; be patient. Something seems to be wrong this time. Why does it not let him see the image of *papäe's* ship? His technique must be slipping. He tries to smooth the new growth on his scalp, and forces himself to concentrate.

But now comes the return of his enemy: fear. The kitchen staff have forgotten to send out his supper. Or else the guard was hit by a wave on his walk here along causeway. What if he never comes? He splutters, which provokes a coughing fit, as he stoops to gather up his trousers. And then his thoughts drift back in time. Back to a frozen mountainside, on which he asked himself how long it would take for someone to find his bones. The oily blackness of the night, the criss-crossing goat tracks through the fog, with now and then some long-since dead tree. But then he smiles as he recalls the rickle of logs he took for a mounted border guard, until the truth gradually dawned. *'Hang onto that part,'* he tells himself. *'It can still see the truth.'*

Hunger brings wakefulness. Until at last, when he is drowsing, a blinding glare dazzles him awake. An indefinable smell, the fleeting gleam of cockroaches scuttering, the scrape of metal on stone. Then the torch beam on the latch leaving him in darkness as the door clangs to, and heavy footsteps die into the night. He devours his cold soup and half the bread. The rest he adds to the stash beneath his mattress. But before he can drift off again and well before dawn, the light from hell is back and breakfast is shoved in his face.

First light brings exercise with a guard at each elbow. Round and round the two sentry towers, staying close to the wall. Seeping through the wall, the gentle lapping sound of wavelets at rest. The black mould seems less toxic now that he can breathe in the ozone. But the wall leaning inward above his head is oppressive, and water pools around its base, sending out fingers of green slime. He looks upward to the small disc of light from the dawn sky, as a guard leans in from his right. He tries in vain to slow the manic pace.

'Mok-pax-gidip...' He tries to ignore the nonsense syllables by listening to the squelch of feet over slime. But the guards lean in harder and shout into his eardrums.' Answer me!' shouts a guard in anger while the other launches a hyena-like laugh.

'*They won't destabilise me,*' he thinks as he lopes round between the burly cretins with their flashing gold-crested armbands. His head up and his sight trained on the crest of the wall. He is imagining Lourenço, another PCP militant, knotting sheets together, scaling down the rocks and slipping into the sea. How, in 1954, could he have stashed that amount of bed linen? He had nine years to collect it, though. Nine years in that vile box. Years, not weeks or days.

But one thing went right. The dispensation he was given to write her a letter, before they brought him to his isolation. And even if she can't write back to him, she will now know why. And then the sobbing of the sea deafens him to everything except the echo of her voice trailing in the wind. And he is grateful for the mounting noise from the waves, as they begin again their daily crashing on the rocks. *There goes one; let it sigh awhile and wait for another*. Round and round they lollop, gathering speed, the guards' grotesque obscenities hurled into a maddened sunrise. Each time they pass the gateway, lights are blinking from the main block. Is Carlos awake yet? João the baker will be up.

He follows the jangle of a keychain along an unlit shale path, until a smudge of blueness appears out of the murky shadows ahead. The smudge becomes a clump of flowers, beside a yellow bridge. He thuds across the bridge, the guard at his back. Part of him can recall how they ambushed him while he slept, the same small part that knows this nocturnal march is to the penitentiary. An archway appears from behind a conference of black palms. He spins round when his name is called, but the guard sends him reeling into the glare from the searchlights of the governor's yard. He blinks at the sodium yellow cistern. He is desperate for a bath. And the tank won't be full of lizards at this late hour of the night.

Up three flights of stairs, neon-lit, *Deliquento politicos* on a sign over a door. *Refeitorio* above another. Can this be the canteen, white-tiled, deserted in the dark? Knives are ranged on a zinc counter, their blades all pointing at him. He hurries past, when he spots his old cell door farther down the corridor. But is it still his cell? He was away for a long time. The collective breathing of the men asleep in their cells seems to pulse through him. Their eyes would see through him too, if they happened to wake. He feels unnervingly transparent.

The guard halts before a door that he recognises at once, the one with its spy hole reversed. The door they would all hurry past on their way back from supper, to avoid hearing the muffled sounds of pain. This grey steel door, identical to all the others, is the *Olho de Judas*.

His knees buckle when a thin voice from within responds to his knock:

'Come in, son.'

He looks around him at a cell not unlike his own, if he remembers rightly. Except that here the three-metre length is stretched to disorienting proportions. The vastness of it makes him yearn to be back inside his 'shell', the solitary chamber he just left. Momentarily he takes the man inside the cell for an intruder, a burglar, or a ghost caught in the act of looking through a file. When he collects his wits, he starts to will his unwashed body odours to dissolve, or at least to go unnoticed beneath the agent's pungent cologne. He finds himself staring anxiously at a pockmarked Roman nose. Except for an old scar, the shape of it resembles his father's. But then the agent turns to a contraption that brings to mind a poor dentist's chair.

Strapped into the chair, he grips the arms and stares at the end wall. At the spot where normally the grille would be with its reinforced glass, but now has blank white ceramic tiles. There is nothing to hold his eye, except for a leather razor strop hanging next to the sink. And a dark stain like a giant Rorschach test that breaks up the parquet.

A spring clip snaps shut. From the corner of his eye, he watches closely his interrogator. In his lap lies a white envelope addressed in handwriting that he knows. And then his blood begins to crawl. His own script is on the paper unfolding in the agent's hands. It is his last letter to Jody. They had allowed him extra time to write it before they led him away. A special dispensation, they said. His eyes dart to a file that lies on the shelf. He can read the label: it says *Graphology Report*.

'So, you know a pretty English girl. Jody. It is an uncommon name. Perhaps the young *senhora* can tell us what we need to know.' The agent studies his letter, while blindly reaching down the file. He took such care to write succinctly in simple English, and now he struggles to comprehend what his words are doing in that lap. And he flushes to his ears, as he recalls how he gave it to them himself. He even thanked them for allowing him to write it.

'You can't touch her. She's in England.'

His words seem to come from someone else in the world outside of that cell. A draught blows across the nape of his neck. A footfall has stopped behind his chair.

'It was kind of you to provide us with her address. Who is Anna? A little child?' His interrogator, without waiting for an answer, turns calmly to the graphology report.

His breathing stops. He starts to panic.

'José Manuel Rodrigues Oliveira de Sà. So you are proud of your ancient family, and so you should be, young man. Defiant, hmm?' The speaker's eyes are like tadpoles; gold-rimmed glasses slide down his nose. 'Intellectual. Imaginative. Reckless. Independent. Oh dear. Sensitive, though. A ray of hope in an otherwise resistant subject. So, Sonny boy, we'll start with the polygraph. These are the organisations we are interested in.' A list appears from a pile of papers. 'Give me your left arm. You can read it while I take your blood pressure. You see, my boy, we already know the crazed gangs that you run with; your friend Miguel has told us everything. The lie detector will confirm his reliability as a witness. Sit forward. These tubes go round your chest.'

So there is no longer any point in denying his connection with Miguel. Ever since the leaving ban was issued, they are thought of as a double act. He makes room for the tubes and watches as his perfumed interrogator fixes metal plates to his fingers. The list of names is nothing. A lot of Ps, a lot of Cs; it can stay in his lap.

'I'll bring the cable over now, and then we'll begin at the beginning. How long have you been a member of the 'Portuguese Communist Party?' The agent crooks two fingers seemingly to emphasise his disdain.

The panel lights are out. The switch is off. Several hours must have gone by. His inquisitor is readying himself to leave. The other footsteps follow him outside. He told them nothing, so perhaps now they will leave him alone. But then the door re-opens with a draught and, suddenly the air is hair-oil sickly. Two thuggish looking aides make for the corners, where they stand poised, which leaves him to his torturer and the overpowering cologne.

'The night can be either short or long, as you wish.'

Wish? Can he still wish? He is struggling to stop something inside him leaching away, something he once vowed he would hold on to at all costs. But without recalling what it was. He fears he is dissolving into the chair.

The agent shakes out a *Camel filtro* and taps one end on the box. Then smoke rises as his ringed fingers run down another list. When he stops shaking his head, the younger and fitter ones leave their corners, their dark bulk obscuring the tiles, their heads brushing the ceiling. One has looped the leather strop round his wrist, next to a watch he recognises. Perhaps they count on the mere threat of violence to loosen his tongue. Or Eduardo was right, and they are not after information. But why the lists? Well, it seems, either way he escapes a beating for now. They are leaving him alone.

It is *his* turn to 'do the statue.' He was ordered to stand motionless at an arm's length from the wall; one fingertip only may touch the wall. Just as in the children's games. Even the littlest ones know how to play *pela estate* in the streets of the Alentejo, while chanting, *Viva Sálazar! But do they know it as the long favoured torture method of the PIDE? The children hear the stories first.* Of grown-ups forced to do the statue for days or weeks without sleeping. Of men's genitals nailed to the wall, if they fall asleep standing. He should have listened to them instead of telling them to stop; they were right. His reflection mocks him from the wall tiles as he tugs the hem of his shirt. *Why are they cut so short?*

So, they have gone and left him with the threat resounding in his ear. 'Don't fall asleep, or else…' The back pain comes first. He was expecting it, but nowhere near as bad as this. And the effort it takes to think of anything beyond his bodily needs and functions and the whereabouts of his trousers, is enough to kill him from exhaustion. At intervals the door will open, a voice will refill his ear:

'You must be feeling guilty, if you flinch before I've said a word.' But soon the voice is gone and he is left with only the smell of toothpaste and garlic.

He shakes a badly swollen ankle as he tries again to resign himself. His finger, swollen and distorted, will likely snap from bearing his weight. It could last for days, this. A week or more. And what do *they* know about guilt? No doubt enough to guess at what is happening to his mind. That he is losing the battle to conceal his guilt from himself. That he is victim to a nasty, creeping paralysis, this inability to stop himself from abusing his own body. To stop it freezing into a solid block of pain. And no one is standing over him with a whip, or even a hammer and nails. There is no one in the cell but him. He alone is there to take the blame, to feel the guilt. The shame of self-harm.

One day, or one night — there is no way of telling which — two of them come and fold him back into the chair. His eyelids droop; they are sore. His head feels too big and lollops around on his numbed shoulders. Perhaps he can just sleep a wink before — A torch beam in his eyes. Slap slap slap and punches to his face. A volley of questions, accusations and obscenities, interspersed with sly promises and each followed by a threat. A short respite, but no time to sleep before it all begins again, with a change of face, new eyeballs and teeth, three heads in rotation until they all spiral into one monster head and pock marks begin breeding like germs.

He wakes to a dull hammering that seems to come from inside his head, which is rolling uncontrollably. And with no idea of how long he has been sleeping in his own cell. He lifts an arm, steadying his wrist with his other hand, and squints at his watch. Midday. But what day? And who strapped on his watch? He is still struggling to dress himself and feeling like a four-year-old, when a key grinds in his lock.

'You may go to the canteen.'

'What day is it?'

'Thursday.'

How long ago did they carry him back to his cell? He shuts one eye to relieve the strain of keeping both open together. And anyway, what is a missed day or two in here? This blinding pain will fade eventually, and his finger could straighten to become useable again. But what about the look of menace that he now sees in every face? That lurks in every voice? Is there no one he can ever trust? And will the memories reverberate forever through his brain? These relics of a mashed selfhood, his pulverised remains. And worse, what the hell did he tell them? He screws his eyes shut, and pulls on his shirt. Screws them even tighter when he bends to ease on a white canvas shoe.

And now the only way to the canteen means walking past that door. Hearing the screams of another wretch, in his place.

He lets down his soup bowl, while he props his tray against a table leg. And then he stands amid the cacophony of the crowded canteen.

'Don't bother to look for João. He was released when you were in the pillbox. But he didn't want to go home. It's the devil, it really is. Happens all the time, though. They almost never want to go back to their former life after being here. No one knows where he went. Perhaps we never shall ...'

'João? Who is João?'

He tastes the thick, grey broth gingerly while Pedro watches at his shoulder.

'There isn't any bread today. They must have put it all in the *açorda*.'

'Remind me to complain to the management, *meu amigo*.' A slap on his back shoots through him and out again from his eyes. Scraping chair legs grate on his nerves. 'I don't expect you to remember me, but I'm Carlos.'

'Carlos. Tell me, how long was I in there? Do you know?'

'In where, amigo?'

'In my sentry box.'

'The pillbox? Eleven days. They think you'll be glad to talk after all that isolation. Not that they are interested in talk. They can't be. The CIA tried to make them stop at the optimum point for that, for getting men to talk, but ... they never want to.' Carlos glances at the guard. 'They're wild animals, savages, incapable of stopping till they have completely and irreversibly broken you. Kaput!'

'And in there? How long was that?' He nods towards the corridor, but has to wait for the white noise in his ear canals to subside.

'You okay, there? You did seven days, man. Sleep torture, I suppose? The statue?'

But that infernal whistle is screaming out through the ventilators again.

***

They are reading out his interrogation report to him in his cell. He learns how he —

'was led to admit to his membership of the 'portuguese communist party' and subversive organisations engaged in clandestine activities against the security of the State.'

As certain as he can be that he admitted nothing of the sort, he nonetheless listens without argument to how —

'the prisoner will not let himself be influenced again or led astray by such irrational and eccentric ideas'.

He signs the paper thrust before him. The agents are already reading from another sheet. Did he hear that correctly? Five thousand escudos, against rising legal costs, may be exchanged for his freedom. What legal costs? With no lawyer and no trial ... But they said, His freedom. His freedom? His miraculous and boundless freedom? He hastily signs both papers with *Oliveira de Sà,* plus a mark to confirm that he is too weak to sign his full name. Three pairs of eyes watch him closely as he fumbles in his rucksack. They even hold it open by the straps.

On the other side of this gate there will be another gate, a huge one with iron bolts so heavy that it takes two men to carry one. But they are bringing him his freedom; and he is very nearly there, at last. The gate clangs shut behind him, as he goes to stand on the bridge. But who are these two overdressed men walking down the path towards him? His escort? He doesn't need an escort. They say they drove here from Lisboa specially to escort him from the gates. But where to? To the station? He wants to catch the train to Lisboa, yes, but only after a plate of sardines and a decent drink. But now they say they have orders to escort him back to Santarém.

The heat. He is unused to it. Sweltering between his minders, he stands and stares at the ancient gate to the famed Cavalry School. He forgot about heat like this, the kind that arrives in early July and burns you to a shrivel. The man on his right turns to him and sneers. There is plenty more sun where he is going, he says, and edges closer. He shuffles to let some air between them and puts on his shades.

The sentries stand motionless at their boxes, real sentry boxes, brushed with broad yellow and red chevrons. High above their heads a bas-relief depicts some great galloping horses in a cavalry charge. Behind his back, a dazzling curtain of water falls from a marble fountain, reminding him that he is in the Gothic capital of Portugal. The pearly city Eduardo reveres with his Alentejan heart, and yet hates as he has never hated Lisboa. The men on either side discuss with reverence a tank parked behind the hedge.

'You are joining one of the oldest armies in the world,' one of them says while giving him a sharp dig in the ribs. And then the gatekeeper opens up.

Within the walls, the *casernas* teem with perspiring young recruits. He tries to make himself invisible among the crowd. A young lieutenant is giving them all an introductory talk, speaking not unkindly, but with authority in his voice. But as for his words, and what it all means, it passes way above his head. At the close of the talk, he is left clueless and quite alone. His eyes are still on the speaker, as he turns and, with his beret tucked into his armpit, leaves the hall. And there he is again, through the window, pausing to tilt his beret. Readying himself to stride across the great quadrangle, his arms held out as if to carry two full buckets.

They give him more food than he can stomach. And he sleeps in a long dormitory, surrounded by men, which takes a bit of getting used to and puts him on his guard. Until, nudged and buffeted and ordered into a life crammed with activity, he is left with very little time for recalling the past. Until the day arrives when it is as if he never had one. Drilling has its own momentum and it sweeps him away, a new broom with which to banish both memory and pain. Discipline, the great amnesiac, purges his days. The nights can tweeze out a splinter or two, can at times open floodgates to unspeakable pain. But even through these nightmares, through the most intimate of flashbacks, a part of him gets the feeling that even they have been programmed. They have been set to drive in a wedge between this soldier and his former life.

Around noon, on a September day, with a strong *Nortada* blowing up. The crowds will recognise his uniform with its stripes as that of militia sergeant. And so will his family, if they can see him through all the heads, assuming they are not too far back. As he leads his men up the gangplank of the converted cruise ship, *SS Patria*, he thinks how it will be their floating barracks for the next thirty days. Until they dock at *Lorenço Marques* in the South of *Moçambique*. The stripes emblazoned on his sleeve do nothing to make this mission seem real. He walks as if in a dream through the soaring cheers, the frantic waves.

The Rocha de Obidos with its vast quayside parade ground, where he was many times among the crowd. And where, somewhere among the dots that cover it today, his mother will be watching him. With his father, if he is ashore, and maybe his younger siblings who will still be on holiday from school. From the corner of his eye, all is a sea of waving handkerchiefs. Eduardo will be there, perhaps with his sister now released from Caxias. Apparently she made Eduardo promise he would bring her for the embarkation. Tiago is still in Caxias, and she is too afraid to come alone.

Once he is on deck, and has dismissed the men, he can take the rail, and can gaze out above the joyous roar. Before the bass note of the ship's horn starts to drown it out with its melancholy. But when it does, his spine still tingles. While his eyes search among the crowd. It should be easy to spot Isabel; there will be a space in front of her, for her mother's wheelchair. He may catch a glint of metal in the sun, from something that could be a wheel guard or the handles that she holds. And he prays that she has stopped teaching illiterates in her mother's attic, and that she hasn't been found out. Is that her? It could be. But Armando is another matter; he is so small. So slight. All these hats and handkerchiefs will bury him. Perhaps they are together somewhere, Isabel and Armando. They were together, when he saw them last in Nicola, on the night before he left.

Twenty-eight

Paris. Late March. 1974

THE GREY Volkswagen Beetle crawls along Boulevard St. Michel. From the passenger seat beside her, Anna counts the iron railings of the Luxembourg, to assure her mother of their progress alongside the wintry gardens. A stray snowflake sails across the car bonnet, melting where it falls. 'It shouldn't snow at Easter, should it, Mum?'

'No, it shouldn't, love; you're quite right. But it does in Paris sometimes and it *is* still only March.' After glancing behind she turns to Anna who is leaning forward to the windscreen, her cheeks fired by a ten-year-old's sense of moral indignation. 'Stay here a minute, will you, while I nip into that bakery. You haven't eaten since we stopped in Alsace, and I can hear your tummy rumbling.'

Back behind the wheel again, she snaps off a piece of *couverture* chocolate, slips it into a split length of crusty, warm bread. 'There you are. *Pain au chocolat.* I'm surprised they open at all on Good Friday,' she says, feeling for the handbrake as the car in front of them stirs. But the cacophony of horns flusters her, and she crashes into gear, just as Anna pokes her hard in the upper arm. 'Ouch! Don't you dare do that when I'm driving!'

'Then tell me. Do they go together?'

'Do what go together?' She bats an eye at Anna's birthday present of an Afghan jerkin and a multi-coloured hand-knitted jumper. 'Yes, they go together perfectly, but stop pulling at the threads. You'll never have another jersey that will keep you as warm as that one. I've had to leave those lovely cones of weavers' wool behind at the commune. We always have to do that, don't we, love? Leave our things behind, leave people.'

Someone's leaning on a horn again. 'All right, I'm going.'

'When I go to see my dad, grandma buys me jumpers out of a shop.'

'Let her.'

'When I grow up I'll buy all of my clothes out of a shop.'

She edges forward in a river of steel, down the length of the railings to where they curve away off the boulevard and round a small square. A parking place becomes free in front of the church of St. Sulpice, opposite the Café de la Mairie du Sixième. A waiter watches from the doorway. She winds the window down and calls out: '*C'est légitime, non?*'

'*Bof. C'est semi-légitime, Madame.*'

Semi-legal? What's that supposed to mean? 'Right. A toasted sandwich for your lunch and a hot chocolate. Cheese and ham do you?'

'Yes please.'

'When you've eaten you can run around in the gardens. And I hope I can then find enough petrol to drive you to the airport and get me as far as Dieppe.'

'You have to. My dad'll be waiting for me in Manchester.'

'Have to? There's an oil shortage.'

'But I want to see my dad.'

'I know you do and I'm doing my best. Ooh, what a long face.'

Dark anvil clouds hang suspended in the sky above the old park. The light has turned apocalyptic. Headlights are blinking on around them, as they dash to the island in the middle of the boulevard. The woman in front stops to check for splashes on the backs of her tights. A small dog trots, nose in the air, through the park gates.

'Hold my hand. Cross now.'

'The car's coming.'

'Quick. We'll make him stop.'

Across the snow-dusted gardens, her gaze follows Anna along a wide pink gravel path, past the clusters of empty green metal chairs around the boxed palms. Then Anna gives a joyous wave; she has seen the model boating lake ahead.

Jody lifts her eyes to the stony white face of a young

woman with long sculpted braids that twist and lose their ends in deep folds of drapery. *Ste. Geneviève, patron saint of Paris*, is inscribed below her sandalled feet. A few yards away, *Marie, Reine de France*, is so small that she needs a higher plinth to stand on. *Mary, queen of France? But she was Mary Queen of Scots.* Her glance alights on a dimpled alabaster chin above a Tudor ruff. Strolling round the great crescent that forms the Terrasse des Reines, she is relishing the air she breathes, the air of a city proud to erect monuments to great women. *And just look at them all!* Men of war on horseback or stern, stony-faced statesmen are all that await her in London.

Anna liked living in Switzerland, especially in the mountains, where she learned to milk a cow. And so did *she*. It still moves her to recall the hands of an old, old peasant woman, who was glad to sell her a trunk full of Edwardian clothes. She's worn the long wool suit as it is; it's too good to remodel. She looks down at the black lace-up grannie boots that just fitted her, and the several thin layers of long skirts that billow in the wind. Anna liked earning extra pocket money with the beads she sold at the flea market. She smiles as she recalls her pride when she told the tourists: 'I threaded them myself.'

But in the wake of a referendum to reduce the number of foreigners, xenophobia began to assault her ears when she took the tram. So she walked more and, with her friends, scoffed at it, believing they would be immune. But those friends have already left, and now she fears the non-renewal of her work permit. She pauses at the last statue and tries to rally her resolve. Come September, she and Anna must have a new place to live, Anna a new school. Anna's going to hate being back in London, that's for sure.

Two impeccably dressed children are nannied through an iron kissing gate. And the clang reminds her that it must be about time to call Anna. But there she is, beckoning, her voice ringing through the frosty air. 'Come here, Mum. Look at all the little boats on the man's trolley.'

They link arms and head for the gate from where they can spot their little car. With all the luggage tied on the roof rack and a cord holding shut the boot, it isn't difficult.

'Can we keep the car, Mum?'

'No, it's only a loan to get us home.' They wait together at the kerb.

'I don't want to go to school in London.'

'Why not?'

'Because in Switzerland I was properly taught. My writing got better, didn't it.'

'Yes it did. Who'd have thought you'd like copying out rows of letters? We'll have to see whether you can transfer it to English.' The look on Anna's upturned face is tugging at a chord within her. She hates uprooting her, but everywhere they live, it ends in the same way. They have to move. 'We can walk from here to the river. But then I must try to find a petrol pump that doesn't have a mile-long queue. Cross now. It's nicer coming through Paris, isn't it?' She still feels nervous at the thought of Anna flying alone. It was Michael's idea. She takes her cold hand and squeezes it as they turn into the rue de Seine. She lingers at a shop window that says: *Librairie des Femmes. The only women's bookshop in Europe.* 'Look, there's a book about mothers and daughters. Fancy that. Ooh, it's too expensive for me. Come on, let's go.'

'Do they have children's books*?*'

'Maybe, but they'll be in French.'

'Oh, I only read Swiss German.'

As they turn the corner into rue de Buci, Anna sees a giant tunny fish flopped across a market stall. 'His eyes are following me. Mum,' she says, as they walk down the narrow street. 'Mum, is it true we turn into a new person every seven years? My teacher said we do.'

'I'm not sure what you mean. Your body cells replace themselves. And situations are meant to repeat themselves every seven years. Though I can't say I've ever noticed.'

'I mean, because now I'm ten, I'm all new again, aren't I? I'm not the same person as when you had me.'

'Let me see. Do you remember when we went to Portugal? No, you were too little.'

Spits of ice in the wind are firing up their cheeks and pinching their noses, as they shelter beneath an arch, their backs to a cathedral-sized door. Next door to the Russian restaurant on the opposite pavement, a tiny gallery has been ensnaring her eye for several minutes. Its half-closed, rusty shutters allow her a restricted view of some canvasses near the door. They have a feeling of authenticity, which is lacking from the sickening commercialism of the street in general. 'Shall we go inside, out of this wind?'

'*Bonjour Madame.*' The red-haired Russian restauranteur grins as they cross the street.

'*Bonjour Monsieur.*'

And then they dive through the narrow doorway into Galerie Almeida, where a small boy is playing in the middle of the floor. A slightly built young woman greets them.

'Daylight harms the paintings,' she says, indicating the shutter. 'Do you know of us? We are a gallery for artists against war. If you would like some more information, we produce a *petit journal.*'

'Thank you. I'll take it with me.'

'You are American?'

'British. You have such a small space here and yet you are hanging large works. I like that. People always think they need room to stand back from big canvasses, but they don't. This work is tactile; it needs to be felt. My French is awful, I'm afraid.'

'You do well. I think you like this artist.'

She looks around the walls at mainly reddish tones that emanate human warmth. And yet there is also stillness and containment. As she lets the canvasses work on her, figures form themselves from fragments, like creation born from destruction. 'It's got a special vibration.'

'You may be feeling what we call the *coup de foudre.*'

'The arrow in the heart? That's really French.' She laughs. 'But I'm no collector. I have a feeling, though, that know this artist, but I can't think who it is. It's funny.' More than funny, it is annoying. Something in this work touches her so directly that it matters. If asked where, she'd say the solar plexus. Slightly fazed, she walks on tiptoe through scattered plastic toys, and carefully round the little boy who kneels on the floor.

A long forgotten image has begun to stalk her mind. A painting that she can no longer visualise fully. But the fragments she can produce are telling her they once belonged to her. The painting that Zé gave her that she never managed to collect? She dreamed once that she set out to search for it again, and that she spoke to a police inspector on the roof of a high building. 'I will find your painting for you,' he said. She thinks he must have been a version of St. Anthony, the saint that helps you to find things that are lost. Dreams are such clever disguises. She moves round to a stack of canvasses propped against the back wall. She flicks through the top stretcher bars, letting each painted surface fall against her soft woollen cloak. 'Come and see the great big ones, Anna. You like that?'

'It's all right.' Anna shrugs. 'They're not as good as yours.'

She lets the stack lean back against the wall, makes it safe and turns to the assistant.

'She is always loyal to me,' she says, smiling down at Anna. 'This artist is dealing with human love, don't you think? Man, Woman, Creation. Procreation too, in that one. But the colours can be quite fierce.'

'I believe he spent some years in Africa. Apart from that, I can't help you. But the owner will be back soon. He works at the Herald Tribune and runs the gallery in the evenings. I'm only helping him this afternoon because it is Easter.'

The signature on a canvas by the open door is just about readable, though small and devoid of flourish. *Rodrigues*. Now she feels the *coup de foudre*, as they call it here, through her breastbone. 'Is this an old work, by any chance?'

'I believe it is current. The paintings in the shows here are always current.'

If it's him ... She steps back and takes a deep breath. *If it's him ... His work has changed, but then it would over time.* And now her voice is coming out squeaky. 'Do you know the artist's first name?'

'I don't, but as I said, my partner won't be very long.'

The boy is waving a model aeroplane up at her from the floor. She stares at it, then remembers they are on their way to the airport. And they can't afford to be late.

'Is he Portuguese …?'

'I think he works here in the Lot. So, wherever he came from, he is a French artist now. *Mon Dieu,* there are plenty of foreign artists here in France. Come to the *vernissage* tonight at seven and you can meet him.'

Meet him? She starts to tremble. She can't meet him! And Zé was such a city person, he couldn't live buried in the Lot. Rodrigues is just a common name, that's all, a really common name. 'No, it's all right, but thank you for the card. I wish I could. He's a good artist. But Anna here flies to Manchester tonight at seven from Charles de Gaulle. And after that I have to drive fast to catch the night ferry from Dieppe. In fact, I still have to find the petrol.'

'She flies alone?'

And Anna, who a minute hence was directing angry looks to her mother, stands tall. A warm blush betraying her consciousness of her role.

'Yes, she'll have her own special stewardess, who will sit with her all the way, at the front of the plane. Isn't that right, Anna? You'll be sitting near the pilot.'

The doorway darkens when a pedlar slaps down a carpet from the pile on his back, and lets loose a torrent of garbled French. With a sigh that seems too deep for her frame, the girl rolls the small woven rug back towards the trader's feet. And Jody seizes the moment to leave. 'Thank you. *Au revoir.*' She waves from the street.

They hurry to the corner, from where she stops to throw a backward glance at the ancient street packed with lit galleries. The owner of the Russian restaurant is outside on the pavement and is talking to a short, dark man with a parcel strung from each hand. He looks at her and half-smiles. She hesitates. She dithers. But Anna tugs at her arm. 'Come on, Mum. You'll make me miss my aeroplane and then I won't see my dad.'

When they pass the Pont des Arts, the same man is wandering among the tourists. Pacing up and down the bridge, his boots thudding on its thick wooden planks. And frowning to himself, apparently enraged at his own thoughts.

Twenty-nine

Paris, 24, April 1974

ZÉ CAN SEE just well enough in his van with the back doors open to secure his largest canvasses to its side walls with a rope. He wipes his brow on his bare forearm, jumps down to the street, and covers the floor at the back with a woollen army blanket and sacks. And then leaning against the side of his old, blue *Estafette transit*, he tilts his wrist to catch the light from the gallery window. Five minutes to eleven.

A wave of laughter escapes from the open door to Ivan's restaurant as Zé returns to retrieve his portable radio from the blanket, and twiddles through to Lisbon Associated Broadcasters. Then, to the sound of Portugal's entry for Eurovision, he lights himself a *Gauloise*. His exhibition is over; he should have known he would fall flat. But the night is loaded with stars, he is with his oldest friends and listening to Portuguese on the radio. Last night at the Café de Flore was almost like the old times back at Nicola in Lisbon. Before they all became exiles. All except for Isabel. He wonders if she still goes to Nicola without them. Probably. It was that kind of place.

'*E Depois do Adeus?* Is that the best they can do for you on your last night in Paris?' Armando has come round the corner from rue de Buci, and has recognised the song. He goes to meet him and they embrace in the glow around the restaurant door.

'Have you come to see me off, *amigo*? Eduardo is about ready to lock up. I'll crash at his house until around five in the morning. I want to make an early start before the Paris rush hour begins.'

'Are the Parisians so keen to go to work? The ones I know aren't. I'll be lucky if I see my students at Le Coq before midday. I'll come with you to Eduardo's for a while.'

Eduardo is behind the van, putting down a pile of small canvasses and wrapping them with the sacks. 'Hold the door for Eduardo, and I'll move this somewhere else.' Armando takes the radio and slips it into the cab. When the small works are all in Eduardo makes a last trip inside the gallery. The lights go out. They wait in darkness.

'Don't forget to bring my *livre d'or*,' says Zé. 'I want it with me in the cab.'

Then a noise like thunder has Armando covering his ears, until Eduardo has finished rolling down the iron shutter. *Armando's never heard shell fire*, he thinks, walking round to the cab and jumping in behind the wheel. Eduardo gets in the other side and lays down his visitors' book in front of the handbrake. 'What do you intend to do about it?'

The book is open at the page with her signature. He would know it anywhere, even though she now signs in her maiden name. If anything it has become larger with the years. And there is no address, just *London*. 'What do I intend? Travel. It would be good to explore London.'

'Yeah, and Jody Smith would be an easy person to find there. Believe me, Zé, I've tried every single Smith in the new directory.'

'So, I should just sit here and wait until it appears? She may not have a phone. Or an address, even. You should have stopped her when you had the chance, or at least, told me about it before the preview instead of waiting.'

'I know, and I've said I'm sorry, but it *was* your first exhibition and, like I said, I thought you'd go off to the airport and blow it.'

But they are moving and it is a matter of weaving through the groups of revellers that flood the passages of the Left Bank at this time of the night. The other two are squeezed together on the same seat and humming to the radio. Heading south on Avenue d'Italie, he sees Moroccans come out of corner shops to take their produce in for the night. While he waits to turn left into Eduardo's narrow street, crates of aubergines and lemons disappear into a *Minimart*.

The radio has changed hands. Eduardo fiddles with the knobs. 'I read a notice in *República*, at work today. It said the Portuguese population here should tune in to *Limite* tonight, on Radio Renascença, and I'm wondering why.' They are parked outside the little house where Eduardo's family is sleeping. Eduardo stops his fiddling and cocks his ear. 'They said the programme starts at midnight.'

Zé checks his watch. 'So why the silence?'

'Sssh. It isn't silence.' Armando peers at them through eyes half-closed, from where he leans against the side window. 'Listen.'

'Not me. I'm too exhausted,' he says, turning off the engine. 'That's a programme for night owls. And I've a long drive in the morning.'

'Found it. Listen.' The radio is on the dash. It begins as a low hum overridden by waves of crackling. As the humming swells it begins to take on the rhythm of marching feet, the form of words. Massed voices are joined in a song which, as it gathers strength, has them glancing from one to the other, perplexed.

'*Grândola-a, vila more-ena. Grândola vila more-ena.*' A sharp intake of breath inside the cab. Eduardo lifts down the radio and shakes it. '*Terra da fraternidade. Grândola, vila morena.*'

'Zeca! It's Zeca!' They all say at once.

Zé is still awake, but slides lower in his seat so that he can rest his head against the back. Eduardo sings along with the radio. It's no use; his spine is tingling. He joins in with Eduardo, lifting his voice and eyebrows to bring Armando in, too. Zeca Afonso's banned folk song erupts from years of enforced silence. Just like the old discoverers returning home to Portugal. To its air thick with emotion. To broad smiles of welcome. Is there a dry eye in the cab? His glasses are steaming up.

'Grândola is in Alentejo,' says Eduardo, with naked pride. And then of course he cannot wait to prove that he knows all of the words. All of them, every verse.

'*In the shadow of a holm oak*
That none now know its age.' And at the end he lets the tears roll.

There are tears in Zé's eyes, too. He only heard the song performed once, maybe twice, before it was prohibited. And the town Grândola has stood in for the song ever since, for everyone, from the region or not. Before he left, he might have said it represented the Alentejan spirit and the region's communist links. '*Revolução,*' he says softly through his teeth. '*Revolução!*' as he looks across at Armando.

'Or another failed bloody coup,' Armando, the devil's advocate, says. 'The authorities put them down at the rate of one a week at the moment.'

'No, I bet that song is the password.' At a noise from overhead, Zé puts his ear to the wheel, to see to the top floor of the house.

'Guys, you'll wake the whole street,' Véronique calls down from a window.

'Let them wake. They won't mind, when they know the revolution is coming,' Zé calls through his side window, giddy at his own words. He lets the others out, and stays behind to lock his paintings in for the night. When he walks into the salon, Eduardo is saying:

'I have a feeling about this. I think this time it's for real.'

'Hold on, old man; wait for an announcement at least.'

'The last time I saw Fernando in Castelo da Vide, he was back from a spell in Guinea Bissau. He said then that something big was brewing. Also that he'd be taking no more men to perish in Africa.'

At the sound of his former captain's name, Zé stands still.

'Fernando? I owe the guy my life. He wasn't like the other captains; he always did his utmost for his men.' But at the first body twitch he stops talking and distracts himself by twiddling through the wavebands on the radio. At this late hour, *Portuguese Radio Club* has normally taken over for the night. It seems there is a blackout perhaps. He yawns and pushes back his glasses. If there's a blackout, something serious is happening in Lisboa. He says nothing to the others and stretches out on the floor. A blend of low voices washes over him and then fades.

He shoots up, to find the radio speaker blaring in his ear. He was right. The station is occupied. Every other station too, if he can believe his ears. The TV studios, the airport, the docks, the Sálazar bridge. *Ah! the bridge is occupied. Meaning what for the Alentejo? It will depend who is occupying.* He lies so still for fear of missing something important that he shivers. His entire being is rooting for the soldiers, egging them on. The tension in his body keeps him hanging on, hoping beyond hope. A medley of popular songs is under way, when at last he shakes the others awake. 'The bridge is occupied.'

'What bridge?'

'The suspension bridge across the Tejo.'

'What?'

By five o'clock the three are sitting on the floor, focused on the radio while they each nurse a bowl of coffee.

'The Portuguese armed forces appeal to all the inhabitants of Lisboa to stay inside their homes and remain as calm as possible.'

He is stunned to recognise Fernando's voice speaking to him through the radio. It seems to echo from a far continent, bringing with it smells of burning, searing heat and scorched grass. Burning oil; charred animal hide; burning flesh … There was the time before Africa and then came the time after Africa. And the only time after Africa that matters is here, in France with his old friends. He looks up. Eduardo is beaming.

'Is Fernando in charge, then?' he asks Eduardo.

'Seems like it.' Eduardo salutes. 'Captain Fernando Maia from Castelo da Vide. I hope Rosa's listening. She was at school with him. Same class.'

'Rosa was an early riser, as I remember.' How much more elation can he contain? Forget about falling flat after the high of his exhibition. He is buoyant. Exhilarated to the limit. And yet, very afraid.

'We sincerely hope that the seriousness of the hour will not be saddened by personal injuries. We therefore appeal to the good sense of all military commanders to avoid any confrontation with the Armed Forces Movement.'

'Well, no one will take the slightest notice of that,' says Armando. 'That's the way to get packed streets. The city will be chaos. Hordes milling about, trying to discover what's going on, and not knowing what to believe. They won't know whether it's a putsch against the new policies by the anti-liberals, or a revolution of the left.'

Zé is imagining the Rossio square packed. He saw it like that once, and violence erupted then. But now Eduardo wants to give them one of his commentaries.

'Listen. I have it straight from the horse's mouth that the Armed Forces Movement came out of Guinea.' Eduardo sits buddha-like, with his chin tucked in, nodding sagely, peering under those eyebrows of his that still meet in the middle. 'The group of young captains out there were the core members.' Then the buddha rises, walks to the kitchen, comes back with a loaf of bread from yesterday and a knife.

'A successful coup has been waiting to happen ever since they asked Spinola to join them,' someone says. They are talking over each other, and joyously, like people just released from a long silence.

'They learned a lot from Amilcar Cabral in Guinea.'

'He's more interesting than Che Guevara ever was ...'

'Spinola really respects him, you know. It's why he wrote his book.'

'It's like Prague Spring in sixty-eight.'

'Except it's all Portuguese.'

Suddenly he thumps hard on the coffee table. 'Stop! We must all go to Lisboa. Did you hear what they just said? You didn't? A column from the Cavalry School in Santarém has got Terreiro do Paço and, so far, they are holding it. They're holding on!' He is shouting between mouthfuls of bread. By six o'clock he is hopping round the room, unable to stay still. 'The Santarém column is leading. They've already laid siege to the ministries and city hall. I can't stay here.' He walks out to the street, where the neighbours' shutters are still closed. 'Come on,' he calls, as he unlocks his van and slides back the cab door. 'I need my radio from the house.'

A sleepy-eyed Véronique wearing Eduardo's pyjamas, has just eased herself between his two friends who stand in the doorway.

'Here. Your radio.' Armando hands it through the cab window without turning it off. 'I think we should at least drive with you as far as the Lot, Zé. Otherwise you'll be off to Lisboa, getting yourself arrested.'

'They can't arrest me anymore. My leaving ban was annulled last year.'

'Only last year? And you've lived in France since seventy-one? It's a joke.' Armando pulls on his jacket and hauls himself into the cab. 'Do they want to keep you in or out these days? Or don't they know?'

Eduardo climbs in last, and they all wave to Véronique.

They eat their second breakfast of the day in a quiet lay-by off the *autoroute* south of Orléans. Each time a tractor or a field wagon rolls by on the side road, they lose a fraction of the broadcast. But it is better than missing everything in a crowded truckers' canteen. And the weather is so mild for April. Since they left the Fontainebleau forest for the open road they have been singing, with the windows open, to the passing countryside. And now his voice is hoarse. The wild open spaces are arms of welcome to his high spirits, as he chases the far horizon. Praying, above all, that this time it won't fail.

'The chutzpah,' says Armando. 'My God, the chutzpah, the bloody nerve.'

The announcement came as he was opening a flask of hot coffee. It made his hands shake, and now his jeans are soaked and his leg burns beneath the wet patch. If he heard rightly, then Fernando, *his* Fernando, his former captain, has arrested — yes, it's what they said — arrested the lieutenant colonel, representative of the government. 'Can he do that? Can he arrest him? Is that even possible?' He looks at the others.

'I like his style,' says Armando.

But then Eduardo is shushing them. There is consternation on the waterfront, it seems. He stops slapping his thighs and dancing around with Armando. They all fall silent. A military frigate has entered the Tagus estuary. It is under orders to fire on the city. On Lisboa. The others are sitting huddled on the ground, their arms covering their heads, as if the Portuguese navy's rockets are aimed at Orleans. His nerves are buzzing with the effort to divine what will happen next. He can already see a massacre, worse than anything he saw in Africa. Because it isn't just machine guns they are talking of. It's torpedoes.

He sits and smokes in the driving seat, one leg swinging outside, his heel making a drumming noise against the metal of the door. His amnesia lifts, and fragments of memory return from Africa. His tank has blown up. The men; where are they? Are they trapped inside there? Dense black smoke is mushrooming, darkening the sky; birds hit the ground; the bush is crackling; all around is a furnace. Blinding him. Choking him. His hair on fire. His scalp. His skin. A foul smell turning putrid; he wants to fight it off, but he must find a way through it, pass out beyond the pain.

Eduardo sidles up. 'All right in there, amigo? They're in the middle of a naval mutiny. Can you believe that? The navy refused to fire.'

'Thank God.' A juggernaut thunders by; he watches it disappear into an underpass. 'Thank God.'

'I'll say.'

His farmhouse is looking less dilapidated than it has done, in this wild valley of the Lot. Tobacco crops once flourished here on the ground between the walnut trees. They are grown too tall now for the harvesting of nuts. Armando and Eduardo sit at the table in his dark kitchen while he improvises lunch. His paintings are safe in the van outside in the front yard. Gazing out through the doorway onto twisted oaks and eglantine, they are tired beyond talking. Heavy smoking is by now the only way to stay alert for further news.

'I ought to telephone Le Coq.' Armando gets up slowly, followed by Eduardo mumbling something about the 'Trib.'

He is staring into his coffee dregs. All through their long lunch, Caetano, Sálazar's successor, has been holed up inside the Carmo Barracks with a handful of his ministers and the National Guard. At the gate stands the column from the Cavalry School of Santarém, at its head the captain with his megaphone is surrounded by and cheered on by an exuberant crowd of civilians. 'I can't stand this suspense.'

He wanders outside, carries in some small paintings from

his van. As he lays them down on a bench, the others are still at the table, speculating.

'He's intelligent, *heu*?'

'But why's the radio so quiet? Has he gone inside the barracks?' says Zé, turning round.

'I don't know. But an engine driver's son, and from Castelo de Vide, taking on the Prime Minister and the National Guard?' Eduardo scratches his head.

He goes to join them. Eduardo bangs the table with a cheese knife each time his eyelids droop. But he dozes off and, with the others, almost misses the next announcement.

' ... *Captain Salgueiro Maia, by means of his megaphone, has issued an ultimatum in the hope of obtaining surrender of the National Guard, and threatened to blow up the gates of their Carmo headquarters. All civilians must now evacuate the Carmo Square.*'

'It is such a well-loved building, the crowds will all stay to watch. There'll be children hiding under tanks.' His kitchen table is filled with bottles and overflowing ashtrays.

They conclude that Fernando has entered the barracks alone. And their debate turns to whether or not he took a hand grenade with him. *What must it feel like to be demanding the surrender of the Estado Novo?* It could happen. Nothing is impossible. Except Caetano has just refused point blank to surrender to anyone below the rank of Lieutenant Colonel. So that the power will not fall to the street. 'The power is already in the street and it had better stay there,' he says. Then, with mixed feeling, he learns of General Spinoza's arrival. And that the aristocrat formally accepts Caetano's surrender. 'It won't make any difference. The power stays in the street.'

'Do you think Fernando is with him?' asks Eduardo.

'With Spinola? No, he sent him to escort Caetano to the airport, I think.'

'Where will he go?'

'Brazil. Where else?'

When the announcement comes that the *PIDE* (now the DGS) is abolished, the sole response inside the farmhouse in the Lot is a stunned silence. *Abolished?* The notion is as difficult to comprehend as a sudden death. How can they not be there anymore? They wander round the kitchen repeating, Abolished. As if the word just appeared in the language with no meaning attached. He still doesn't trust them. *That last announcement is a hoax.* 'Abolished. Is that all?'

A faction of the old *PIDE* is still holding out at their headquarters. But then they surpass all expectations. From their window, they open fire directly on the crowd with a machine gun. Four civilians are killed. Forty-five are wounded. And they are still fighting on in Caxias. Until the paratroopers arrive.

'*Laws dismissing the fascist leaders, abolishing the DGS, The Portuguese Legion and The Portuguese Youth Movement, have been passed. The navy is caring for political prisoners, who will all be released tomorrow. The sick will be treated in hospital.*'

'What about reprisals?' Zé springs to his feet.

'*The Armed Forces Movement thanks the people of Portugal for their patience and co-operation. All will be back to normal tomorrow. Thank you and good night from Portuguese Radio Club.*'

'I said, What about reprisals? They're bound to turn on the political prisoners in Caxias.'

'*Nao,* not with the navy taking care of them all.' Eduardo's hand is on his back.

'I'm going there for the release. But haven't we all got friends in Caxias? Or Aljube?'

'You're right, Zé.'

'We'll go tomorrow, Zé.'

'Then come outside and help me finish unloading the van.'

Thirty

A SOUTH LONDON housing estate. Not a bad one: red brick, cream-painted copings, an outside iron staircase. Macramé hanging baskets fill the kitchen window, not her own kitchen window, with Busy Lizzies. And a horse chestnut drops its candles on the grass two floors below. Sturdy pine shelves support earthenware pots of scented geraniums among the whole grains and pulses in recycled jars. From the food co-op, all of it. She would love to have such a kitchen.

'Don't cry, Mum.'

'I'm not crying.' She folds a telegram into the pocket of her dungarees.

'Is he marrying another lady?' Anna whispers in her ear.

'Trust you to guess.' She unwraps Anna's arms from around her shoulders. 'But don't worry, I'm not sad about that. We'll have a new place to live soon, you'll see, and then we'll find you a school. A nice one. We're always lucky with things like that, aren't we, you and me? Of course we are.'

The doorbell chimes. The door opening to the sound of a man's voice.

'Goody. Alistair. Can I go, Mum?'

'Yes, if you want to.'

She has Alistair to thank for finding her this place to stay while she house hunts. And it should have worked out fine, even with the age gap between the girls. He meant well; they all meant well. But it's awkward when the girls fight, and she feels beaten by the situation. By the dearth of any place that's vacant, or likely ever to become vacant, let alone within her means. She hasn't viewed a single place yet, in a month of searching every day. And all her friends can say is: 'It's dire.'

The sound of raised voices from the front room interrupts her thoughts. Alistair has been diverted. And her ears are starting to burn. 'No, don't go just now, Anna, you had better stay in here with me.'

She feels unable to deal with obstacles the way she did when they were in Switzerland. Although she knows what she's doing wrong. She stays within the same neighbourhood, pounds the same Georgian terraces with half their houses boarded up, instead of searching elsewhere. Because elsewhere is frightening; it is lonely and filled with strangers. A tap on the door to the kitchen interrupts her thoughts. 'Alistair?'

'Hey, good to see you. But why such a worried look? Hallo, cheeky girl.' Jody likes the new Alistair, no longer the jaded ad-man, but happy in a job he likes. And she can walk along the south bank to his office at the GLC. As the door closes the geraniums waft their lemon scent in her direction, and she steels herself for what she has been expecting him to say.

'You need to compromise. In the end, you'll have to squat like the rest of us, or move in with the group at the church in Camberwell Green.'

'I've been there, but they're full. And I need my own place with space to work.'

'Well, we'll sort something out soon. But what about the goings on in Portugal, eh? What? You don't know? Don't you ever watch the news? There's been a bloody revolution. I should have said a bloodless revolution. The swiftest, most efficient coup ever, done and dusted in a day. People are going nuts over there, throwing carnations around. Women climbing onto tanks and sticking them into the soldiers' gun barrels; little children do it, too. So how about you and Anna come home with me for the weekend? Then you can watch it on my telly. It'll be a break. Whoah, Anna. Don't crush me to death,' he says, unclasping Anna's arms from round his waist.

'Okay, but where are you taking us? The Brixton squat or the Oxfordshire manor house?' She bites her lip; she oughtn't to have said that. She knows he only squats in Brixton so he can help people there. And now he looks hurt.

'We'll go to Steeple Hey.'
'Only joking. I'll go and fetch our coats.'

From the relative comfort of a lilac leather beanbag, she stares at the television. Seeing Lisbon again shocks her, pictures of the Rossio most of all. The pavements made of little black and white stones they used to call *calçadas*. She recalls how smooth they were to walk on. And in the Rossio, those wave patterns … Her eyes begin to scan the shop fronts for a façade that she will recognise. Perhaps one with Nicola carved into the stone.

'It's all still there, Alistair.'
'Of course it's still there.'
'Look, there's the doorway.' She gets up to point it out on the screen.
'Hmm. Art Deco. Well, the goods in the shops will change, but beautiful architecture will survive.'
'You'd die, if you saw inside.'

The breathless TV commentary is drowned out by a swell of cheering from an uproarious crowd. Soldiers look bemused to find themselves marooned on top of their tanks, which are now islands in a sea of faces with jubilant smiles. One great extraordinary grin. She tries to dam a well of feeling, to stem the tears that threaten to flood, conscious that Alistair is standing at her shoulder. She looks up. He's polishing a lump of oily metal with an old vest.

'That's beginning to look to me like a party not to be missed. What d'you think? If we left tonight in the van, we could be there for May Day. Say something, will you?' It seems that Alistair's eyes also find it hard to leave the screen.

'You are joking, of course.'

How can he even think of it? How can he make light of all that happened? 'Where's Anna?'

'Playing in the garden. I'm going out to the shed, when I've washed my hands. I want to try to get you enough water for a bath out of our solar system. My brother helped me set it up. Will lukewarm be all right? And while you get yourself together, I'll have a go at mending the van.'

'What's wrong with it this time?' she says, without turning

from the screen. Without intending to, she has begun to comb through the faces in the crowd, begun to scrutinise the features of every soldier that appears in close-up. To will others to turn around. 'This is getting ridiculous. I can't watch any more. Do you know what I'm doing here? I'm searching for a man who's dead.'

'Now, now. You don't know that.'

'No, you're right. And I think I'd know if ...' She stretches her neck to try to loosen a knot of tension at the nape. 'He won't be there, you know. So what's the point? I've come to the conclusion that if he's anywhere, he's in Paris. And he's painting. He always wanted to go there. And when he's ready, he'll come.'

'You still believe that?'

'I suppose, although I never think about it. I've moved around so much, haven't I? I'd be very difficult to find.'

'It didn't even cross my mind that we should go looking for Zé.' He stands back, scratching his stubble. 'But look at all those faces. Don't they make you want to be there? Your story is a part of all that! Any chance of cuppa? And then I'll go out and fix the heater.'

She dreams her way across the room and down the steep step into the kitchen. As she holds the kettle to the tap, she thinks about the paintings she saw in Paris. Nearly a month ago now. It is as if they had been put there to alert her to something, but she doesn't quite know what. In fact it doesn't seem to matter now, if they were his work or they weren't. What matters now is what life wants her to remember, and why. When she has carried in the tea tray, a folded slip of paper appears on it. *The telegram.* She feels in her skirt pocket. *It must have fallen out.*

Alistair is watching her closely. 'That settles it. You need a break.'

'That doesn't bother me.' She tears the telegram and throws the pieces in the grate.

'A break from house-hunting and the tension at the flat would do you good. And once we're back from Lisbon, I'll open up an empty house for you. You move in overnight and then it's up to you. You could write to the council, let them know you're there and offer to pay rent.'

'That was my idea, to offer rent. It's better than declaring myself homeless.'

'Can you be ready in time for the night ferry?'

Lisbon. May Day 1974

Anna knows she must hold on to their hands and not let go.

'Or you'll be swept away in the crowd and that'll be the last we see of you; we'll never find you in this,' Jody says.

Pressed forward by the human surge from behind, suddenly they are spewed into the vast square of the Rossio. And are caught up in the street party, the sounds of mass euphoria. When a small patch of the square clears for a moment to reveal the wave pattern, she lets out a squeal. Five days have passed since the coup. The flower stalls in front of the theatre have run out of carnations. The crowd is trampling blooms underfoot and no one has room to bend down and pick them up. Swaggering bands of men link arms. Long, swaying lines of women shout out in unison as they dance. Soldiers grin incessantly as they gather in the flowers, while the younger women haul themselves up onto their tanks with offerings of newspapers, sandwiches, cigarettes. From the ground, others blow kisses, flaunt themselves, entice the soldiers to dance.

Holding onto Anna's hand, Jody tries to see through the crowds to the edge of the square. Which side of the square Nicola was on, she cannot recall. And then she falls and takes Anna down with her, struck by marauding pamphleteers. They pick themselves up, and then need to step backwards again. A band is on its way towards them, belting out *The Internationale*. Even in Portuguese, she can tell that news is buzzing round the square. Every now and then somebody makes a flamboyant entrance, is then lionised, hoisted up and passed above the heads of the crowd. She would love to know who they are. The next time it happens she will ask.

A volcanic force is erupting, spilling out, as people, too long silenced, at last find their voice. Everyone is either clamouring or queueing to sign up for something. A trade union. A women's group. The women seem to hold sway. Marauding gangs of them, dressed to the nines, release newly formed slogans like a popcorn machine. '*Liberdade sexual! Homen em cozinha! Liberdade sexual!*'

'Men into the kitchen!' she calls to Alistair, and laughs. He can't hear. It is the best May Day ever. A country's whole population on the streets. A once-sedate city fizzing.

At the cooling end of the day she longs to slip away and find a quiet spot.

'I want to walk in the Baixa,' she shouts to Alistair. 'Anna needs to calm down.'

'Okay, but we stay together,' he shouts back.

With a sense of relief she wanders through the smooth pedestrian streets, looking in shop windows, oblivious to what is happening. Except that Alistair has disappeared, after insisting they stay together. She looks around, hoping to spot him, but then brutally stubs her toe. She hops around, cries out and bends down to rub a sore shin. She has just saved herself from falling onto an old lady in a wheelchair.

'*Perdão. Desculpe.*' She has been apologising all day.

'I'm terribly sorry. I was looking the other way.' The young woman at the handles of the chair is speaking to her in English. 'Please let me take a look.' Then she crouches to check Jody's bruise.

'It's not your fault. I should look where *I'm* going,' Jody says to the back of a head. And when the young woman is upright again, Jody takes Anna's hand, prepared to walk on, but instantly pauses. *This is stupid,* she tells herself, *as stupid as in the Rossio.* When she was looking out for Nicola, as if he would still be there. Nicola! That was it! She turns back to where the young woman still stands leaning on the handles. *That prominent forehead ... the look of a sage.* 'I'm sorry, I thought I knew you for a moment, but it's me.' ... *the look of a sage.*

That's funny. I was just wondering if you once knew a friend of mine. You're not Jody, are you?'

'You can't be Isabel. You are, aren't you? You're Zé's old

friend Isabel. You know, I kept your address for years. I don't know how I lost it, but I've moved around such a lot ... Nothing changes here though. Oh, excuse me, this is Anna. She was little when Zé knew her.' As she turns round to look at Anna, Alistair reappears out of nowhere. 'And this is Alistair, a friend from England. Alistair, I used to know this girl. She was meant to be my contact to find Zé.'

'And you lost the address. Sorry, I went look in the old tobacconists across the road, but I knew where you were.'

'Pleased to meet you, Alistair. But you know, Jody, it wouldn't have changed anything. Zé left without giving me your address, and then we lost contact. I couldn't reach him.'

'Nor could I. He only ever had my workroom address anyway. And I left it, when I left my husband in 1968. I now hear it was demolished, soon after, so. Look, can we get tea or something?'

'Yes, so long as we can sit outside or else get the wheelchair through the door.'

'What about these tables on the street? There's one on the outside that looks about ready to empty.' Alistair goes across and hovers nearby until the people leave, when he quickly pounces on the table.

As he moves a chair to make space, he says he needs a beer before he dies of thirst. Jody has seen the custard tarts being carried to some other tables, and so she orders a large plateful. Anna sneezes when the icing sugar gets up her nose. Jody keeps wanting to ask Isabel about Zé, but she stops herself and listens, ever more incredulous as the time wears on. Until, at last, she finds the courage.

'The last I heard from Zé was when he wrote to me from Santarém prison. I wrote back straightaway, but then I never heard from him again. Eduardo told Kay a friend of mine was on his way to England, and I waited, but he never came. That was awful. When I moved to London, I had in mind to go to Africa eventually, but the embassy fobbed me off. I've moved a lot, I suppose. I can't seem to stay anywhere for long.' She looks at Anna, who is busy licking her fingers. She looks happy enough.

'When Zé came home from Africa, the *DGS* — it used to be the *PIDE* — imposed such restrictions on him that it was the same as before he left. So he decided he could only live in exile, and went to France. He'd been burned badly, when his tank caught fire. He's still receiving treatment in France, as far as I know.'

'He lives in Paris?'

'No, in the South, in the Lot valley.'

Oh, no! She lays a hand to her chest, as if she's been winded. And when the fluttering has died down, she starts to tell Isabel about the paintings she saw in the gallery in Paris.

'They were signed Rodrigues, and that was all, and it is such a common name. I should have known though, but I just couldn't imagine him in the Lot.'

'You saw it? His exhibition in Eduardo's gallery? It's over now, and they've all come to Lisbon for a few days.'

'All? You mean he's married?'

'I mean he came with Armando and Eduardo. They live in Paris now.'

'I can picture them both, still.'

'We went to Caxias together yesterday, for the release of the prisoners, because we all had friends in there we hadn't seen for a long time. Zé had someone from way back, when you were here; I think you knew him. He owns a café up the coast.'

'The yellow place. Amarela. The owner there was called António.' She looks at Alistair, who is listening. 'Are you following this?'

'I think so.'

'I heard Zé telling António that he would visit him there today. He's probably up there now.'

Alistair chokes on his cake and reaches for his beer. She hopes he doesn't see the panic she is in. She can't go there. Her knees are shaking. She couldn't get on a train. She can't ... But Alistair is already asking Anna if she wants to go to the seaside. Of course she does.

In truth, he cannot say he missed the sound of water rushing through the old sluice down below the café Amarela. But now he does. It was the bass line of the soundtrack to his family's summer holidays. As much a constant as the big red suns that plopped into the Atlantic at the ends of long summer days. In sixty seven, when the Free Waters Aqueduct was deactivated, and thus the sluices of the seaboard, he wasn't even here. Probably he was somewhere in the Spanish plains by then. But throughout the summers that he spent here as a child and later as a student, that sound had provided him with a connection to Lisboa. To the aqueduct, their greatest monument, his own Great Wall of China. To his city and his home.

Sitting at his old table out on the terrace, he lets his eye wander along the peeling promenade. Well, that hasn't changed: the wall still flakes its paint, upholding the reputation of the town. He smiles. The promenade has some new built-in changing rooms now, and an ice-cream parlour with a spare room where deck-chairs are stacked. And the café still serves cool Sagres and good *galãos* as it always did. He used to like the smell of oil lamps at night, but now, when he turns around, he sees António standing beneath a string of fairy lights. A much thinner António, without eyelashes. Here he comes.

'My son has found his feet now, Zé; he runs the place well, in his way. My wife has kept an eye on things, too. It all goes smoothly. Are you staying for the party here tonight?'

'Yes, but only for a while. My friends will wait for me in Nicola in the Rossio. It seemed strange there, too. I missed the men in dark suits huddled round the door. I kept looking out for them. Abolished.' He shakes his head.

'Yes, and no more swimsuit police here. You heard about the topless ones? It will be an interesting summer.'

'I think perhaps your wife will do the policing instead.'

'*Bem*. It's good to see you back anyway. Seven years, eight; I don't know where they go. I don't expect you hear from the English girl any more?'

He gives a wry smile and stands. 'You've moved the men's room, I see.'

'Inside now, through the bar.'

When he returns he finds António behind the bar, busying himself with a new coffee machine. And he decides to take a short stroll. The sun is low and is reflected in a calm sea tonight. He likes the soft sound the ripples make, when they are only flirting with the shore.

A man and a young girl are running round in circles on the beach below, scattering the blushed sand and calling out in English. He sighs. And there, a dark silhouette against the gold, a woman stands quite still. And then she turns and walks up the sandy beach towards the zigzagging slope.

He stops and stands beside the parapet, looking down onto a rather small white pennant of a beach. And lets his eyes move along the wall as far as the spot. The empty spot. Looking back, his long search for her was nothing but a sea of straw. There are still some upturned fishing skiffs, he notes, but not so many as before. The beach looks smaller too, like every place from childhood, or from a long time ago. He watches as the woman pauses, and then purposefully begins to climb the zigzagging slope. There was something about the turn of her head ...

THE END

About the author

Julia Sutton is an artist and writer from East Anglia, who has lived and worked for much of her adult life in continental Europe. Following eleven years in Paris, she returned, in 1997, to her native Suffolk coast, where she now lives and writes full-time.

A Sea Of Straw is her first novel.

This book is just a work of fiction, but readers who would like to explore further Portugal's history may like to turn to the following books: Paul Hyland's *Backwards out of the Big World*, *Oldest Ally: A Portrait of Salazar's Portugal* by Peter Fryer and Patricia McGowan Pinheiro, and *Freedom Fighters* by João Freire, translated by Maria Fernanda Noronha da Costa e Sousa.

Printed in Great Britain
by Amazon